JUSTICE DENIED

THE SEEKING JUSTICE SERIES

SARAH HAMAKER

ISBN: 978-1-958375-10-5

Cover design by 100 Covers

Edited by Liz Tolsma

 Created with Vellum

Also by Sarah Hamaker

The Seeking Justice Series

Justice Delayed

Justice Denied

The Cold War Legacy Trilogy

The Dark Guest

The Dark Atonement

The Dark Reckoning

Love Inspired Suspense

Dangerous Christmas Memories

Vanished Without a Trace

Standalone Romantic Suspense

Illusion of Love

Protecting Her Witness

Novellas

Christmas Cold Case

Deadly Diamonds

Mistletoe & Murder

PRAISE FOR SARAH HAMAKER

—Faith Ijiga, author of *Jungle Justice*

What a ride! Twists and turns that I didn't see coming. A must read for all suspense lovers.

—DiAnn Mills, bestselling and award winning author of Lethal Standoff (Tyndale September 2024)

Justice Delayed is a page-turner of suspense with a strong faith component. Hamaker once again establishes herself as a master of the genre! Readers won't stop reading until they finish this heart-wrenching tale.

—Carrie Fancett Pagels, award-winning author of Mackinac Cottages series

Sarah Hamaker's *Justice Delayed* held my attention from the first page. The characters were authentic, and the story's twists and turns kept me guessing all the way to the end. If you love sweet romance combined with thrilling suspense, then don't miss *Justice Delayed*.

—Robin Patchen, USA Today bestselling author

WHAT OTHERS ARE SAYING ABOUT *THE DARK GUEST*, BOOK ONE IN THE COLD WAR LEGACY SERIES

"Once I started reading *The Dark Guest*, I could not put it down. The story captures the reader in the first chapter and doesn't let go until the last. Sarah Hamaker has created wonderful characters to root for as she takes them on a dangerous, twisty journey to the truth."

—Patricia Bradley, author of The Natchez Trace Park Rangers Series

"Sarah Hamaker has crafted a novel that makes you think long after you've turned the last page. *The Dark Guest* draws past sins into the present and highlights the freedom that only true repentance brings."

—Jodie Bailey, CBA bestselling author

"This book drew me out of my reading slump and into its sticky web of spies and Cold War intrigue. In this high stakes tale, the well-crafted characters overcame their pasts and fought for the truth to come to light using code breaking and investigation to bring it all to a satisfying conclusion. Highly enjoyable."
—Lisa Phillips, USA Today bestselling author

"Filled with engaging characters, page-turning intrigue, and a sweet romance, *The Dark Guest* is a riveting political thriller you won't want to miss."
—Kelly Goshorn. award-winning author of *A Love Restored*

"Sarah Hamaker has done it again! *The Dark Guest* is an edge-of-your-seat suspense that kept me turning the pages well into the night. She's managed an exquisite blend of danger, action, espionage, and double-crossing that kept me wondering who was who. Yet in this great story where you never know who is telling the truth, she's woven in a magnificent hero and a true-to-life heroine, as well as a love story for the ages. In a time when most main characters are picture perfect and physically impeccable, hers are neither. I couldn't put this book down until I finished it, and you won't, either. Highly recommended."
—Donna Schlachter, author of *Always a Wedding Planner*, *Double Jeopardy*, and other mysteries and suspense

"As the threads of the mystery come together and the suspense builds, *The Dark Guest* becomes a book you can't put down. Engaging characters and a beautiful romance make Hamaker's book one you will remember long after you finish reading.
—Nancy J. Farrier, author of the Driftwood Cove Series

My God, my Father, blissful name!
O may I call thee mine?
May I, with sweet assurance, claim
A portion so divine?
This only can my fears control,
And bid my sorrows fly:
What harm can ever reach my soul
Beneath my Father's eye?

From "My God, My Father, Blissful Name" by Ann Steele, 1790

CHAPTER

ONE

J etta Ainsley stood at the kitchen counter sorting through the mail from the past two days. She'd forgotten to empty her mother's mailbox after a long day spent clearing out the three bathrooms in the house. She rubbed her lower back with one hand while tossing grocery store flyers and postcards from political candidates into a growing pile for the recycle bin.

She separated the bills into a stack to take to Mom, who was in a rehab facility recovering from a nasty leg break after tripping and falling on the escalator at a crowded shopping mall. A battered envelope with a barely legible address piqued her curiosity. She used her mother's letter opener to slit the brown envelope and dumped the contents onto the counter.

The top paper was a typed, undated note addressed to someone named Jay. Jetta gasped as she realized the letter had been written to her late father. Who would be so cruel as to send a letter to a long-dead man?

Before reading the missive, she checked the envelope for the postmark. Uncertain she'd read the year correctly, she used her phone's camera to zoom in on the numbers. Sure enough, the postmark bore a date fifteen years ago—two days before her father's death of a heart attack.

Jetta started a text to her mother to let her know about the envelope but decided to read the papers first. After all, her father was deceased, so it wasn't like she was violating anyone's privacy. Given the doctor's strong recommendation to move to a home with one-level living, Mom had been a little down lately. To leave the home where her mother had spent most of her married life and raised five children hadn't been an easy one. But at least Jetta had been able to step in and help with the clear out while Mom concentrated on healing.

The letter's opening words puzzled her.

Dear Jay,

I'm sorry. It's all my fault you're in this mess. Believe me when I say I had no intention of blaming you. I'm too much of a coward to confess my part in all of this, but my conscience wouldn't let me do nothing, and so I'm sending you what I can. I know it's not enough to completely exonerate you, but it should point FinCEN in the right direction.

No signature adorned the printed page, leaving her no clue as to the author's identity. Jetta shuffled through the rest of the papers. Account statements from a Cayman Island bank plus several Excel spreadsheets. The numbers meant nothing to her. While her father had been a whizz with digits, she hadn't inherited his acumen with math. But why would someone send Dad financial documents and apologize for not doing more to exonerate him—from what, Jetta hadn't a clue. She decided not to text Mom but would bring the papers during her visit tomorrow morning. That way, Mom wouldn't be able to brush her off like she'd done whenever Jetta asked questions about Dad, who had had a fatal heart attack when Jetta was eleven.

Bingley, her golden retriever mix, bumped her leg, his signal for attention. She scratched his head and glanced at the stove clock. Five fifteen. Time for a quick ball toss in the backyard before she thought about what to eat for dinner.

When she headed to the back door, Bingley pushed ahead of her, his tail wagging. Once outside, she threw the battered tennis ball across the yard, sending Bingley racing after it with a happy bark. He would chase the ball for as long as she tossed it, and she had to admit her oldest sister Jenna had been right in convincing Jetta to adopt the dog when she moved back to the family home six months ago. It had been almost as if Jenna had known Jetta would need a companion as she sorted through the detritus of their parents' lives.

Bingley trotted up and dropped the ball at her feet. Jetta obliged with another toss, this time sending the ball to the back fence line with the canine in hot pursuit. Her dog panted up, the ball once more in his mouth. She gave it another throw, the rhythm of the game more soothing than she'd anticipated.

But her mind refused to settle down, her thoughts swirling around the mysterious envelope. She flung the tennis ball again to the far corner of the yard, Bingley running all out. Maybe she would finally learn some new information about Dad. While she missed him, she had more memories of her life without him than with him. That had definitely played into volunteering to sort through their parents' things ahead of putting the house up for sale. Her four older siblings—sixteen, fourteen, twelve, and ten years older than her— had had more time with Dad, although they too rarely talked about the man who had raised and loved them.

Jared, the oldest, had rebuffed her attempts to find out more about their father, while Jenna, the next sibling down, had flat out refused to discuss "the man who ruined our lives." Jason, preoccupied with his twins and business, never had time for serious conversation. Jade, the youngest of her siblings, had shared the most, but even Jade hadn't been able to fill in many of the blanks in Jetta's mind. All of her siblings had either been in college or living on their own at the time of their father's death.

Bingley nudged her leg with his nose, reminding her to uphold her end of the game. She picked up the tennis ball and complied. Her phone rang, and she pulled it out of her back jean pocket to check caller ID. Jason, the brother who came behind Jenna in birth order. "Hey, what's up?"

"Just checking in to see how my sis is doing." A shouting match in the background, the voices high and childlike, made her grin. Mervin and Millicent, no doubt.

"I'm doing okay." She took the ball from Bingley and walked back to the outside storage bin to deposit it, signaling playtime was over. "Got through the bathrooms today."

"Find anything interesting?"

She sank into a plastic Adirondak chair as Bingley sniffed along the far-left side of the fenced yard. "Not really, just a lot of expired medications."

"You know Mom never thought expiration dates applied to her."

"So true. Didn't she try to give you an antacid that was eight years old?"

"Yes, she did, telling me there wasn't anything in there that could 'go bad.'" He laughed. "I refused and later secretly toss the bottle in the outside garbage can."

Jetta leaned her head against the chair back. "I did find a bottle of antidepressants with Dad's name on it under the sink in the ensuite bathroom off Mom's room. The medication inside had turned to mush, probably because of the moisture of the bathroom, but the label was still legible. I didn't think Dad had been depressed."

Jason sighed. "I forget how young you were when he died, so you probably have no idea."

When he didn't continue, she pressed. "No idea about what?"

"That Dad had been accused of embezzling millions of dollars but had a fatal heart attack before anything came of it."

"Wait, what?" Jetta sat bolt upright, her stomach churning at the news. How could her family have not told her this vital piece of their history? "What are you talking about?"

"I told the others we should have said something to you, but none of us wanted to revisit that particular time."

"I'll address the idiocy of that statement later—spill it. Now." Bingley sank on his haunches, laying his head in his lap. She smoothed his silky ear while she listened to her brother tell her about how Topher Robotics, where their father had worked as chief financial officer, had presented evidence he had siphoned off millions over a five-year period, cooking the books to hide the withdrawals. "I can't believe none of you told me about this. It must have been big news."

"Mom never said anything?"

Jetta rubbed the bridge of her nose. "To be honest, I never asked her too many questions about his death because talking about Dad made her so sad. Which makes more sense now that I know the whole story."

"I'm sorry—we should have told you. But I think we all wanted to forget, to move on. Jared had joined a prestigious litigation firm in Boston when Dad was arrested, while Jenna was in the throes of her residency at John Hopkins University Hospital in Baltimore. Jade and I were still in college."

His explanation made sense but it still didn't excuse their continued silence. A sharp yell from his end of the phone blasted her ears. Jason shouted something she couldn't decipher, then he said, "I've got to go. Looks like Milicent whacked her brother in the noggin with his favorite blue truck again."

The antics of her toddler niece and nephew quirked her lips into a smile as she said goodbye, her mind filled with the weight of a family secret everyone else had been carrying but her. Although, to be fair, she was carrying another secret that would soon be out in the open. She rested her hand on her belly, which grew bigger by the day as her due date neared. Mom was the only family member who knew and that was only because Jetta hadn't been able to hide her pregnancy.

She patted Bingley's head, her attention straying back to the envelope with its financial documents. The short note made more sense given the context of her father being accused of embezzlement, but she still hadn't a clue what those papers could do to exonerate a dead man.

All problems for another day, as Mom liked to say in a thick southern accent as she mimicked Scarlett O'Hara. Jetta heaved herself out of the low-slung chair and tucked the phone into her pocket. After she scrambled an egg for dinner, she'd do some internet sleuthing. Millions of missing dollars would certainly have made headlines. Once she had the facts, she could grill her mother about why no one had told her. Being the youngest by so many years meant her siblings and Mom often treated her like a child even though she'd been an adult living on her own for five years now.

"Come on, Bingley. Let's go inside." She headed for the sliding doors, but her dog didn't bound after her. Instead, he staggered, his body shaking violently before he threw up in the grass at the verge of the brick patio. "Bingley!"

She rushed to his side as the dog collapsed in a heap beside the patio, a little foam at his mouth. She laid a hand along his ribs, thankful to feel him breathing. After whipping out her phone, she noted the time—closing in on six. Her regular vet closed at five. "Hang on, Bingley." Somehow, despite her shaking hands, she managed to Google the nearest emergency vet clinic. There was one on Leesburg Pike, a seven-minute drive away.

Bingley heaved again, spewing more of his stomach contents onto the grass. She laid a hand on his head to reassure him. "I'll be right back." Jetta hurried into the house for her keys and a towel to wrap Bingley in.

Back at his side, she placed the faded beach towel around his still body and attempted to lift him into her arms. But no matter how many angles she tried, she couldn't get the seventy-pound dog more than a couple of inches off the ground. Tears of panic and frustration clouded her vision. She couldn't lose him!

"Is everything okay?"

The sound of a male voice brought her head up. Seth Whitman, her next-door neighbor, stepped into her backyard through the side gate, his T-shirt accentuating his bulging biceps. "No." Her voice broke on a sob. "Bingley needs to go to the vet, and I can't lift him."

He handed her a set of keys. "I'll drive so you can sit in the back with him. The back seat should be clear, so open the door and I'll get the dog."

Relieved he hadn't asked delaying questions, she dashed for the gate, leaving it open and headed to his SUV sitting in the adjacent driveway. All the while, she prayed her dog would survive whatever was ailing him and thanked God for bringing Seth to her aid at the right time.

SETH CROUCHED BY THE STILL CANINE, THEN REACHED HIS ARMS UNDERNEATH the dog, being careful to keep the faded pink towel wrapped around Bingley's lower body. Good thing he regularly dead lifted three hundred pounds or more during his workouts. Carrying the medium-sized pooch wouldn't be a problem. He rose, the inert dog held easily in his arms.

"Door's open." Jetta hovered by the gate as he strode as fast as he could without jostling the animal. After gently laying him on the back seat, he repositioned the towel over the dog and stepped back. She passed him his keys, then hopped in beside Bingley, moving faster than he expected for someone as pregnant as she was. "It's the Veterinary Emergency Group on Leesburg Pike."

"Got it." He closed the back door, then slid behind the wheel, connecting his phone to the vehicle's Bluetooth. He hit the "Ask Siri" icon and fed the virtual assistant the clinic name to get directions. In less than ten minutes, they arrived at the clinic. He carried Bingley into the office, where staff immediately directed him to an empty exam room. After depositing the dog onto the stainless-steel table, he stepped back to allow Jetta access to the table.

A male tech came in, along with an older woman wearing a lab coat and stethoscope around her neck. "I'm Dr. Williams and this is Nolan, one of our techs. What's going on with this handsome guy?"

Jetta swiped at her cheeks with her fingers. "I'd been playing fetch with Bingley and his favorite tennis ball in the backyard when he suddenly started vomiting and then collapsed."

"How many times did he throw up?"

Seth gave into his impulse to move closer to Jetta, wanting her to feel she wasn't alone. He stood by her right shoulder as she stroked Bingley's head while the tech checked the dog's vitals and answered their questions. "At least twice."

"How long ago did this happen?"

She shrugged. "I'm not sure, maybe fifteen, twenty minutes? Not more than half an hour."

"I think it was less than that," Seth inserted, not wanting to interrupt, but he had to correct Jetta's statement in case it was important in figuring out what was going on with Bingley. "When I arrived, it was five-fifty-eight. It's now six-ten, so it's probably closer to fifteen than twenty minutes."

The doctor nodded. "Good. Now I'm going to ask you both to step out so we can pump Bingley's stomach and see if we can get out the rest of whatever he ingested."

Jetta opened her mouth as if to protest, but the tech added, "It's not something you really want to see. We'll take good care of Bingley."

"Come on, let's let them get Bingley better." Seth gently touched Jetta's arm. He guided her back to the waiting area.

"Ma'am? Would you come check in now?" The receptionist beckoned Jetta over to the counter.

"I'll grab a seat." Seth wanted to stay with her but wasn't sure if his presence would annoy or crowd her. Best not to chance it. He picked a magenta plastic chair and settled into it, the molded frame groaning under his bulk.

He prayed Bingley would recover from whatever ailed the dog—he could see how much the animal meant to Jetta. He'd always wanted a pet, had even enticed a stray cat into their apartment one summer. Seth hadn't thought about that feline in years. He'd named the small tabby Buttercup because of her very light, almost yellow stripes. Buttercup had been his companion nearly all summer until his mom had caught him pouring milk into a saucer for the cat. Seth shifted uncomfortably as the memory of his mother's anger and her man-of-the-moment's vicious kick that sent Buttercup over the Rainbow Bridge, as he'd later learned people say when a beloved pet died.

"Guess we wait now." Jetta dropped into the seat beside him, a hand on her belly. "I'm so glad you came by when you did. I couldn't have lifted Bingley myself."

Her praise warmed his heart—and his neck. He instinctively rubbed the back of his neck, as if his movement could erase the tell-tale signs of his embarrassment. "I'm happy to help."

A tear slipped down her cheek. "You've been so kind to me."

How could he not be? His protective instincts had kicked in the moment her mother had introduced Jetta to him on the grassy strip between their driveways when Jetta had brought Bingley home from the pound. A light breeze had carried the fruity scent of her shampoo to tickle his nose. Since he had often assisted Emily Ainsley with household tasks, he had continued to do so with Jetta after Emily's accident.

Breathing deeply, he caught a whiff of that same citrusy smell underneath the antiseptic of the vet's waiting room. "How's your mom doing?"

"She's impatient with the slow recovery." Jetta sighed. "Her leg isn't healing as fast as the surgeon would like, and there's talk she may not fully recover the ability to walk unaided."

"I'm sorry to hear that." Emily had become a dear friend in the three years he'd rented the house next door, and his heart ached for the older woman's not-so-great prognosis. "I guess it's a good thing she'll be moving to one-level living soon."

"I guess."

Her desultory response reminded him she was clearing out her childhood home. Seth couldn't fathom having such a connection to a house. He and his mom had moved countless times, and he'd had even more moves after social services stepped in and removed him when he was nine. He envied her stable childhood, although losing her father at eleven meant it wasn't without pain. At least she'd known who her father was, something he had no idea of how to find out for himself, since his mother had left him no clues as to where he might look.

"Ms. Ainsley?" Nolan stood a few feet away.

Seth rose along with Jetta.

"Yes?"

"Come this way." The tech walked toward the examine room.

Jetta hurried after Nolan without looking back or asking Seth to accompany her. The story of his life—always destined to stay on the fringes of any friendship. But there was one thing he could do from afar, and he bowed his head to pray again for Bingley's recovery. If he gave into temptation and added a line or two that his lovely next-door neighbor noticed him beyond his helpfulness, then that was between him and God.

TWO

In the exam room, Jetta rushed to Bingley, who lay covered in a blanket and motionless on the table. Seeing his chest rising and falling stemmed her tears.

"I'll get Dr. Williams." Nolan slipped out the exam room's back door.

She turned, expecting to see Seth beside her, but he wasn't there. While she stroked Bingley's head, disappointment flooded her that Seth hadn't accompanied her. Anyone else would have simply followed her into the room, but not Seth. He never overstepped whatever boundaries she put up—or didn't realize she'd constructed, like right now. Seth, with his gentleness despite his huge size, continually surprised her.

She swiped a stray tear from her cheek as she waited for the vet, her thoughts still on her neighbor. Seth had never commented on her pregnant state or lack of a husband. His only acknowledgement of her increasing belly was his insistence on taking her trash and recycling bins to the curb and his standing offer of assistance with any heavy lifting. Her mother encouraged her to tap into his willingness to help, relating how good a neighbor he'd been for the past few years.

When Dr. Williams entered with Nolan behind him, she pushed thoughts of Seth aside and focused on her dog. The vet's serious expression did little to soothe Jetta's alarm.

"What's wrong with Bingley?" Her voice choked on the name. The dog had wormed his way into her heart these past six months, and she couldn't imagine life without him by her side.

"We suspect ibuprofen poisoning."

"Ibuprofen? Like for people?" Jetta could hardly wrap her mind around the idea that what she sometimes took for headaches could cause such harm in a dog.

The vet nodded. "Given the symptoms you described, I was pretty sure he'd eaten something he wasn't supposed to, so we induced vomiting." He handed her a plastic zipper top bag containing three reddish pills she recognized as a popular over-the-counter brand of pain reliever.

"How did he get hold of these?" Jetta laid the bag on the counter beside Bingley. "There wasn't any Advil in the house." She reached for her purse, then remembered she'd left it on her kitchen counter. At least she had her driver's license and credit card in her phone case. "I'll check my purse when I get home, but I'm sure he didn't dig around in my bag to scarf down pills in a plastic bottle."

Dr. Williams frowned. "You're sure there wasn't a way for him to ingest ibuprofen?"

"None comes to mind." She'd been very careful with the medications from the bathroom cabinets and a few hours ago had taken everything to a local pharmacy with a medicine disposal kiosk.

"He must have eaten a fair amount to display these symptoms."

She rubbed the dog's silky ear. "I didn't even know ibuprofen was so dangerous for dogs."

"The Pet Poison Helpline receives more than four thousand calls a year about dogs being exposed to the pain reliever. Even small doses can trigger adverse effects in dogs and cats." Dr. Williams must have clocked Jetta's increasing distress because she hurriedly went on. "But we caught it quick enough in Bingley, and he should make a full recovery."

Jetta tightened her hand on the counter as relief turned her legs into cooked spaghetti. "Thank God." And Seth for his strength in getting Bingley to the clinic.

"We would like to keep him overnight for observation and to replace some of the fluids he lost due to vomiting."

"Okay, if you think it's necessary."

The vet leveled her with a stern look reminiscent of her mother when she caught Jetta disobeying instructions. "This will also give you time to check your house and yard to see where Bingley might have gotten the pills. His system might not recover if he eats any more so soon."

"Oh, I will." She would scour every inch of her mother's house and property to ensure her dog didn't come in contact with those drugs again.

The back door opened, and another tech tugged a stainless-steel trolley into the examining room. "We're ready to move Bingley to the kennel."

Dr. Williams nodded. "Someone will call you in the morning when he's ready to be released, probably around ten, after the morning checks."

"Okay." She patted Bingley's head again and stepped back as Nolan and the other tech prepared to transport Bingley.

Nolan added, "The front desk will have the paperwork for his overnight stay."

Jetta took that as a hint to move out of their way and exited the room. She paused by the reception desk to wait for the person in front of her to finish and drew in a deep breath to steady her nerves. She'd nearly lost Bingley, who had somehow managed to get hold of ibuprofen pills. The baby kicked her ribs, the movement a reminder of why she was sure she didn't have any of that over-the-counter medicine, since it wasn't advisable for pregnant women to take ibuprofen. So how had Bingley gotten access to those pills?

"Is Bingley okay?"

She stifled a gasp as she spun to see Seth. For a big man, he moved with the stealth of a cat. "You startled me."

He ducked his head. "Sorry about that."

His chastised posture chided Jetta to consider her tone probably had been harsher than she'd meant. "No, I'm sorry." She laid a hand on his arm briefly, then recounted the vet's diagnosis. "Bingley's going to be fine, but they're keeping him overnight to pump more fluids into him."

"I'm glad he'll recover." He shifted on his feet, reminding her she was keeping him from whatever plans he had for a Tuesday evening.

"Let me check in with the front desk and we can go."

He returned to his chair, the faint whiff of bergamot orange teasing her nostrils. It was a scent she'd begun to exclusively associate with Seth. At the counter, the perky receptionist presented her with an iPad to sign her permission for Bingley's overnight stay.

"That will be $1,437 for the exam, treatment, and overnight stay. How would you like to pay?"

Jetta swallowed her protest at the high bill, which would put a dint in her bank account. Staying at Mom's house saved on rent, but not working meant her balance wasn't increasing. Eventually, she would need to land a job, but with the baby's due date in six weeks, she'd decided to wait until she'd figured out whether she would keep the infant or give it up for adoption. She handed over her credit card and waited while the receptionist ran the card. After signing the receipt, she folded a copy of the bill and turned to find Seth.

"I'm ready," she told him. Worry for Bingley and her mother's recovery nibbled at her nerves, making her itchy with unease.

"Have you eaten dinner?"

Seth's question triggered an answering growl from her stomach. "No." She mentally reviewed the contents of her fridge and bit back a groan. She recalled finishing the eggs last night and meaning to make a trip to the supermarket today, which hadn't happened. A nap had derailed her afternoon. "Maybe we could grab dinner on the way home?"

As soon as the words left her mouth, she wished they hadn't. Seth was a nice guy, one she suspected had a crush on her, if his frequent blushes around her were any indication. She had vowed yesterday to be kind but distant in order not to lead him on. She most certainly was not in a good place to fall in love, not when the last man she'd been involved with had led to her current state. She shot him a glance to gauge his reaction to her question.

"Since you must be tired, we could hit the drive-thru at McDonald's, Taco Bell, or Chick-fil-A on our way home."

Relief poured through her like hot fudge on soft serve ice cream at his suggestion. "I never turn down the chance for a cookies-and-cream milkshake and chicken nuggets from Chick-fil-A."

His eyes crinkled as he smiled. "I'm partial to their chicken strips with sriracha sauce myself."

As he moved to open the door, Jetta caught the receptionist, a young woman around her age, eyeing Seth while she spoke on the phone. She couldn't blame the other woman, as he was a fine specimen for someone in the market for a man, which Jetta most certainly wasn't. With full lips, chiseled cheekbones, and a strong jawline, he was, in a word, gorgeous. Long dark eyelashes framed chocolate-brown eyes. The word brawny came to mind when describing his build. Not over-the-top sculpted like a serious body builder, but definitely a lot more muscles than the average man. If she had to guess, the man had not an ounce of fat on him anywhere. A man who would make any woman feel safe and protected. Not like her ex, Kyle Franklin.

The efficiency of Chick-fil-A's drive-thru had them on their way, and before long, he was pulling into his driveway. She grabbed the food bags and waited for him to open her door. She had been surprised when he'd asked her to wait for him the first time they'd ridden together, but she soon learned being courteous came second-nature to Seth.

As he climbed out and shut his door, she tried to remember if Kyle had ever once opened a door for her during the eight months they'd dated. Nope, Kyle jiggled his keys if she took too long to get out of the car and always walked ahead of her through the business doors, never bothering to step aside and hold the door for her.

Seth pulled her door open, then closed it after she'd exited. "Thank you."

He gave her a sweet smile, but it fell off his face as he stared past her toward something in her side yard. "Wait here, please."

While Jetta couldn't see what had captured his attention, the concern in his voice kept her glued to the side of the car. Her heart pounded as she considered what might lay outside her sightline—and if it would be connected to what she'd left behind in Chicago.

Seth crouched next to the dark furry object lying in the grass near the half-closed back gate of the Ainsley residence. He grabbed a nearby stick and poked the still raccoon. No movement. Dead. Using the toe of his sneaker, he nudged the animal over onto its back. Vomit coated the animal's mouth and nearby ground. The odor assaulted him, but he ignored it. He'd smelled worse and had grown immune to the scent of regurgitation.

With his phone's flashlight to illuminate the mess on the grass in the darkening shadows, he spotted the remanent of a reddish-brown pill in the masticated stomach contents. The animal must have gotten into the same stash as Bingley.

Rising, he hustled to his SUV to usher Jetta into her house with their dinner. "There's a dead raccoon, so why don't you go inside your house with our dinner, and I'll take care of it."

She frowned. "Did the neighborhood fox get it?"

"I don't think so. It appears the animal found whatever Bingley ingested. Let's go around the back of the SUV so you don't ruin your appetite with the view."

She grabbed the food bag and he got the drink caddy from the SUV before he led her to the kitchen. "I'll be back in a few minutes. I don't want any other animals getting into the mess."

"You don't mind? It must be really gross."

"I can handle it." Good thing he had an iron stomach—hardly anything bothered him. Not too surprising, given his childhood. "I'll be back in a flash."

He hustled to his house for several black yard trash bags, a snow shovel he unearthed from a back closet, and a ratty old towel. After taking photos of the animal and the surroundings, he used the shovel to move the raccoon onto the towel, then folded it over the still form before sliding it into one of the trash bags. He tied it off, then inserted the bag inside a second trash bag, repeating it until the raccoon's remains were concealed under three layers of heavy plastic.

Seth placed the bag inside his outdoor trash can, then returned to the scene with a small plastic to-go container. With his hands inside plastic sandwich bags, he scooped up as much of the vomit as he could into the container, sealing it with the lid. He put the container on the ground next to the trash can before heading inside to thoroughly wash his hands.

The sickness of Bingley and the death of the raccoon bothered him. He wanted to check to see if the raccoon had indeed ingested ibuprofen like the dog had. Tomorrow, he would take the container to the vet to see if they could run determine whether it was similar to what Bingley ate. In the morning, he would search Jetta's backyard— after securing her permission—to make sure nothing remained of what he suspected had been contaminated meat, given the couple of chunks near the raccoon's carcass. The look on Jetta's face when she'd come for his help with Bingley tugged at his heartstrings. He never wanted her to have such a look of anguish again.

His phone buzzed, and he paused on the sidewalk to read the text from his colleague and friend, Brogan Gilmore, before knocking on Jetta's door.

Hey, Melender canceled on me, so want to grab a bite at Ireland's Four Provinces?

Seth usually enjoyed listening to the Irish musicians who often entertained the crowds at the popular bar and restaurant.

Not tonight.

You said you didn't have plans…

Well, plans change.

He hoped Brogan would leave it at that, but wasn't surprised when another text flashed on the screen.

What's her name?

Seth balanced the phone in his hand, debating how to answer. He decided the truth would be best—just not the whole truth.

I'm helping my next-door neighbor.

Brogan would think Seth meant Mrs. Ainsley, since he often helped the widow.

And here I thought you'd finally met a girl. Guess it will be me enjoying the band solo tonight.

Seth let his colleague have the last word and pocketed his phone. As he crossed the lawn to the Ainsley's, he tamped down his hopes that Jetta had meant she wanted to enjoy a meal in his company. Jetta put out a strong I-just-wanna-be-friends vibe and he respected that. If only his foolish heart would stop leaping to unwanted conclusions every time she smiled at him or touched his arm, then he would be fine. He could do the friend thing with her, especially because he sensed a world of hurt behind her sunny façade. His hands curled into fists and he purposefully shook them out. As much as he wanted to punch the guy who'd made her so skittish—and who'd left her pregnant and alone—violence only created more problems than it solved. He ought to know. One act of violence had changed his life.

Emily Ainsley shifted in the chair lounge. She shouldn't have let the aide help her out of the wheelchair and into the chair without finding out how long she'd have to sit there before she could return to bed. The single hospital bed, with its crisp white sheets and lightweight blanket, stood not ten feet from her chair but there might as well be the Atlantic Ocean between them. Emily couldn't traverse even such a short distance without assistance, not with her leg still encased in a cast from hip to toes.

A sharp knock, then the door opened and an older woman wearing the plum-colored scrubs of an aide entered. Emily bit back a caustic request to wait for a reply to the knock before barging in, but she'd been in the rehab facility long enough to know it would make no difference.

"Oh, good. You're sitting in the chair. You'll get better faster if you move around more." The aide regarded her with one of those cheery smiles the healthy gave the sick.

Emily swallowed another sarcastic reply that hovered like a bee above a blossom on her lips. Instead, she viewed her left outstretched leg on the recliner's footstool. She still had at least another week to wear the blasted thing.

The aide refilled the plastic mug with water. "Anything else I can help you with?"

"Yes, I'd like to return to the bed. Please." Emily waited for the reprimand about doing it on her own.

The aide huffed, displeasure written on her expressive face, but she complied and soon Emily was ensconced in the bed. She thanked the aide, then took a sip of water before logging onto her tablet to check her email.

Still no reply from Topher Robotics about her emails, the most recent sent a week ago. She tapped the side of the case as she considered calling. She should have done this years ago, but raising her fifth child as a single mom while grieving the loss of her husband hadn't left much bandwidth for Quixotic quests. Having enforced immobility since her accident six weeks ago had meant more time to think, which translated into more time to remember the injustice done to her husband.

She considered what she knew about Topher Robotics. Founded and run by the Topher family, the company had expanded beyond robots to artificial intelligence and other cutting-edge technologies. Jay had worked his way up to chief financial officer from the accounting department, spending most of his career at the company. Emily hadn't particularly liked the Tophers, but then again, she had only encountered them at office parties and a few charity events.

Before sending her email, she'd refreshed her memory about who still worked at the company. Peter Topher, who'd founded the company in 1970, had retired from the day-to-day operations twenty years ago. Emily recalled Jay saying Peter frequently came to the office to check in on how his adult children were handling things.

The current CEO, Ryan, was Peter's oldest child and had taken over the reins from his father. Gene Topher, Peter's middle child, now held Jay's former position as CFO, while Yasmine, the youngest and only daughter, was chief operating officer. Other Tophers, which

Emily assumed were the progeny of the Ryan, Gene, and Yasmine, populated the middle management positions. Very few outsiders held leadership positions—Topher Robotics was the quintessential family-owned and -run business—which made their circling the wagons against her husband not surprising.

The stricken expression on her husband's face when he'd informed her of the embezzlement accusations the day before his death flashed into her mind.

"All of them were there—Peter, Ryan, Emil, Yasmine—when Ryan told me I was fired for embezzling millions from the company over a five-year period." Jay had slumped on the couch, his voice a mere whisper, as if saying the words softly would negate their terrible meaning.

Emily hadn't understood what her husband was saying, not right away. She'd stammered something about it being a mistake Jay could explain, but he'd only shaken his head. "I tried to tell them I was innocent, but they had spreadsheets and bank account statements supposedly showing how I had siphoned off the money. I'd never seen those papers or accounts before in my life, but that didn't matter." He put his head into his hands.

She rushed to his side, kneeling on the floor beside him. "We'll fight this together. I don't care what papers they have—they must be fake! You're the most honest man I've ever known."

When he raised his head, the grief and hurt in his eyes sent her stomach to the bottom of the ocean. Without a word, she enveloped him into her arms and held him tight. The next morning, while they sipped coffee after a restless night for them both, officers from the Falls Church Police Department arrived to enact an arrest warrant from Fairfax County for Jay. She closed her eyes as memories of that awful sequence of events replayed in her mind in slow motion.

Jay standing, his face ashen. One of the officers extending his hand with handcuffs dangling from his fingers. Her husband meeting her gaze, his own filled with sorrow and pain. The click of metal as the policeman secured Jay's hands in front of him. Then Jay moving his cuffed hands toward his chest, his eyes widening as his knees buckled. The officer holding his elbow attempted to help him into a chair, but Jay somehow ended up on the floor.

Her scream echoed off the walls as the officers tried to resuscitate her husband, but Emily had known the moment his body hit the floor, Jay was gone. For days after his death from a heart attack, the papers had been filled with a constant stream of articles, each one with another sordid detail of the fraud and embezzlement Jay had supposedly committed. Without him around to defend himself, he was easily convicted in the court of public opinion.

Emily closed her eyes, trying to recover her equilibrium after her dip into the past. Her husband had mourned the loss of his good name as much as he had the fact someone was getting away with the money. That the men and women he'd worked with as employees or clients thought he'd taken money that wasn't his had cut him to the quick.

Drawing in a breath, she pulled up the number to Topher Robotics and dialed it on her cell. Punching through to speak to the receptionist, she requested Ryan Topher. A series of clicks, then someone answered.

"Ryan Topher's office, Mae Stanhope speaking."

"Hello, I'd like to speak to Mr. Topher please." Emily interjected a smile into her tone.

"I'm sorry, Mr. Topher isn't available. May I take a message?"

Emily had expected this. "Yes, this is Emily Ainsley."

A soft gasp from Mae told Emily the other woman recognized her name. Good, that would make things easier. "I'm calling to get an answer to my emails."

"Your emails?" Mae had recovered her professionalism, her voice crisp and calm once more.

"Over the last couple of weeks, I sent Mr. Topher several emails regarding the embezzlement charges levied against my late husband by the company fifteen years ago."

"And the message?"

"That I'm through waiting for a reply. I've given him ample time to respond to my request to officially clear Jay of any wrongdoing. Now I will take the necessary steps to do so myself."

"Would you please hold, Mrs. Ainsley?" Mae didn't sound quite so confident.

Emily listened to the classical hold music, wondering if Mae was the same Mae who used to work in accounting under her husband. Maybe she would ask when the woman came back on the line, but the call disconnected abruptly. She debated calling back but decided she would wait before poking the bear again. As she considered her next move, an idea blossomed, one that might accomplish two things at the same time. She would suggest Jetta help her clear Jay's name with the assistance of Seth Whitman, that nice young man who lived next door and worked for *The Herald*. Reporters knew all about ferreting out secrets, didn't they?

But she would have to tread carefully and make it seem like Jetta's idea. Her youngest had an independent streak a mile wide and didn't like to be told what to do. Emily had a feeling that attribute would come in handy in the search for the truth about who'd gotten away with millions—and falsely blamed her husband for the crime.

JETTA TOOK THE FINAL SIP OF HER COOKIES-AND-CREAM MILKSHAKE. WHILE she'd been hungry earlier, hearing about the dead raccoon had zapped her appetite, and she'd thought she wouldn't be able to choke down any food. But during their meal, Seth entertained her with hilarious tales of photographing events for *The Northern Virginia Herald*, and before she realized it, she'd eaten all of her nuggets and waffle fries.

"So there's the Falls Church mayor chasing his ball cap down the sidewalk as the wind keeps tossing it hither and yon." Seth held out his phone to show her the picture he'd snapped.

She chuckled at the usually dignified mayor running after the cartwheeling Nationals ball cap. "Did the paper run the photo?"

He shook his head. "No, my editor went with the more formal one, but the one I showed you is my favorite of that series." He gathered their wrappers and put it in the kitchen trashcan.

"Thank you."

"For what?" He washed his hands in the sink.

"For taking my mind off of what happened to Bingley and that poor raccoon."

"My pleasure."

The simple words rang with such sincerity, she believed him.

"I should be going. Before I head to work in the morning, I can check your yard for what Bingley and the raccoon ate."

His offer didn't surprise her, but she reminded herself that the more she relied on him, the more he might think she cared for him beyond friendship. "I don't want to put you out. You've already done so much for me with Bingley and taking care of the raccoon."

"I don't mind."

That was the trouble—he liked helping her, and while she knew he didn't expect anything in return, the lopsidedness of their relationship had begun to grate on her nerves. But that could be her advanced state of pregnancy talking. Everything had started to irritate her. Even her mother had commented on Jetta's snappiness of late.

She rubbed the small of her back as the baby stretched in her belly, then capitulated as gracefully as she could manage. "Then I accept."

"Consider it done." But the lines across his forehead deepened instead of receding with her acquiescence.

Usually he seemed pleased when she accepted his help. "What's the matter?"

"I was thinking how weird it is your dog and the raccoon both ate ibuprofen. I mean, it's not like people dump bottles of the stuff around a neighborhood." He paused, as if debating with himself on whether he should continue. Staring down at the granite countertop, he spoke to the slab. "I looked more closely at the raccoon's, er, vomit when cleaning it up, and it appeared the pills had been mixed with chunks of meat."

"What are you implying?" But her mind had already gone there, and she placed her hand on her chest to still her suddenly racing heart.

"I think someone might have deliberately tried to poison your dog."

"But why would anyone do that?" Jetta couldn't believe anyone would want to harm Bingley. She might not have had him very long, but he was a wonderful pet.

"You haven't had any run-ins in the neighborhood about Bingley?"

"No, everyone seems so nice. He's a friendly dog. I grew up in this neighborhood. It's a safe place." But it didn't feel so safe now, if he was right about it being a deliberate act.

"You don't have any enemies?"

"No." But even as she denied it, a face contorted with rage flashed in her mind's eye. Kyle was in Chicago and wasn't stupid— surely, he wouldn't do anything to revoke his plea agreement. She interpreted Seth's raised eyebrows as indicating his skepticism of her denial. She would probably not believe herself either.

When she stayed silent, he broke eye contact but not before she glimpsed sadness in his chocolate-brown eyes. "I'll let you know where I find any contaminated meat or pills."

"Thanks again." She closed the front door behind him. Then his last sentence snagged her attention. Seth hadn't said *if* he'd find something but *where*, as if he fully expected to locate the source of Bingley's sickness and the raccoon's death. Her denials notwithstanding, Seth believed someone had indeed deliberately targeted her dog—and by extension, Jetta herself.

CHAPTER

FOUR

Jetta punched the body pillow in the hopes she could get it into a shape suitable for sleeping. Seth's assertion he would find evidence someone deliberately tried to harm her dog had her insides tied up with more knots than ropes on a ship. To focus her thoughts on something else, she'd read everything she could find online about her father and the embezzlement charges. Learning the sordid details of the crime had merely revved up the baby, who had somersaulted for hours, keeping her awake.

She tried to pray but couldn't form the words with her thoughts all jumbled. While raised in church, her mother hadn't attended much after her father's sudden death. Now that Jetta knew a bit more about the circumstances surrounding his fatal heart attack, she wondered if church members had snubbed them because of the embezzlement accusations. In her teens and college years, Jetta had allowed herself to drift away from the things of God, but her current situation had driven her back into the arms of her loving Savior. Jetta had begun to memorize Scripture to bolster her fledging faith, and now a recent verse from the Psalms flitted through her mind. "The

29

Lord is my light and my salvation; whom shall I fear? The Lord is the stronghold of my life; of whom shall I be afraid?"

Jetta repeated Psalm 27:1 over and over, whispering the words until her eyelids dragged downward and her heart rate slowed. Her phone buzzed on the nightstand, jolting her back from the edge of sleep. One a.m. She pushed up onto her elbows and checked the incoming call. Jade, the last sibling who hadn't called after she'd texted their group chat about Bingley's trip to the vet, keeping the reason vague.

"Hey, sis." Jetta flopped onto her back. "Do you know what time it is?"

"Girl, why didn't you call me? I had to find out by text?"

Jade's manufactured outrage made Jetta grin. She did enjoy riling her older sisters, Jade in particular, who hated being the last to know any family news, but living in California with the rest of her siblings on the East Coast meant Jade missed some things. But her smile fell away at the serious nature of the incident. "Sorry, wasn't feeling up to talking."

"Yeah, it must have been rough." Her sister's voice softened. "But I'm glad Bingley will be okay. You haven't told Mom, have you?"

"I'm planning to when I see her first thing in the morning."

"What did the vet say was wrong with him anyway?"

Jetta contemplated the ceiling, trying to figure out how to tell the truth without alarming her sister with all the details. "He must have eaten something that disagreed with him."

"You'll need to keep a close eye on him, since you now know he's apt to get into things he shouldn't."

"I most certainly will." Jade's assumption Bingley had been the culprit instead of someone who wanted to harm him eased some of the stress building inside Jetta. She wouldn't have to share her suspicions that someone had deliberately poisoned her dog. If her siblings found out, one of them would be on their way to Falls Church on the next available flight—and would find out about her delicate condition. She most certainly did not want them butting into her life.

Hiding her pregnancy felt like lying to her brothers and sisters—okay, it *was* lying by omission—but she couldn't handle their questions and well-meaning directives, not when she was still sorting through her options.

Before Jade could launch into another topic, Jetta asked, "Why didn't you tell me about Dad?"

"What about Dad?"

Jetta rolled her eyes at Jade's obvious attempt at dissimulation. "You know very well what I'm talking about—the embezzlement charges."

"We—"

"And don't tell me I was too young. I haven't been too young for years now."

"You're right." Jade's voice softened. "We should have told you. But honestly, we didn't want to ruin your memories of him like ours were ruined."

"Wait, you think he was guilty?" Jetta couldn't believe what she was hearing. While she knew only what she'd read online, she didn't for a minute believe the man who had tried to find the owner of a dollar bill he'd found on the sidewalk outside a store could have embezzled millions.

Jade's breath sounded suspiciously like a huff, something her sister did whenever she thought the other person was having a "duh" moment. "It didn't impact you as much as it did us. We had to deal with the fallout of having a father accused of embezzling millions from a cutting-edge company working on developing robotic prosthetics, among other things."

Jetta hated to push, but she needed to know where Jade stood. "You didn't answer my question."

"Yes and no."

"What's that supposed to mean?" Usually Jade wasn't one to mince words, so her reluctance to say what she thought of their father made Jetta wonder how the accusations might have hurt her sister, who'd been at Boston College at the time of the arrest.

"As chief financial officer, he had to know about the missing money. He was very good at his job." Jade paused, then continued, her voice soft yet firm. "So either he didn't know and therefore wasn't paying close attention to the books like he should have been or he turned a blind eye to whoever was taking the money."

Jetta mulled that over before positing her thoughts. "Mom always said Dad was a straight arrow."

"Until this happened, I would have agreed."

"Then there must be a third option."

"What's that?"

"What if he knew someone was taking the money but was trying to find the evidence to prove it?"

Jade stayed silent for so long, Jetta checked to make sure her sister hadn't hung up. "Jade?"

"While I'd like to think that, if I recall from what the articles—and Topher Robotics—said, the evidence against Dad was overwhelming."

Jetta opened her mouth to refute Jade's claim, but she didn't know how because she hadn't investigated beyond the news stories. Best take a closer look at what happened, then she could persuade her siblings of their father's innocence.

Before Jetta could end the call, Jade asked, "Hey, Mom says you've been spending time with your hunky neighbor."

"Seth?" The name burst out of Jetta before she had time to consider what it would telegraph to Jade. She mentally slapped herself in the forehead for giving her sis ammunition to pummel her with about her lack of a love life.

"Ha, I knew it! Spill it."

Jetta sighed. She'd have to throw her sister a bone or Jade would never let her go and get some sleep. "He rescued Bingley tonight." Then gave an abbreviated version of the events surrounding Bingley's trip to the hospital.

"I knew he was more than a pretty face." Jade's grin came across loud and clear on the phone. "Like your own personal knight in shining armor with arm muscles are to die for. Besides, Mom approves of Seth, and since you're not dating Kyle anymore, you're a free agent."

Jetta bit back a groan at her older sisters' meddling in her life. Lately, they had morphed from trying to control her career to finding her a man. "What would your husband think of your drooling over another man?"

"He'd understand I'm only doing it to get my younger sister to see the potential right under her nose."

Jetta stuck out her tongue. Jade wouldn't be so gung-ho if she could see Jetta's predicament. No one would want to date her, much less marry her, in her current situation. "You get married and suddenly, everyone has to be partnered with someone?"

"Can I help it if I want you to experience marital bliss like me?"

"Yes, you can." She yawned. "Listen, it's after one here and I'm beat. I'll have to get up early if I want to visit Mom before getting Bingley from the vet."

"Right. I still can't keep this East Coast-West Coast time thing straight. Sleep tight, and let us know how it goes with Mom."

"Will do." Jetta ended the call and checked that the phone charger was still connected. She tried a different position in bed but still couldn't get comfortable. With a sigh deeper than the ocean, as Dad used to say, she closed her eyes. Maybe more prayers would help her find rest. She prayed she would be able to get Mom to talk about the arrest and evidence against Dad when she visited her tomorrow. Sleep began its gentle pull on her body once more as she snuggled deeper into her covers.

Seth Whitman popped into her mind. His effortlessness in lifting the seventy-pound Bingley coupled with the gentleness of his movements made him an attractive package. His kindness toward others shone through in every encounter. Her mother might vouch for him, but Jetta couldn't rely on her own instincts, not when the result of her last judgment call in trusting the wrong man kicked her in the ribs. Sleep nudged her into dreamland before she could resolve the problem of how to keep Seth in her life without leading him on, because she could use a friend like him.

RYAN TOPHER EYED HIS OLDEST SON, FREDERICK, OVER THE RIM OF HIS CUP. The boy—he still thought of him that way despite Frederick's forty-four years—had his habitual petulant look, his lips pursed as though sucking on something sour. Frederick held a cup and saucer but hadn't taken a sip of the excellent coffee Ryan had flown in every quarter from a Hawaiian coffee farm. Ryan waited for Frederick to state why he'd requested this meeting. Frederick's duties as vice president of operations meant he reported directly to Yasmine and not his father, which curtailed the interactions Ryan had with Frederick, something Ryan appreciated more as the years passed and what had been cute when Frederick was younger morphed into something else entirely.

Frederick set his untouched beverage on the coffee table. His leg jiggled up and down once before he stilled it with a hand on his knee. Ryan inwardly winced at the telltale sign. Money. The kid wanted more money.

"How much this time?" Ryan kept his tone bored and low.

His son jerked as if Ryan had shot a cannon off in the spacious corner office. "What? No, I mean why would you assume I want money?"

The manufactured outrage on his son's countenance usually made Ryan laugh, but not today. "I don't have time to dance around the issue. If I misunderstood, I apologize." He drained his coffee and set the cup beside his son's untouched one on the table. "Now, I have a board meeting to prepare for, so if there's nothing else, I'll see you Saturday for your mother's birthday dinner."

Frederick shot to his feet. "Well, the, um, thing is..." He rubbed his hands together, a boyhood tick that signaled Ryan wasn't going to like what came next. "The fees for Ridley's boarding school went up way more than we'd anticipated, and Macey won't graduate from college for another year."

Ryan waited a beat. The cost of two kids in private schools must be enormous, but then again, Frederick took home a handsome salary, plus the use of a company vehicle, so he should be able to cover the expenses without a problem. A red flush crept up Frederick's neck and onto his cheeks. Interesting. He didn't usually blush when asking for a loan from his father.

"The thing is, Dad, that, uh..." He choked on the words.

Ryan didn't have time to coax it out of him, not when he had to contend with an antsy board and rumors about a hostile takeover from a rival technology firm. "Spit it out or leave it for another time."

The words came out harsher than Ryan had intended, but he wasn't about to apologize. Frederick's eyes widened, but he squared his shoulders and blurted, "Cynthia said she's leaving me."

Cynthia, still a beauty at forty-one with her ice-blue eyes and naturally blonde hair, had struck Ryan as the pragmatic type who would stick by her man come what may. Ryan leveled a hard stare at his son. "What did you do?" He held up a hand to forestall the protest he was sure would be rising to his son's lips. "And don't tell me nothing. Cynthia's not a fool. She's put up with a lot from you over the years."

"She found out about Natasha." Frederick's gaze skittered away from his father's.

Ryan firmed his lips. "I warned you about flaunting your mistresses."

Frederick waved his hand as if brushing away a pesky fly. "Cynthia and I have an understanding."

"Then what's the problem?" Ryan pointedly glanced at his phone, letting Frederick know his time was running out.

"Natasha's pregnant."

Ryan had to hand it to his son—he hadn't been expecting that bombshell.

"Won't you talk to Cynthia, get her to see how damaging it would be to the family for her to leave?"

The whine in Frederick's voice grated on Ryan's nerves. It was past time for his son to live with the consequences of his actions. "No."

"But—"

"Getting your mistress pregnant is something no wife should have to tolerate." Ryan stared straight into his eldest son's eyes, which begged to make his problems disappear. He firmed his lips, tired of always bailing out one of his three children. If only his wife had been more supportive of his decisions related to raising their brood when the kids were younger, he wouldn't be having this conversation now when he needed to focus on saving the company. "If Cynthia has decided this is the final straw, I will not intervene."

"She'll clean me out!" Anger laced Frederick's words. "Plus I'll have to pay Natasha child support. She's already told me she's keeping the baby."

Ryan refrained from rolling his eyes at the expectation he would once again step in and untangle the trouble Frederick had made. "Of course she is—that's her ticket to at least eighteen years of monthly payments from you." He pointed to the door. "You made the mess, you sort it out. I have a board meeting to prepare for."

Frederick stormed toward the door, yanking it open. "I can't believe you'll let her destroy my family."

"You did that all on your own." Ryan turned away, his attention on how to calm the jittery board members. He barely noticed his son's departure as he focused on the spreadsheets showing rising profits and a rosy outlook for the rest of the fiscal year. The numbers should be enough of a distraction from any takeover rumors. His desk phone buzzed. The temptation to ignore it warred with the knowledge Mae Stanhope, his long-time assistant, knew not to bother him with unimportant matters during his board prep time.

He snatched up the receiver. "Yes?"

"Mr. Topher, I have Mr. Conner on line two."

Blake Conner's timing was as impeccable as always. "Thank you." Ryan punched in the number. "Blake, good to hear from you."

"It's not good."

His long-time friend's voice was hushed. Ryan's stomach clenched. "What does that mean?"

"It means the rumors are true—Maxwell Technology is putting together a hostile takeover bid."

This could not have come at a worse time, with the board breathing down his neck and the delay of Vie, an AI-powered wearable device. He pinched the bridge of his nose. If he could keep his father from getting wind of this new development, he could find a way out to retain control of the company and bring Vie to market within six months. He had to manage this or his father would come out of retirement to oust him. Ryan had to keep that from happening or he'd lose more than his title at the company. "Thanks for the heads-up."

"I don't have to tell you what could happen if this goes through."

He certainly did not, but his siblings would help him come up with a plan to salvage the company. After talking about getting together for a golf game next week and exchanging goodbyes, Ryan disconnected. As he replaced the receiver, he hoped that would be the end of the bad news coming his way today.

But the phone buzzed as soon as he'd lifted his hand. "Mae, I'm busy—"

"I'm glad to hear it, son."

His father's gravelly voice punched him in the gut. "Dad, sorry. I'm prepping for the board meeting, and—"

As usual, his father didn't give him a chance to finish. Whatever Peter had to say was always more important than anyone else. "Consider this a courtesy call letting you know I'll be attending."

"The board meeting?" Ryan blurted the question before he could curb his tongue. His father coming would only complicate an already delicate dance.

"Of course the board meeting. Are you sure you're up to running things? You seem a little distracted."

"Frederick just left with the news Cynthia's leaving him." Ryan hoped their family drama would distract his father from commenting further on Ryan's behavior.

"Found out his mistress was pregnant, did she?" Peter chortled. "Guess even Cynthia has her limits."

"You knew?" Ryan shouldn't have been surprised. His father had spies everywhere. He made a mental note to sweep his office for bugs again, as Dad wasn't above using whatever means possible to meddle in the company and his children's and grandchildren's lives.

"Stop asking dumb questions and get ready for the board meeting." His father hung up, leaving Ryan vacillating between amused and annoyed at Peter's interference.

Thanks for upping the ante, Dad. Ryan blew out a breath and made a mental note to have Mae schedule a massage for him before work tomorrow. Then he buckled down to prepare for the board meeting that might determine the fate of the company, his own job—and perhaps even his life.

CHAPTER

FIVE

Seth hefted the free weights to his chest, sweat running into his eyes. He blinked to clear his vision as Clancy Meadows—a former Grand Prix Pennsylvania champion bodybuilder—spotted him.

"You've got this. Easy does it." Clancy talked him through several reps of dead lifting four hundred pounds. "That's enough for today."

Seth wanted to argue for more time but instead lowered the weights to the floor in a controlled movement.

Clancy clapped him on the shoulder. "Your mind isn't here today."

Seth mopped the sweat from his face with a clean towel. The older man was correct in his assumption. Seth wasn't concentrating on the workout, usually one of his favorite parts of the day. Instead of working his muscles until they ached, his mind kept drifting to a blue-eyed strawberry blonde. "Sorry about that."

"Son, there's no need to apologize. You're a hard worker, but I can tell something's bothering you." The owner of God's Body Gym grinned. "I bet it's your young lady, am I right?"

Seth should never have let slip his interest in Jetta, and nothing he'd said since had convinced Clancy she was way out of his league.

Clancy nudged his shoulder. "Hey, man. I was only teasing."

"I know." Seth glanced around the gym where mostly men worked on toning their bodies while instrumental hymns played through the sound system. No one seemed to be waiting for Clancy's attention, so he decided to see if the older man had any advice. "I had an unusual encounter with Jetta yesterday."

"Ah." Clancy placed a ten-pound weight to its proper slot on the rack.

His roommates would have pounced on his statement with rapid-fire questions, but Clancy's noncommittal response loosened Seth's tongue.

"Her dog needed help." Seth relayed the info about what happened to Bingley and the raccoon as succinctly as possible.

"You're worried someone's targeting her."

Seth hadn't breathed a word of his suspicions, but Clancy must have picked up on his concern. "It definitely didn't seem random."

Clancy cocked his head. "What are you going to do about it?"

"I checked her yard and found some bits of ground beef by the back fence, which I cleaned up."

"That's a good start."

The older man's direct gaze made Seth think he'd missed a question on a quiz he'd forgotten to study for, but he didn't know what else the man wanted him to do.

"I was married once."

"You were?" Seth had been going to the gym for nearly three years and had thought he and Clancy were friends, but he'd never known this bit of the other man's history.

"I was. She died much too young. Never wanted to try my luck again, she was that special."

"Oh." Seth cleared his throat as he took in the sheen of moisture in the older man's eyes. "I'm sorry."

"I am too, that you never met my Raylene." Clancy swiped a tear from his cheek without apology. "But she told me something I never forgot—that a kindness done is one a woman always remembers. Seems to me, you did your young lady a kindness more than once these past months."

Seth mulled that over, hope beating to life in his heart. Maybe Jetta was waiting for him to move their relationship beyond friendship. "That may be, but that doesn't mean she's amenable to going out with me."

"My advice?"

Seth nodded while Clancy gathered some dirty towels left beside the bench press machine before continuing. "Don't overthink it. If she's special enough to catch your attention, then she's worth putting yourself out there to let her know that."

Seth absently rubbed a towel over his shoulders as the older man left to answer another patron's question. Jetta had responded to his text about his backyard find with a thumbs-up emoji. Maybe he should have looked around the house as well to make sure it was safe for Bingley. He checked the time. If he hustled, he could do that before he showered and headed to his next assignment photographing the unveiling of a new eco-friendly mixed-use building with residential and retail offerings.

After parking in his driveway, he noted Jetta's vehicle wasn't in its usual spot in front of the garage. She probably had left already to stop by Emily's before getting Bingley from the vet. He hustled over and started with the back of the house. Nothing out of the ordinary around the foundation. He moved to the sides, then tackled the front. A piece of paper wedged behind one of the potted mums sitting to the right of the door snagged his attention.

When he unfolded it, he frowned. At first, the words made no sense, then their meaning became clearer.

He fumbled for his phone and snapped several photos. Not his best work, but despite the crumbled paper, the words printed in block letters in a thick, red marker couldn't have been clearer. Gripping the paper by an edge, he returned to his house and slipped it inside a plastic zipper-top bag.

"I thought you'd gone to work." Wade Frazier strolled into the kitchen, coffee mug in hand.

Before Seth could reply, his roommate pointed to the bag on the kitchen counter. "What's that?"

"It's a note I found on the front porch of the Ainsley house."

Wade raised his eyebrows. "Stalking her now, are you?"

Seth resisted the urge to rub the back of his neck as heat climbed up and into his cheeks. "No, I was checking close to the house to make sure nothing would harm her dog." He quickly recounted what had happened to Bingley yesterday evening and what he'd found this morning.

"Wow, that's terrible." Wade nodded toward the table. "You think this means the poisoning was deliberate?"

"What else could it be?" Seth hadn't wanted it to be true, but finding the ground beef plus the note meant someone had targeted the Ainsleys.

"Have you told Jetta yet?"

Seth shook his head. "She's gone to visit her mom, then she'll swing by to get the dog. I wasn't sure this was something I should text. But I need to get cleaned up and to work, so I can't wait until she returns to show her in person."

His roommate put his mug into the dishwasher. "Seems to me like sending a text is the next best thing." He checked his phone. "Gotta run. See you at Bible study tonight?"

"I should be able to make it, unless something comes up at work." Seth sighed, then composed a text to Jetta describing how the note had been found. He selected the best picture of it and attached it to the message. His thumb hovered over the send arrow, re-reading the stark words on the page once more.

Consider this a warning. Next time, it won't be an animal that gets hurt.

～

MAE STANHOPE REREAD THE EMAIL, HER HEART RATE RISING WITH EACH word. No, no, no! This couldn't be happening again. She'd put this all behind her years ago, repaid the debt with interest, and still it hadn't been enough. She slumped in the chair, tears pressing at the backs of her eyelids. Why couldn't they leave her alone? She'd had to live with the guilt of what she'd done to cover her own tracks, but it had been worth it to ease the end of her father's life. Instead of his last days in a state-run nursing home with indifferent staff, he'd had a private room and round-the-clock nurses to care for him as the cancer enjoyed its last meal on his frail body.

"Honey? It's nearly eight."

She exited out of the email program on her phone as Anderson, her husband of thirty-eight years, entered their bedroom. "I thought you said you needed to be in the office by eight-thirty for some big meeting."

Mae raised the phone. "Got caught up in checking email and lost track of time." She rose. "I'm off. I might be late coming home because of the emergency board meeting."

The disappointment that drew down his features usually made her reassure him that she would soon join him in retirement. Then the two of them would start traveling like they'd always planned. Instead, she planted a quick kiss on his cheek and hustled down the stairs, her mind whirring with how to respond to the email.

During the drive to Topher Robotics, the words her anonymous tormenter had written replayed in her mind like the banner under a news program. This time, it wasn't a coverup they requested but spying. Who did they think she was? A female James Bond? No, she wasn't cut out for espionage. She might have taken some money, but she hadn't hurt anyone. And she'd been paying it back with interest when the first email had landed in her personal inbox eighteen years ago.

At the gate, she used her employee ID card to gain access, then proceeded to the employee parking lot. Before going into the building where she'd worked for more than twenty years, she opened the email again. The sender had demanded she respond by text to an included number. Mae keyed it in, then typed her reply.

> Impossible. I'm no spy and would get caught immediately.

Her phone dinged as soon as she'd closed her car door.

> You're perfect. No one notices middle-aged women.

The words slapped her across the face with their poignant truth. The sender was right—no one noticed her and hadn't for years. That's why she'd gotten away with the original crime. She'd flown so low under the radar, no one could imagine her guilty of taking so much as a paperclip without permission. While she had only siphoned off enough to help her father's last days be more comfortable, someone had found out and used her to redirect millions. Framing Jay Ainsley hadn't been part of the bargain. She'd done nothing to implicate him, but her contact had ensured he took the fall for all of it—the money Mae had taken on her own plus the extra dough she'd been roped into stealing.

Her phone buzzed.

> I want to know what was said in the board meeting as soon as it's over.

"Hi, Mae."

She waved at a colleague as she went into the building, her mind whirring like the windup toy monkey banging cymbals she'd played with as a child.

You got that?

The impatience ignited a spurt of anger, but she tamped it down and responded with a thumbs up emoji. At her desk, which sat outside Ryan Topher's office on the top floor, she put away her purse and phone, then booted up her computer.

"Ready for the meeting, Mae?"

Ryan held a cup of coffee, as if to silently reprimand her for having to get it himself from the small kitchen down the hall.

"Sorry I'm late. Traffic..." She grabbed her steno pad and sharpened pencils. Ryan refused to allow her to take notes on a tablet or laptop during board meetings, preferring her to record the minutes in shorthand. No matter it made extra work for her to transcribe them afterwards. At least Peter Topher, her former boss, had the decency to remember her birthday and ask after Anderson sometimes. Peter had even sent flowers to her father's funeral, something Ryan had failed even to acknowledge.

Ryan turned on his heel and retraced his steps to the large conference room where the board always met, leaving her to scurry behind him. She slipped in, taking her usual seat in the corner next to the vent, which blew cold or hot air directly on her, depending on the season. Today, the air blew cold since the outside temperatures were expected to hit the low eighties. Another touch of summer even though the calendar said late September.

"Are we ready to begin?" Ryan settled into the chair at the head of the table and opened a folder.

"Isn't your father joining us?" Chester Cane, a long-time board member folded his hands on his folder.

"Since my father no longer runs the day-to-day operations of this company, I don't think his presence is necessary." Ryan's smooth tone belied the tightening of his mouth.

Mae recognized his annoyance and mentally sighed. If this didn't go well, Ryan would be in a foul mood all day and make her life even more difficult.

"But this isn't about the daily operations," Brooke Williams protested. "This is about the bid for a hostile takeover from Maxwell Technology."

"Which is why I decided to attend." Peter Topher shut the door with enough force to rattle the china coffee cups in their matching saucers. He glared at his oldest son, who hadn't moved from his place.

"Then by all means, join us." Ryan nodded to an empty chair near the foot of the table.

Mae moved her pencil over the page, quietly recording all conversation. This wouldn't be included in the official meeting minutes, but her tormentor would want to know exactly who said what.

Peter shrugged and took the open seat. But if Ryan thought not giving his father the head seat would send a message as to Peter's importance in the meeting, Chester disabused him of that by directly asking Peter what they should do to combat the takeover bid.

Mae effortlessly kept up with the torrent of words as the atmosphere in the board room heated up. Good thing the A/C was on today—maybe it would cool things off. As she flipped to a fresh page, she worried about what the next assignment from her mysterious contact would be, because she had no doubt this was only the beginning of round two.

SIX

Jetta hadn't believed her mother could ever look frail, her personality had always been so larger-than-life. After her father had died, Mom had returned to teaching high school English, spending most of her academic career at a Title I school in Washington DC. Her stories of facing down student gang members had made Jetta's hair curl but most of her students had loved her.

Now as Jetta hovered in the doorway of the physical therapy room at the rehab center watching her mother lift weights with a therapist's assistance, she noted new lines on her mother's face and pain pinches bracketing her mouth and eyes. Learning the additional burden her mother had carried about her husband being accused of embezzlement made her admire how Mom had shielded Jetta from the truth. But that admiration didn't excuse her mother's failure to inform Jetta about what happened to her father.

"One more, Emily. You can do it." The therapist's gentle but firm encouragement seemed to spur Mom on to finish the rep. "All done for today. You did good."

"I don't feel like I'm making any progress. Probably won't until this blasted cast is off." Mom wobbled a bit, and the therapist guided her to a waiting wheelchair.

Jetta stepped into the room. "Hi, Mom."

"You're early." Mom still sounded grumpy, but Jetta didn't take it personally. Her mother never liked to be seen as weak by anyone, even one of her daughters. "But since you're here, you can take me back to my room."

"Yes, ma'am." Jetta gave a mock salute.

"I don't need your sarcasm, young lady. I brought you into this world—"

Jetta finished the familiar saying with her mother, "And I can take you out of this world."

A faint smile creased Mom's face. Jetta dropped a light kiss on her forehead, then aimed the wheelchair toward the door. "Ready, set, go!" She pushed the chair as fast as she could, sliding out of the door and into the wide hallway.

"Jetta! It isn't a race." The banked laughter in her mother's voice gave lie to the scold.

"Yes, ma'am." She slowed her pace a fraction to make a right turn, then sprinted down the long, empty hall. The wheels sped along the polished linoleum.

"Wheee!" Mom pumped a fist in the air.

Jetta dug in her heels to slow the chair as they neared another turn, this time to the left. Her foot slipped, but she managed to keep her balance and the chair upright. She leaned into the chair, using the momentum to turn it without more pressure.

"What is going on?" An older man, his face suffused with red, blocked their way a short distance down the hall. "This isn't a roller derby."

Jetta slowed the chair to a halt a couple of feet in front of him. Mom smiled up at the man. "Mr. Danvers, have you met my youngest daughter, Jetta? Jetta, this is the daytime manager, Mr. Danvers."

"Nice to meet you, Mr. Danvers." Jetta held out her hand to the man, but he ignored it.

"Mrs. Ainsley, you must not allow your family members to behave in such a way. It's simply not how we run things at Sunshine Rehab Center."

"Perhaps it should be, Mr. Danvers." Mom craned her neck to catch her daughter's eye and winked. Then she slumped in the chair, the picture of fragility. "Please take me to my room. I'm feeling tired all of a sudden."

"Yes, ma'am." Jetta nodded at Mr. Danvers and hustled her mother down the hall to her room. Once inside, she shut the door and helped her mother to the easy chair. "Do you need anything else?"

"Some water, please." Mom gestured to the plastic cup with a lid and straw on the end table.

After filling the large mug with water, she returned. "Here you go."

"Thank you, my dear." Mom took a long swig. "And thanks for the ride."

"I hope I didn't get you Mr. Danvers' bad graces."

Mom waved her hand. "I can handle Mr. Danvers. He thinks much too highly of himself as it is, so I never pass up the opportunity to tweak his nose a bit."

Jetta filled a plastic cup with water from the adjourning bathroom for herself, then took the window seat. She should tell Mom about what happened to Bingley but wasn't sure how to phrase it so as to not alarm her. She also wanted to bring up the subject of Dad and the charges leveled against him, but seeing how exhausted Mom appeared, she decided to wait before opening that particular can of worms.

Her mother set the mug on the tray table. "I have something to tell you."

The serious expression on her mother's face sent her heart rate soaring. Was her mother's condition more serious than she'd thought?

"I'm fine, at least physically."

Mom's ability to read Jetta's mind hadn't dimmed over the years. "That obvious?"

"Only to your mother." Mom sighed. "I should have told you years ago, but it's something I wanted to forget."

Jetta suspected she knew the topic. "It's about Dad and the embezzlement charges, right?"

"How did you know?" Mom narrowed her eyes. "Did one of your siblings tell you?"

"Jason and Jade did, but not until I asked them yesterday when they called me." Before her mother could ask her further questions, Jetta tugged the envelope from her purse. "This came in the mail, addressed to Dad."

Her mother took the proffered envelope. She ran a finger over the address, then pulled the envelope closer to her face. "This was mailed fifteen years ago?"

"I think so, as the postmark appears genuine, especially when you read the note inside." Jetta waited while her mother extracted the papers and read the top sheet before shuffling through the remaining pages.

A few tears trickled down Mom's cheeks. "Oh, if only this had arrived on time, your father might still be alive." She blotted her cheeks with a tissue. "I never doubted his innocence. Your father had more integrity in his little finger than most people had in their entire bodies. There was no way—No. Way.—Dad would have taken that money." She gripped the envelope. "Someone framed him, and now we have proof."

Math had never been Jetta's strong suit—she much preferred wordsmithing to addition or subtraction. The spreadsheets and bank accounts with all those numbers meant little to her. "So you under-stand what the enclosed pages mean?"

"I haven't a clue. I've been thinking a lot about that time since

I've been laid up with this monstrosity." She thumped her leg cast. "Hindsight does give you clarity, and I wish I had pushed more to clear your father's name."

"Why didn't you?"

"Grief, then trying to simply survive. I did talk to a lawyer but was advised to let it drop lest Topher Robotics take me to court to recover the millions Dad had been accused of embezzling. I couldn't afford that, so I convinced myself the wisest course of action would be to do nothing."

Jetta mentally reviewed all the information she'd read online. "I read the newspaper accounts from the time, but most of the stories after Dad died rehashed the charges. Did they ever find the money they said Dad had taken?"

"No. After Dad died, Topher Robotics hired a forensic accountant to go through the books to figure out where the money had gone. They tracked down about two million in an offshore account in the Cayman Islands Dad allegedly opened and recovered that money. But eight nor nine million was never recovered."

"I don't understand how the accusations against Dad stuck in the first place."

"Someone needed a scapegoat, and he was the only C-suite executive who wasn't a Topher."

Jetta considered the information while taking a sip of water. "You think the true embezzler was someone connected with the Topher family."

"There are certainly lots to choose from." Mom's dry tone eased some of the concern in Jetta's chest. Her mother sounded more like her old self. "Take a look at the About page on the company website, and you'll see it's stuffed with Tophers."

"Were most of them there when Dad was?"

"Yes, the executives, vice presidents, and directors are all Tophers and had been at the company when Dad was CFO. I did try to get a copy of the forensic accountant's report but was rebuffed." Mom sighed, a long, drawn-out sound that seemed to mirror her frustration. "I wasn't surprised. Dad was the outsider, the one Peter Topher, who founded the company, brought in over the objections of his sons and daughter."

Jetta digested the info as more questions pounded through her mind. Her phone buzzed, and she glanced at the screen to see an incoming text from Seth. She'd read it later, not wanting to be distracted from this conversation.

"As I mentioned, I've been thinking about this, and I've come to a decision. I'm going to pursue justice for Dad."

"What do you mean?"

"Last week, I emailed Ryan Topher, CEO of the company, and demanded he clear Dad's name by reopening the investigation into who took the money."

"Have you heard back?" Jetta was curious how the company would react to such a direct request.

Mom shook her head. "Not a peep, so yesterday I called and spoke to his administrative assistant, Mae something or other, but the call dropped before I was connected to Ryan."

"They hung up on you?"

"Maybe, but once we get this new evidence interpreted, we'll have more ammunition to force them to say Jay wasn't involved in the embezzlement."

A knock on the door preceded a woman entering wearing Snoopy scrubs and a red bandana. "Mrs. Ainsley, it's time for chair yoga."

"Okay, Alison."

Jetta moved out of the way as the aide helped her mother back into her wheelchair. "Give me a minute to say goodbye to my daughter."

"Sure, Mrs. Ainsley." Alison turned to Jetta. "Just push her chair to the hallway when you're leaving."

Jetta nodded. Her mother didn't speak until the aide had left the room. "Did you make a copy of the papers?"

"In the envelope?" It hadn't occurred to Jetta to do so.

"Yes." Mom interpreted Jetta's question as a negative response. "Would you? I'd feel better knowing this wasn't the only copy."

"Why would you say that?" Jetta frowned, as Seth's insistence in checking her yard for evidence of whatever sickened Bingley and killed the raccoon filtered into her mind.

"Because whoever stole that money has gotten away with it for years." Emily gripped the envelope. "Please make a copy of these papers."

"Of course." Jetta took the envelope, then kissed her cheek. "You sure you're okay?"

"Determined to see this through." Mom chuckled. "I've probably watched too many Hallmark Mysteries lately and see intrigue behind every shrub."

"Perhaps lay off those shows for a bit?" She pushed her mother's wheelchair through the door and into the hall. "But I'll follow your advice and make copies."

"When will you be back?"

Alison came out of another resident's room and headed toward her mother.

"I'll see if I can return later today."

"You'll bring me dinner?"

The hopeful look on her mother's face brought a smile to her own. "A number nine sub from Jersey Mike's?"

"With extra lettuce and pickles." Mom waggled her fingers at Jetta as Alison took charge of her wheelchair.

Once outside in the bright fall morning, Jetta breathed in deeply to calm her mind. She slid into her vehicle before she remembered Seth's text. She'd read it before going to pick up Bingley.

> Checked the yard and found bits of ground
> beef near the back right corner of your yard.
> I also looked at the outside of the house but
> found nothing. Well, nothing related to
> whatever Bingley and the raccoon ate. I did
> find a piece of paper on the stoop near the
> front door. I'm not sure what it means but I
> kept it. Let me know when you'll be home,
> and I'll bring it over.

He included a picture of the paper. Jetta had to read it twice before her brain could comprehend the message:

Consider this a warning. Next time, it won't be an animal that gets hurt.

～

A FIRE AT A CONSTRUCTION SITE OCCUPIED THE REST OF SETH'S MORNING. As he snapped photos, he resisted the urge to constantly check his phone to see if Jetta had responded to his text. The eleven-story mixed-use complex had been halfway completed when flames erupted shortly after workers arrived for the day. Activists had vehemently opposed the building with its eight hundred luxury condo units and space for up to ten retailers on the ground and second floors because it would remove ten acres of woodland. The environmental protestors had been demonstrating in front of the site for weeks, leading to increasingly violent scuffles between the workers and demonstrators. Seth had visited the site several times to photograph the protestors.

As he focused his camera on the still smoldering area, speculation that the activists had started the fire spread through the gathering crowd. Seth doubted the group had orchestrated the fire, given their heroic efforts to assist construction workers fleeing the flames. He counted at least a dozen people—both activists and workers—

being treated by paramedics, but he hadn't been able to ascertain the extent of the injuries.

Brogan Gilmore jogged up, notebook and phone in hand. "Hey, Seth. What have you gotten so far?"

Seth gave his *Herald* colleague a run down on his photos, then pointed toward the far end of the site where a group of firefighters in protective gear used long-handled sticks to sort through one section of the smoldering ruins. "I was heading over there to see if I could get another angle on the firefighters."

Brogan nodded his approval. "After that, do you think you could photograph the crowd without anyone noticing?"

"In case the arsonist is admiring his handiwork?"

"Exactly." Brogan paused. "Although no one's officially saying it's arson."

"No one besides the rumor mill." Seth adjusted the lens to take a long shot of the firefighters.

Brogan leaned closer. "One of my sources says the owner has run into money trouble and can't make this month's payroll."

He lowered the camera. "You're thinking this might be insurance fraud."

"It's possible. Gotta go catch the fire marshal. Let me know if you see anything interesting." With a wave, Brogan hurried toward an older woman wearing full protective gear huddled with a police officer and another firefighter.

Seth inched closer to the fencing, taking several photos of the firefighters among the building's ruin. Then he slipped behind the front of an idling ambulance to surreptitiously take pictures of the crowd, which had swelled in numbers. His phone buzzed but he ignored it until he was satisfied he'd gotten all the shots he could from his vantage point.

Pulling out his phone, he glanced at the screen. Dismay punched him in the gut at the sight of a missed call from Jetta. A quick check showed she hadn't left a voicemail. He hit her name on the recent call list to return the call.

"Hello?" She sounded breathless.

"It's Seth. I missed a call from you?" He winced at the question in what he'd meant to be a statement. What if she'd pocket dialed him?

"Seth, thank goodness you're there."

He slipped through the crowd toward his vehicle as the sense something wasn't right with Jetta firmed with every step. "What's wrong?"

"I think someone's following me."

"Where are you?" He chirped open his Rav4 hybrid.

"I'm on my way to pick up Bingley from the vet's on Route 50 near Graham Road."

He slid his camera into its case in the backseat before climbing behind the wheel, starting the engine to connect the call to Bluetooth. "What makes you think someone's following you?"

"There's a white pickup that has been a couple of cars behind me for miles, maybe ever since I left the rehab center in Reston."

He programed the Happy Animal Clinic address into his car's GPS. "I'll meet you at the vet's."

"Thank you." Her voice hitched as if she was choking back a sob.

"Are you okay?" Dumb question, considering the message he'd found and texted her.

"I don't know." She blew out a breath. "My mom has started looking into what happened to my dad."

"I thought you said your father died when you were a kid?" Seth should have couched the question with more sensitivity, but her comment had caught him off guard. He turned onto the road out of the complex parking lot.

"He did, but apparently, there's more to the story—much more —than I ever knew. And now I don't know what to think or do."

"I see." He didn't, but maybe when he saw her, she would elaborate more.

"I—"

Her scream cut off whatever she was about to say.

"Jetta!" Seth slammed on his brakes to avoid ramming the car in front of him, which had stopped at a traffic light. The call dropped before he could hear a reply. His heart pounded faster than a heavy metal drummer. GPS informed him it would take twenty-three minutes to reach the clinic. Jetta had said she'd been near Graham Road and 50, so he reprogrammed the GPS to that location and shaved four minutes off his arrival time. Still too long. With a prayer for Jetta's safety, he reined in his impatience and concentrated on making the drive as quickly as possible.

CHAPTER

SEVEN

The impact of the truck into her smaller crossover vehicle snapped Jetta forward, her seatbelt holding her in place. She mashed on the brake pedal and wrenched the wheel to the right to avoid clipping the car in front of her. By some miracle, she managed to maneuver onto the grassy verge and out of the traffic lane. The pickup roared off, weaving in and out of traffic until she couldn't see it any longer.

Her phone had flown from the console onto the floor of the front passenger seat. She trembled so violently, it took her three tries to put her car into park and cut the engine. She set the emergency brake and hit the flashers before releasing her seatbelt. Her shoulder and hips ached but she was in one piece. At least the airbag hadn't deployed. Rubbing her belly, she prayed her baby was okay too.

Reaching over, she snagged the phone and placed a call to 911. A knock on the passenger side window, which she'd lowered a couple of inches, triggered a scream.

A man held up a phone, his forehead creased. "I called 911. Police and ambulance are on their way. Are you okay?"

"911, where's your emergency?"

Jetta raised her finger to the man to indicate she was on a call and replied to the dispatcher. "Someone clipped me with their vehicle and fled the scene, but another driver called it in, so I think I'm good."

"What's your location?"

"I'm on 50 near Graham Road." Jetta clenched her fingers together to stop the shaking.

"I'm showing emergency personnel are on their way to that location. Are you in a safe place to wait?"

"Yes, thank you." Jetta disconnected the phone and turned to the man. "Thank you for calling. I think I'm okay. Did you see what happened?"

"Yeah, a white truck with Florida plates clipped your bumper." He craned his neck as if to see the back of her vehicle. "Your left rear bumper is toast. I was sure you were going to smash into other cars."

"Me too." She leaned back against the seat as the sound of sirens filled the air. Seth! She'd been talking to him when the accident occurred. Before she could hit redial, an ambulance screeched to a halt, along with a fire truck and police cruiser. Opting instead for a quick text, she let him know she was fine.

The next moments blurred as she repeated what had happened to a Fairfax County police officer, then allowed an EMT to check her over for injuries in the back of the ambulance. He gave her over-the-counter pain medication and an ice pack for the darkening bruises on her shoulder and hip. He strongly recommended she report to her OB-GYN to check on the baby.

"Jetta!" She turned from the back of the ambulance as Seth raced up, his face pale. "Are you okay?"

"Just some bruises, thank goodness."

His concerned expression nearly made her rush into his arms, but she hugged herself instead. Hadn't she learned her lesson in Chicago about letting her feelings push her too quickly into a relationship?

"What happened?" He reached out a hand as if to touch her

shoulder but dropped it without making contact. "I was so worried when the call dropped after you screamed."

She drew in a breath, then recounted the accident. "A bystander snapped a photo of the fleeing truck, and the police officer said the vehicle was reported stolen."

"Have they recovered the truck?"

"I don't know." She shivered. Seth stepped closer, his bulk soothing instead of intimidating her like a man of his size would normally do. So unlike Kyle, who used his height to get his way. She'd thought Kyle had a kinder side too until he'd proved her wrong. Better to remember that and not get fooled again. Seth's caring veneer might hide a darker underbelly.

A light touch on her arm brought her out of the painful memories and back to the side of the road. Seth's gaze fastened on hers, his brown eyes dark with compassion.

"Sorry, trying to make sense of it all," she said, not bothering to explain what was on her mind. Let him think it was the accident rather than her ex.

The Fairfax County Police officer—O'Brien, Jetta recalled—returned. Jetta introduced Seth as her next-door neighbor and indicated the officer could talk in front of him.

"Ms. Ainsley, we have reports of a truck abandoned at a Safeway parking lot a few miles from here with the driver gone. We'll tow it to our forensics lab to see about any prints and to match the damage on the vehicle's front bumper with your car."

By the skepticism she detected in the officer's voice, Jetta said, "But you don't think we'll catch whoever hit me."

O'Brien shook her head. "My guess is whoever stole the vehicle clipped your car by accident as they attempted to put as much distance between where they got the truck and wherever they were headed."

"You don't believe Jetta was deliberately targeted?" Seth's question was one Jetta hadn't considered.

"Why would you think that?" O'Brien raised her eyebrows as she looked from Jetta back to Seth.

"Because someone deliberately poisoned her dog yesterday and killed a raccoon," Seth said.

"Tell me what happened." O'Brien pulled a notebook from her breast pocket and jotted down Jetta's account of Bingley's trip to the vet. "Where's this dead raccoon?"

"In my trashcan," Seth said. "I checked her backyard this morning and found traces of ground beef near the left back corner fence line." He showed several photos of the flecks of hamburger on his phone to the officer and Jetta.

O'Brien frowned. "I'll send one of our animal control officers over to recover the raccoon's body and do a thorough search of your yard. Do you have any security cameras installed on the property?"

"Not that I know of, but I'll ask my mom." Jetta explained about her mother's accident. "I'm cleaning out the home so Mom can put it on the market. She needs to live in a one-level home when she gets out of rehab." Too much information the officer didn't need to know, but Jetta couldn't wrap her mind around the idea of someone after her. Kyle had harassed her, but his MO was to use his current love interest to do his dirty work for him. Except for...

Jetta clamped a hand over her mouth as bile rose in her throat. She stumbled toward a bit of land between the pavement and a parking lot curb and heaved the contents of her stomach onto the straggling grass. She leaned over, hands on her knees until the nausea passed. After straightening, she wiped the back of her hand over her mouth. Yuck. She needed something to swish out the aftertaste.

"Here." Seth handed her bottle of water. "It's a little warm."

She accepted it and used a mouthful to rinse her mouth, spitting it out onto the grass. Then she drank some of the water. "Sorry about that."

"No need to apologize." His gaze flicked down to her extended belly, then back to her face. "It happens."

"Ms. Ainsley?" O'Brien called. "Are you feeling better?"

Jetta nodded, then returned to where the office stood by the crushed back bumper of her car. She couldn't dredge up another apology for her unruly stomach.

"Is there anything else I need to know?"

"Yes." Seth showed the officer the photo of the note. "I found it on her front porch this morning when I was checking the outside of the house for any more contaminated meat."

The officer read the note. "What do you think it means?"

"I have no idea." A headache gathered strength behind her eyes. "I've only been home for the past seven months."

"Where were you before?" the officer asked.

"Chicago." Jetta didn't provide additional info, not wanting to go down that particular rabbit trail.

"And you're helping your mom?"

"Yes." Jetta had nothing else to add, fatigue pulling at her body as the adrenaline drained away.

"I put the note in a plastic bag. It's at my house," Seth put in.

"I'll tell the animal control officer to pick it up when she comes to do the sweep of the backyard." O'Brien closed her notebook. "I'll let you know if forensics recovers anything useable from the truck."

"Do you think this is related to the string of carjackings and stolen vehicles?" Seth inquired. *The Herald* ran a story about the uptick in those kinds of crime last week."

"Possibly." O'Brien firmed her lips, indicating she wouldn't be saying anything more. "Here's my card. Your vehicle appears to be drivable. Contact me in a few days for a copy of the accident report."

"I will, thank you." Jetta pocketed the card, then checked her phone. 11:45 p.m. "I need to pick up Bingley from the vet by one."

He glanced toward the traffic moving at a steady clip on the busy road, then back to her. "I had to park across the street." He pointed to the parking lot of a Latino grocery store. "Would you like me to follow you to the vet and home?"

Relief coursed through her at his offer. She hadn't realized how nervous she was about driving anywhere by herself. "Sure."

He nodded, then waited for a break in traffic before jogging across the street. She climbed into her vehicle and started the engine as she waited for him to come her way. The emergency vehicles cleared the area and traffic soon returned to normal. When Seth pulled behind her, her heart skipped a beat—because she was relieved to have someone following her home, not because of his concern for her. Jetta didn't want to focus on the latter, no matter how much her heart told her otherwise.

SETH HURRIED FROM HIS DRIVEWAY TO JETTA'S, CATCHING UP WITH HER AS she inserted her key into the deadbolt at the front door. Bingley milled about her feet, his leash looped over her wrist. By the slump of her shoulders, exhaustion had staked a claim on her body, probably aided by an adrenaline crash. While he needed to go through the fire scene photos and submit some with captions to his editor, he had to ensure Jetta and her dog were safe and sound first. She'd hardly said a word at the vet, who had declared Bingley fully recovered.

While he didn't want to overstep, he did want to do what he could to help. "If you'd like, I could take Bingley to my backyard until you're settled inside."

She removed the key before turning to him. "Would you? I'd forgotten I can't let him out back until animal control comes by to check the yard."

"Happy to." He held out his hand, and she placed the leash in his open palm. "Take your time. We'll be fine. Come on, Bingley." With a wave to Jetta, he jogged back to his house, pausing at his side gate to open it. Once inside the enclosure, he secured the gate, then released Bingley to explore the space. The dog raced from one area to another, sniffing furiously before selecting a corner of the yard to do his business. That morning, Seth had done a sweep of this space as well as Jetta's to ensure it would be safe for Bingley—a precaution he was glad he'd taken. He found a sturdy stick near the fire pit and tossed for Bingley to chase, having seen Jetta throw balls with the dog.

"Hey." Jetta closed the gate behind her and joined Seth. "Thanks for this."

"Anytime. We hardly use the backyard, so you can let Bingley play here for as long as you need to."

The dog bounded up and dropped the stick at Jetta's feet. She obliged with a toss, and Bingley ran after it. "You work for *The Herald*, right?"

"I do, mostly as a photographer, although I do write some of the shorter news pieces." As if on cue, Seth's phone buzzed, probably Fallon or Brogan harping about the fire pics.

"Do you have to get that?" She nodded toward his pocket where an incoming call buzzed incessantly. Bingley brought the stick back, then flopped down in front of them to gnaw at it.

He glanced at the screen. Brogan. He let the call roll to voicemail. "I'll get it later."

Her gaze directed toward the dog, she hunched her shoulders. "Being a journalist, you know how to find things out, don't you?"

He nodded. Her mouth pinched, and a line creased her forehead. Something was bothering her beyond the accident. He recalled she'd mentioned something about her father but had given no details. When she didn't expound, he prompted. "What do you want to find out?"

"Whether my father was guilty of embezzlement." She shot him a glance as if to gauge his reaction.

Seth didn't respond, letting her tell the story in her own way. He thought he might have passed a test because her shoulders relaxed.

"It's been fifteen years since he was accused of taking millions from Topher Robotics, where he was the chief financial officer. When the cops came to arrest him at our house while I was at a friend's house, he collapsed with a heart attack. He didn't make it."

"I'm so sorry." Seth responded to the pain in her voice, although he couldn't imagine actually missing the man who'd fathered him. He didn't know if his dad were alive or dead—and he didn't care to find out. Not after the childhood he'd had. But he shoved those memories back into their scarred box hidden deep in his heart and refocused on Jetta. "What happened with the embezzlement charges?"

She shrugged. "I have no idea. I only found out about the accusation yesterday. I was still in elementary school, but my brothers and sisters were either in college or already working their first fulltime jobs." Her lips quirked upward. "My dad always called me his little unexpected caboose."

"How many siblings do you have?" He couldn't recall how many kids Emily had mentioned over the years and envied Jetta her obviously close-knit family.

"Four. Jared's the oldest and sixteen years older than me. Then comes Jenna, who's fourteen years older." Jetta ticked off siblings on her fingers. "Jason comes next, and he's a dozen years older, and Jade's only ten years older. All are married, but only Jared and Jason have kids."

"What about you?" Heat climbed the back of Seth's neck at his inane question. Obviously she was about to have a baby.

She chuckled, the sound thready. "I've sworn off men."

His heart sank at the pain and determination in the words. He wanted to press for an explanation but instead turned the conversation back to her father. "You said they all knew about your father's, er, problem?"

"Yes." She directed her gaze to him. "Then this morning, I opened a package addressed to my dad that arrived in yesterday's mail. It had a note saying the enclosed documents could help clear my father's name."

"Wow."

"Yeah, right?" She reached down to scratch Bingley's head between his ears. "The first I hear about Dad's past is when this mysterious—and anonymous—package shows up saying he's innocent. But that's not even the really strange part."

Seth raised his eyebrows. "It's not?"

"The postmark is from fifteen years ago."

"How could that happen?"

"Who knows? The mail service can be erratic, but losing a package for more than a decade seems extreme. So of course, I Googled 'lost mail' and saw a news article about a letter that finally made it to the recipient a decade after it had been mailed. A US Post Office official said in the article that sometimes mail gets jammed behind the automatic sorting machines and isn't discovered until the piece is moved for cleaning or repairs."

"Weird." A piece of information related to lost mail pushed to the front of his memory. "I think I read somewhere about a letter delivered in England more than a hundred years after it had been mailed, plus another letter in the US that had been lost since World War II."

"Makes me grateful this one made it to us sooner than that."

"What was in the envelope?" Seth figured he could ask since she'd been so open with him about the situation.

"Spreadsheets and bank statements." Bingley nudged into Jetta, the movement drawing her attention to the animal. "Oh, right. I should feed you." She patted the dog's head. "The thing is, my mom said she's determined to find out the truth behind the accusations, and I want to help."

She bit her lower lip. "I'm not sure where to start, but maybe you could help?"

"I'd be happy to." His heart thudded at the thought of spending more time with Jetta. He sternly told himself it was because she needed his assistance, not that she wanted an excuse to be with him. Besides, she basically indicated she wasn't ready for another relationship.

"You would?" The smile blossoming across her face stole his breath.

He should have said no, palmed her off on Brogan. His heart

would not be safe if she kept looking at him with those big blue eyes and smiling so broadly. His phone buzzed again.

"You need to get back to work, but why don't you come over for dinner and I can show you the papers?"

Seth agreed before he could think better of it. "Sure. What time?"

"How about around six?"

"I'll be there. Can I bring anything?"

"I think I've got it covered, but thanks." She snapped a lead on Bingley's collar. "I appreciate your help with my dog and coming out to the accident scene. I'd been feeling overwhelmed lately and praying about cleaning out the house, my mom, and ... things."

He didn't miss the hesitation between the last two words, wondering if her swearing off men had anything to do with the "things" that had been overwhelming her.

"You've been an answer to prayer."

Her words jolted him to the core. Of all the things he expected her to say, that hadn't even occurred to him. He'd never been anyone's answer to prayer, and he liked hearing her say so. She seemed to be expecting a response, so he said, "I'm honored you would consider me so."

His statement brought another dazzling smile to her lips. She tugged on Bingley's leash. "Well, then. I'll see you in a few hours."

"See you." He walked her through the side gate, then headed to his own front door while she and the dog went inside her house. He had to sort through the fire photos and check in with Brogan. Perhaps he'd even have time to a little research into who Jay Ainsley was.

He hesitated before calling Brogan as he reviewed the series of events over the past twenty-four hours. Jetta might not see them as connected, but to his mind, a very clear pattern was emerging. Someone was targeting Jetta—and it was his job to make sure she stayed safe.

CHAPTER

EIGHT

Jetta pulled the roasted chicken thighs with butternut squash and kale from the oven, the familiar scent of rosemary filling her nostrils. Kyle had refused to eat anything with kale—or nearly any other veggie—so she'd adjusted her cooking to accommodate his needs. Now that she no longer had to consider his opinion, she'd been making all her favorite recipes with the green leafy veggie, including the knock-off version of Olive Garden's Zuppa soup.

With his rippling muscles, Seth struck her as someone who ate his veggies, so she'd decided to make the chicken and autumn squash recipe. She surveyed the kitchen table, set with Mom's floral everyday china. She'd been tempted to pull out her parents' wedding plates but decided that would be overkill on their first date. Her hand flew to her mouth as the thought settled like a falling souffle. Would Seth consider this dinner one?

No, of course not. Besides, she was in no condition to think of any man that way. A man as handsome as Seth must have plenty of opportunities to date, and despite his blushes around her, he would recognize her invitation as one extended to say thank you for his assistance with Bingley. That was all. Nothing more. She would make it clear she needed his expertise as a journalist, not as a potential mate.

The doorbell rang, sending Bingley, who'd been snoozing in his dog bed right outside the kitchen, into a frenzy of barking. Butterflies in her stomach joined him as she hurried to open the door.

Seth stood on the porch, a plate covered in foil in his hands. "I brought brownies for dessert."

"How thoughtful, thank you." She stepped back to allow him to enter before closing the door and flipping the deadbolt, a habit she'd acquired since Chicago.

He sniffed, an appreciative look crossing his face. "It smells delicious. Is that butternut squash I detect along with the chicken?"

"Good nose—you're right." She led the way down the short hallway to the kitchen at the back of the house to where the pan with the chicken, squash, and kale rested on a hot pad. "I hope you also like kale."

"I do." He set the plate on the counter. "I make a mean kale smoothie."

"Kale smoothie?" She carried the pan to the table tucked into what her mother had optimistically called a breakfast nook. "I'll have to try that one day."

"I'm happy to make you one the next time I have one myself." Bingley nudged Seth's leg, drawing his attention. "Hey, there." Seth tousled the dog's ears, then scratched behind them. The dog leaned into him, tongue lolling in canine bliss.

"You keep that up, and he's yours for life." Jetta filled a glass with sparkling water from her Soda Stream bottle, then asked Seth what he'd like to drink.

"What you're having sounds good." He gave Bingley another pat on the head, then gently moved the dog out of the way to wash his hands in the sink.

She set his glass on the table, then jumped when he reached

around her to pull out her chair. "Sorry, I'm not used to the royal treatment."

He pushed in her chair, then took a seat across from her. "My grandfather drilled into me to treat women with respect."

"Oh." She wanted to ask more about his grandfather, but that might give Seth the wrong idea about this dinner, so she reached for the serving spoon to fill his plate.

"Do you mind if I say grace first?"

"You're a Christian?" In all their interactions over these past months, they had never discussed faith.

He met her gaze, his brown eyes steady on hers. "Yes, I accepted Jesus in college."

Her shoulders relaxed. "Me too." Maybe that was why she felt so drawn to Seth—she subconsciously sensed his love of Christ. "Please say the blessing."

He reached for her hand, and she slipped hers inside his larger one. Instead of feeling uneasy about his strength like she had with Kyle, holding hands with Seth made her feel safe and secure, like a cherished family heirloom.

"Dear Jesus, please bless our food and our conversation. In your name, amen." He squeezed her hand gently before releasing it. "I can't wait to try this. It looks and smells amazing."

She served him two chicken thighs and a big spoonful of veggies. "It's a pretty simple recipe, but I like the way the chicken juices flavor the squash and kale."

He waited until she had food on her plate before picking up his fork for a bite. "Delicious," he concluded after finishing his first bite. "Would you mind sharing about your faith?"

While they ate, Jetta recapped her own journey to Christ, then asked Seth about his own.

"I attended George Mason University in Fairfax, and one day, in the student union, a church was handing out free Bibles. I took one and started reading Genesis." Seth neatly cut his chicken off the bone while he spoke. "I couldn't stop, and by the time I got to the Gospels,

I knew I wanted to leave my old life behind and become a new person."

"God indeed changes us, doesn't he?" She chewed and swallowed a bite of chicken. "I was raised in church but didn't really think about my own faith until moving back here."

"I'd prayed to God as a child, so perhaps the faith of our youth really doesn't leave us."

"That's a good way to look at it." She sighed. "I feel like my faith would be stronger if I hadn't let it wither for so many years."

"Maybe, but didn't Jesus say even a mustard seed of faith was enough?"

His reminder eased her anxiety. "Where do you go to church?"

"Covenant Community Church. It meets at the Falls Church High School. It's a Presbyterian Church of America church plant from McLean Presbyterian Church."

"Maybe I'll check that out one Sunday. I haven't found a local place to worship yet. Back in Chicago, I attended a nondenominational congregation." She stacked their plates, then rose. "Would you like any decaf coffee or tea with our dessert?"

"I'll stick with water, as I haven't had enough today." He carried the baking dish with the leftovers to the island. "If you'll direct me to your containers, I'll pack this up."

She started to object he didn't have to help, then shrugged. She pointed to the appropriate cabinet and turned her attention to loading the dishwasher. Within minutes, the dishes had been done and they'd decided to have their dessert on the back patio, keeping Bingley safely locked inside.

"Have you heard from animal control about the yard?" He settled into one of the lawn lounges and set the plate of brownies on the small table between them.

"Got a text before you came over that someone would stop by first thing in the morning." She put her mug of decaf coffee on the table and reached for a napkin and brownie. "These look yummy."

He picked one up and consumed it in two bites. "It's my secret recipe."

She bit into the gooey chocolate and chewed. The flavors burst onto her tongue. "Wow, these are so good." She closed her eyes as she took another nibble, trying to decipher the ingredients.

"Trying to guess what's in them?"

Gazing straight into his eyes, she burst out laughing. "Yep."

He polished off another brownie, then sat back with his arms crossed. "Give it your best shot."

"Cocky, aren't you?"

He moved one massive shoulder up and down. "Confident you'll never guess all the ingredients."

She started with the usual brownie ingredients. "Let's see, flour, sugar, some sort of oil, vanilla. How am I doing so far?"

"So far, you've only said what's in nearly every brownie recipe." He sipped his water while she ate more of her square.

"I'm going with cocoa powder instead of melted chocolate for the chocolate part."

"Go on." His eyes twinkled, giving his face a delightfully roguish gleam that made her heart do a funny little flip inside her chest. A girl could get addicted to making Seth Whitman look at her like that, but she wasn't that girl.

She returned her attention back to the brownie, but even after adding chocolate chips to the list, she couldn't figure out the last ingredient. "Okay," she admitted after another serving still didn't give her a clue, "I give up. What am I missing?"

He leaned across the table and motioned her closer. "Zucchini."

She frowned. "The green summer squash?"

"My secret ingredient in 'Legit Brownies That Happen to Be Vegan and Contain Zucchini.'"

As the recipe title hit her, another chuckle burst from her. "That's what you call these?"

"Yep. Fits, right?" He wolfed down another square. "I sometimes use vegan chocolate chips, but this time, Wegmans was out, so these are technically only 'Legit Brownies That Contain Zucchini.'"

"Glad we cleared that up." She firmed her lips but couldn't corral the smile that spread across her face. Seth kept surprising her, his thoughts and actions running counter to everything she thought she knew about muscle-bound men. A gentleness underscored his entire being that warmed her to her toes. Time would tell if his actions reflected a genuine heart or if the façade she saw hid an ugly core.

SETH COULDN'T REMEMBER A TIME WHEN HE'D BEEN THIS COMFORTABLE with a member of the opposite sex. Too bad Jetta wanted to keep him at arm's length, but he'd respect her wishes and pray God would change her mind. So while he was enjoying this relaxing time with her, he'd better redirect their attention before he started dreaming impossible dreams. "You said something about papers?"

"Right, the papers." Before he could ask where they were, she leveraged herself out of the chair and went inside. She returned shortly with a brown mailing envelope in hand. "Here you go." She handed him the package, then retook her seat next to him.

He extracted the papers, noting two separate accounts at two different Cayman Islands banks with account holders as New Horizons LLC and Jay Ainsley, each listing this Falls Church address. One account held $1.4 million while the other had $1.2 million. Deposits into each account ranged in increments of $50,000 to $100,000 over a six-month period, with daily and sometimes twice daily wire transfers. The other papers detailed a spreadsheet, showing similar payments to various vendors over the same time period. He reshuffled the papers, reading the letter that had accompanied them.

"I'm no financial expert, but it appears these show someone using fake vendor invoices to siphon off money from Topher Robotics into these Cayman bank accounts." He rubbed the back of his neck, a habit he'd had since childhood when he was thinking through a problem—or embarrassed by his tendency to blush. "But the note mentions FinCEN, so maybe we should start there."

Her shoulders sagged and disappointment flashed across her expressive face. He wished he could tell her the papers were indeed a smoking gun proclaiming her father's innocence, but he didn't have the expertise to solve this particular problem on his own.

"I keep forgetting to look up what exactly FinCEN is."

"That I can answer. It's the US Treasury Department's Financial Crimes Enforcement Network." His cheeks warmed as her jaw dropped opened, then she snapped it close. He'd obviously surprised her with this knowledge, so he hastened to explain. "Brogan wrote a story a few months ago about the director's appearance at a local high school on educating teens about financial crimes. I snapped pics during the event."

He plucked his phone from a back pocket and scrolled to find Leslie Updike's contact info. "I have one of the agent's numbers in case we needed to follow up. I'll send her a text and see if she can lend us a hand with deciphering these. She might even remember your dad's case."

"Thanks."

He wanted to flash her a quick grin, but this wasn't about impressing a young woman. It was about finding out the truth about the embezzlement accusations levied at her late father. "All sent. I'll let you know what she says."

"I appreciate your help." Her voice trembled a bit and she broke eye contact with him.

He put his phone away, not sure what to say or do. He neatly put the papers back into the envelope. "We'll figure this out. May I make a copy of these papers?"

He had trouble catching his breath at the hurt in her beautiful eyes. The urge to draw her into his arms nearly overwhelmed him, but a lifetime of not pushing physical contact on anyone held him still.

"Would you make two copies?"

"Sure. I can do that at work in the morning, then drop them by later tomorrow."

She sniffed, then gestured to the plate. "You'd better take those with you, or I'll eat all of them tonight."

"I'll leave you some if you'd like."

"Sure." She led the way back into the kitchen and opened a drawer, then fished out a plastic zipper-top bag. After plopping a couple of brownies into the bag, she gestured toward the plate. "Plenty left for you."

"I'll have to hide them from my roommates, or they'll be gone by morning."

That brought a hint of a smile to her lips. "I forget how much guys can eat without packing on the pounds."

His chest tightened as unwanted memories of what people said to him about his weight pummeled his mind. He was not that four-hundred-pound teenager anymore. He didn't use food to escape his reality. Several years of counseling with a food addiction specialist, coupled with weight training, had helped him identify his triggers and work through a lot of his painful childhood. But offhanded remarks like this could drag him back into the mire again.

"Seth?"

He shook himself like a dog getting rid of water. "Sorry, lost in thought." He drew in a breath. Her expression showed she wasn't quite buying his explanation, so he added, "Trying to figure out where to hide the brownies."

That smoothed out her features, making his heart light. "Now I'd better go, as I have an early morning photo shoot with some fisherman trying to catch an elusive channel catfish in Burke Lake."

"Sounds exciting." She walked him to the door.

"This is take two, as last week, the rain and fog made any chance at a photo to document the catch impossible. Tomorrow's weather looks clear." He paused on the front stoop. "Thanks for the delicious dinner."

Their eyes locked, the tension building slow and easy like a spider spinning a web. Again, that tug toward her, the desire to brush his fingers across her cheek to see if the skin was as smooth as it appeared. He forced himself to step back, breaking the gossamer thread. "Please use my backyard as much as you need to with Bingley."

"What?" She blinked, as if coming back from the same dream he'd been caught up in. "Oh, right. Will do."

A strand of auburn hair fell across her cheek. He curbed the impulse to tuck it behind her ear. "See you later."

An emotion he couldn't decipher flickered in her eyes as she repeated his goodbye, then closed the door with a soft click. He strode across the lawn to his front door, frustration nipping at his heels. He entered the house, glad his housemates weren't in the common areas, although he could hear Wade's music blaring from his bedroom. He headed for his own room, taking the plate of brownies with him and quietly closing the door so as not to alert Wade to his presence. While he often enjoyed his company, he didn't want to be grilled about where he'd been.

Flopping onto his bed, Seth stared at the ceiling fan as he reviewed the evening's ending. Was she disappointed he hadn't offered to comfort her with a hug? Or was she relieved he hadn't presumed such intimacy? Questions that wouldn't be answered tonight, but perhaps, if he studied really hard, he might be able to figure out the correct answers before they solved her father's case and Jetta returned to her life in Chicago.

CHAPTER

NINE

As darkness fell outside, Emily settled back against the pillows. More details from the days leading up to the arrest and Jay's heart attack had been filling her mind. Fresh grief over her husband's untimely death assailed her, coupled with a determination to take a clear-eyed view of those events.

When Jay finally told her what had been worrying him for weeks, she had been horrified. It explained his long hours and haggard appearance in the days before the arrest, which lended credence to his fatal heart attack. As sleep continued to elude her, she relived the memories playing like a movie across her mind's eye. Putting aside her own reactions and emotions as best she could, Emily concentrated on seeing everything as unambiguously as possible.

Fifteen years ago

Emily poured two cups of coffee, delighted Jay hadn't rushed off to work this Saturday morning as he'd done the past couple of months.

79

While she understood his concern about who had embezzled the money, she hoped he wouldn't have to go into the office today. She stirred a dollop of cream into his, adding sugar and cream to her mug. Then she pulled the pan of homemade cinnamon rolls from the oven, the aroma of sugar and spices filling the kitchen.

"Smells good in here." Jay crossed the room dressed in jeans and an old college sweatshirt, the lettering no longer readable. Instead of reaching for a roll, he wrapped his arms around her. Nuzzling her neck, he said, "I'm yours for the entire day. What shall we do?"

Delight zinged through her at the unexpected gift of time with her husband. "Jetta spent the night at a friend's and they have plans for a zoo trip this morning. I was going to check out the 'Murder is Her Hobby' exhibit at the Renwick Gallery. Want to come along?"

"Intriguing title." He took the plate with a roll she offered, then followed her to the small breakfast nook with its floor-to-ceiling windows overlooking the small, fenced backyard.

"It's about Frances Glessner Lee and her Nutshell Studies of Unexplained Death—kind of like dioramas of twenty real-life murders, suicides, and accidental deaths she made to help law enforcement learn forensic science techniques." She sipped her coffee as Jay downed the roll in several big bites.

"Sounds a bit gruesome," he winked at her, "but the perfect way to spend a Saturday."

She grinned, happy that Jay seemed more like his old self. They chatted about inconsequential things as they finished their coffee and rolls. While she loaded the dishwasher, Jay went upstairs to retrieve his phone. A pounding on the front door made her jump. Who would be calling at eight on a Saturday? The doorbell pealed, accompanied by more pounding. She dried her hands and hustled to answer it.

The doorbell rang again as she yanked open the door. The annoyed response died on her lips at the sight of two uniformed police officers plus a woman dressed in a navy-blue pants suit. "I'm Detective Serenity Washington with the Falls Church Police Department." She flashed her badge so quickly, Emily couldn't read the words. "Is Jay Ainsley here?"

Confusion and a growing sense of unease snaked its way up Emily's spine. "He is."

"We need to speak with him immediately. Please step aside." The detective took a step forward, and Emily automatically retreated until the woman and two officers were in the foyer.

"What's going on?" Jay walked down the stairs, his eyes briefly meeting Emily's before returning to the police.

"Jay Ainsley?" Detective Washington addressed her husband, who had reached the bottom of the stairs.

"Yes, I'm Jay Ainsley."

"Jay Ainsley, I'm arresting you on charges of embezzlement and fraud." The detective nodded to one of the officers, who produced handcuffs and reached for Jay. "You don't have to..."

Emily tuned out the rest of the Miranda warning the detective recited as the officer cuffed Jay's wrists in front of him. Her husband kept his gaze directed at Emily, the anguish in his eyes nearly undoing her composure. His face had lost most of its color, leaving him a pale imitation of his former robustness. Her heart squeezed as thoughts of how this could be happening pummeled her mind.

She touched his arm, earning a frown from one of the officers. "Ma'am, please stay away from the prisoner."

Prisoner. Not her Jay. "Honey, I'll call..." She couldn't think of the attorney's name, the one who had helped them revise their will after Jetta's birth.

"Call Peter Long. Name's in my phone contacts list." Jay squared his shoulders as the officers flanked him. "He'll know what to do. I love you. Tell the kids how much I love them."

"I will." She covered her mouth as if to stifle the scream threatening to erupt. She wouldn't give into the rising panic. She would call Peter Long, who would straighten out this mess and get her husband back home where he belonged.

As they led him to the front door, Jay raised his cuffed hands to his chest, then his body sagged, nearly dragging the two officers to the ground. One of them yanked up on Jay's arm, but her husband's knees hit the entryway rug with a thud before he collapsed onto the ground.

This time, she let out the scream as she sank to the floor to cradle her still husband in her arms.

EMILY SWIPED TEARS FROM HER CHEEK AS MEMORIES OF THE OFFICERS working to restart her husband's heart assailed her. She'd wanted to tell them it was too late—Jay was with his Savior, leaving her to soldier on through the accusations that had tainted their family ever since. But maybe this time, she would find the answers as to who had set up her husband to take the fall for the fraud and embezzlement. For never once over these past years had she doubted he was innocent of all charges.

Not for the first time, she wished she'd pushed for a second autopsy on her husband, one that would run a fuller tox screen than the usual tests for alcohol, amphetamines, barbiturates, marijuana, and opiates. Back then, her gut told her Jay's heart attack wasn't the result of stress of his being found out but because someone didn't want him searching for answers.

But with the Tophers threatening to sue for recovery of the money Jay supposedly stole—and wasn't accounted for in the offshore bank accounts linked to him—and their circle of friends shrinking each time another story hit the papers, she didn't have the energy or the funds to pursue it on her own. Maybe it wasn't too late to re-examine her husband's body, but she'd tackle that question once she had enough evidence to reopen the case.

Emily moved again on the bed, still unable to get comfortable. Her leg and hip ached. Why hadn't the nurse come back with her pain meds for the night? She reached for the call button and pressed it.

A few minutes later, the door opened, and a figure dressed in scrubs stepped inside, leaving the door ajar. Emily raised the head of the bed slightly. "Did you bring my pain meds? I'm really uncomfortable."

"These will make all of that go away." The voice, muffled by a facemask, didn't sound like the usual night nurse.

In the darkened room with only the light from the hallway, Emily couldn't make out the nurse's identity but could tell it was a man by the height and breadth of his shoulders. No soft round curves on his body.

The nurse handed Emily a paper pill cup. "Here you go."

Emily stared into the cup, noting the oblong, rather than round, shape of the pills. "These look different."

"We were running low on the usual ones, but these will work just fine." The nurse held out Emily's plastic water mug. "Down the hatch."

She wanted to press the man for an explanation, but some instinct told her to appear to comply. She tossed the pills from the cup into her mouth, then took the water and sipped, swallowing the water but keeping the pills tucked into her cheek.

The nurse appeared satisfied with her performance because he patted her shoulder. "You'll feel better soon." Then he walked out of the room, closing the door behind him.

Quickly, Emily spat out the pills into the empty water cup before using some water to swish out her mouth. She removed the lid to spit the water back into the plastic mug. Then she mashed down the call button over and over again until her door burst open.

"Ms. Ainsley, are you okay?" The usual nighttime nurse rushed to the table, a paper cup in her hand.

Emily burst into tears. "I think he tried to kill me."

"What?" The nurse—Merena, Emily recalled from other nights— flipped on the overhead light, flooding the room with brightness.

"Someone came in dressed like a nurse and gave me those pills." She pointed to the paper cup on the bedside table. "But they didn't look like the ones I usually take, so I pretended to swallow them and spit them out when he left."

"Let's take a look." Merena dumped the contents onto the table. Three purple capsules rolled a few times on the surface.

The nurse frowned. "These are not on your pill list. I'm not sure what's in them." She handed Emily a pill cup. "These are your extra strength Tylenol the doctor prescribed for your pain."

"Would you please get me some fresh water?"

As the nurse complied with her request, Emily verified the pills were indeed Tylenol. She then took the Tylenol to ease the discomfort. "What about the other ones? And the male nurse who tried to give them to me?"

Merena scooped the purple pills back into the cup. "I'll take these to our lab and see what's inside them, then stop by security to mention the nurse. Can you describe him?"

Emily gave as many details as she could about the man, which was precious little given the room's darkness and his face mask. Merena left with assurances they would be extra vigilant the rest of the night with plenty of extra checks on Emily. Emily wanted to press for more, but without knowing the contents of the purple pills, it wasn't clear what the man's intention had been. Emily had no doubt the pills would contain something designed to kill her. Why else would someone sneak into her room to give her the pills?

Then she remembered Jetta and the papers someone sent Jay. Would her daughter be in danger now too? First thing tomorrow, Emily would contact the detective who had come to arrest Jay. The woman had seemed to care, even coming to Jay's funeral—something not even many of their so-called friends had done in the aftermath of the embezzlement accusations. Maybe seeing the papers and whatever the lab found out about the purple pills would be enough to propel Detective Washington to open a new case to find the real embezzler—or at least look into her nighttime visitor. And she would warn Jetta to be very careful.

As sleep finally reached out to embrace Emily, one question

circled round and round like the Johnny Cash album her husband played on their stereo system. In trying to clear her husband's name, had she brought evil into her life?

RYAN TOPHER ADJUSTED HIS RED POWER TIE, THE SILK BRINGING TO MIND A slash of blood against the stark white dress shirt. He shrugged into the custom-made navy-blue suit jacket and buttoned the top button. The full-length mirror in his executive suite bathroom showed a man in his prime, ready to take on the world. He'd need that persona if he were to convince the board and their largest shareholders to reject Maxwell Technology's hostile takeover bid.

His desk phone buzzed, and he punched the speaker button. "Yes?"

"Mr. Topher, Dr. Willis and Dr. James are here," Mae informed him.

"Send them in." He sank into the high-backed leather office chair, letting his gaze roam around the well-appointed space. From his antique banker's desk polished every evening to a high shine to the Persian carpet overlaid on the more serviceable wall-to-wall carpet to the small paintings and objects d'art placed strategically to show off his impeccable taste, Ryan prided himself on his excellent taste. He hadn't spent the last twenty years acquiring the trappings of wealth to lose it in a hostile takeover.

The man and woman who entered wore white lab coats, attesting to the fact he'd pulled them from their work in the company's research wing. Dr. Jana Willis strode to his desk, stopping inches from it. "What do you want?"

Her clipped tone indicated his summons had better be for an excellent reason, or she'd carve him up for lunch. He hid his amusement at her directness, which he put up with because she was one of the nation's brightest robotics engineers. "Dr. Willis, I need an update on the project." No need to designate which project—there was only one that interested all three of them.

She removed her glasses, polishing them with the hem of the lab coat. "As I told you last week, we are very close to a workable proto-type." Replacing the glasses, she glared through their thick lenses. "This is not something to be rushed."

Dr. Brian James added, "There has been progress over the past week. We've isolated the problem that caused the malfunction of the previous prototype and are now testing solutions to fix it."

Ryan regarded them steadily, his mind whirring with how to spin this to convince the board and shareholders to not accept the takeover bid. "What's the new timeline?"

The doctors exchanged glances, then Dr. Willis shrugged. "Perhaps another six months."

Ryan slammed his fist down on the desk, and the two scientists flinched. "We don't have that long. Do you not understand what might happen in forty-five minutes? The shareholders of Topher Robotics with the full backing of the majority of the board are likely to vote to accept Maxwell Technology's takeover bid. You know what Maxwell Technology does to tech companies like ours? They strip it of all saleable assets, then leave it a hollow shell of its former self."

When neither scientist spoke, he added, "They will take your work—all of your hard work—and shove you out the door without so much as an acknowledgement of your contributions to the project."

Dr. James's face lost its color, but he lifted his chin. "Then I think it's best if you allow us to get back to work."

Ryan considered the man's request, then waved them off. "Keep me informed—and only me."

He'd hoped to have more ammunition to tease the shareholders with visions of tech glory—and riches from the AI-powered wear-able technology. He suspected several shareholders were behind the takeover bid, and he had to keep the exact nature of the project a secret, or Maxwell Technology would press harder. Ryan discarded several scenarios before coming up with a plausible story, one that should ignite interest and hold the wolves at bay for a few more weeks. With any luck, it would quash the takeover bid entirely, although he'd be satisfied with a stay of execution. Anything to stop a close look at the company's books.

TEN

Seth liked working in the quiet of a usually busy newsroom. While *The Herald's* staff of eight was small, the crowded office space meant a louder work environment as the trio of advertising and classified ads reps made calls and the two other reporters spoke with sources. He'd awakened early, and, after a run through the pre-dawn air, had gone to Burke Lake to photograph the fishermen attempting to land the record catfish at dawn. Unfortunately, the fish they'd caught wasn't the prizewinner, but he'd gotten some decent pics of their valiant effort. Then he headed to the office to research Jay Ainsley. As the sun rose higher, he read through the numerous articles centering around Jay's death after being charged with embezzling nearly $10 million from Topher Robotics. He printed a few stories for background, then switched to investigating Topher Robotics.

The top search returns focused on Maxwell Technology's bid for a hostile takeover of the family-run firm. Interesting. He hit print for the most comprehensive article, then delved deeper, going back more than fifteen years to see what the company's status was prior to Jay's embezzlement charge. Most of the stories centered around

Topher Robotics' new products, such as innovative prosthetics and automated robots for cleaning and delivery. Then one piece snagged his attention.

FOUNDER OF TOPHER ROBOTICS REFUSES TO STEP DOWN

BOARD INSISTING PETER TOPHER HAND OVER THE REINS TO HIS ELDEST SON

STERLING, Va.—Peter Topher, who founded Topher Robotics in 1970 at a time when few were investing in robots, has said he will not relinquish his position as chairman of the board to his eldest son, Ryan Topher. Ryan has been tapped as the heir apparent to the company and had long been rumored to want to take the company public in order to expand its R&D department. This puts him at odds with his father, who has stated emphatically he does not want the family to give up its majority stake in the company.

The article quoted numerous sources, some named and some anonymous, adding credence to the growing rift between father and son. Seth thought he'd seen the company listed as one publicly traded, and when he checked, found that Ryan had won that round with the board. Digging deeper revealed the Topher family collectively held forty percent of the company's stock and was still among the largest shareholders. The current list of executives on the Topher Robotics website showed Peter as emeritus chairman of the board with Ryan as CEO and his two siblings filling out the rest of the C-suite executive positions. Other Tophers, presumably the grandchildren of Peter, held middle management positions, while Avery Lassiter had been chairwoman of the board for the past decade.

Seth made notes about his findings, his mind spinning with possibilities. When he spotted Brogan, he hailed the reporter. "Got a sec?"

"Let me finish this text." Brogan bent over his phone while Seth curbed his impatience. "Okay, what's up?"

As succinctly as possible, Seth outlined the embezzlement case.

Brogan frowned. "Doesn't seem like there's a story if the accused is dead and the company isn't pursuing it."

"On the surface, yes, but then Jay Ainsley's widow received this in the mail." Seth handed photocopies of the envelope's documents to Brogan. "Along with this note." He slid over the note on top.

Brogan scanned it, then tapped the page. "But why send this to a dead man?"

"They didn't." Seth explained about the postmark on the envelope. "Must have gotten lost in the mail for fifteen years."

As he'd hoped, that nugget of information snagged Brogan's attention. "Interesting, but I'm not sure there's much here beyond a quirky human-interest story about lost mail being delivered years later."

"There's more." Seth mentioned the poisoning of Bingley and the death of the raccoon. "Jetta will let me know what animal control finds when they search her yard, but it appears someone tried to kill her dog."

"There's no direct connection between what happened to her dog and a case that doesn't need solving."

"Then there's the note I found." He showed his colleague a photo of the threatening words. "Plus, someone tried to run Jetta off the road yesterday."

"Do the police have this info?"

"Yes." Even as he relayed the info, Seth could see how flimsy it was.

"I get you're concerned about Jetta's safety, but we need something new to start an investigation."

He blew out a breath in an attempt to tamp down his growing frustration. "You didn't have anything new when you agreed to help Melender re-investigate the disappearance of her cousin—and she had been convicted of the crime."

Brogan sighed. "That was different because we had a story angle about a convicted murderer trying to clear her name."

"While I only have a daughter trying to clear her father's name of a crime in which he was never tried or convicted." He fisted his hands on his hips, irritation radiating throughout his body. "So when it's a woman you're interested in, you'll go the extra mile, but not when it's me?"

"If you're asking if this merits an investigative story, then the answer is no. You need more than some bank statements and a spreadsheet." Brogan gave the papers back. "But good to know you find Jetta interesting."

Seth ignored the teasing note in his friend's tone as the reporter hustled to his cubicle to pick up his ringing desk phone. He wouldn't tell Jetta that Brogan passed on opening an investigation. He'd look into it himself. After all, he majored in journalism and photography, and wrote short pieces for *The Herald* all the time. Granted, he'd never tackled a story this complex, but he knew how to research.

First, he had to check the rest of his assignments for the day. Fallon would not be happy if he dropped the ball on his work. Two popped up in his inbox—one at noon to snap a pic of the Rotary Club's handing out its fall scholarship to a local student and the other right afterward to photograph the City of Fairfax mayor as she read to a group of kids for the elementary school's fall fundraiser read-a-thon.

His cell buzzed and his heart twisted when he saw Jetta's name as the sender. *Settle down. She's probably only telling you the results of the animal control sweep of her backyard.* But his sensible admonition did little to slow his heart rate.

Do you have time to talk?

He frowned. That didn't sound good. Maybe she would tell him to forget the whole investigation thing and to never darken her doorway again. In his experience, answering that question only led to disappointment. But putting her off wouldn't change the outcome of the conversation, so instead of replying, he hit the call button.

"Seth? Oh, thank God."

The tears in her voice coupled with what sounded like relief made him forget his fears about what topic she wanted to discuss. "What's wrong?"

"I'm with my mom." She sucked in air, then blew it out in a whoosh. "Someone tried to kill her last night."

"What?" He was on his feet and heading toward the exit, every instinct driving him to get to Jetta as quickly as possible. "How?"

"We're still getting the information. I've called the police, but could you come?" Her voice hitched. "I can't think straight, I'm so scared."

"I'm on my way. Text me the address."

"Will do. See you soon." She ended the call, and Seth's phone buzzed a few seconds later with the rehab facility's address.

A quick check of the time showed he had a little under two hours before he had to be at the Rotary Club in Falls Church. Once in his vehicle, he cross-checked the drive time from the rehab center to the Rotary Club. Fifteen minutes. Good, that gave him a bit of a cushion. He prayed he would be able to support Jetta and not have to rush off to snap the photo. He couldn't afford to lose this job, not if he wanted to pay his rent. His side hustle photography business had been growing, but it still wasn't steady enough to pay his bills.

After arriving at the center, he jogged toward the rehab facility entrance. What Jetta said reverberated in his mind—someone had tried to kill her mother. Surely that was tied to Emily's desire to prove her husband's innocence. Because if Jay Ainsley was not the embezzler, that meant someone had gotten away with millions fifteen years ago—and had even more to lose now because of the potential acquisition.

Jetta held Mom's hand as she recounted what happened with the male nurse the night before. The rehab facility's in-house lab had discovered a lethal dose of fentanyl in the purple capsules they'd examined first thing this morning. The daytime manager had immediately phoned the police, and now Detective Patrick Brady questioned her mother while two Fairfax County police officers talked to the staff. Jetta had texted Seth as soon as her mother had called with the news. She'd already been on her way to visit her mother when the call had come in, so she had arrived within minutes.

"Mrs. Ainsley, do you know of any reason why someone would attempt to kill you?" Detective Brady had kind eyes bracketed by lines, as if the man smiled more than he frowned. His salt-and-pepper hair reassured Jetta he had the experience to thoroughly investigate the attempted murder, and she'd hoped it meant he might have been on the force fifteen years ago.

Mom squeezed Jetta's hand. "Yes, I do."

Her answer must have startled the detective because his eyes widened slightly. "What reason would that be?"

His tone, although cordial, held a hint of skepticism. On the surface, Mom appeared to be a widow in her early sixties, someone whom no one would give a second look, and with whom no one would hold such a grudge as to warrant murder.

"Because I want justice for my husband."

Detective Brady didn't jot that down. "Why is that?"

"He died fifteen years ago after being accused of embezzling millions from Topher Robotics." Mom withdrew her hand from Jetta's to point a finger at the detective. "I think they killed him to stop any further investigation into the theft and now they want to silence me because I'm looking into it again."

"I think you'd better start at the beginning, Mrs. Ainsley." He leaned back in the chair positioned next to Mom's bed, his posture relaxed and interested.

"Certainly." Her mother recounted the events leading up to Dad's arrest and heart attack, the aftermath with the Topher family lobbing accusations about Dad, then her email and phone call to the company requesting an investigation to clear his name. She ended with the arrival of the envelope two days ago. "My daughter," she indicated Jetta, "is looking into it for me, to see if there's anything we can do to exonerate Jay's name."

"I remember the case. Hard to forget hearing about a suspect who died upon arrest." Detective Brady tapped the screen of his iPad, where he'd been writing notes with a stylus pen. "Wasn't my department, but I think one of the original investigators is now the head of fraud. I'll get in touch with her and see what she remembers about the case."

"Thank you." Mom's quiet words reminded Jetta how much her mother still missed her father.

"Did you tell him about Bingley?" Seth stepped into the room, his large presence filling Jetta with relief. She hadn't realized how much she'd been longing for him to arrive until he was here.

"Bingley?" The detective stood as Seth approached Jetta, who introduced him to the detective.

"My dog." Mom's close call had shoved Bingley's incident to the back of Jetta's mind. "He ate some raw meat mixed with smashed ibuprofen tablets and nearly died two days ago. A raccoon ate some of the same meat and did die."

"What did animal control find?" Seth moved to stand beside Jetta's chair as Detective Brady retook his seat.

Jetta explained about the morning's sweep of her backyard. "The remnants of ground beef with traces of ibuprofen on the left corner of the fence facing the sidewalk—the opposite side where you also found a few bits of meat. They think someone shoved it under the wooden fence planks."

"That's dreadful! Bingley's okay?" Mom grasped Jetta's hand again, concern etched on the lines of her face.

"Yes, he's fully recovered." She glanced at Seth. "The animal control officer took the raccoon to see if it had ingested the same thing as Bingley."

"Plus, someone tried to run her off the road yesterday," Seth added. "And left the note on your front porch." He showed the detective the photo of those awful words.

Jetta shifted in her chair as her mother gasped.

"You didn't tell me any of this."

Jetta hastened to reassure Mom. "I didn't want to worry you. Besides, there didn't seem to be a connection. The truck had been stolen, and I just got in the way." Based on the determined looks in her mother and Seth's eyes, her attempt to downplay the incidents fell flat.

"I don't like this." Detective Brady met Jetta's gaze. "This smacks of escalation from leaving notes to harming and potentially killing a dog to attempted murder."

"Do you think everything that's happened so far are connected?" Seth asked.

"The stolen truck is the only outlier, in my opinion, as, like Ms. Ainsley said, it could have been she was in the way of a car thief. But the dog poisoning and note are directly tied to Ms. Ainsley," Detective Brady said. "Would you have the vet send me a copy of his findings about Bingley?"

Jetta agreed, making a note on her phone to do so.

"I'll follow up with Animal Control and get the report from their sweep of your yard." The detective eyed Jetta and her mother. "In the meantime, be careful. Someone appears to be targeting you two, and until we know why, be on your guard."

"What happens next?" Seth laid a hand on Jetta's shoulder, as if he'd known she needed comfort.

She leaned into his side, wanting closer contact and hoping his strength would rub off onto her. Her mind overflowed like a fast-moving stream with too many disconnected thoughts.

"We're finished here for now and will return later to talk to the night shift," the detective said. "In the meantime, I've alerted security to be extra vigilant."

"What about the embezzlement?" Mom asked.

"I'll check with my colleague and see what I can find out about the original investigation." He stood. "If we find a connection between the embezzlement and the attempt on your life, we'll reopen your husband's case. Until then, I'll treat it as background."

Mom's lips tightened in the way that indicated she wasn't pleased with that answer, but she didn't contradict the detective and thanked him again.

After the detective left, Mom sighed. "At least he didn't laugh at me for suggesting Jay's case had something to do with these attempts."

"I think he will look into it." Jetta thought the detective had been sincere. "In the meantime, we'll keep digging and see what we can come up with. What did your colleague say?"

Seth ran a hand along the back of his neck, a gesture Jetta noted he did whenever he was nervous or embarrassed. "Brogan said there wasn't enough new evidence to warrant opening an investigation. But I did find out something interesting about Topher Robotics. Maxwell Technology is trying for a hostile takeover."

"What does that mean exactly?" Jetta voiced the question she'd seen on her mother's face as well.

"It means Maxwell Technology will try to convince the majority of the shareholders to vote for their offer to acquire Topher Robotics without the board's approval," Seth explained. "I don't know all the ins and outs myself, but I do know since Topher Robotics went public a few months after your father's death, the Topher family has had less control over the company. They're still the largest shareholders with forty percent of the stock, but they no longer hold the majority position."

Jetta rubbed her temples as a headache inched its way into her skull. "All this financial mumbo-jumbo is confusing. I didn't get Dad's affinity for numbers and spreadsheets."

"You have a good head on your shoulders." Mom patted her hand. "Now you two run along and start sleuthing."

Jetta frowned. "You heard what the detective said—we need to be extra careful. I'm staying here with you until that man is caught."

"Absolutely not." Mom shot Jetta The Look, the one that said *I will not be gainsaid about this.* "That detective will do his best, I'm sure, but the poor man is overworked, and since I didn't die, this isn't going to be at the top of his list. He will ask questions and do a thorough job, but he will not delve too deep into the embezzlement. That's up to you two. I've waited fifteen years to prove Jay's innocence. There's no more time to waste."

"Yes, ma'am." Seth gave her mother a salute, then winked at Jetta. "Shall we grab a cup of coffee in the cafeteria and plot our next move?"

Mom made a shooing motion with her hand. "I'll be fine. Go."

Jetta kissed her mother on the cheek. "I'll stop by before I leave."

An orderly, one Jetta had seen several times before, came into the room as Jetta and Seth left. "Time for your PT, Mrs. Ainsley."

"She'll be in good hands, now that the staff is alerted," Seth said as they made their way to the cafeteria. "The best thing we can do is figure out the truth about who stole that money."

"I suppose you're right, but I'm worried." Jetta paused outside the bustling café. "First Bingley and now my mom. This is serious. Maybe we shouldn't..."

Seth gently turned her to face him, his light grip on her upper arms sending tingles throughout her body. "If we don't, someone will get away with not only embezzling millions but also the attempt on your mother's life."

He guided her into the cafeteria. "The best way we can keep your mom safe is to find out who's behind the embezzlement."

Jetta wished she had confidence they would uncover the culprit after all these years, but as she'd painfully learned with Kyle, people were very good at hiding their true colors. And when faced with exposure, they could react in very unexpected ways. With the attempt on her mother's life, Jetta had no doubt whoever was behind the events was playing for keeps.

And would stop at nothing to keep their secrets hidden.

CHAPTER

ELEVEN

Seth focused the lens on the smiling group of fourth graders surrounding Mayor Susan Birmingham as she read "If You Give a Mouse a Cookie" from a rocking chair and snapped several photos in quick succession. He checked the compositions on his camera to ensure at least one would be usable. "Thanks, everyone."

He said goodbye to front office staffer who'd accompanied him to the classroom before slipping out of the school. With any luck, he'd have the captions written and the photos sent to his editor within the hour, freeing him up to follow up with Leslie Updike, his FinCEN contact. She hadn't responded to his text yet, and he was too impatient to wait for her to do so. A phone call might produce better results.

Less than sixty minutes later, he punched connect on his cell and prayed Leslie would pick up his call.

"Leslie Updike."

"Leslie? It's Seth Whitman." He paused, then added, "from *The Northern Virginia Herald*. We met..."

99

"At the director's talk at Fairfax High School a while back. Hold on a sec."

In the background, he heard muffled speech, then a few seconds of quiet before Leslie returned to the phone. "Sorry about that. Just finished a meeting. What can I do for you?"

Before he could mention his text and Jay Ainsley, Leslie continued, "Oh, sorry, you texted me and I totally blew you off."

"It's okay." Seth was used to be women blowing him off. "I know you're busy."

"Not too busy for an afternoon coffee if you're buying."

The teasing lilt to her voice caught him off guard. She wasn't flirting with him, was she? If she was, how was he to respond to that? Indecision froze his tongue.

Leslie chuckled. "It's only a mocha, and I have a boyfriend. Besides, it will be easier to talk about the case you mentioned in the text outside of the office."

"Right, sorry. Where and when?"

They settled on Basecamp Coffee Roasters in thirty minutes. After getting her beverage order, Seth checked in with his boss to let him know he'd be out of the office the rest of the day. He arrived at the coffeeshop before Leslie and ordered an iced green tea concoction for himself and a mocha for Leslie. Leslie arrived as he carried the beverages to a corner table.

"Ah, good. I can use a pick-me-up." She settled into the chair opposite him and grabbed her drink. "The ambrosia of the gods."

"If you say so." Seth had never understood the frothy coffee drinks packed with sugar and syrups, but mostly kept that opinion to himself. "Thanks for meeting with me."

"I must admit to being intrigued by your text. What old case are you interested in?"

He glanced around the half-filled shop, then leaned forward. "Jay Ainsley."

Her brow furrowed as if she was trying to recall the name. "Not ringing any bells."

"Fifteen years ago, he was accused of embezzling close to ten million from Topher Robotics but had a fatal heart attack when the cops came to arrest him."

She snapped her fingers. "Now I remember. I had joined FinCEN only a few months before that. It was big news. Only a couple of million dollars was recovered from an offshore account, right?"

"Less than a million in an account with Jay Ainsley's name on it and another million or so in an account under New Horizons LLC." His research had uncovered a person didn't actually have to visit the Cayman Islands to open a bank account but simply provide the relevant documents, meaning anyone could have set up the account as Jay Ainsley. "Was your office involved in the investigation?"

"Like I said, I was new so didn't have any direct knowledge of the case, but my former boss, Frank Warner, would know details. He's now retired." She sipped her drink. "I can introduce you if you'd like."

"That would be great." Seth tamped down his disappointment at not getting answers immediately, but at least they had another lead.

"I'll text him right now." Leslie did so. "Why are you interested in this old case?"

"Well, I, um…" He should have come up with a reason before meeting with Leslie, but couldn't think of a plausible one. Instead, he blurted out the truth. "His daughter asked for my help in clearing his name."

Her eyebrows rose. "Ah, I see. Pretty, is she?"

His neck heated. Seth resisted the urge to rub it, taking a gulp of his iced green tea to occupy his hands.

"Hey, I'm only teasing." Leslie tapped his forearm. "It's a bad habit of mine, and I should learn not to do it with acquaintances."

"It's okay." He swallowed more tea. "I appreciate your help."

Her phone buzzed. "Looks like Frank remembers the case and is willing to talk with you. I'll tell him I'm sharing his number with you now."

His phone alerted him to the incoming text. He quickly composed a new message to Frank, who replied immediately.

I recall the Ainsley case. Happy to discuss.
Free this afternoon at four.

I can do four. Where?

My house. 6909 Bright Avenue, McLean.

I'll be there.

Leslie drained the remainder of her drink. "I gotta run. Good luck with Frank."

"Thanks for your help." Seth decided to finish his beverage and plot out the questions he wanted to ask Frank Warner about the Ainsley case. He texted Jetta a quick update and asked if she wanted to accompany him to Frank's. Her affirmative response made him smile. Too bad it was because of minuscule progress in the case and not to spend more time with him.

"Are you going to tell me what's wrong?" Emily raised her eyebrows as her daughter glanced at her. Jetta had been milling about her room ever since Seth left.

"Someone tried to kill you last night." Jetta slid her gaze away.

Children might grow up, but a mother always knew when they weren't telling the entire truth. Jetta's tell was that slight ducking of the head as she broke eye contact. Emily would have smiled had she not been worried about what her youngest was keeping from her. She might have trouble walking with this blasted cast, but she still had a sharp mind.

"Jetta." The single word snapped her daughter's attention back to Emily. "I'm your mother. I know when something else is bothering you."

Tears tumbled down Jetta's cheeks. She dashed them away with the back of her hand before turning her back on Emily. Her posture stiff, she spoke to the window. "Oh, Mom. I made a huge mess of things, and I'm afraid I'll do it again."

"About what?"

"I thought Kyle loved me, that we had a future."

Emily waited for her to say more, grateful her daughter was finally opening up about what happened in Chicago. She hadn't wanted to push for answers when Jetta had come home seven months ago, drawn and pale, but as her pregnancy became apparent, Emily had known as mothers do something dreadful had happened to her youngest.

"Then Kyle became more and more possessive."

As Jetta outlined a few examples, Emily's heart ached as she revealed how bad it had become with her boyfriend.

"I realized I had to break up with him, that this wasn't normal behavior. He didn't take it well, said no one broke up with him. Threatened me, but thank goodness I had the foresight to do it during dinner in a crowded restaurant, so there wasn't much he could do. I left, having arranged an Uber to pick me up. I thought that was that—he would realize it was over and move on to the next girl." She huffed a laugh. "I knew he'd already lined her up."

"He was seeing someone else while dating you?" Outrage on her daughter's behalf slipped out before Emily could stop herself.

Jetta shrugged. "It was the way he operated, I learned later. He'd begun to come onto me while dating the woman before me. I was foolish and stupid and got sucked in by his charm and good looks, and yes, money. He took me to expensive restaurants and concerts, bought me pricey jewelry. He was older—in his late 30s—and I thought I was so sophisticated, so special. It was all an act he used on young women."

Concern over the direction the tale was taking inched up Emily's spine, but she stayed silent as Jetta continued her story.

"Then a few weeks after the breakup, I woke up in the middle of the night to find Kyle in my bedroom."

Emily's heart stuttered. *No, please God, no.*

"Earlier, he apparently had taken my key ring without my knowledge and made a copy of the apartment door key. He told me no one walked away from him. Then he..." She hiccuped as sobs tore through her body. "He, he...he raped me."

"Jetta, come here. It's okay. It wasn't your fault." Emily coaxed her daughter into her arms. Jetta flew into them, rocking Emily back onto the bed. Pain flashed along her leg in its cast, but Emily ignored it. Her daughter needed her. What was a little pain in light of the burden Jetta had been carrying for months?

After Jetta's tears subsided, she sat up on the side of the bed. "I reported him, Mom. I almost didn't because he said no one would believe it hadn't been consensual and that he had friends in high places. And he did. He knew the mayor personally and other Chicago bigwigs. But I decided that even if no one believed me, I would tell the truth. So I did."

"Did they believe you?" Emily brushed a strand of hair from her damp cheek.

"Yes, they did." Jetta's mouth turned down into a grimace. "Mostly because of the physical evidence."

Emily again praised God for the support Jetta had gotten when reporting the heinous crime. "You'll need to go back to Chicago for a trial?"

"No. Kyle somehow finagled a deal with the prosecutor's office for twelve months' probation and rehab, claiming he'd been high on drugs when he'd come to my apartment. He also insisted I'd given him a key. Since the key was my word against his, it weakened my case. I did get the prosecutor to add a restraining order forbidding Kyle from contacting me in any way."

Jetta blotted her face with a tissue from the bedside table. "I couldn't stay in the same city with him. That's why I quit my job, sublet my apartment, and moved back home." Fresh tears spilled out. "I don't know what to do."

Emily enfolded her into her arms again. "We'll figure it out with God's help. Don't worry." She hadn't always been one to point her children to God. Her anger over Jay's death and the unresolved charges against him, plus the way many members of their church had shunned her in the aftermath, had lingered for years. But recently, she'd realized her mistake in pushing God away when she should have been clinging closer and had reconnected with her Savior at a new church home.

After her daughter's tears lessened, Jetta laid her head on Emily's shoulder. "Would you pray for me?"

"Of course." Emily brought all their concerns before their Heavenly Father, praying for wisdom and peace. When Emily said "Amen," Jetta stood beside the bed, her hand holding Emily's.

"Thanks, Mom. I feel better. I didn't know how to tell you. Even though I knew it wasn't my fault, somehow it felt like it was since I'd gone out with Kyle for nearly a year."

Emily squeezed her hand. "It wasn't."

"I know that in my head, but my heart is another matter." She gave a watery smile. "I'm terrified Kyle will find out about the baby, and I don't even know if I should keep it or give it up for adoption. What if he wants some sort of custody?"

"Those are all questions we'll figure out together," Emily reminded her.

"Okay." She sniffed, then blew her nose. Her phone buzzed and she checked it. "It's Seth."

"He's a fine young man." Emily had been impressed with her young neighbor and his willingness to help her out at times. "I think he likes you."

A faint flush stole up her daughter's cheeks. "It wouldn't matter if he did, not with the baby. Plus, I thought I could trust Kyle and look how that turned out."

"Seth doesn't strike me as a man who would hold your circumstance against you in any way."

"Perhaps you're right." Jetta pocketed the phone. "But I'm not ready to think about dating anyone right now. To completely change the subject, he's found someone to talk to about the embezzlement, so I need to go meet him." She hugged Emily. "Love you."

"Love you too." As her daughter left with promises to let her know how the meeting went, Emily once again approached the throne of God with her petitions for Jetta's safety, for the health of her newest grandchild, and for resolution in the years-old mystery of who embezzled millions and blamed her husband. For good measure, she threw in a prayer that Jetta and Seth would find happiness together, for her mother's intuition told her the two would be good for each other.

CHAPTER

TWELVE

J etta parked behind Seth's car, her emotions more tangled than a kitten playing with a ball of yarn. Mom's words about Seth being a kind man repeated in her mind. Her heart thumped a little bit faster as he waited for her on the sidewalk. Something about this big man with his peaceful spirit drew her to him. The desire to know more of who he was pulsated through her veins. While her mind screamed caution, given her colossal mistake with Kyle, her heart kept nudging her to let Seth into her life.

"How's your mom?" He motioned for her to proceed him up the walkway.

"Still a bit shaken but okay. Detective Brady will send an officer to sit outside her room at night for at least a few days." She sighed, worry for her mother's safety nibbling at her frayed nerves. "Apparently, the person avoided the security cameras and wore gloves, so there's not much evidence to figure out their identity. Mom thinks it was a man, but she can't be a hundred percent certain."

"I'm happy to keep watch overnight too." He flashed her a soft smile, one that made his chocolate brown eyes sparkle.

She placed a hand on her suddenly racing heart. Why had she

107

never noticed how expressive his eyes were with their impossibly long lashes? He seemed to expect a reply, but she couldn't remember what he'd said. She drew in a deep breath to give herself time to recall. Right. He'd offered to keep an eye on Mom at night. "Thanks, I'll keep that in mind."

"Good." He found the camera doorbell and rang it. When a strong male voice requested their identities, he replied with their names.

"Ah, right on time. Come on in."

The door lock disengaged with an audible click, and Seth pushed it open, then stepped back to allow Jetta to pass through first. As she moved past him, the scent of cedar mixed with a light soap wafted over her, igniting an urge to bury her face on his broad chest and cling to his strong arms. What was wrong with her? She shouldn't want to fling herself into another man's embrace given her pregnant state.

A tall, silver-haired man came into view from a doorway a little way down the hall, interrupting her thoughts. "This way, please."

Seth's hand at the small of her back as they walked down the hallway warmed her, easing some of her tension. The pleasant room with a large bay window overlooked the backyard, which at first glance resembled an overgrown jungle. Jetta drifted to the window for a better view. Closer inspection revealed order with enclosed beds holding wildflowers gradually going to seed while stone walkways intertwined among them. Mature trees dotted the landscape, with neatly trimmed bushes serving as boundary markers along the edges.

"You like it?" The man joined her. "I spent the first six months of my retirement redoing the bland grassy expanse into something more interesting."

"I do." She smiled. "It's messy but organized."

He laughed. "That's exactly it. Most people simply see the overgrowth and assume I've let it go to pot."

"You've created something for the pollinators and other insects and animals, not necessarily for humans."

The man clapped Seth on the back after his observation. "Another insight many do not get. Frank Warner."

"Seth Whitman," he said, then touched Jetta's arm. "This is Jetta Ainsley. Her father was Jay Ainsley."

Mr. Warner sobered. "I'm so sorry about your father, Ms. Ainsley."

"Thank you, and please, call me Jetta." She turned away from the window. "We appreciate you talking about the case with us."

After asking if they'd like a beverage, which they declined, Mr. Warner said, "Let's have a seat." He chose a leather club chair while Jetta plopped down on the loveseat, Seth beside her.

His thigh pressed lightly against hers, then he shifted his away. She refrained from scooting closer to him, missing the feeling of safety.

"What would you like to know?"

She spread her hands out. "Anything. Everything. I recently learned of the embezzlement charges, so I only know what I read in the news."

Mr. Warner steepled his fingers. "My office never officially launched an investigation into the embezzlement at Topher Robotics."

Seth frowned. "I thought FinCEN was the source for the Fairfax County Police Department's probe."

"No, Fairfax came to us with the evidence against Ainsley."

Jetta digested that bit of news. "Why would they come to FinCEN?"

"At the time, they didn't have the resources to launch a deeper investigation into Topher Robotics and were hoping we would."

"So the cops suspected the embezzlement was the tip of the iceberg," Seth said.

Mr. Warner nodded. "In cases involving this much money, that's usually correct. However, when Ainsley died, the investigation did too."

"You never looked into the company's finances?" Jetta curbed her frustration. She'd been hoping for answers, not more questions.

"Not officially."

She picked up on Mr. Warner's word choice. "But unofficially?"

"I didn't like the way the Topher family went after your father so viciously in the press. Your mother should have sued them for slander, since your father was charged but not convicted of embezzlement. But with the case essentially closed, my hands were tied." Mr. Warner sighed. "I've known Peter Topher for years. At the time of your father's death, he was transferring more power to his three children. His wife had been pushing him to retire so they could travel more."

Seth leaned back, slipping his arm along the back of the loveseat behind her. Jetta gave into temptation and rested her back against the cushions, shifting toward him a little and hoping he'd wrap his arm around her shoulders. He didn't but he also didn't move his arm.

"Peter came to me a couple of weeks after Ainsley died, asking if I would take a look at the company books—strictly off the record and without his kids' knowledge."

When Mr. Warner stayed quiet, Seth prompted, "Did you?"

"I did. As I said, Peter was an old friend." Mr. Warner again didn't continue for several seconds. Then he stood. "I'll be back in a minute."

After Mr. Warner left, Jetta swiveled to face Seth. "Where do you suppose he's going?"

"To get his copy of the books."

"What? You think he made a copy of the company financial statements? Wouldn't that be—"

"Unethical?" Mr. Warner re-entered, a bulging accordion folder in his hands. "Perhaps a little, but I had Peter's permission to examine the documents, and my gut said something wasn't right. My initial perusal showed nothing out of the ordinary, which was what I told Peter. By then, he expressed regret in bringing me in and said he was satisfied everything was as it should be. I returned the documents but not until I'd made a copy."

"Why?" Seth asked the question burning in Jetta's mind. Mr. Warner exuded integrity and had been a higher up at FinCEN for years before his retirement.

"Because I wasn't convinced of Ainsley's guilt for one." Mr. Warner retook his seat, setting the folder on his lap. "And because the financial documents were a little too neat. Nothing I could point a finger at, but something about them didn't sit well with me."

"What did you find?" Jetta gazed at the folder, praying it contained concrete evidence exonerating her father.

"Nothing because I never looked at them again." Mr. Warner placed a hand on the folder. "My wife received a cancer diagnosis a few weeks later, and I completely forgot about Topher Robotics. She lost her fight three years ago."

"I'm so sorry for your loss," Seth said, the compassion in his voice evident.

Mr. Warner nodded, the tears glistening in his eyes reminding her of her mother's abiding love for her father. No one spoke for a couple of minutes, then Jetta asked, "Will you look at the documents now?"

"Yes, I will." He touched the folder. "It will take a while."

"Is there anything we can do to help?" Seth removed his arm from the couch back.

"Actually, there is." Mr. Warner unfastened the string holding the folder together and extracted a bundle of papers. "These are invoices from outside vendors. It's not every invoice, of course, but I'd asked for at least one from each vendor they paid over a two-year period prior to Ainsley's death. Would you check each one to see if they did the work or sent the goods listed on the invoices?"

"We'll verify these." Seth accepted the papers.

Jetta caught onto the importance of checking the vendors. "Because you can siphon off money through fake invoices."

"Exactly. I'll give you my email address. Update me as you work your way through the invoices." Mr. Warner provided the address. "May I ask why you're looking into this now?"

Jetta shot a glance at Seth, who nodded. She explained about her mother's fresh desire to clear her dad's name, plus the envelope that had taken fifteen years to arrive. "My mom wants me to find out what I can. I think cleaning out the family home while she's in rehab has also brought it all back."

"A letter accompanied the statements and spreadsheets?"

"Yes, written on a computer with nothing to identify the author." Jetta wished she'd have thought to bring a copy of the envelope's contents to let Mr. Warner have a peek.

"Finding out who sent the documents would shed more light on who could be responsible for the embezzlement," Mr. Warner said.

"We can probably get a list of employees at Topher Robotics from that time, but I wouldn't know where to start IDing the letter writer." Seth set the stack of invoices on the coffee table.

"It's usually someone who had access to the money in some fashion," Mr. Warner pointed out. "I'd start with the finance department, but also look at any position that could submit invoices. Oh, and I'll bet the embezzlement started out with small amounts. Once the person realized no one noticed, she could increase the amounts."

"She?" Jetta hadn't considered a woman as being behind the embezzlement.

"Oh, yes. Embezzlement of this kind—stealing from the company directly, not some sort of Ponzi scheme—is usually done by a female employee." Mr. Warner got to his feet. "I have a garden club dinner I need to prepare for, but please don't hesitate to ask if you have more questions."

Seth rose, holding out his hand to Jetta, who accepted his assistance in rising from the loveseat. "Thank you for your time."

"If I can help right a wrong, I'm happy to do it." Mr. Warner walked them to the front door. "However, I must warn you that if I find your father did indeed take that money, I'll report that as well."

Fear that she might not be able to prove her father's innocence swept over Jetta. Then her mother's determined face, her certainty Dad had been framed, washed away the fear. "I have to know for sure whether he's guilty or innocent."

On the sidewalk beside their vehicles, Seth checked his phone. "I've got to cover the City of Fairfax's City Council meeting for *The Herald*."

"Oh, okay, see you later." Disappointment slumped her shoulders, but she squelched it by straightening her spine. She was the one who constantly reminded Seth he was firmly in the friend zone by her actions, so why should she be disappointed when he went to work rather than suggesting dinner with her? Perhaps because she wasn't as indifferent to his presence as she tried to pretend she was.

Mae resisted glancing behind her as she walked through the research facility, something she did frequently enough no one paid her the least bit of attention. However, this time, she wasn't on a mission from her boss but for her mysterious contact. After she'd sent the board meeting minutes, all had been quiet, lulling her into thinking she was once again home free.

When she'd arrived home yesterday, a package with a burner phone had been delivered, and she'd known the meeting minutes had only been the first salvo in a protracted siege. Once she'd powered up the phone, a text demanded she make a trip to R&D and discover as much as she could about Project Z. This morning, she'd easily uncovered the project wasn't on the official list of R&D projects, which stumped her. How could she find out info about a nonexistent venture? Then she realized her position as the CEO's administrative assistant gave her leave to request info with Ryan's implied authority. Thus her end-of-business day trip to R&D.

She checked the list of projects against rooms as she worked her way down the long hallway. All listed projects had corresponding labs, but the two doors at the very end of the corridor were blank. A keypad with a smaller, fingerprint scanner beside one of the doors alerted her she might have found Project Z. All the other labs had keypads, not biometric scanners.

This time she gave into the urge to look over her shoulder. No one lingered in the hallway. Drawing in a deep breath, she squared her shoulders and knocked firmly on the door. Silence. She knocked again, louder, allowing her frustration and fear to power her knuckles. This time, the door opened to reveal a man about her height wearing a white lab coat.

"Who are you?"

She ignored the snap to his tone. "Mae Stanhope, Ryan Topher's personal assistant."

The man didn't move from the doorway or relax his scowl. "What do you want?"

"Mr. Topher requests an update on Project Z." She'd rehearsed what to say and the words came out with authority.

"He does, does he?" The man crossed his arms, his frown deepening the lines bracketing his mouth. "Why didn't he come himself?"

"Because he's too busy trying to save this company from a hostile takeover." She put a hand on her hip.

The man huffed. "You can tell Ryan the test went as planned and we're moving into phase two."

She nodded as if she knew what he meant. "He'll be pleased to hear that. What's involved in phase two?"

The man's eyes narrowed. "That's all you'll get out of me." The door swung shut in her face.

Mae shrugged, then returned to her desk to retrieve her belongings before hustling to her car. Once off campus, she pulled into a grocery store parking lot and texted her contact.

> Project Z is a secret. Work behind an
> unmarked door on the research floor.
> Security keypad and fingerprint entry. Going
> to phase 2.

She hit send and waited, sure her contact would respond quickly.

Good. Need more details. Take photos.

Mae muttered a word her father had often used when frustrated.

How? Very secure unit. It was hard to pry
that info out. If Ryan finds out…

I'm sure you'll think of something.

She wasn't a superspy, for goodness' sake. Her phone vibrated again.

You have until next Tuesday.

The coffin emoji next to an older man emoji shocked Mae. She'd considered only of her own exposure, not that her husband would be threatened. But the emojis spelled out her contact's intent to kill Mae's husband if she didn't comply. She rested her forehead against the steering wheel, tears slipping from her eyes. Not for the first time, she wished she'd resisted temptation to fudge that initial invoice and pocket the difference. The bills for her father's care had been mounting faster than she and Anderson could pay, and they were dangerously close to losing their house. Anderson had no idea how fast and loose she'd been playing with their finances, wrongly assuming her father had had enough on his own to cover his expenses. That might have happened, but Mae found out a nursing home staffer had convinced her father to open a separate bank account in her name and transfer regular payments there. The woman had been caught, but the money would never be recovered. Moving him to a facility with more oversight had been the only way she could ensure he wouldn't lose the remainder of his money. But the new place had cost twice as much, and soon she was dipping into her retirement funds to pay the hefty monthly fees.

That ran out fast too, so she'd "borrowed" enough to fund her father's stay. However, the easy money had enticed her take a little bit more to replace the retirement account money until, at the time of his death eighteen years ago, she had embezzled nearly a quarter of a million dollars. A life insurance policy she hadn't realized her father had taken out replaced $150,000 of that amount, with her working overtime to return the remaining $100,000. Her husband thought the extra hours were her way of coping with her father's death and hadn't asked too many questions.

She still hadn't told him she couldn't retire as planned, given how depleted her own 401(k) was. And now this. She rubbed her head and started the vehicle. She had less than a week to figure out how to uncover more details about the secret project. Even if she could get in, how on earth would she know what to snap pics of?

As she headed for home, she discarded scenario after scenario until she finally had a possible solution. She would go in on the weekend and sweet-talk her way into the room by saying Ryan needed something ASAP. Yes, that might work. Ryan always golfed with three friends Saturday with a standing 2 p.m. tee time. He also kept his phone on silent during the outings, berating any staffer who tried to contact him during his golf game.

Now that she had a plan for how to get into the room, all she had to do was come up with a solution to keep her visit a secret. She had no intention of becoming a scapegoat for her unknown tormentor. She parked in the driveway, mentally noting Anderson had yet to clean out the garage as he'd promised. Maybe she could suggest he tackle it on Saturday while she nipped out ostensibly to the store but really to work. That would occupy him enough that he wouldn't notice how long she'd be gone.

With the first phase of her plan in place, she pasted a smile on her face and greeted her husband. After kissing his cheek, Mae caught the scent of oregano and garlic. "Something smells good in here."

"I made my favorite girl my famous spaghetti and meatballs." He guided her into the living room. "You put your feet up while I get you a glass of wine. You've been working way too hard. Dinner will be ready in about ten minutes."

She caught his hand in hers. "You take such good care of me."

He dropped a kiss onto her head. "You deserve a little pampering."

No, she didn't, but with luck, he would never find out what she'd done to ensure their lifestyle didn't have any major roadblocks along the way.

CHAPTER

THIRTEEN

The itch near her knee under the cast was driving Emily crazy. Only a few more days to suffer through the heavy plaster keeping her left leg immobile. While her doctor hadn't committed one way or another, Emily had read between what he hadn't said to realize she might not regain full mobility because of the multiple breaks in the appendage, which meant moving to a single-level home made even more sense.

Her bedside clock registered close to midnight, but her mind wouldn't stop whirring. Jay used to call it her "whirling Dervish" brain when she couldn't get it to shut off for the night. He'd had a few tricks up his sleeve that had helped, but since he'd been gone, she had had less success in silencing the inner thoughts.

Her door stayed cracked a sliver, allowing a narrow beam of light from the dim hallway to spill onto her floor. The police had stationed someone outside her door, but he'd been called away to a six-car pileup nearby around nine, with assurances the rehab security would be keeping a close eye on her. She wasn't reassured—after all, someone had breached security to get to her room last night.

A shadow blocked the light from the door. Her heart rate lurched

119

into high gear. She closed her fingers over the call button as the door slowly opened and the outline of a big man filled the doorway.

"Mrs. Ainsley? It's Seth Whitman."

She relaxed her hand on the call button. "Seth, you gave me quite a scare. Come in."

He did so, returning the door to its original position. "Can't sleep?"

"No, and I didn't want to take any sleeping pills." She raised the head of the bed, then pointed to the chair next to her bed. "Have a seat and tell me why you're here at this hour of the night."

"Has Jetta called you?" Her alarm must have shone on her face because he quickly added, "She's okay."

"No, she hasn't."

He looked down at his clasped hands, big, strong hands capable of protecting her sweet youngest daughter. That he cared for Jetta was apparent to Emily, although she doubted Jetta could see it. The man kept his emotions well-hidden, but Emily had learned a thing or two about reading a person as a high school teacher, and she could see his interest in the way he hovered around her daughter. "What's going on?"

When he stayed silent, she prodded. "You're here at this hour in my room because you're worried about Jetta."

"No, ma'am." His swift denial gave her pause. "Not Jetta. I'm worried about you."

"Me? I have someone keeping an eye on me. The officer will be back soon." And he would be, but not until the tomorrow night's shift.

"I don't think that's entirely accurate."

Emily bit back a smile at his tactful way of calling out her half-truth.

"I stopped by the security office when I didn't see the officer outside your door, and he told me about the callout. So you don't have protection." He leaned forward. "Which is why I'm here."

"To protect me." Emily regarded the brawny young man.

"Yes."

She thought about sending him home, but something in Seth's eyes told her he would simply sit outside her room instead of leaving the facility. She decided to find out what had prompted this visit. "What happened?"

He had the grace not to pretend he didn't understand her question. "Jetta's fine."

"But..." She hadn't raised five kids to not know when something was being left unsaid.

Seth acknowledged her prompt with a slight smile. "But she's worried about your safety."

"As I'm worried about hers." She settled back against the bed, but the pillow had shifted down. Seth adjusted it for her without her having to ask, cementing her first impression of a sensitive man. Perfect for her youngest daughter—not that she'd tell either of them that. At least not yet.

"When did you first move into the house?"

She considered his question, glad for the distraction from fresh worries about Jetta and the grandchild she carried. "Let's see, we moved to Virginia from Indiana when I was pregnant with Jason, our third child. That would have been nearly forty years ago."

"Then you're not the first owners of the house."

"Not by a long shot." Memories of the 1950s kitchen and 1970s shag rugs made her smile. "We did buy it from the kids of the original owners, who had been a bit of a do-it-themselves when it came to renovations. Our first Christmas, when Jason was a newborn, I insisted on a live Christmas tree. Jay wrestled it through the door and onto the stand, nearly taking out the chandelier in the foyer in the process. When we had it up and decorated, he flipped the switch for the lights and promptly blew a fuse. That wasn't the first time we'd run into circuits being unable to handle whatever we turned on or plugged in. The previous owners had done some DIY electrical work that ended up costing us a small fortune because we had to get the entire house rewired."

She shared a few more stories of their early life in the home she now had to leave.

"Sounds like you have many good memories of living there."

The wistfulness in Seth's voice made her think his upbringing wasn't nearly as idyllic as the one she'd given her children. "Yes, I do. Mixed with the not-so-good too, of course."

"It must be hard to contemplate leaving."

In the low light of the room, his features lay hidden in shadow, but she detected a yearning in him for such memories of his own. "It is." She sighed. "But I've sensed God nudging me to let go of the past and embrace my future with him more and more." She tapped her leg cast under the covers. "It took an accident to push me to finally make the changes I should have made years ago."

She yawned as sleep began to press down on her shoulders and eyelids. She lowered the head of the bed so she was more reclined than sitting up, allowing the quiet inside the room to lull her toward sleep.

"Why are you so certain your husband didn't embezzle the money?"

"Because I knew Jay." She smothered another yawn. "You know that adage about looking up a word in the dictionary and finding that person's picture? You would find Jay's photo next to the word *honest*. He went out of his way to be above board in every aspect of his life. Did you know he pushed for annual audits by an outside firm the first year he was at Topher Robotics? Peter Topher nixed the idea, saying he didn't want outsiders messing with his books, but every chance he got, Jay hounded Peter, and then Ryan, Peter's oldest son, for yearly audits. Maybe if he'd been successful, the embezzlement would have been uncovered sooner."

"But it was uncovered eventually and all evidence pointed to Jay."

Emily shook her head. "Jay never talked much about his work— another hallmark of his integrity—but he did let it slip once a few years before the accusations against him that he thought someone was stealing small sums of money from the company. He must have been thinking out loud and immediately clammed up when I asked him what he'd meant."

"Can you remember his exact words?"

She closed her eyes, willing her mind to dredge up the long-ago conversation she'd deemed unimportant at the time. "I did mention it to the police after his death, but they weren't interested in investigating any longer since the person accused of the crime couldn't be prosecuted. It might be in the police report, if it has been kept somewhere." She breathed in and out slowly, casting her thoughts back to the April day. Rain poured down, and she'd talked Jay into taking Jetta to school rather than making her wait in the deluge for the bus, which usually ran late on days like this.

He'd agreed, but clearly had been distracted because she'd seen him put on his trench coat while Jetta was still eating breakfast. Emily had hustled to catch him before he could leave the house and that's when she'd overheard his muttering. Her eyes popped open. "I remember. He said, 'It has to be one of three people, but why would any of them take such a risk for so little money?'"

"One of three people taking small sums of money," Seth repeated.

"That's all he said. He dismissed it as a work issue when I asked him what he meant." Sleep beckoned more insistently as she fought to keep her eyes open.

"This could be helpful. I'll pass it along to the former FinCEN agent who's helping us with the financial side. Now, rest easy, Mrs. Ainsley. I'm not going anywhere until the morning."

"Thank you, Seth." She lowered the bed's head until it was nearly horizontal, her preferred way of sleeping. Emily allowed her body to fully relax for the first time that night, closing her eyes. *Lord, thank you for bringing Seth into Jetta's and my life. Heal the hurt I sense behind his kind exterior. And I also pray you would bring the two of them together, if it is your will. Help us uncover the truth behind what happened to Jay too. Amen.*

~

SETH SHIFTED IN THE CHAIR NEXT TO MRS. AINSLEY'S BED, DRAWING THE light blanket he'd found in the closet onto his chest. While it had been comfortable when he'd first sat down, a few springs had sprung in the seat. No matter how he maneuvered, one of them dug into his backside. Mrs. Ainsley's soft breathing assured him she had fallen asleep, something Seth had been hoping to do until the chair declared war on his body.

He rose and paced to the windows with floor-to-ceiling drapes. After slipping behind the heavy curtains, he gazed out onto an inner courtyard. Garden lights framed paved walkways that wound around mulched beds. The bright moon, coupled with the low lights, illuminated the space. Flowers in muted fall colors of orange, red, and yellow had been tucked in among shrubs and small trees. The mix of greenery with color created a welcoming oasis at odds with the sterile interior of the facility.

Leaning his shoulder against the window, he allowed himself to revisit the memories talking with Emily had dragged to the surface. Despite Jay's death, she had created a loving environment for Jetta and her older children. His own childhood had been so different.

The memories played like a jerky home movie across his mind's eye. The fights between his mom and her man-of-the-moment that always escalated into broken dishes and smashed knickknacks. Then the awful yelling that went on for hours before the boyfriend slammed out of the house. His mother gathering up whatever things he'd left behind and chucking them out of the apartment window to the street below. The curses raining down along with shirts, shoes, and toothbrushes.

Her anger spent, his mom would then shout for him to clean up the mess because she was going out. Which translated into heading to the nearest bar to find another man. Somehow, she always did, and the next morning, a new face would be across the breakfast table. He never bothered to learn their names. Instead, he'd watch their eyes to see if they would be nice or mean. If a mean one, he would find more excuses not to come home. For a nice one, he'd try to weasel out some cash for food or a needed clothing item.

The predictable, familiar cycle rinsed and repeated every few months throughout his childhood until one day, Hunter Thomas flipped the script. Definitely not the time to revisit that particular memory, not when he needed to stay alert to keep Mrs. Ainsley safe.

He peeked around the curtain to ensure Mrs. Ainsley slept, oblivious to his inner churnings. In some ways, that night made him into the man he was today. It certainly was why he'd chosen to keep watch over Mrs. Ainsley. He'd vowed to never let a woman get hurt on his watch again.

Seth returned his gaze to the courtyard, seeing not the peaceful space but Jetta's lovely face. Her skittishness reminded him of his mother, who tried to hide the bruises from her revolving-door lovers. He didn't think Jetta played the field like his mother had, which meant her ex-boyfriend must have been a piece of work. If Seth ever saw the man, he'd be hard put not to plant a fist in his jaw for the way he'd treated Jetta. How men could use their strength to dominate women, Seth would never understand. Women should be treated with respect, with dignity. He would never treat a girlfriend in such a way. Not that he'd ever had a chance to find out.

All he knew for sure was he wouldn't keep his distance, not when someone was trying to hurt Jetta and her mother. The next time might result in injury or worse. But keeping them safe meant risking his own heart. Jetta had slipped past his defenses before he'd been aware the fortress he'd constructed around his heart had been breached.

Not that it mattered. Long ago, he'd resigned himself to spending life alone. He was too broken to ever be whole enough to be loved. No matter how much he wished it not to be so. A lifetime of experience had taught him that simple truth.

He shoved away from the window and quietly returned to Mrs. Ainsley's bedside. She hadn't moved, her features relaxed in sleep.

His own mom had never relaxed, her movements either jittery or abrasive, depending on her mood. He ignored the torture chair and snagged the blanket. Moving back to the window, he stretched out on the floor, covering his body with the blanket. Within seconds, sleep claimed him.

FOURTEEN

Seth craned his neck to see if Jetta had taken Bingley outside for his morning walk. He'd arrived home a few hours earlier, having slipped out of her mother's room at the rehab center around six when the day shift brought more people to the floor. While he had slept a few hours on the hard floor, scenes from his childhood had made his rest less than peaceful. He tightened the laces on his running shoes.

Another glance out of the living room window showed Jetta emerging from her house with a leashed Bingley. He quickly pulled open his front door and jogged down the sidewalk. Bingley barked at his appearance, drawing his owner's attention in the early morning light. Seth had been prepared to wait at least another hour before Jetta left her house, as seven was early for her.

"Seth, hi." She tugged Bingley to a halt a few feet from him under a still-lit street light. Dark smudges under her eyes attested to her own restless night. "I didn't expect to run into you."

Bingley leaped about him as if the dog hadn't seen Seth for days instead of mere hours. He focused on the dog instead of responding to her question. "Hey, boy. How are you?" He knelt to allow the dog to slobber kisses on him as he petted Bingley.

"You're going for a run?"

He straightened. "Yes."

She thrust the leash toward him. "Mind taking Bingley along with you?"

"Happy to." He accepted the leash. "I'll be about half an hour."

"Sounds good." She trudged back to her house.

He waited until she entered, then said to the dog, "Guess we're going for a run."

Bingley barked his agreement, and Seth started down the sidewalk, mentally mapping out a shorter route. He didn't want to overly exert the dog, since Bingley was used to more leisurely walks with Jetta. As he jogged, the dog panting beside him, he prayed again for Jetta. Something was weighing her down, and he suspected it was more mental than physical.

Sweat dripped down his face as he rounded the corner to his block. He slowed his steps to catch his breath, not wanting to show up on Jetta's doorstep breathing hard. When he came to his house, he decided to take Bingley inside for a water break before letting Jetta know they'd returned. "Come on, boy. Let's get a little cleaned up before we see her, yeah?"

The dog simply panted as Seth led him up the walkway and into his house. He found a bowl suitable for water and filled it from the tap for Bingley. Then he drank a glass of water himself while the dog lapped from the bowl. Seth used one of his workout towels to mop the sweat from his face.

"Ready?"

The dog lifted his head and woofed as if replying yes. Seth grabbed the leash and headed next door. As they crossed Jetta's driveway, Bingley growled, low and menacing, the sound raising the hairs on the back of Seth's neck. The dog lunged toward the house, jerking the leash from Seth's hand. "Bingley!" He darted after the canine, registering the open front door as he followed the dog inside.

Something wasn't right.

Bingley raced upstairs, Seth several steps behind. The dog moved as if propelled by a cannon. Bingley disappeared through an open door at the end of the hallway into the primary bedroom. A cry, then a crash had Seth putting on a burst of speed into the room.

Bingley had a man wearing ballcap and a facemask cornered. The dog bared his teeth as he growled and barked at the intruder. Seth swept the room but found no sign of Jetta.

"Where is she?" He approached the man, who had a knife in his hand.

"If you don't want this dog dead, call him off." The cold tone informed Seth the man was serious.

"Where is she?" He repeated the question, standing with the bed between him and the intruder.

"Dog. Now." The man brandished his weapon with the easy confidence of one who knew how to use it.

"Bingley, come." Seth had no idea if the dog would obey or not.

The dog growled again, his head low and his teeth still bared.

Seth sharpened his tone. "Bingley, no. Come." He decided to add what might make the dog obey. "Find Jetta."

With one final growl, the dog whirled and dashed from the room, leaving the two men eyeing each other.

"What now?" Seth hadn't moved from his place across the bed.

"Now I'm going to deliver the message." The other man's grin upped Seth's heart rate considerably. This was no ordinary bulgar. This was a professional, one who enjoyed striking fear into his victims.

Seth crossed his arms, his biceps rippling. Might as well see if using his considerable muscle would intimidate the other man or merely make him mad.

Neither, as it turned out. "Tell your girlfriend and her mother to stop meddling."

"Meddling in what, exactly?" Seth figured he knew, but clarifying would give Jetta time to call the cops if she hadn't already.

The other man's eyes narrowed. "Don't play dumb with me."

Seth shrugged but didn't reply. The distant sound of sirens drew his attention—and the intruder's.

"But since it appears I'm out of time, I'll spell it out in words even someone with your brawn but not brains can understand. Lay off your harassment of Topher Robotics."

"Or what?" Seth cocked his head, his calm demeanor a front as he digested the man's words.

Without answering, the man moved toward the door, the knife still visible in his hand. Seth mirrored his steps, arriving at the door at the same time. He stared into the intruder's hard eyes.

Bingley barked, the sound coming from downstairs. The man took advantage of Seth's momentary distraction to slip through the door. Seth flew after him, pounding down the stairs. He caught the man's arm on the threshold of the open front door, but he whipped around, knife gleaming, and sliced Seth's bicep.

Pain exploded and Seth reflexively let go as blood spurted from the vertical gash across his upper arm. He gritted his teeth, his right hand covering the wound on his left arm. The man disappeared from view a few minutes before a police vehicle roared to a stop.

Bingley nudged his leg as he stood dripping blood in the entryway. Jetta! He stumbled as a feeling of lightheadedness washed over him. He wouldn't pass out, not from a little blood loss. He had to stay strong and find Jetta.

"Halt! Police! Show me your hands."

Seth stopped a few feet from the front door. "I'm injured in my left arm, but I don't have any weapons." Blood continued to drip onto the hardwood floor, giving his statement credence.

"Turn around slowly," the male officer commanded.

Seth did. When he came face to face with the officer, he squinted, blinking sweat from his eyes. "Trevor?"

The officer frowned. "Seth? What are you doing here?"

Seth nodded toward the gun his Bible study mate still pointed at him. "Mind lowering your weapon?"

Another officer approached the house as sirens indicated more help had arrived. "Hawks, what you got?"

Falls Church Police Officer Trevor Hawks holstered his gun. "Not sure, but this man needs medical attention. He's Seth Whitman, a photojournalist with *The Herald*."

Seth breathed a prayer of thanks that the responding officer was a friend. "I'm fine, but Jetta Ainsley, the daughter of the home's owner, is somewhere downstairs, and she might be hurt."

Trevor stepped into the house. "You wait here and tell Fleetwood what happened." He moved around Seth as the other officer came up to Seth.

Officer Fleetwood said, "The ambulance is here, so let's get that arm looked at while you tell me what occurred here."

Seth didn't want to leave the house, not before finding out where Jetta was, but as another police vehicle pulled to a stop at the curb, he allowed himself to be guided to the ambulance. As an EMT cleaned his wound, Seth relayed what had happened, along with a description of the intruder and which direction he had gone after leaving the house.

By the time the EMT had bandaged the cut and directed him to see a doctor as he was certain it would need stitches, Seth could hardly stay still, the need to see Jetta racing through his veins. "Thanks."

He bounded out of the back of the ambulance, swaying a bit as his feet hit the pavement, then he ran toward the house, shouldering his way past the officer at the door. "Jetta!"

Bingley woofed, directing him into the living room. Seth screeched to a halt in the doorway as another EMT crouched by Jetta's side as she sat on the couch.

"Jetta." He breathed out her name at seeing her. They hadn't rushed her to the hospital, so perhaps that meant she and the baby were okay.

Jetta raised her head and met his gaze. The smudges under her eyes appeared more pronounced than they'd been less than an hour earlier. Bits of something black bracketed her mouth. "Seth." Tears streamed down her cheeks as if seeing him released a dam inside her. Her eyes widened. "You're hurt!"

"It's nothing." He weaved his way around Trevor talking to another cop to reach her, dropping onto the cushion at her side.

The EMT packed her bag. "Check in with your OB-GYN if you feel anything unusual with the baby."

"Will do, thank you." Jetta swiped tears from her cheeks with her fingers.

Seth handed her a tissue from a box decorated with fall leaves and pumpkins. "Hey, it's okay."

"No, it's not." She used the tissue on her face. "It's not. You could have been killed."

Her concern for his wellbeing warmed his heart. Surely the fear in her eyes meant she cared for him more than a friend, but he'd tuck that away to exam later. Right now, he needed to know what had happened during his run with Bingley.

"Ms. Ainsley?" Trevor came over and stood by the mantel. "Do you feel up to telling me what happened?"

She reached for Seth's hand, and he willingly gave it to her, noting the same black residue around her wrists, which had pink welts. The sight made him firm his lips to keep from blurting out his anger at the intruder, who must have bound her wrists and mouth with duct tape. If only he hadn't gone for the run or hadn't been vain enough to want to clean up a little before returning Bingley, she might have been spared this. Once again, his inability to think about someone else before himself had resulted in someone he cared about being hurt. It was a lesson he seemed doomed to repeat, but one he vowed he would master before something serious happened to Jetta.

JETTA GRIPPED SETH'S HAND AS IF IT WERE A LIFELINE. AND MAYBE IT WAS because she couldn't stop crying because of what that masked man had done. When he'd come up behind her while she washed the breakfast dishes, she hadn't had time to scream before a piece of duct tape slapped across her mouth silenced her. Then he'd roughly shoved her onto a chair and duct taped her hands together in front of her before wrapping her ankles to the two front chair legs.

Terror had nearly made her pass out as images from her ex's assault mixed with the morning's attack. The masked man, his anonymous identity jacking her heart rate up even higher, had smiled when she'd peed her pants, her bladder no match for her willpower. The baby moved, rippling her stomach and reminding Jetta she had to hold it together for her little one's sake. When the man had left her alone to search the house, if the sounds of doors opening and closing were any indication, she had prayed for Seth to come. But as the minutes dragged on, anxiety over what might happen when Seth did return had her frantic with worry.

Then she spotted the landline phone on the counter, a relict her mother insisted on keeping. The man had bound her hands in front of her, but her feet to the chair legs. If she could move close to the counter, she could grab the phone and call for help.

A crash above her told her the intruder was in one of the bedrooms. She wobbled the chair, rocking it enough to move it slowly across the floor. Once, she thought it would tip over, but her prayers were answered, and she stayed upright. Soon she had the phone and had dialed 911. Somehow, through the duct tape, she managed to convince the dispatcher it was an emergency. Bingley's growl had alerted her to Seth's return. As soon as the police officer had come into the kitchen and released her, she had insisted on changing out of her urine-soaked clothing before answering any questions. What she didn't tell the cop was that she had no intention of discussing the incident until Seth was beside her. She needed his comforting presence to make it through the telling.

Now, holding his hand, she managed to get out the salient details of the attack.

"Once he had you secured, did he say anything?" The officer

asked.

She'd forgotten his name, but he seemed to know Seth, which reassured her enough she could tell what happened. Now she frowned, struggling to recall the exact words he'd murmured in her ear. Her fear had sent blood rushing into her ears, making it difficult to hear what he was asking. That's right, a question.

"He wanted to know where the papers were." She was proud she remembered that much.

"What papers?"

Of course the cop would need to know specifics. "He didn't say." If he had, she would have gladly handed them over.

"I think it might be the papers you got in the mail," Seth interjected. "He told me he was supposed to deliver a warning for us to back off our investigation into the embezzlement."

The officer looked from Seth to Jetta. "I think you'd better start at the beginning."

Four hours later, Jetta rubbed her wet hair with a towel. While she had showered already today, the need to wash away the man's rough touch when he'd tied her up had driven her to take another one once the police had finished with forensics and their interviews. Because the man had worn gloves, she wasn't surprised when the crime scene techs turned up nothing useful.

At her urging, Seth had gone to urgent care to get his arm looked at, since the EMT thought stitches might be necessary. He promised to return with soup from Panera, about all Jetta thought she could choke down. A call to her OB-GYN had reassured her that the baby should be fine, given she had only been tied up for a short period of time.

Seth's revelation about the man's warning shook her. Her mother's desire to clear her father's name had set off a chain of events no one had anticipated. Part of Jetta wanted to stop searching for the real embezzler, but another part—the louder voice—insisted that they had a right—no, a duty—to proceed because it was obvious Dad was innocent. Otherwise, why would someone care if they investigated or not? If Dad was guilty, then all they would find would be proof of his involvement.

Bingley's bark alerted her that Seth must have returned.

"Jetta, it's me." His voice reassured her as did his intuition she would need to know who was in her house.

"I'll be down in a second." She swept her damp hair back into a ponytail, then went downstairs to find Seth unpacking containers on the counter. The scent of tomato basil soup triggered a growl from her stomach. Maybe she would be able to manage a bite or two after all.

Once the food had been laid out on the table, he said grace, then dug into his broccoli soup. They ate in silence. After a few bites, she pushed her container away. "What am I going to tell my mom?"

"The truth?" He spooned more soup into his mouth.

The way he said it sounded so simple. "She'll be worried." *And I've already given her more than enough to worry about.*

"Emily is tougher than you think."

"You don't know that." Irritation crept into her tone.

"I know you're scared." His direct gaze, those amazing brown eyes seeing far too much, did little to quell her rising panic.

"Scared? You bet I'm scared. Someone broke into my house and assaulted me, all because I wanted to help my mom clear my dad's name of something he didn't do."

"Do you want to quit looking for the embezzler?"

His question diffused some of her growing anxiety as she contemplated the answer. While she had only learned of the accusations, the unfairness of it pulsated throughout her body. The thought someone had gotten away with it all these years, had stressed her father into having a heart attack, made her angry. Despite her fear for her mother's safety and the reminders of Kyle's assault the morning's attack had brought on, she did not want to stop. If she did, that meant the embezzler won again.

"No, I don't."

Her response brought a smile to his face. She grinned back, glad to have something to smile about after her terrifying morning. Impulsively, she touched his hand. "I'm glad you're investigating with me. I wouldn't be able to do this alone."

He turned his hand over and intertwined his fingers with hers. She should pull back, lest he think she liked him more than a friend, but she couldn't. Not when the feel of his hand gave her such comfort and, if she were being honest, a little thrill. Seth, with all of his obvious strength, never pushed her to accept more than she wanted to receive. To avoid making the same mistake meant she was wearing blinders when it came to Seth. His actions to her mother and to her these past months showed a caring Kyle had never possessed. If only she could convince herself Seth wouldn't change like Kyle had.

"I'm glad to be of service." He squeezed her fingers. "I should tell you where I was last night."

She cocked her head, not sure where this was going. "Where were you?"

He rubbed the back of his neck. "I, um, spent the night in your mom's room."

"What?" She hadn't been expecting that revelation.

"In a chair, or rather the floor." He fumbled to explain. "I was worried about her safety, and I knew you were beat, so I thought…"

Gratitude for his thoughtfulness filled her entire being. "So you went over there to keep an eye on her."

"Yes, and I'm glad I did because the officer assigned to keep watch left to respond to a massive traffic accident."

"Thank you." The words seemed inadequate, and she leaned across the table and brushed her lips against his cheek. "You're one in a million, Seth Whitman."

A blush stole up his neck and across his cheeks. A man who blushed yet made her feel safer than anyone she'd ever met might be a keeper, as her grandmother used to say. Time would tell whether he would be willing to raise another man's child, if she decided to keep the baby.

FIFTEEN

Seth refrained from touching his cheek where the impression of Jetta's lips remained. He told himself to not get his hopes up that her feelings were warming toward him. An incoming text was the distraction he needed. "I'd better get this, as it might be work."

She stood. "I'll clear."

Seth checked the incoming text from Brogan.

> Hope you don't mind, but I mentioned your quest to Fallon since Topher Robotics is in the news with rumors of a hostile takeover.

Seth furrowed his brow. His colleague had been adamant about not being interested in clearing Ainsley's name, but having the veteran investigative reporter's assistance would provide invaluable guidance.

> What did he say?

He's intrigued, wants a full report on what you're doing and what happened 15years ago. Stop by his office when you're in.

If Fallon assigned a story to Brogan, it might give the investigation the juice it needed to progress at a faster clip. While he was texting Brogan, Seth decided to see if Brogan's girlfriend was available, as he could see the mess the intruder and the crime scene techs left behind.

Hey, is Melender up or sleeping?

Up. She's off for the next few days. Why?

Someone broke into the Ainsley home this morning and messed some stuff up. She's okay, but the intruder got away. Jetta could use some help cleaning up.

I'll ask her to text you if she's free.

Brogan sent a winking face emoji, which Seth ignored by replying only with a thumbs up emoji. Jetta had taken Bingley out to the backyard, so Seth finished his unsweetened iced tea while he waited for Brogan to get back to him. His phone dinged with a text from Brogan saying Melender would be on her way in fifteen minutes. He sent another thumbs up emoji.

"I hope you don't mind, but I asked Brogan's girlfriend, Melender, to help get the house cleaned up," he told Jetta when she and Bingley returned to the kitchen. "She works for Squeaky Clean, so she's really good."

Jetta frowned. "I suppose Mom can pay for the help, but I wish you would have asked before hiring someone."

Seth realized his mistake. "Oh, I should have explained. She's not coming as an employee of Squeaky Clean but as a friend."

"But I don't even know her."

"That doesn't matter to Melender. She has an interesting story to tell about her own journey to justice."

A knock at the door tugged his attention away from Jetta. Bingley barked and raced for the door.

"I'll get it." Seth could see Jetta was a little spooked by the earlier intruder.

Melender Harman stood on the porch with a plastic caddy of cleaning supplies. "Hey, Seth."

"Melender, thanks for coming." Seth gestured her inside. "Come on in. Jetta's in the kitchen."

Melender stepped inside, Bingley shoving his nose into her side. "Who's this beautiful boy?"

"This is Bingley." Seth led the way back to the kitchen, where Jetta was wiping the counters. "Jetta, this is Melender. Melender, Jetta's working on getting the house ready to sell since Mom needs to move to one-level living."

Melender raised the caddy. "Jetta, I have two things to tell you. One, I'm bossy as all get out when it comes to cleaning, and two, I'm so sorry this happened to you."

"Thanks." Jetta wrung out the sponge and put it back on the sink. "I wasn't too happy when Seth told me you were coming, but now I can see we'll get along fine."

Seth hid a smile as the two woman began planning how they would clean the house. Good, Jetta could use a friend and help in tackling the mess inside. He said a quick prayer of thanks that Melender came over.

"I'll leave you two alone." Then he remembered Brogan's text. "I forgot to tell you that Brogan texted me our boss wants to hear about your dad's case since Topher Robotics is in the news."

"The hostile takeover?"

At his nod, Jetta continued, "Do you think Brogan might be assigned to look into it?" The hope in her eyes made him want to promise her the moon, but he tempered his reaction.

"Maybe, but we should work on the invoices ourselves. Perhaps

Mr. Warner will find something too. I've got to cover a ribbon cutting at three. I'll let you know as soon as I've talked to Fallon."

Seth left, his heart aching for all the burdens Jetta was carrying. At lease he'd been able to ease her physical work with Melender onsite. His thoughts turned to his meeting with Fallon. He prayed for a good outcome because he would need all the help he could get to convince his boss to open an official investigation into Topher Robotics.

"Any other business?" Ryan Topher eyed his siblings over the rim of his coffee cup.

Yasmine, the company's chief operating officer, cleared her throat. "Daniel Pluris in communications fielded a call from a local reporter, Brogan Gilmore, asking for an interview with you."

Ryan replaced his cup carefully on its matching saucer, relieved his hand had stayed steady and not betrayed the roiling emotions inside. "What would the interview be about?"

She consulted her iPad. "A profile of Topher Robotics was all Gilmore told him."

"Hmm." Ryan regarded his sister. "What do you think?"

"I think we could use all the positive PR we could get." She leaned across the small conference table in Ryan's office. "We could feed Gilmore hints about the wearable AI your team is developing."

"It could work in our favor with our shareholders too," Gene, their chief financial officer, chimed in. "We barely won the vote this time. I doubt Todd Griffin and Mari Rawls will give up now that they smell vulnerability. They'll try again with another attempt at a hostile takeover from Maxwell Technology."

"I agree." Ryan, along with their father, had rallied the long-time shareholders into banding with the family and repulsing the initial takeover bid, but the margin had been slim. One misstep, and they could easily lose a second vote. "Who is Gilmore?"

"He's with *The Northern Virginia Herald*, hardly a hard-hitting news outlet, but it does have a decent circulation online and a print run of 300,000 readers." Yasmine's tone dismissed the paper as inconsequential, but Ryan knew the power of the local press shouldn't be discounted so easily. "An interview with Ryan would be a coup for any reporter, let alone one of his stature. We should be able to manipulate him to say what we want and get a nice puff piece out of it."

"Don't be so sure." Gene crossed his arms, his lips set in a smug line Ryan recognized all too well. The middle child, Gene constantly needled their younger sister as if needing to prove his seniority again and again. "A few months ago, he broke that case involving the wrongly convicted woman, Melender Harman, and he was a former investigative reporter with some big-name newspapers."

Yasmine raised a single eyebrow. "You should have dug a little deeper, brother. Gilmore had a spectacular fall from grace for fudging sources. Yes, his stories about that ex-con got picked up by the Associated Press and sent around the country, but he's still near the bottom of the journalistic heap."

Ryan rolled his eyes at the interplay of one-upmanship between the two of them. As the elder brother, he tried to stay well out of their petty squabbles. But he agreed with Yasmine's assessment of the reporter. "The bottom line is that Gilmore, having gotten a taste of the big times again with the Harman story, is probably eager for another feather in his cap."

"Exactly." Yasmine shot Gene a triumphant glance, which he ignored. "But to be safe, I could invite him here for a background interview, strictly off the record, and get a feel for the story's direction. Then if we're satisfied he'll report what we want, we'll give him access to you, Ryan."

Gene opened his mouth, but Ryan cut him off before he could muddy the waters. "That's an excellent idea. Set it up for this week if you can."

"Will do." She made a notation on her tablet, then stood. "I've got an appointment, so if you'll excuse me…"

"Who is he this time?" Gene's casual question stopped their sister halfway across the room.

She spun around, fire dancing in her eyes. "If you must know, dear brother, it's with my gynecologist, a follow up appointment to discuss the results of the biopsy I had a few weeks ago."

Her news pulled Ryan to his feet. For all their arguments, the three of them were a tight-knit bunch. "Are you okay?"

"Why didn't you say something?" Gene also popped to his feet.

She waved them off. "It's a small mass on my left ovary. It's not cancer, but we need to discuss whether or not it should be removed." She offered a saucy grin. "I didn't tell you two because I knew there would be an opportunity to spring it on you and wanted to enjoy your reactions when you found out. It was so worth it."

When the door closed behind her, Gene gathered his notebook, preferring paper and pen to technology for meetings. "She'll be the death of me."

Ryan leaned against his desk. "Me too."

"How's Dad doing?"

"I think the close vote shook him." Ryan winced at the memory of Peter's fury and his caustic words about how his children were ruining Topher Robotics. "But we're very close to announcing the new wearable AI device."

"The sooner the better," Gene said. "Some of the shareholders who voted with us only did so because of loyalty to Dad. They'll jump ship if we can't prove we're growing the company as fast as they'd like."

"Don't worry. I've got it under control." Ryan returned to his desk as Gene exited his office. He would do whatever it took to ensure the company his father built stayed in the family's hands. While his father railed about preserving his legacy, Ryan had more practical matters to think about if Maxwell Technology succeeded in its bid for control. For one thing, he didn't care for another company to take credit for the technology his team was developing. On the other hand, he wasn't sure their books could withstand close scrutiny such a takeover would unleash. No, much better to use this reporter to burnish the reputation of Topher Robotics. After all, it wouldn't be the first time he manipulated the press to make a potential problem disappear.

CHAPTER

SIXTEEN

Seth uploaded the photos from the early afternoon assignment, then stretched his arms over his head. He had planned to hit the gym after his morning run, but the intruder had derailed that plan. Now he probably wouldn't make it there today because he wanted to use his spare time tackling his half of the invoices. At least his quick conversation with Fallon had resulted in the green light for Brogan to write something about Topher Robotics and the hostile takeover bid. The paper's editor said they'd need more evidence before a full investigation into the embezzlement would be prudent.

A tap on the outside of his cubicle preceded Brogan poking his head around. "Pencil in Friday at ten a.m."

Seth pulled up his calendar to scan Friday—wide open in the morning. "Where we going?"

"Topher Robotics to interview Ryan Topher." Brogan's grin widened. "Yep, the top man himself."

"How'd you score that?" Seth entered the info to block off the time on his calendar.

"I might have let them believe it would be a puff piece on the company and Ryan." Brogan raised his eyes to the ceiling as if trying to project his innocence. "I convinced Yasmine Topher, the youngest sibling and the company's COO, I had no ill intentions during a phone screener."

"I'm impressed, as from what I've read about her, she's a tough cookie." Seth rested back against the chair. "But I guess with the takeover still a possibility, they need some positive publicity touting Ryan's excellent leadership."

"Exactly. We'll make a bona fide reporter out of you yet." Brogan winked at him. "Said I would be bringing a photographer, and they were extremely happy to hear that."

"I bet they were." Seth evaluated his colleague. "What's your plan of attack for the questions? I assume you'll be asking about Jay Ainsley and the embezzlement charges."

"We'll have a tour of the research facility first with Ms. Topher, then sit down with Ryan in his office. I'll cover all the softball questions while you take photos, then slip in some he won't be expecting."

"What's Fallon's take on your strategy?"

Brogan responded with a thumbs up. "Gotta run. Have an interview with the fire chief about the what caused the fire at the construction site."

Seth finished captioning the photos and sent them to Fallon, then he decided a trip to the gym would help him more than puzzling over the invoices. Ten minutes later, he set the pin low on the bench press and settled in for twenty reps. Sweat beaded his forehead as he considered how best to tackle the invoices. Google the company names, then crosscheck with the online yellow pages. Some invoices had numbers he could call for more information, but he'd need a cover story first. While lying used to be a large part of his past, since he became a Christian, telling even the slightest untruths didn't sit well with him.

Moving onto a machine to work his shoulders, he reviewed and discarded scenarios as he completed several sets of fifteen reps. As he made his way around the circuit of machines, he kept puzzling over the best—and most honest—approach, to no avail.

"Hey, Seth. Don't often see you here at this time of day." Clancy joined him as Seth wiped down the final machine in the circuit.

"Been too busy to come after work, so thought I'd fit one in now." He moped his face with another towel.

"Something troubling you? That young lady, perhaps?" The older man's eyes twinkled as he asked the questions.

Seth's cheeks heated with more than sweat from the workout. Ignoring the second question, he replied to the first. "I need to call some companies to ask about old invoices, but I don't want them to know why I'm calling, and I don't want to lie."

"I see." Clancy crossed his well-muscled arms over his barrel chest. "Would you call what you're doing an audit of sorts?"

"Maybe." Seth caught onto where he thought the gym owner was heading. "Perhaps I could say I'm reviewing the invoices without mentioning who I'm with or why."

"Most people are too busy and wrapped up in their own lives to ask a bunch of questions, so you're likely to get the info you want without too much fuss." He slapped Seth on the shoulder. "Good luck, and bring that young lady of yours around sometime."

"I will." Seth didn't bother explaining Jetta wasn't his young lady. Not yet. Her buss on his cheek gave him more hope than he'd had in a while, though he could tell by Jetta's wide eyes, her action might have startled her as well.

Back in the office after a quick shower, Seth checked his email for any last-minute assignments, and, finding none, started verifying the invoices. An hour later, he blew out a breath. All of the companies had what appeared to be legitimate websites. Time to start calling. The first call went as well as Clancy had predicted. The person in accounting simply took his word about an audit and assumed Seth was with Topher Robotics. Seth gained confidence with his cover story as the pile of invoices dwindled. But as each invoice proved legit, the thought of this being a wild goose chase took firm hold in his mind. He dialed the twelfth company, SafeSense Technologies, a firm that manufactured sensors.

When he explained what he wanted to the woman in accounting, she agreed to check and put him on a brief hold, which stretched to nearly five minutes. Seth was beginning to think she'd disconnected the call when a different person came on the line.

"This is Huey Reinhardt," a man said. "After all this time, why are you asking about this invoice again?"

Seth immediately latched onto the last word in the question and pivoted away from his prepared speech. "As you know, Topher Robotics recently repelled a hostile takeover bid from Maxwell Technology."

Before he could continue, Reinhardt broke in. "And you need to make sure we aren't going to say something? Seriously? I told Ryan then and I'll tell you now—we had no idea Dolores had been submitting fake invoices to Topher Robotics. She'd been an exemplary employee for more than a decade. When we discovered what had happened, we took immediate measures to change how we submit invoices, and we fired Ms. Green. We were assured by Ryan fifteen years ago this would not be brought up again. Good day."

The man hung up. Seth replaced the receiver on his desk phone, his mind churning with the information he'd gleaned. Someone named Dolores Green at SafeSense Technologies had faked invoices to Topher Robotics, which had been discovered presumably as part of the internal investigation into the embezzlement Jay Ainsley had been accused of. The mention of Ryan Topher's name was interesting. Seth quickly composed an email recapping the conversation and sent it to Brogan for background ahead of their interview.

Then he returned to SafeSense's website, having earlier spotted a tab for company newsletters. As he'd hoped, the quarterly newsletter stretched back more than two decades, with older versions available as PDFs. He did a name search for Dolores Green to see if any of the issues mentioned her. A few hits returned, the top one being the winter edition from sixteen years ago. She sat in the front row of an accounting department photo beside a Christmas tree decorated with money symbols and dollar bills. Dolores appeared to be in her mid-50s, a plain, nondescript woman with faded brown hair scraped back into a tight bun.

The second issue from the following spring had a story about donations via a Caring Bridge page set up to help Dolores with medical bills related to Roxy, her beloved shiatzu's cancer treatment. He clicked the Caring Bridge link, expecting it to be a dud, but to his surprise, the page pulled up. Although the donation button had been turned off, the text related Roxy's fight, and it gave a south Arlington home address. He jotted it down, then closed out of his searches. He'd text Jetta and see if she wanted to stop by in the event Dolores Green still lived there and would talk to them about those fake invoices.

Mae Stanhope marched down the hallway of the research wing of Topher Robotics, her stride at odds with her jelly-filled insides. Her mysterious contact had texted the death emoji several times over the past couple of days, but Mae ignored it. She had to come up with a plausible reason to get the photographs the person wanted, and that couldn't be rushed. Ryan had left for a round of golf with some of the board members, clearing the way for her late afternoon visit. Her boss never answered texts or calls on the course.

Reaching the door to the secret project, she paused and drew in a breath. She could do this. She had to. After knocking on the door, she waited, slowly counting to sixty before knocking again. She repeated it several times before the same man, wearing the same irritated expression, yanked open the door. Mae stepped forward immediately, her movement pushing the man back into the room. As she'd hoped, he closed the door behind her.

"What do you..."

Mae didn't give him a chance to finish the question. "Ryan Topher needs a video of Vie in action. Now."

The man crossed his arms over his chest. "I've heard nothing of this."

Mae leaned closer, channeling her boss's most irritated tone. "Of course you wouldn't have because emails and texts and phone calls can been compromised. That's why he sent me directly. So are we going to stand here arguing, or are we going to get that video?" She waited a beat, then added, "Or do you want to see all your hard work vanish when Maxwell Technology takes over the company?"

She'd guessed right that the man feared his research would go to another company. He shrugged. "Come on back."

Hiding her elation, Mae followed him deeper into the building. He used his handprint to open a door on the left. The windowless room had bright lights, gleaming white counters, and three people working on separate stations.

Her heart sank when she recognized Dr. Brian James and Dr. Jana Willis. She'd been hoping for more low-level employees where her status as Ryan's personal assistant would carry more weight.

"What's she doing here?" Dr. James charged toward them.

Mae let the other man explain, figuring he would want to justify his decision to let her into the inner sanctum.

"Don't look at me. Ryan sent her to video Vie in action," he snapped.

The other scientist joined them, her eyes narrowing. "I heard nothing of this."

Mae stepped in. "You wouldn't have because he gave me the order right before he left to make tee time." The mention of golf—and the implication of Ryan being unavailable—gave the two scientists pause, if she correctly gauged their expressions. "Look, he wants a short video to show the board members in order to stop another takeover bid. The danger of Maxwell Technology swooping in isn't over yet. There will be another vote, and soon."

She debated whether to add anything about Maxwell Technology's reputation for gutting a company of its most valuable assets and siphoning off promising research but decided not to overplay her hand. The scientists exchanged glances, then the woman firmed her lips and gave a small nod.

"One video only. We will provide no commentary." Dr. James spun on his heel and marched to the table and conferred with the room's third occupant, a young man who looked barely old enough to shave.

Mae nodded her agreement, then cued up her phone's camera and waited for the demonstration to begin. Soon Dr. James waved her over.

"You may begin filming and must stop when we say."

Mae held up her phone without bothering to agree. The device, which appeared to be similar to a smart watch, buzzed and lit up, its small screen going through a series of changes. She couldn't tell what was special about Vie but figured it didn't matter. Getting the video was all that did.

"That's it," Dr. James intoned.

She hit end on the video.

"Get what you needed?" Dr. Willis's question was tinged with impatience.

"Yes, thank you." Mae lowered her phone. "I'll be sure to let Ryan know about your cooperation. He also asked for an update on the timeline."

"And we told him soon is the best we can do," said Dr. James. "Now leave us to work in peace."

Gladly. Mae hustled toward the exit, the man who'd let her in at her heels. He let her out, then practically slammed the door on her. His actions screamed good riddance, but she wasn't offended. She was more than happy to be done with this particular assignment.

Ten minutes later, Mae hit upload and sent the video to her contact, then typed up the minutes from Ryan's Saturday morning emergency meeting with the executive board. As she finished her tasks, she hoped the person would be satisfied with the video and ask no more of her, but she wasn't confident that would be the case. The thought she should simply retire now crossed her mind. She had calculated she'd need to work another two years to replace the money in her retirement fund, but perhaps they could manage on what they had now. But to do so would mean telling her husband what she'd done, and she wasn't ready to have that conversation. She doubted she ever would be.

CHAPTER

SEVENTEEN

Across the street from Dolores Green's modest brick home in south Arlington, Jetta wedged her vehicle between a pickup truck and an older model sedan. She winced afresh at the dented and mangled rear bumper now bungee-corded in place. She needed to get it fixed but hadn't had time to figure out where to take it. Maybe Seth would have advice.

The man uppermost in her thoughts exited his vehicle and joined her on the sidewalk in front of the Green residence. When he'd texted her about his idea to drop by unannounced, she built all sorts of scenarios about the woman who had implicated her father in the embezzlement scheme, painting her like some femme fatale of 1940s noir films.

Now surveying the flower beds that lined the walkway to the home, a surge of pity batted away those images as she noted signs of neglect. Paint peeled from the shutters framing two windows while the concrete stoop crumbled at the edges as if too tired to hold itself together anymore. It was also one of the few original homes left intact on the street. On either side, larger, more modern houses had probably replaced similar 1950s abodes.

"It always saddens me to see neighborhoods turn over because so many times, it means tearing down the old and building the new." She'd seen the same kind of changes in her mother's neighborhood and wondered if whoever bought her childhood home would tear it down to start again.

"Sometimes the old needs to be torn down and rebuilt into something new." The bitterness behind the statement surprised her, but he changed the subject before she could delve deeper into what he meant. "How do you want to play this?"

"Maybe you should take the lead." Although she had taken a short nap after Melender left, she still wasn't feeling herself.

He nodded, then knocked on the door. Jetta stood on the walkway below the one step leading to the stoop.

An older woman wearing stretchy pants and a flowery top stood to the left of the now-open door. "If you're selling, I'm not buying."

"We're not selling, Ms. Green." Seth's easy reply did little to eliminate the suspicion hovering in her eyes.

"How do you know my name?" Dolores swiveled her gaze from one to the other.

"Ms. Green, I'm Seth Whitman, and this is Jetta Ainsley. We're hoping you could help us."

"With what?" She planted a hand on an ample hip and narrowed her eyes. "I haven't got all day, so spit it out." Her annoyance played a band concert of discordant sounds.

"Ms. Ainsley's father, Jay Ainsley, worked for Topher Robotics. He was accused of embezzling a lot of money, but he died before he could prove his innocence." Seth let the statement hang in the air like a basketball player going for a slam dunk.

Jetta watched as emotions she couldn't identify flashed across the older woman's face.

For a moment, Dolores didn't respond, then she huffed a sigh. "You'd better come in."

Jetta entered, Seth at her heels, as Dolores led them into a living room crammed with knickknacks on every available surface. Upon closer inspection, the glass and ceramic figurines appeared to all be dogs. She didn't know how the woman lived in such a cramped space, but Dolores didn't seem to mind. Their hostess crossed her arms, her stance radiating distrust and tension.

Seth pointed to an amateurish watercolor still life of a body of water with what Jetta supposed was a duck floating on the surface hanging above the mantel. "That's Burke Lake, isn't it?"

Dolores uncrossed her arms. "Yes, my grandson painted that for my birthday years ago."

"How old was he?"

"Ten."

"Impressive that he could capture the essence of the lake at such a young age." Seth sounded genuinely impressed.

"That's why I display it." Dolores joined him in front of the painting. "He's now studying art at the Pratt Institute in New York. He's given me better paintings, but this was his first watercolor. Every time he visits, he begs me to replace it with a more recent, better executed painting, but I enjoy gazing at the potential you can see in his brush strokes than his later polished pieces." Some of the stiffness eased from her shoulders. "Have a seat and tell me why you think I can help you."

Seth and Jetta both took the couch while Dolores choose a well-worn easy chair.

"Mrs. Green," he began.

"Please, call me Dolores."

"Dolores," he started again, "as I mentioned, we're looking into the embezzlement charges levied against her late father."

Dolores held up her hand. "And you discovered an anomaly with some of the invoices from SafeSense that were attributed to me."

"That's correct."

Jetta repeated to herself she would trust Seth knew what he was doing, allowing the silence to grow rather than filling it with the evidence they had about the fake invoices.

"I couldn't believe it when Mr. Reinhardt called me into his office and accused me of tampering with invoices." The older woman's voice hitched. "I had no idea what he was talking about, but he showed me the invoices I had sent to Topher Robotics."

"They had been altered after you'd sent them?" Seth's voice had a gentle tone at odds with his beefy physique.

Jetta admired him for not throwing his weight around to intimate the other woman to get what he wanted.

"They must have been as I didn't change the amounts." Dolores dabbed at her eyes with a tissue, alerting Jetta to how troubled the older woman was about the invoices. "I tried to tell Mr. Reinhardt I wouldn't do something like that, but he wouldn't listen."

"We believe you didn't have anything to do with the altered invoices."

Jetta shot Seth a glance, but his attention remained fixed on Dolores. The woman could be upset merely because she'd gotten caught.

"You do?" The older woman deflated as if someone had let the air out of her. Her hand fluttered to her chest, resting there for several seconds.

"Yes, we think you were targeted much like Jetta's father was." The conviction in Seth's voice told Jetta he was convinced of Dolores' innocence.

"But why would someone do such a thing?" Dolores swung her gaze from Seth to Jetta, then back to Seth.

"That's what we're trying to find out." Seth opened a notebook, poising his pen above a blank page. "Would you walk us through exactly what happened?"

Dolores straightened with a decisive nod, her attitude a complete one-eighty from her earlier demeanor. "The thing is, I brought one of the altered invoices to the attention of my supervisor a few weeks before Mr. Reinhardt accused me of stealing money."

"What did your supervisor say?"

"That she would check into it. I forgot about it until that meeting with Mr. Reinhardt." Dolores shuddered. "It was awful. When I arrived at work, I couldn't log onto my computer, but before I could call tech support, Mr. Reinhardt's admin called me into the meeting."

"Who was there?" Seth inquired as he wrote down the details.

In spite of her skepticism, Jetta found herself drawn into Dolores's story.

"Mr. Reinhardt, who was the head of accounting, and my immediate supervisor, Fiona Everly."

"The one you'd told about the invoice?" Seth clarified.

"Yes." Dolores firmed her lips as if stopping more words from spilling out. She appeared to be fighting for composure with deep breaths and rapid eye blinks. Then she continued, her voice not as steady as before. "I still didn't suspect anything until Fiona laid out a stack of invoices for Topher Robotics with the one I had brought to her attention on top. She then asked me to explain why I had been changing the invoice amounts and where the extra money had gone."

As Dolores explained how the duo had harangued her to confess what she'd done with the money and why she had committed fraud, Jetta saw similarities between Dolores's story and her father's. According to her mother, Ryan Topher had engineered a meeting with his two siblings and Dad, laying out the embezzlement charges and requesting Dad's cooperation in returning the money.

"Mr. Reinhardt even had statements from a bank account in the Cayman Islands in my name showing I had deposited several thousand dollars that corresponded with two of the invoices." Dolores shook her head. "No matter what I said, no one would believe that I hadn't done this."

"How did things end?"

Again, Jetta was struck by the empathy in Seth's tone and posture.

"They decided they wouldn't prosecute me if I agreed to resign and pay back the money they said I took." The bitterness in Dolores's voice told Jetta what she thought of that deal. "I'd worked for Safe-Sense for twenty-five years, and they threw me out like garbage."

"I'm guessing you took the deal." Seth closed his notebook.

"I had no choice, not when they threatened me with prison if I didn't." She sighed. "I wanted to call their bluff and insist on a full investigation, but I had no resources to fight them. I did call a couple of law firms and see if someone would take my case pro bono, but no one would." She crossed to an old-fashioned secretary and lowered the lid. She removed a brown envelope similar to the one Jetta's mother had received.

"Here." Dolores thrust the envelope at Seth. "This is the agreement they forced me to sign. They wouldn't broadcast what I had done, but they would if I ever worked in an accounting position again."

Seth extracted the papers and Jetta leaned closer to read, smelling the cedar and soap combination she now associated with him. She skimmed the legalese until she came to the amount Dolores had been accused of stealing. "Eighty-seven thousand dollars."

Dolores twisted her fingers together on her lap. "I've worked two retail jobs—the only work I could get outside accounting—for the past fifteen years and still owe more than $25,000. But as the agreement states, as long as I pay something each month, I'm safe from prosecution."

"You've thought about not paying?" Seth asked.

"I've been too afraid to see what would happen, but yes, I have thought of it. Talking about it with you has made me realize the only proof they had was the bank account in my name and the altered invoices."

"The bank account could have been opened by anyone with your information, and just because you handled the Topher Robotics account doesn't mean you were the only person with access to the invoices."

Dolores relaxed her hands at Seth's statement. "Exactly. In fact, I heard that Fiona left SafeSense to work for Topher Robotics a few months after I was let go.”

“Do you know if she’s still there?” Seth reopened his notebook and jotted a note.

“According to the company website, she’s now the head of accounting, answering to Gene Topher.”

Jetta found that very interesting. Something worth following up. Seth thanked Dolores for her time, and the woman walked them to the door.

“You’ll let me know what you find out, won’t you?” The hope in Dolores’s eyes mirrored Jetta’s own.

She touched the other woman’s hand. “We will.”

Back on the sidewalk, she turned to Seth. “You think Fiona altered the invoices and blamed Dolores for it?”

“That’s one possibility.” Seth put the reporter’s notebook into his back pocket. “The other is Fiona knew who at Topher Robotics altered the invoices and decided to jump ship to cash in on that knowledge.”

A sharp crack sliced through the end of his sentence. Jetta screamed as a second bullet tossed a chunk of concrete into the air. Someone was shooting at them.

Seth pushed Jetta to the ground, covering her body with his as gunfire erupted around them. Dirt, grass, and bits of concrete flew up at them as the hail of bullets continued for what seemed like minutes, but he knew would only be seconds. Then the squeal of tires and the roar of an engine replaced the shots, leaving behind the acrid scent of smoke and gunpowder in his nostrils. An all-too familiar smell, but he didn’t have time to dwell on those horrific images, not when he needed to make sure Jetta was unharmed.

He lifted himself on his elbows to gauge whether it was safe to rise.

"Are they gone?" Jetta's voice quavered.

"Maybe." Her face, streaked with dirt and blood, made him gasp. "You're hurt." He touched her cheek where the blood streamed from a cut, alarm reigniting the adrenaline. "Are you shot?"

"I don't think so." She twisted as if to check herself. "What about you?"

"I'm fine." Anger that someone had taken potshots at them burned deep in his belly.

"I've called 911." Dolores stepped off the sidewalk. "I know this isn't the same neighborhood I grew up in, but we've never had a shooting in broad daylight."

Jetta rolled to a seated position.

"Oh, you poor dear. Come inside to wait for the ambulance. Is your baby okay?" Dolores fluttered her hands.

"I'll sit on the step." Jetta sent him a look he interpreted as needing his help, and he leaned down to assist her to her feet. Her body, with its distended belly, pressed against his side.

With the utmost care, he assisted her to the top step leading to the sidewalk. "Here you go." He looked over his shoulder at Dolores. "Would you bring Jetta a glass of water?"

"Of course." Dolores disappeared inside the house as sirens rent the air, sounding close.

Bits of grass tangled with Jetta's strawberry blonde hair, and she had a few cuts on her arms and one on her cheek from flying debris, but thank God she appeared otherwise unharmed. He couldn't live with himself if he hadn't been able to protect her. Her arms crossed across her stomach, drawing his attention to her midsection. "You sure you're okay?"

"I'm fine, just shaken." Her sharp tone almost made him smile. "I've had a rough day."

"That you have," he agreed, his tone mild. "But maybe you should get checked out by your doctor to make sure the baby's okay."

"I said I'm fine." The glare she sent him could have curdled milk, but he couldn't help the worry nibbling at his mind like a mouse with a hunk of cheese. A flash of memory pummeled his mind. His mother, holding her middle as blood pooled at her feet, her eyes begging him for help he couldn't give. His seven-year-old self scrubbing the evidence from the bathroom floor. The baby sister he never got to hold.

"Seth?" Concern knitted her brow, her lovely blue eyes pools of worry. "I'm really okay, and so is my baby. See?"

He dragged himself from the memory pit that threatened to swallow him whole and cleared his throat as she reached for his hand and pressed it to her stomach. A firm kick from the baby startled him, followed immediately by what felt like a punch. His eyes widened.

She laughed, leaning closer to him with her hand still on his resting on her belly. "Amazing, isn't it?"

"It is." The baby kicked again, bringing a grin to his face.

Jetta moved her hand from his and touched his cheek, her fingers lightly caressing the smoother part of his face.

Seth sucked in a breath, his chest tightening as her hand cupped his jaw. The desire to kiss her made him drop his eyes from her face to her mouth. His breath whooshed out as she raised her lips and touched his own.

The shock of Jetta's mouth against his reverberated through Seth's body. The very action he'd only dared think about was happening. The softness of her lips, the feel of her body resting lightly against his, spiraled through him. His very first kiss wasn't at all what he'd expected. It was so much more. His internal body temperature shot up so fast, he groaned against her lips. A warning bell chimed incessantly in his mind, and somehow, he managed to heed its call. Breaking off the kiss, he rested his forehead against hers.

"Oh, my." Dolores's voice doused him with cold water. "I, um, brought Jetta's water."

"Thank you." Jetta moved away from Seth, accepting the glass with a smile while Seth could barely catch his breath.

His first kiss had been everything and nothing he'd ever imagined. Despite Dolores hovering behind them, he had to tell her so. "I never imagined my first kiss to be so wonderful."

"Your first kiss?" Her jaw dropped, then snapped close.

"Yep." He leaned back on his hands, trying to project confidence with the statement. "I've never been kissed before in my life. Well, I don't think I can count the pecks my mother or grandmother bestowed on me as kisses, right?"

"But you're a good-looking guy."

Good to know she thought so, but he merely shrugged. "Guess no one's noticed until now." He added a wink.

His phone buzzed, and he grabbed it from his back pocket, thankful their dive onto the ground hadn't cracked the screen. Caller ID showed it was Fallon.

"My boss." He answered the call as the sirens grew louder. "Yes, sir?"

"Where are you? You're supposed to photograph the winners of the Meadowlark Gardens flower arrangement contest, but I got a call from the organizer to say you hadn't arrived yet."

Seth groaned. He'd forgotten about the assignment in his haste to visit Dolores Green. "I'm sorry. I'm in south Arlington and am not going to make it."

A police car turned onto the street, sirens blaring.

"Is that sirens I hear? What's happening?" Fallon clipped out the questions in his trademark staccato.

Seth gave his boss a quick overview, adding he needed to go as an ambulance arrived, followed by more police vehicles. His boss harumphed once, then snapped, "You'd better be in my office as soon as you're able—with all the details on the shooting for Brogan to write up."

Fallon hung up before Seth could agree. The next hour whizzed by as more officers and crime scene techs arrived, and Seth and Jetta gave statements to uniform police officers as to why they were at Dolores's home. Dolores confirmed their story and plied the emergency responders with tea and homemade oatmeal cookies, which Seth found quite tasty. Dolores had finally convinced Jetta to return to the house, but Seth stayed outside to record the details for a potential story.

"Mr. Whitman?" A tall man, his jet-black hair worn short at the sides and longer on top, flashed a badge. "I'm Detective Oldfield. I know you've spoken to uniform about what happened, but I'd appreciate it if you would walk me through it as well."

"Sure." Seth complied.

Detective Oldfield lightly slapped his notebook against his leg. "This embezzlement happened fifteen years ago?"

"That's right."

"Dolores Green was involved how?"

Seth walked the detective through Dolores's small part in the scheme. "She says she never altered any invoices but didn't have the funds to fight SafeSense."

Detective Oldfield made some additional notes. "She walked you two outside when you left?"

"No, we said goodbye at the door." He rubbed the back of his neck as the terrifying memories of the bullets flying so close to them returned.

"Then someone started shooting."

"That's about the size of it." Seth wasn't sure what else to add, given he'd gone over this several times already with the first responding officers.

Detective Oldfield handed him a business card. "I'll be in touch if I have any other questions."

Seth texted Brogan with a few additional details he'd gleaned from the detective, then went to Dolores's house to see if Jetta was ready to leave. They hadn't had a chance to discuss the kiss, and he hoped she wasn't regretting it. He most certainly was not.

"I think she might have fallen asleep on the couch," Dolores said when he knocked on the door. She pointed to where Jetta sat on the sofa with her head resting against the back and her eyes closed.

"Thanks, I'll wake her, since we can leave now."

"I hope you can find out the truth after all these years." Dolores's earnest expression reminded him Jay's wasn't the only life upended by the embezzler.

"We'll do our best." He prayed God would use their best to uncover the truth as he entered the living room and sat down beside the woman he was falling in love with. For a moment, he allowed himself the privilege of watching her sleep, her features soft. His eyes dropped to her belly, love for the child—Jetta's baby—swelling inside him. If she'd let him, he would love her and her baby for the rest of his life. "Jetta?"

She stirred but didn't open her eyes. He brushed a stray strand of hair from her face, reveling in the smooth texture so unlike his own skin.

"Ummm." Her eyelids fluttered, then sprang open, alarm widening the pupils.

"It's okay. You fell asleep in Dolores's living room." He rubbed her arm as if soothing a startled animal.

"Why is this happening?" Her soft question, punctuated by a sob, tore through his heart.

"I don't know. But you know who does?" He waited a beat before answering his own question. "God. He's not surprised about any of this. It's all part of his plan and for our good."

"How could it be for our good? Someone is trying very hard to prevent us from finding the truth." Anguish tinged her words.

"I don't claim to fully understand these things, but if we can't trust God has this—the entire world and everything in it—under his ultimate control, then we're in a pickle."

His word choice brought a faint smile to her lips. "A pickle, huh?"

"Definitely a pickle." He nodded when what he wanted to do was cover her mouth with his to taste her sweetness again. But this wasn't the time. Besides, before he kissed her a second time, he needed to make sure she didn't regret the first kiss.

"Thanks."

For a moment, their gazes held. Heat flickered in hers, igniting the flame in his own heart. Then she glanced away and brushed her hands together. "I need to go see my mom."

The abrupt change in topic jarred him, but Seth tamped down his disappointment. "And my boss will want my photos of the shooting pronto."

After thanking Dolores for her hospitality and promising to be in touch with any updates, he walked Jetta to her car. He opened her car door and waited until she slid behind the wheel. Then he gathered his courage and asked, "Shall I cook something for dinner tonight?"

For a moment, she seemed to hesitate, then she smiled. "That would be lovely. Text me the time, and I'll be there."

He agreed, then shut her door. He stood on the curb watching her drive away and take another little piece of his heart. He should be worried at giving her so much of that vital organ, but somehow, he couldn't be bothered. As he climbed into his SUV and drove toward *The Herald*, he reflected how much he had grown to care for this intriguing woman. He only prayed their digging into the past would bring closure to her family—and not the end of their lives.

EIGHTEEN

J etta's phone rang as she chirped the car locks outside the rehab facility. A smile stretched across her face, thinking it was Seth. She swiped to answer. "Miss me already?"

Silence.

She frowned. Wrong number or spam call. But before she could disconnect, a voice said, "Next time, the bullets won't miss."

The cold, arrogant tone sent a chill down her spine. "Why are you doing this?"

A soft chuckle from the caller. "That doesn't matter. What matters is you and that muscleman stop sticking your noses into where they don't belong."

"But—" The caller hung up before Jetta could formulate the rest of her thought. Anxiety made her shoulders slump, but Seth's words about God being in control strengthened her. She would not be cowed by these circumstances. After sending Seth a text outlining what the caller had said, she squared her shoulders and marched into the rehab center.

She signed in at the front desk, then made her way to her mother's room, only to find it empty. Maybe she was in PT. She returned to the nurse's station and waited until for a nurse to finish a phone call.

"May I help you?" The older woman wore impatience like a shawl, her tone indicating she hoped she could send Jetta on her way fast.

"I'm looking for Emily Ainsley."

The nurse huffed and pointed to the room. "That's her room."

"She's not there. I wondered if she might be in physical therapy?" Jetta kept her tone light and friendly, though she was a bit put out by the woman's unhelpful attitude.

The nurse frowned and tapped the computer keyboard. "She's not scheduled for anything else today and should be in her room." She craned her neck to look past Jetta. "Nurse Chara, do you know where Mrs. Ainsley is?"

"In her room."

"Not there." The concern Jetta had been wrestling with broke out of her hold and filled her body. "I didn't see her wheelchair either. She's not able to get around herself, so someone must have helped her."

The panic climbing in her voice must have transferred to the seated nurse because she stood. "Right. I'm calling security, and we'll do a search of the hospital."

"I'll check her room again." Nurse Chara headed into Mom's room and Jetta followed.

While the nurse did a cursory sweep of the room, then left, Jetta decided to do a more thorough search. The nurse was looking for Mom. Jetta was looking for clues as to where her mother might have gone. Initially, she spotted nothing out of the ordinary until she got on her hands and knees to peer under the bed. There, one slipper lay on its side. She plucked it out to examine it. The right slipper, the one Mom wore on her good leg, rested in her hand. She got down on all fours and used her phone's flashlight to see if the left slipper had been pushed farther under the bed. Nothing but a few dust bunnies.

Jetta frowned. Mom wouldn't have put the wrong slipper on her bare foot. Even though the difference between the right and left slipper wasn't that noticeable to the eye, Emily insisted she could tell when the left slipper was on her right foot. Having helped Mom to wear the slipper during her rehab stay, Jetta could attest to the fact Mom would never have put on the wrong slipper. While she couldn't wear the left one because of her cast, she'd insisted on having it with her for when the cast came off.

"Ms. Ainsley?"

Still holding the lone slipper, Jetta sat back on her heels to see a tall, angular woman standing in the doorway. "Yes?"

"I'm Holly MacNamara, head of security." The woman come into the room, bright from the sunlight spilling into it from the two large windows. "We're conducting a search of the hospital and grounds for your mother."

Jetta held up the slipper and explained its significance. "She would never deliberately put on the wrong one."

Holly furrowed her forehead, but before she replied, her radio squawked something Jetta couldn't understand. "Repeat please." The woman put the radio closer to her ear but this time, Jetta heard the words loud and clear. "We found a woman's bedroom slipper near the hedges at the east end of the property."

"I'm on my way." Holly turned to Jetta. "You stay here."

Shaking her head, Jetta followed the security guard out of the room. "I'm coming with you. It's my mother who's missing."

Holly didn't reply but powerwalked to the closest exit and pushed open the door. Jetta kept up as the other woman veered to the left on one of the many paths crisscrossing the open expanse of the outer lawn. The facility was essentially a rectangle with an inner courtyard of flower beds, shrubs, and small trees with concrete walk-ways and benches for the patients to use. Manicured lawns surrounded the building with woods along one side, residential homes on the opposite side, and thick hedges where it backed up to farmland. Jetta tried to pray for her mother's safety as she jogged after Holly, but the words jumbled together in her mind. Three people wearing similar uniforms to Holly stood in a clump near a gap in the hedge.

"What did you find?" Holly barked the question as she approached the group.

"A woman's slipper." A chubby man with a bald head hitched his duty belt, then pointed to the slipper lying on the ground.

Jetta immediately recognized it as the mate to the one she suddenly realized she still clutched in her hand. "It's my mom's." Her voice wavered and she cleared her throat. "It's a match to this one."

All four guards stared at the slipper in her hand, then at the one near the hedge. "It appears to be the other one," Holly agreed. She leaned forward as if peering through the narrow pathway in the hedge. "There's a bit of fabric snagged on the branch near the exit too."

"What does that mean?" Jetta asked the obvious question to which she was sure she didn't want to know the answer.

"It might mean someone has taken your mother against her will," Holly said, her voice firm but gentle. "I'm calling this into the police as a possible kidnapping."

Jetta gasped, bringing the slipper to her chest as she blinked back tears. Crying wouldn't help them find her mother and would only distract them from their work. While Holly phoned the police, Jetta stood, unable to move her gaze from the slipper resting so peacefully on the dirt. *Please God, keep Mom safe!*

After she finished her call, Holly addressed her people. "Clive, go back to Ms. Ainsley's room and shut the door. Then stand guard outside of it. No one goes in or out until the police arrive. Javier, you'll do the same here—no one touches anything until the cops arrive. Make note of anything you see or hear while you're waiting. Vicki, you'll come with me and start reviewing the security footage. Ms. Ainsley, it's best if you come back to the facility, as the police will want to interview you right away."

Jetta nodded and trudged behind the two women as they made their way back to the building. Once inside, Holly guided her to a small conference room, assuring her she would send the police to her as soon as they arrived. Alone, Jetta gave into temptation and buried her head in her arms as the sobs engulfed her, the prayer to God for Mom's safety looping in her mind.

EMILY SLOWLY OPENED HER EYES. THE ROOM DIDN'T SPIN QUITE AS BADLY has it had the first couple of times she'd attempted to return to the land of the living. Maybe whatever they'd given her was wearing off. She lay on a thin mattress on the floor of a bare room. Light spilled in from two un-curtained windows, telling her wherever she was, she wasn't close enough to any other house that they feared discovery. Her head ached like the time she'd drunk too much champagne at a New Year's Eve party and Jay had to practically carry her home. She'd vowed never to indulge like that again and hadn't, but she still recalled the awful feeling.

She became aware of pain building in her leg as she continued her inventory. Sweat beads popped out on her forehead and she bit her bottom lip to stem the whimper rising in her throat. The door opened and a figure entered. Fear gripped Emily by the throat, but she couldn't move her limbs at all, much less try to see who was in the room.

"I see you're awake." The voice, muffled by a facemask, sounded neither male nor female. "But you're in pain. I do apologize for that and brought you something." The person squatted and set down several prescription bottles on the floor near Emily's head, along with a bottle of water. She recognized the labels as hers. The thugs who took her must have swiped her pills as well.

"I'll be back in a bit, once you're feeling better." The figure rose and left Emily alone again.

She struggled to sit up, propping her back against the wall. Despite its bare appearance, the room was clean, the linoleum floor dust-free, and the mattress covered in a clean sheet. The cinderblock walls had a fresh coat of white paint, if the faint scent she now discerned was any indication. She managed to snag all of the bottles and took a long drink of water before examining the pills. Yes, these were indeed her prescriptions. She fumbled to open the one with her pain pills and popped two in her mouth, followed by another swallow of water. Then she rested against the wall to wait for the pain to recede.

Emily wasn't sure how much time had passed, as she must have fallen asleep. She stretched her neck to relieve a crick from sleeping slumped to one side, but at least the pain in her leg wasn't as sharp as before. The sunlight wasn't as strong either, leaving the corners of the room in shadows. Jetta must be frantic with worry, as surely her presence must be missed by now. Emily prayed for her daughter's safety, for someone to find her soon, and for this entire ordeal to be over. Thoughts of her late husband filled her mind. All she wanted was to restore Jay's good name so he wouldn't be remembered as someone who'd bilked his company out of millions but as someone who tried to do the right thing. Her older children refused to discuss their father, his fall from grace hitting them harder than it had Jetta.

But given all that had happened, Emily wasn't sure her quest was as noble as she'd thought. She didn't think it would put her daughter in danger, much less herself. At least this had brought Seth more into Jetta's life. Emily had liked the big young man from the moment he'd jogged over to help her move the pile of mulch in her driveway around to her flowerbeds a few years ago. She'd been calling herself all sorts of a fool for continuing the practice of loose mulch that needed a wheelbarrow and shovel to haul rather than hiring a land-scape company to pretty up her beds. She hadn't wanted to admit her body wasn't up to doing the things it once accomplished with ease. But Seth hadn't minded, and from then on, he always appeared exactly when she needed brawny assistance.

Her daughter deserved someone who would treat her right. Emily had never liked Kyle, even though she hadn't met the man in person. What Jetta said—and didn't say—about her boyfriend had told Emily all she'd needed to know, but she could only offer a listening ear and snippets of advice as Jetta struggled through the relationship. When they'd broken up months ago, Emily had been thrilled. But learning about Kyle's attack on her sweet Jetta, leaving her pregnant, made Emily's heart ache.

She wasn't sure whether Jetta would keep the baby or not, but Emily had the sneaking suspicion Seth wouldn't mind raising another man's child. In fact, she was sure he wouldn't. If only Jetta would be able to overcome her fear of trusting the wrong man and see Seth for the godly man he was, then things might turn out okay for her youngest.

The door opened and the same person came back, this time carrying a tray. "I brought you some soup."

The scent of chicken broth triggered an answering rumble in Emily's stomach. She straightened as best she could as the figure unfolded the legs on the tray and set it before Emily. A bowl of steaming soup and another bottle of water rested on the tray.

"Eat before it grows cold." The person stepped away as Emily picked up the spoon and savored the soup.

When she'd finished, the figure placed the tray by the door before returning to crouch in front of Emily.

"You have been busy digging up the past, despite your injuries."

Emily stayed silent, waiting for the other person to come to the point of her kidnapping.

"Your husband stole that money, Mrs. Ainsley. All the evidence points to that."

She could keep quiet no longer. "No, he did not. Evidence can be manufactured, and Jay was gathering proof of his innocence before he died."

"Maybe so, but that was a long time ago. Why pursue this now, especially as your husband is dead?"

"Justice." Emily nearly hissed the word, her anger at her captor's cavalier attitude toward Jay's tarnished reputation growing by the second. "He was innocent—and I intend to prove it."

A rough chuckle emanated from the person. "You're tilting at windmills. There is no proof to exonerate Jay Ainsley because he was guilty, guilty of more than just the money."

"What are you talking about?" The question burst out of her like a bullet.

"You don't want to find out. Stop this quest now, or you'll regret it."

Emily shook her head but didn't bother asking what she would regret. She would not halt her search for the truth, not while she still had breath in her body. Despite being snatched from her rehab room, she could sense no ill will from her captor, only a sense of frustration overlaying another emotion she couldn't identify. What was clear was that this person needed something from Emily, something that could only be obtained from a face-to-face encounter. "If all you wanted to do was threaten me, why kidnap me? Seems like quite a risk to warn me off."

The figure rose, pacing to the other side of the small space and keeping their back to Emily. "I shouldn't have underestimated you."

The hushed words made no sense. Emily hadn't made much progress in proving Jay's innocence, but maybe Seth and Jetta had? Jetta had been coming by to see her when Emily had been taken. The person whipped around, the dark eyes visible above the surgical facemask blazing with fury. "But you shouldn't have meddled with Topher Robotics."

The increased anger shocked Emily. Before, when discussing the embezzlement, her captor had seemed almost pleasant, but now their fury blasted her like a hot oven, sizzling her entire being. "I'm only looking into who could have embezzled the money."

"Liar!" The person narrowed their eyes to slits. "You have been poking around Project Z. Don't bother to deny it. I saw through your minion's pathetic attempt to gather information. It was clever of you to use someone close to Ryan for the job, less likely to run into questions from the staff. But you miscalculated they wouldn't report the unusual request to the boss himself."

Emily shook her head. "I have no idea what you're talking about. What's Project Z?"

For a moment, her captor stared at her, the tension rising like flood waters coming closer to swamp her. Without another word, the person left the room, slamming the door so hard, the windows rattled. The snick of a deadbolt brought Emily a measure of relief that her tormentor wouldn't be returning soon. But the questions being asked made her tremble in fear for herself and for Jetta and Seth. For she caught a glimpse of something bigger than embezzlement going on at Topher Robotics. And she feared they would be caught in the crossfire.

CHAPTER

NINETEEN

Seth sorted through the photos from his last assignment before selecting three for Fallon's final approval. He wrote captions for the pictures, then hit send. He'd already written up the shooting as a short news piece, leaving out his presence at the scene as requested by Fallon. Now he picked up his cell to check to see if Jetta had called or texted. She hadn't responded to his text about the timing of dinner, and he hadn't seen any other communication from her. It had been several hours since he'd sent it, so worry took up residence in the corners of his mind. Some people might think he was overreacting, but his gut told him otherwise. He'd learned from an early age to always listen to his gut. It had saved him and his mother more times than he cared to recall.

"Ready for tomorrow?" Brogan slapped the top of the cubicle with a notebook.

Right, the Topher Robotics interview. "Yes. Should we meet at headquarters or drive in together from the office?"

"Headquarters. I've got an appointment at noon." His colleague appeared to be suppressing news by the way his fingers tapped out a rhythm that had a familiar cadence to it. *Da, dum-de-dum. Da, dum-de-dum.*

The sappy grin gave Seth the final clue. "You're picking up an engagement ring."

Brogan's smile widened. "I knew you'd figure it out."

"Have you asked Melender yet?"

"No, want to have the ring first." Brogan waved a hand. "And no, I didn't ask what kind of ring she wanted. I figured that out for myself."

"Good for you. When you do plan on asking her?" Seth admitted Brogan and Melender's sweet romance had given him hope he might one day find his own happily-ever-after. Connecting more with Jetta had given fuel to that hope, although his confidence in their own happy outcome wasn't as high as Brogan and Melender's must be.

"Saturday. I've planned a hike in Shenandoah National Park. She knows about the hike but not exactly where or the special picnic I've planned when we get to the waterfall."

"Sounds romantic." From what he knew of Melender, it would be the perfect spot for a proposal.

"It should be, if the weather holds. Right now, it's showing a cool, sunny day, but that could change in an instant in the mountains." Brogan gave the cubicle top a final tap. "Gotta run but will see you tomorrow at 9:45 in the parking lot so we can get our strategy set before the interview."

"Sounds good." Seth waved bye, his thoughts returning to Jetta's silence. Rather than continue to stew about it, he would call her. The phone rang once, twice, three times.

Then Jetta answered. "Hello?"

The pain in her voice cut him to the quick. "It's Seth. What's wrong?"

Sobs greeted his query. He gave her a few minutes to regain control before softly voicing his question again.

This time, she managed to reply. "It's Mom."

His heart dropped to his toes at the despondency in her voice.

Surely Emily hadn't died? He waited for her to explain rather than pepper her with the questions swirling in his brain.

"She's missing." Jetta cleared her throat. "Someone's taken her!"

"She's been kidnapped?" Seth was on his feet and moving toward the door. "I'm on my way."

"No."

The single word stopped him in his tracks, sending his heart plummeting to the bottom of the ocean. She was regretting their kiss and was regulating him once more to mere friends.

"I need you to continue our investigation. It has to be the reason for them taking her."

He returned to his workstation, his mind racing with which lead to pursue. One rose to the surface. "Brogan and I are going to talk to Ryan Topher tomorrow morning, so I'll research the central cast of characters there more, including Fiona, the woman Dolores said moved to Topher from SafeSense."

"Good idea. I'm going to work through the rest of my invoices. I have about ten more to go." She sniffed. "There's not much else I can do while I'm waiting."

"Do they know what happened?"

"They're certain she was kidnapped because the security footage had been tampered with during the twenty minutes an incident involving two residents took place."

"Was the incident staged?"

"Not sure, as these two residents often kick things off between them. The police think the timing is suspicious as it drew staff and security guards away from my mom's room."

The weariness and concern underneath her words made Seth question his acquiescence to stay put. "Are you sure you don't want me to come there? You sound like you need a hug."

"More than you know, but"—her voice grew stronger—"I need you to help me figure this out. I believe this will be the key to bringing my mom home safely."

"If you're sure." He frowned as he realized dinner would not be happening, at least not in the way he'd anticipated. "How about if I text you in a few hours to see how you're doing?" He decided not to mention dinner but would figure out how to bring food to her when the time came.

"Sounds good." She sniffled. "You haven't mentioned the phone call."

"What call?"

"I texted you a few hours ago."

"Let me check." He did so, but nothing had come through from Jetta. "I don't see anything."

"Oh, wait, now I see it didn't send. I was going to follow up with the detective after I visited with my mom but forgot. I'll resend the text. Would you pass it along to the detective?"

"Sure." He wanted to ask about the phone call now, but the weariness in her voice made him hold off. He wouldn't press her. He was about to sign off when he remembered there was something he could do for her, and it didn't necessitate being with her in person. "May I pray with you?"

"Would you? I've been praying for Mom's safety, but I've run out of words."

"It would be a privilege." Closing his eyes, Seth bowed his head and lifted up the situation to their heavenly Father. He had prayed in public only a handful of times, but he felt no awkwardness as he bared his heart to the One who cared about them.

"Dear Lord, you know how scared we are for Jetta's mom. Please keep Emily safe from harm. Let her rely on you for her strength of body and mind. Give Jetta peace during this difficult time of uncertainty. Help us to peel back the curtain on the lies surrounding the embezzlement and find the truth. Let us not grow weary of fighting for justice for her father. Let us be successful if it is your will. In Jesus' name, Amen."

Jetta sniffled again. "Thank you, Seth. I feel better already."

"I'm glad." His heart swelled with purpose and a growing affection for this woman God had brought into his life, for he had no doubt who had orchestrated their meeting.

Muffled voices came over the line, then she said, "I've got to go, as the police are here with an update. Not on the location of my mom, but on the circumstances of her abduction."

"Let me know what they said when you can."

Jetta assured him she would, then disconnected the call. Seth held the phone to his chest and prayed again for Jetta and that Emily would be found safe—and soon. Then he dialed Detective Oldfield's number to report the anonymous call Jetta had received.

After identifying himself when Oldfield answered, Seth said, "Jetta received a phone call telling her next time, the shooter won't miss."

"From an unknown number, I'm guessing."

"Yes." He outlined the warning to back off the embezzlement investigation.

"I'll log it in my notes, but I'll be honest—it will be next to impossible to trace the caller."

"We know that." Seth drew in a breath. "There's more. Her mother's been kidnapped from a rehab center."

"What happened?" The detective's voice sharpened.

Seth gave the scant information he had. "Jetta said she was meeting with someone from the police a few minutes ago, but as far as she knew, her mother's whereabouts are still unknown."

"Okay, I'll see who from our department is working the case."

"You think they're connected?"

"It's too much of a coincidence in my book for it to be otherwise. From what I've researched about the Ainsley family, they're not the typical family to be targeted by kidnappers looking to score a big payout."

The fact that Detective Oldfield was taking the embezzlement connection seriously made Seth feel marginally better. "So you'll be looking into the original embezzlement charges?"

"Let's just say I'm keeping an open mind."

Seth ended the call, both troubled by the increasing danger related to their investigation and a little elated that someone thought they were making progress. He sent yet another prayer for Emily's safe return and for God to comfort and sustain Jetta. Then he logged onto Topher Robotics' website and found the list of personnel. First he pulled up data on Fiona Everly, whose photo showed a striking woman in her late forties or early fifties.

"Good write up on the shooting." Fallon's comment made Seth jump. "Startled you, huh?" The older man chuckled as he leaned a shoulder against the cubicle doorway. "How're you holding up?"

It took Seth a moment to realize Fallon was referring to being shot at earlier that day. Had it really only been a few hours ago? "I'm okay."

His boss raised a salt-and-pepper eyebrow. "I can see that it's not been top of mind for you."

Seth shook his head. "I've had other things on my mind."

"Related to that embezzlement story you've been pushing Brogan to investigate?"

Nothing got past the editor-in-chief, something Seth would be wise to remember. "I think so."

"Spill it." Fallon crossed his arms, his posture not as combative as it might appear, as Seth had learned it meant the boss was listening hard.

Seth relayed the kidnapping of Emily Ainsley, Jetta's anonymous warning, and his research into Fiona Everly, who had jumped ship from SafeSense to Topher after Dolores was fired. He also recapped the info Dolores had given them about her own involvement—or lack of involvement—in the altered invoices. "It can't be a coincidence that Fiona left SafeSense and moved into a higher position at Topher Robotics."

"You're thinking the person who hired Fiona might be your head embezzler?"

Seth shrugged. "Could be, so I think it's a lead worth following up."

"Good. Don't let your assumptions lead you in one direction only. It's entirely possible Fiona got the job all on her own merit and it had nothing to do with the embezzlement." With a nod, Fallon continued on his way.

Seth appreciated the reminder he shouldn't get his hopes up that discovering how Fiona got her job would close the fraud case. Instead, he made a note of the names of those in the Topher HR department to call in the morning before his visit to see if he could glean who hired Fiona Everly. Then he spent some more time praying for Emily Ainsley to be returned home soon—and for her daughter to trust in God. He also added a petition for himself for patience and understanding as Jetta decided how to respond to their kiss and whether she would make room in her life for Seth.

IN THE EASY CHAIR IN MOM'S ROOM, JETTA RUBBED HER BELLY AS THE BABY somersaulted. Seth's easy acceptance of her pregnancy had been one of the things that had initially drawn her to him. He never looked at her as if she had committed a sin because she was expecting and not married. He also never directly asked her where the baby's father was. Instead, he simply treated her like a fragile egg, making sure she called him for any heavy lifting and always taking her trash and recycling bins to the curb with his own.

Maybe she should call a Chicago attorney and explore her rights to exclude the father from her baby's life. Jetta still couldn't decide on whether she'd keep the baby or give it up for adoption. Asking a man to raise someone else's child would be a huge undertaking, and she wasn't sure she could handle raising a child on her own. Seth popped into her mind. His tenderness spoke of a man who would love unconditionally. Would that love extend to a non-biological child? Somehow, she thought it would, but she knew so little about his past, she couldn't be one hundred percent sure.

"Ms. Ainsley?" A woman wearing a pantsuit stood in the doorway, her long black hair a stark contrast with the cream of the jacket. "I'm FBI Special Agent Alisha Keen." She flashed her credentials. "The Fairfax County Police Department asked the FBI to consult on your mother's kidnapping."

Jetta shook the woman's hand. "Is there anything new?"

"Not yet, but one of the officers said you had a theory as to why she was taken." The agent called to someone outside the door. "Would you please bring in another chair?"

A moment later, a security guard entered with a plastic lobby chair and set it where the agent indicated. "Thank you." She situated herself in the chair, a tablet and stylus in hand, then addressed Jetta. "Tell me everything."

So Jetta did, starting with her mother's accident, her siblings' revelation about their father's embezzlement, Bingley and the raccoon's poisoning, the mysterious envelope, her car accident, the home burglary and assault, and the shooting outside Dolores Green's house.

The agent listened, interjecting questions a few times for clarification. "What have you and Mr. Whitman found out in your investigation?"

"Not much." Jetta blinked back sudden tears of frustration at their lack of progress. "We keep pulling strings to unravel more information and it simply leads to more strings and not answers."

Agent Keen smiled. "Welcome to the drudgery that is real police work. In other words, that's pretty normal. We all expect things to wrap up neatly like in those TV crime shows, but real-life investigations are a series of false starts and rabbit trails. Eventually, if we're lucky, we stumble upon something that's the key to the entire crime, but more often than not, it's a slog through mounds of misinformation to get to the truth."

"Now I'm really depressed." Jetta laid a hand over her stomach, where her baby had settled down. "But still determined to figure this out."

"You say you've spoken with someone from FinCEN?"

"Seth did, but he hasn't heard back yet." Jetta made a mental note to follow up with Seth about his contact. Probably too soon for her to have gotten any information about the original investigation, but it wouldn't hurt to check.

"This Warner fellow—he provided you with copies of invoices?" Agent Keen made notes on her tablet.

"Yes, and that's how Seth found Dolores Green." Jetta shuddered as memories of the shooting a few short hours ago flooded her mind. Maybe she shouldn't have encouraged Seth to continue the investigation rather than come here. She would give anything to have his presence beside her now.

As if her thoughts had conjured him, Seth stepped into the room, holding a plastic takeout bag in one hand. "Hey, Jetta. I brought some food."

Without thinking, she pushed out of her chair and threw herself onto his chest. His arms came around her, the bag bumping into her back. Being supported in his embrace released the torrent of tears that she had been blinking back ever since she learned her mother had been kidnapped.

"Shhh, it's okay. I'm here." Seth's whispered nothings triggered more tears. He rocked her in his arms as she let all her fears and worries flow out as she sobbed.

Her anguish spent, she raised her head to meet his gaze.

"Better?" He made no move to loosen his hold, for which she was grateful. She didn't think she would be able to support her weight on her own quite yet.

"I think so." She rested her forehead on his chest again, concentrating on her breathing to regain control of her emotions. Mom had been right—being pregnant did mean you wore your emotions close to the surface. Jetta had never been much of a crier, but she'd shed more tears over the past few months than she had in years. While she longed to stay within his arms for a while longer, she also wanted him to meet the FBI agent. Reluctantly, she placed her hands on his front and applied slight pressure to break his embrace.

Immediately, he dropped his arms, but he didn't move away, as if unsure she would be steady enough on her feet.

"I'll be okay." She offered him a quick smile, then made her way back to the recliner.

The FBI agent looked up from her phone. "I take it this is Seth Whitman."

"Yes." Jetta willed the blush threatening to stain her cheeks to recede. She had nothing to be embarrassed about—her mother had been kidnapped, for goodness sake. She was entitled to comfort from a friend. And if that friend happened to be male and handsome, well, that was just a bonus, right?

Seth put the bag on the bedside table, then offered his hand to the agent. "Nice to meet you."

Agent Keen introduced herself but didn't show him her badge. "Ms. Ainsley was telling me what you had discovered."

"May I see your credentials first, please?" Seth's question startled Jetta, but she supposed it was a natural question, given how easily her mother had been snatched.

The woman handed him her badge folder. Seth examined it but didn't return it. "What office do you work out of?"

"DC."

"I'm going to verify you are who you say you are." Without asking permission, he tapped on his phone, then lifted it to his ear.

"I'm sorry about this," Jetta said in a soft voice to the agent.

"I understand his wanting to make sure I'm the real thing." The agent appeared relaxed as she leaned back in her chair.

"Hello?" Seth moved to the other side of the room and turned his back on the two women.

Jetta couldn't hear his side of the conversation, but the agent prompted her to continue telling what they'd learned so far about the embezzlement.

"I'll wait for Seth, since he'll have info to add." Jetta crossed her arms over her stomach as an uncomfortable vibe settled over the room.

Seth whirled around and held the phone up toward the woman, the flash indicating he'd taken a photo. The woman frowned, then rose. Jetta thought she would ask for her creds back from Seth. Instead, she headed for the door.

In an instant, Seth had blocked her exit. "You're not going anywhere."

The woman knocked the phone out of Seth's arm, but he blocked her next blow. Jetta couldn't keep up with the flurry of movement as they grappled together. She prayed for Seth to get the upper hand because it had become apparent the woman wasn't an FBI agent after all. Then Seth whipped the woman's right arm behind her and pinned her to the wall. She snarled but he held firm, using his body weight to subdue her.

"Jetta, get a police officer in here now."

She scurried to comply, returning quickly with two officers. When Seth explained the woman was impersonating an FBI agent, one of the officers handcuffed her and began Mirandizing her. He retrieved his phone and apologized for the disruption before handing the false agent's phone and badge to the other officer.

He came to Jetta, who had returned to her chair, adrenalin pulsating through her body at how much she had revealed without a second thought.

"The badge is real, but Agent Keen is out on maternity leave."

"How did you know she wasn't a real agent?" Jetta felt all kinds of stupid for missing that. Was she doomed to repeat her mistakes in judgment the rest of her life?

"It seemed too soon. Your mom's only been gone a few hours, and usually the FBI doesn't get involved in adult kidnappings unless they have reason to believe the victim has been taken across state lines or there's been a ransom demand."

What he said made sense. "I should have known she wasn't a real agent."

He crouched beside her chair and took her cold hands in his, rubbing them lightly. "Don't beat yourself up. Your focus was on your mother and her safe return."

Now that Seth was here and the false agent gone, Jetta replayed the conversation. "You know what was strange?" She didn't wait for his answer. "I could have sworn she was surprised to hear about some of the things that had happened. Not Mom's kidnapping, but her eyes widened slightly when I mentioned Bingley's poisoning and the raccoon's death."

Seth moved to the chair the agent had occupied. "That is weird. If she was here to find out what we'd learned, you'd think she would have known about the attacks designed to make us stop our searches."

"Exactly." The aroma of Chinese food wafted toward her. "You brought Chinese?"

"Yes, sweet-and-sour chicken and Mongolian beef, with rice and egg rolls."

Her stomach growled at the mention of the food. "I'm starving."

"I forgot to bring plates." He started to rise but she waved him back.

"Let's be decadent and eat directly out of the cartoons."

He hesitated but then nodded. "Sure." He got them paper cups of water from the supply in the bathroom while she unpacked the food. Soon they were eating and sharing the main courses. By mutual agreement, they avoided talking about the fake FBI agent and her missing mom but instead discussed their favorite books. Seth read widely, more fiction than she'd expected, so they'd had a rousing debate on the merits of different genres.

Jetta set down her chopsticks. "I'm stuffed. Couldn't eat another bite."

Seth dug around in the bag. "Good thing there are no fortune cookies."

"Those never have fortunes anyway, but weird sayings like, 'Take advantage of your opportunities,' and 'You are kind and friendly.'" A burp surprised her. "Excuse me."

"No worries. My mom always burped more when she was expecting." Seth stuffed the empty containers into the plastic bag.

"I didn't know you had a brother or sister." She handed him her cup.

"I don't."

The anger behind the denial startled her into probing deeper. "But you just said your mom—"

"She lost the babies." Seth wouldn't look at her, but the rigid set of his shoulders told her how upset he still was over the deaths of his baby siblings in utero.

His hands fisted, crinkling the plastic bag. "No, she didn't lose them. They were taken from her."

CHAPTER

TWENTY

Seth tied the bag and tossed it into the trashcan, glad for the distraction to get his emotions under control. He couldn't believe he'd shared that much with Jetta, but the truth had popped out when she'd asked her innocent question. The urge to tell her the rest of the story welled up inside him. "The first one was supposedly an accident, if you can call keeping my mom drunk for weeks even while knowing about the pregnancy an accident. The second time she gave into the pressure from the father to have an abortion. The third time, she was nearly seven months along, but babies can't withstand hard punches to the abdomen."

"I'm so sorry." Her eyes grew wet with tears. "How old were you?"

"Old enough to know what was going on and young enough to have no power to change things." He huffed out a breath, as images of the blood and his mother's screams overwhelmed him. "Until the last one."

He wanted to take back his words, but now that he'd begun to tell the darkest of his secrets, one he had never shared with another living soul, he couldn't stop. "His name was Hunter Thomas, and he ruled our little patch of earth as his own kingdom. He ran drugs, girls, you name it. If it was illegal, he took a cut. For some reason, Hunter took a fancy to my mom. Not sure why because drugs and booze had made her too skinny, I thought. But she was the most beautiful and exotic creature I'd ever seen, with her long, honey-colored hair and big brown eyes."

Seth sank onto the chair as the story spilled out, his attention not on Jetta but on the pictures flipping through his mind. "At first, it seemed good to have Hunter around. He treated Mom better than her previous boyfriends and tolerated my presence too. But when Mom became pregnant, things started to change. The larger Mom's belly grew, the more Hunter was absent, which made Mom sad. When Hunter did come around, they would fight something fierce, mostly with words, although he occasionally slapped her."

He laced his fingers together to avoid punching something as the emotions from those days boiled his blood. "Mom was about seven months pregnant when they had their last fight. Hunter had left some drugs in the apartment, which Mom had found. Mom was furious because social services had been sniffing around for a couple of years and she was terrified someone would come by unexpectedly, find the drugs, and take me—and the baby when it was born—away from her.

"Hunter didn't care. He laughed and said he was through with her and her brat, that he even doubted he was the baby's father. That set Mom off, and she flew at him, slapping and hitting. He responded by punching her in the stomach over and over again."

Memories of his mother's screams, her vain attempts to get away from Hunter, seared into his mind. His anger at the man hurting his mom and baby sister burned hotter and hotter. "I grabbed the iron skillet Mom had left dirty on the stove and ran into the bedroom, where Hunter was kicking my mom, who lay on the floor trying to protect her baby with her arms."

He could still feel the weight of that heavy pot in his hands. "I swung it with all my might at Hunter's head."

He focused on his hands, which trembled in his lap as the memory of the impact, blood splattering over him, played in his mind. His mother's whimpers. The blood pooling underneath her intermingling with the blood flowing from Hunter's head as he lay on the floor not moving.

"How old were you?" Jetta's soft question drew him back to the present.

"Seven, nearly eight." He cleared his throat and raised his head. The compassion and understanding in her blue eyes eased some of the guilt he still felt over taking another man's life. "Mom lost the baby, a little girl she named Sadie. Before she passed out, Mom told me she would say she was the one who hit Hunter with the skillet, that she told me to bring it to her and that's why I got blood spatter on me. It was the last thing she ever said to me."

"Oh, Seth."

"I never said anything different because I was afraid I would get my mom into even more trouble if I told the truth." He breathed out a sigh, the burden of carrying that secret alone all these years easing from sharing. "The cops called social services."

"Foster home?"

"Homes." He gripped the back of his neck with a hand. "At first, I kept running away, trying to get back to my mom. She needed me. If I wasn't there, she might not remember to eat." Tears dotted his eyes, but he refused to let them fall, wanting to get the rest of the story out. "So I was moved farther and farther away until I stopped trying to find her. By then, I was so angry, many foster parents didn't want to deal with it."

"What happened to your mom?"

"One day, when I was around ten, a social worker came to tell me my mom had died. Drug overdose. I knew better. She'd given up on life because she didn't have me." Sorrow clogged his throat. She might not have been a perfect mom, but she had loved him and tried her best.

Clearing away the lump, he continued. "They couldn't trace any relatives on my mom's side—she never talked about any siblings or her parents—so I finally ended up in a group home run by a young couple. By then I was fifteen and had gained a lot of weight. It was my way of coping with all the stress and trauma. I went to counseling for a few months, but since I refused to talk about my mom or our life together, they stopped making me go."

Those bleak years of fear, anger, and despair were behind him. Being a follower of Christ had accelerated the healing process. "When I attended George Mason University, I went back to therapy, which helped me a lot, but I never mentioned the murder."

"You were a kid trying to protect your mom. It was self-defense."

"The cops concluded it was self-defense for my mom back then too. She was never charged with any crime." He paused. "I was messed up for a long time, and I still can't stand to see any man treating a woman with disrespect."

A slight smile turned up the corners of her mouth. "I know, it's one of your best qualities. You make me feel safe and secure."

Her words soothed the raw edges of his emotions, filling in a little bit more of the hole the trauma of Hunter's death and his removal from his mother's care had created all those years ago. It gave him hope that one day, the entire hole would be gone. He couldn't believe he'd told Jetta his deepest, darkest secret without her recoiling from him. Maybe she was beginning to care for him like he cared for her.

RYAN PLACED THE BALL ONTO THE TEE, THEN LINED UP HIS CLUB. He channeled all his anger into hitting the ball as hard and as far as he could. It sailed through the air and temporarily disappeared before bouncing onto the green on the sixteenth hole.

"Nice shot." Luis Skyler, his former college roommate and corporate attorney for a pharmaceutical company, slapped him on the back. "You've been in attack mode all afternoon." He shouldered his bag and waited while Ryan picked up his.

The two of them played a game whenever they could squeeze it into their busy schedules, and Ryan had been more than happy to ditch the office for a few hours when Luis called him around lunchtime with an offer of a 3 p.m. tee time. "Have I? Guess I'm carrying my work into my game."

"You mean the possibility of Maxwell Technology's hostile takeover of Topher Robotics."

Ryan shouldn't have been surprised Luis had heard the rumors. "That and other things."

"The wearable AI."

This time Ryan stopped walking and waited for his companion to do the same. He had worked much too hard to have knowledge of the secret artificial intelligence device leak out. The suspicion this hadn't been a random invitation burst into his mind with the force of a cannonball. "What's going on?"

His friend tried a jovial smile. "Two old college roommates playing a game of golf."

Ryan saw through the lame attempt at levity. "Don't mess with me."

The smile dropped from Luis's face, and he stepped closer. After glancing right and left, as if ensuring they were indeed the only two people on this particular bit of the golf course, he lowered his voice. "I'm in negotiations to work for Alternative Realities as vice president of their legal department. During the final interview with a handful of their board members, one mentioned you and I must have attended university at the same time, and he wondered if we'd known each other. I, of course, spilled the beans that we roomed together all four years. Afterward, this board member pulled me aside and asked if I knew how close you were to having this AI device ready for action."

Ryan digested the information. "How did you respond to that?"

"That I had no idea, since you hadn't mentioned it to me." He shrugged. "Then someone else came up and that was that."

"When was this?" Ryan allowed his frustration to give a snap to his words.

"Two days ago." Luis held up a hand. "Before you ask, I haven't said a word to anyone else."

"What else have you heard?" Luis had earned a reputation in college for sniffing out the facts behind many a rumor and used that knowledge to his advantage. Although he never resorted to blackmail or was particularly malicious, his friend firmly believed knowledge was power.

Luis rested his bag on the ground. "That Maxwell Technology caught wind of it and that's the real reason for their hostile takeover bid."

The bottom dropped out of Ryan's stomach as his greatest fears were confirmed. He'd strongly suspected Maxwell Technology knew about Project Z because of their continued hard press after the initial rebuff by the board. Could a board member or one of the shareholders have tipped off Maxwell Technology about the project?

"Thanks for letting me know." Ryan didn't elaborate, and his friend took the hint and changed the subject to the upcoming game between the Washington Commanders and the Dallas Cowboys as he hefted his bag and resumed walking toward the next hole.

Ryan followed, his mind spinning. Word had leaked out about his supposed secret project. Would that help or hurt his bid to keep the company in his hands? He would have to return to the office instead of heading home. Cynthia would understand his skipping their dinner engagement at the Gordon-Lightsmiths. He'd always detested Dalia and her insipid conversations revolving around her darling grandchildren or her dogs, so missing it would be a relief. His wife only cultivated the acquaintance because Michael Gordon-Lightsmith was chair of the board of her favorite charity, and she felt a few dinner parties a year was worth it to stay in his good graces.

Ryan finished the last couple of holes on autopilot, his mind busy with how to use the information that Project Z had become more common knowledge to his advantage. The board had narrowly voted against recommending acceptance of Maxwell Technology's bid, but one member had called for a special shareholders meeting in one week's time. Peter had railed at Ryan, calling him incompetent and worse for allowing such a meeting to be scheduled. This time, rather than ignoring his father's rant like he usually did, Ryan had responded in kind, reminding Peter he had approved the bylaws when he had taken the company public, bylaws that allowed for that circumstance to happen.

His lips thinned as he relished the memory of his father's face. The older man had gaped, as Ryan's hit had found its mark. Then Peter rallied, insisting if Ryan were a better leader, no board member would have dared to call for such a meeting.

"Good game, Mr. Topher?" Ryan jerked, so caught up in his thoughts he hadn't realized he and Luis had arrived back at the clubhouse. The head caddy, who took care of making sure his clubs were cleaned and stored in the Topher locker at the clubhouse, reached for his bag.

"Yes, Juan. Thank you." He slipped the man a $20, then turned to Luis. "I've got to run—dinner date with the wife and some people I can't stand."

"See you at the Children's National charity tournament in two weeks."

Ryan nodded, then slipped out of the clubhouse. Instead of waiting for the valet to bring his car up, he grabbed the keys and walked to the parking lot. An idea formed in his mind about how he could use the rumors to his advantage. The sure knowledge one of his siblings had sold him out burned bright in his mind. He would find out who was behind the leaks, solidify his grip on the company, and make sure other potential problems wouldn't surface to play into the hands of those plotting for his—and his company's —downfall.

TWENTY-ONE

Jetta rested her hand on Bingley's head, which lay in her lap as she sat at the kitchen table. The dog hadn't left her side since she'd returned home from the rehab facility as if sensing Jetta's worry over her still-missing mother. The baby stirred but the dog didn't move. She rubbed Bingley's silky ears, her body tired but her mind unable to focus on any thought but her mother's safety. *Please God, don't take her from me. I need her now more than ever.*

The doorbell rang. Seth had followed her home, then left to snap pictures of another construction site fire, this one on the opposite side of the county from the first one. He wouldn't have returned so fast. Rapid knocking on the door followed another peal of the doorbell. Maybe the police had found Mom. She refused to believe the visitor was bringing bad news.

Jetta heaved herself to her feet and made her way to the front door. She hesitated, then peeked through the peephole to find Melender standing on her stoop, her long, silvery-blonde hair escaping from a single braid down her back. Jetta yanked open the door.

"Oh, thank God you're okay." Melender placed a hand on her

chest. "When Brogan told me about your mother, I tried to call you, but your phone rolled over into voicemail. With Seth at the fire, I thought you might like some company, but when you didn't answer my text, I was concerned something might have happened to you as well."

Jetta frowned and checked her phone, which had registered several texts and a missed call from Melender. "Sorry, I have it on silent and must not have heard the buzzing."

"No problem." Bingley shoved past Jetta to greet Melender. "Hey, boy. You keeping a close eye on your mistress?"

Jetta blinked back tears at the other woman's thoughtfulness. "You came all the way over here to check on me?"

"Of course." Melender smiled. "What are friends for?"

Her innocent question brought forth a gush of tears. Melender nudged Bingley out of the way, then guided Jetta back into the house and into the living room. "I'll make some herbal tea." She gave her a push toward the sofa. "Put your feet up, and I'll be back in a jiffy."

Jetta sank onto the couch, toeing off her shoes and swinging her legs up on the cushions. Her mother would be appalled to see feet—even sock feet—on the sofa, but Jetta didn't care. Tears eked from her closed lids as she battled to regain control of her emotions. By the time Melender re-entered the room carrying a tray with a teapot, Mom's honey jar, and two cups on saucers, the tears had stopped.

"I seem to cry at the drop of a hat these days." Jetta accepted a cup of tea into which Melender had put some honey. She drew in a breath, the scent of lavender wafting to her nose. "I smell lavender but something else too."

"Chamomile." Melender sipped from her cup. "It's Yellow & Blue from Harney & Sons Teas, one of my favorite tea purveyors. I love this blend as it's caffeine-free and it tastes good. Yes, I brought some with me just in case."

Jetta tried a small sip. "The honey is a nice change from my usual sugar as the sweetener."

The two sipped their tea while Bingley rested on the floor.

Melender put her empty cup back onto the tray with a click. "How are you holding up?"

Jetta sighed. "Not too well." Tears pricked the backs of her eyelids, but she refused to let them fall. Enough with the weeping. "The police said there's nothing to do but wait. I could tell the rehab staff was uneasy about my staying in Mom's room, so I came home."

"Anything new in the investigation? Brogan only gave me a bare outline."

Jetta filled her in on Seth's invoice sleuthing that led to Dolores Green, and then the shots fired at them.

"Wow." Melender sat in silence for a moment, then pointed to the clock on the mantel. "It's four p.m. Why don't we tackle the rest of your invoices?"

Jetta couldn't believe it wasn't late evening, so much had happened that day. "Sure, I only had time to call a couple of them, but they seemed legit. I'll get them."

Melender waved her back to the couch. "Tell me where and I'll grab them."

Jetta directed her to the study next door and waited until Melender returned with the stack, plus pens and clipboards for both of them. She handed Jetta a stack and took the rest for herself. "Start with the ones on the East Coast and then work your way westward. That way, we'll make the time zones work for us."

"Good idea." Jetta was grateful for Melender's take-charge attitude, as hers seemed to have fled with her mother's kidnapping. She sorted the invoices by time zone, then picked up her phone and started dialing. With any luck, she'd find another anomaly.

Forty-five minutes later, Jetta set aside her final invoice. All appeared to check out with legitimate expenses. Melender shook her head as she ended her call. "Nothing on my end."

"Mine either." Jetta stretched, her movement sending the baby into somersaults. "Oh, he's getting active."

"You're having a boy?" Melender gathered all the papers together in a neat stack on the coffee table.

"No idea, so I switch up calling it him or her. *It* sounds too imper-sonal." She winced as the baby's foot caught her ribcage. "She's prac-ticing for the Olympics gymnastics team today. I can't believe I have seven more weeks to go."

"I remember my aunt saying she felt as big as an elephant the final trimester." A shadow crossed Melender's face, but it was gone so quickly, Jetta thought she might have imagined it. "Do you have names picked out?"

"I don't even know if I'm keeping the baby or giving him up for adoption." Jetta clapped a hand over her mouth. "Oh, you won't say anything? I haven't been broadcasting that."

"No worries, I won't say a word to Seth." The other woman leaned closer. "But he's a really good guy, solid and trustworthy."

"I got that sense too, but..." Jetta wasn't sure how to put into words her trepidation at making another mistake with a man whose outward appearance hid a rotting inside. Something about Melender made her want to try. "It's like that book we read in high school about the portrait of a man who stays young in appearance as he ages but the painting of him turns ugly and old."

"*The Portrait of Dorian Gray*?" Melender shuddered. "That story gave me the creeps. But Seth isn't at all like that character."

"You can't be sure, though, can you?" All her concerns about the past, present, and future rushed together, jumbling her brain. Her colossal mistake in trusting Kyle mixed with her worry about her missing mother, driving her fears to greater heights. "But you don't know him that well, and I barely know him. Sure, he seems like a nice guy, but then again, don't most psychopaths?"

"I doubt Seth is anything like a psychopath. He's..."

But once the words began to tumble out of her mouth, Jetta couldn't stop them. "That's my point—you don't think so, but how can you be sure? Have you heard about his upbringing? He spent his early years with a drug-addicted mom who had all manner of mean boyfriends in her home." She nearly blurted out the secret Seth had shared with her, but somehow managed to keep that bottled up inside. She might not fully trust him, but she also didn't think he had been lying about killing his mother's violent boyfriend to save her life when he was so young.

"That doesn't mean he's anything like those men. Brogan has only good things to say about Seth. Besides, Seth is a believer."

Melender's soft rejoinder did little to quench the flow of words. All the pressure on Jetta, from deciding what to do about the baby to cleaning out her parents' home to clearing her father's name, exploded inside her. Like a volcano spewing lava, her voice rose. "He's a former foster care kid! I worked on a project about foster care, and the stats are troubling. More than half of boys in foster care as teens go on to commit a crime as an adult. Plus, you've seen the size of him. He's a big guy. If I'm wrong about him, he could use his strength to hurt me or the baby, and I couldn't stop him."

"I'd never do that."

Seth stood in the doorway, his face pale. A faint whiff of smoke filled the space, reminding Jetta of his work photographing another fire.

Jetta crossed her arms, unable to retract her words as her emotions seesawed between embarrassment at him overhearing part of her diatribe and her uncertainty of his character. When she stayed silent, his lips firmed, drawing her attention and reminding her of the gentle kiss they'd shared hours earlier.

"Because I'm big, therefore I can't be trusted." Sadness tinged his words. For the first time since she'd met him, he looked smaller than usual. He dangled his hands at his sides as if the air was slowly leaking out of his body and draining it of its vibrancy.

Melender cleared her throat. "I'd better be going."

"You don't have to…" Jetta began, not sure she wanted to be alone with Seth, but the other woman shook her head.

As she passed her, Melender patted her shoulder. "Let me know if you need more help, and I'll be praying they find your mom soon."

The mention of Mom brought fresh tears to Jetta's eyes, but she blinked them away. She was so done with crying. "Thank you."

Seth stayed where he was, his body dejected and his face toward the floor. When he spoke, he didn't meet her eyes. "Do you want me to leave too?"

If she said yes, he would slip out after Melender and wouldn't bother her again unless she reached out to him first. She opened her mouth, but no words came out. He lifted his head, his eyes fastening on hers. The sorrow etched on his face broke her heart, but she couldn't find the strength to retract her harsh assessment of him.

She still hadn't answered his question, but he nodded once as if she'd spoken and left. When the front door closed with an audible click, the flood gates on her tears released. Sobs tore through her body as she cried. Her words replayed over and over in her mind as did the look of utter misery on Seth's face. As her tears eased, one thought pushed its way to the surface. Seth hadn't seemed surprised by her conclusions. He seemed more resigned, as if it was what he'd expected. That reaction told her volumes about his upbringing, a background he had shared in confidence with her hours before only to have her use it against him. Maybe Kyle hadn't been the entire issue after all. Perhaps she had been more to blame than she wanted to think.

TWENTY-TWO

Seth didn't want to go into his house where he might encounter one of his roommates since both of their vehicles were parked outside. Instead, he shoved his hands into his pockets and headed down the sidewalk. Jetta's words had been like the cliché dagger to the heart, piercing him with an almost physical pain. Other voices joined Jetta's in his mind, calling him names or making fun of his large size. A tear trailed down his cheek, and he let the light wind dry it rather than wipe it away.

He'd known she had a world of hurt behind her pregnancy. His childhood in and out of foster homes had developed his ability to spot the pain behind the masks people wore. But since their kiss, he had let himself begin to hope this time that the relationship would develop into a forever one, rather than the temporary unions he'd become accustomed to. He pulled out his phone and sent his therapist's assistant a text to see about any openings. He hadn't spoken to Dr. Finnegan in almost a year, but his confidence had taken a direct hit with Jetta's harsh opinion of him.

As his stride put more distance between him and Jetta, he couldn't help but consider the situation from her perspective, something he'd always defaulted to. Dr. Finnegan had helped him see that while empathy and the ability to consider the other person's point of view were admirable traits, they could also push Seth into dangerous territory by not holding others accountable for their actions or offering excuses for their behavior.

He attempted to look at the current situation with a clear eye. It was true they hadn't known each other long, so on the one hand, her concern was warranted. However, Seth had developed a years-long relationship with her mother, so that should have given Jetta some reassurance as to his intentions.

Seth turned a corner, passing a group of kids chasing each other, their happy squeals and mock screams tugging at his heart. He had let himself dream of raising Jetta's child as his own, and, maybe one day, adding a couple of more kids to the mix. For all her bravery on the outside, Jetta had been deeply hurt by someone who had gotten her pregnant, then abandoned her. The urge to pray for her made him pause, close his eyes, and pour out his heart to the one who understood all his pain and Jetta's. After his silent amen, he continued, thanking God for Dr. Finnegan's wise counsel in helping him wrestle through his childhood hurts and his teenage angst.

He wasn't sure how long he had been walking and giving his feelings for Jetta and the situation to God when a familiar bark brought him up short. Jetta and Bingley stood a few feet in front of him on the sidewalk.

Bingley, straining at the leash held tightly in Jetta's hand, wagged his tail in welcome, but Seth couldn't distinguish Jetta's features in the twilight.

"I'm sorry." Jetta's voice sounded rough, as if she'd been crying a lot. "I'm sorry for saying I thought you might be abusive."

Seth sensed she had more to say, so he came closer to let Bingley lick his hand.

"I said some terrible things about you. I..." Her voice cracked. She breathed in and out slowly before continuing. "I have no excuse for my actions other than I'm scared. Scared for my mom. Terrified about what I'm going to do once the baby comes. Worried I'll make another mistake and mess up her life."

"Jetta." The pain in her tone made him want to draw her into his arms.

She held up her hand. "Please, let me finish. You've been the perfect gentleman in all of our interactions. You've never asked about the baby's father, but you deserve to know why I'm such an emotional mess."

"You don't have to tell me." But oh, how he hoped she would.

"Yes, I do." She held out the leash to him. "I think I can get the words out better if we walk and talk. Would you mind?"

"Not at all." He accepted the leash, tugging Bingley to get him moving again. Jetta fell into step beside him, her arm brushing against his. Every fiber of his being wanted to take her hand in his but he would keep his distance so she could tell her story. While she had apologized, it didn't mean she was ready to welcome him into her life.

They walked nearly an entire block before she spoke. "He never hit me." Her quiet words eased some of the worry Seth hadn't realized he'd been carrying. "But he tried to control me in other ways."

When she let the silence build, he filled in the blanks of a story he'd seen play out more often than he liked to remember with some of his mother's men. "By belittling you and isolating you from your friends and family."

Surprise widened her eyes. "How did you know that?"

He drew Bingley to a halt to face Jetta. "My therapist helped me see that's what some of my mom's men did, even when I couldn't articulate why their behavior bothered me so much."

Jetta appeared to mull that over, then she continued walking. "I met Kyle at the mega church I was attending in Chicago. While the pastor did preach the Gospel, what attracted me was the way I was able to slip in and out without many people noticing me. It was easy to think I was doing the right thing without the accountability. In hindsight, that's why Kyle liked the church too."

No wonder Jetta had thought Kyle was a safe bet, meeting him in a house of worship.

"At first, I was flattered by his attention. He was older, in his late-thirties, and seemed so sophisticated. Unlike men my age, he had more money, and he liked to spend it on theater tickets, high-end restaurants, and box seats at sport events. Dating him was like nothing I had ever experienced, and for a while, he treated me like a queen."

Seth braced himself as she shared more details as Kyle niceness wore off, telling himself she had gotten away from the man who had hurt her so deeply in Chicago.

"He was so good at making me believe his demands were reasonable that I didn't realize what was happening until one of my sisters visited me."

Jetta paused the story as if lost in the past. He prompted her with a question. "Which sister?"

"Jenna, the oldest one. Kyle was supposed to go to dinner with us, but he backed out at the last minute because a friend had gotten courtside seats at a Chicago Bulls game. I wasn't about to ditch Jenna and accompany Kyle, who blew up for disobeying his command." She huffed a laugh. "He didn't use those words. That's how I saw it later, when the scales had fallen from my eyes."

"So no one from your family ever met Kyle?" Seth tugged Bingley away from a flower bed as the streetlights came on to illuminate the dusk.

"No. Jenna asked the right questions about his over-reaction to a change in plans, but I wasn't ready to hear it. I still thought he hung the moon, as my grandmother used to say."

Bingley barked at a neighbor walking a black lab, and Seth tightened his grip on the leash. They passed a neat brick house with a freshly mowed lawn and few ghosts hanging from the small tree in the front yard.

"I don't get why people decorate for Halloween." Jetta pointed to the extremely tall skeleton on the lawn. "It's not even October."

"I guess because pumpkin spice comes out in early August, people think it's time to break out the Halloween decorations in late September."

"Maybe." She swiped across her face with the back of her hand. "I'm so tired of these blasted tears. Every time I turn around, I'm bawling like a baby." She pointed a finger at him. "And don't you dare say that's because I'm having one."

His lips twitched, but Seth managed to turn his head so she wouldn't see his almost-smile. "Yes, ma'am."

"I found out Kyle's true colors around Halloween last year, two months after Jenna's visit. It was such an ordinary day. We were supposed to go to a Halloween party, one of those adult dress-up affairs. He'd bought costumes for us but hadn't shown me the outfits, saying he wanted it to be a surprise." She snorted. "He certainly succeeded. He came dressed as a pirate complete with swashbuckling sword and eyepatch. My outfit was much skimpier. The skirt, if you could call it that, would have barely covered my rear. The top consisted of a laced corset type thing, a bustier I think they're called. I took one look at the scraps of fabric and said no. Kyle was furious. He exploded in a rage, calling me all sorts of nasty words and threatening to leave me if I didn't go get dressed in the wench's costume."

Seth was glad Kyle was in Chicago because the urge to plant one in his face grew with each snippet of Jetta's tale. He never understood the sheer selfishness of some men in the way they expected their women to behave.

"So I called his bluff and said fine, leave me. I wasn't wearing the outfit."

They had rounded the block with their houses in sight. Seth said a prayer of thanks for her courage in extracting herself from such a volatile relationship. Although if she broke up with Kyle last October 31, then the baby must not be his because the math didn't add up. Babies didn't take eleven months to be born.

"He stormed out and didn't call me for two weeks, during which time I had a good, long think about our relationship."

"What did you conclude?"

"You mean besides the fact that I was better off without him?"

"Yep."

"That I had been a fool, but at least God had opened my eyes at last." She halted at the walkway leading to her front door and laid a hand on his forearm. "Seth, I'm so sorry for those terrible words I said about you. You've been nothing but kind and generous and caring toward me and my mom, and I let my fear about my mom and uncertainty about my own future cloud my judgment. I hope you can forgive me and that we can be friends."

His heart, which had begun to beat faster at her light touch and her complimentary words, slowed as she friend-zoned him. "Of course I forgive you." *I'm in love with you. I'd forgive you anything.* He swallowed the words he wanted to say, knowing it wasn't the right time. It might never be the right time, not if she continued to vacillate between flirting and friending.

She squeezed his arm. "Thank you. I don't deserve someone like you."

"I think you do, but that's a conversation for another day." He handed over Bingley's leash. "You look about to drop on your feet."

She stifled a yawn behind her hand. "The day's caught up with all of a sudden."

"I'll keep praying for you and your mom. Sleep tight, Jetta."

With a wave, she trudged up to her door. He watched from the sidewalk until she and the dog disappeared inside, then went to find something to eat. He hoped his roommates hadn't eaten the leftover chicken, or it would be cereal for dinner. If only his love life could be so easy to solve as feeding his stomach.

Mae huffed as she searched the shelves in the supply closet for binder clips. The office manager assured her the company had recently ordered more, but Mae had yet to find them. Ryan preferred the clips to staples on his reports, so she regularly ran through her desk supply. She made a mental note to assign the office manager with the task of organizing the spacious closet on the upcoming office cleanup day. Mae would attach Ryan's name to the order so the woman wouldn't dare not comply. Samantha Layne would know it was Mae's revenge for the binder search, but she would still have to re-organize the supplies.

Mae moved to the far corner of the room where a stack of boxes had been opened but not put away. She grabbed a single step stool to use to peer into the box, which held packages of multicolored sticky notes. Moving the top box to the floor, she tried the middle box. Rubber bands, dry erase markers, and Sharpies. After stacking the middle box on top of the former upper box, she sat on the stool to go through the bottom one. This one held even more of a hodgepodge of supplies.

She dug into the box, shifting the contents around as much as she could without removing anything. Ah, there at the very bottom sat a box of binder clips. She excavated her find but froze as the sound of voices filtered to her.

"What did you find out?" a familiar woman's voice said.

"You sure we're alone?" a male voice answered.

"Still scared of closets like when we were kids, Gene?"

Mae put a name to the taunting feminine voice. Yasmine Topher, who, in her opinion, had more brains than her two brothers but because she'd been born female—and the third child—she'd been largely regulated to the sidelines. But Mae saw through her façade of indifference and spied a woman hungry for power, which spelled trouble for Ryan. The middle child, Gene, struggled to find a place to shine outside of Ryan's shadow. Gene wasn't as brilliant as his older brother and not as engaging as his younger sister. If they found out she was eavesdropping, Yasmine would give her an earful or perhaps even complain to Ryan. Mae would simply shrink down even farther to avoid detection.

"We don't have time for your pettiness." Gene's voice sounded too close for Mae's comfort, but she didn't dare move to check on their proximity to her hiding place. "We have a much bigger problem at hand."

"Which is what?" Yasmine sounded bored. "Everything's going according to plan."

"So you say. The last vote wasn't even close to passing in favor of the takeover. You promised you had info to make it happen."

"Be patient. There will be an emergency vote in a few days."

A phone buzzed. For an instant, Mae was terrified it was hers. But Yasmine answered with a sharp, "I told you not to call me at this number."

Mae's heart rate began to slow to normal speed. Maybe they would leave now, and she could take her binder clips and forget she'd ever heard them plotting against her boss. Ryan never remembered her birthday, but he always respected her abilities as his personal assistant. He didn't deserve to be undermined by the two people who should have his back. Mae would have to do some digging to discover how the siblings would benefit from a takeover.

"I see." Yasmine's voice had grown cold and hard. "What have you been up to?"

"What do you mean?"

Even Mae, who could only hear the conversation, could tell Gene knew exactly what his sister was asking from the tone of his voice.

"You've always been a terrible liar. I hear you've been dabbling in a little kidnapping."

"Kidnapping? What are you talking about?"

Yasmine cursed so creatively, Mae would have applauded her performance if she'd been able to without giving herself away.

"I'm talking about Emily Ainsley. You had her kidnapped."

"I did no such thing."

His sister clearly didn't believe him. "You panicked after the last vote. I told you I had everything under control. The Ainsley widow wasn't even close to figuring out who embezzled the money—all the evidence still points to her saint of a dead husband. Your little stunt could cost us everything we've worked for."

"You said someone had info about Vie, so I thought maybe she'd uncovered something."

"I also said I would find out and take care of it," Yasmine hissed. "Now you've simply given me a bigger mess to clean up."

"She won't connect anything to me." Gene's whine grated on Mae's nerves.

Mae avoided contact with the second son as much as possible because of his constant attitude of "not my fault" related to everything. If he hadn't had such competent underlings, the operations part of the company would have collapsed years ago.

"She's never seen anyone's face. There's no need for anyone to get hurt."

Yasmine must have been considering her brother's words because she was silent for nearly a minute—the seconds of which Mae ticked off in her head. "If you're wrong, you will regret it. I haven't worked this hard to lose over something as stupid as this."

"I'll take care of it. The Ainsley woman will never know anything about you or me. I promise."

Mae expected him to add "or hope to die," as the childish saying went.

"See that you do." Yasmine's heels clicked on the concrete floor. Mae breathed a sigh of relief as the door opened and closed.

Then she heard Gene's voice again. Drat, he must have not followed his sister out and was making a phone call. She'd have to stay hidden a while longer.

"It's me."

She strained to hear his side of the conversation as he spoke softer.

"Have you gotten anything from her?"

He shuffled back and forth.

"No, if she hasn't talked now, she doesn't know anything about Vie."

More pacing. "Taking her was a mistake." Another short moment of silence before he whisper-yelled, "I am not authorizing that. I'm not a killer. Let me think."

Mae's heart raced as she listened to Gene negotiate with the kidnapper on what to do with Emily Ainsley. Gene must have found out about the email Emily had sent and the phone call asking for a new investigation into the embezzlement.

"No, here's what you'll do. There's an old cemetery called Tippit's Hill near Route 28 and Pacific Boulevard. Leave her there and make sure there's nothing to tie her to us."

A few seconds later, he uttered a curse word that lacked the force of his sister's. "I'm the one calling the shots, so you listen to me. You will not get the last half of your payment until you send me photographic proof she's in the cemetery, alive."

That must have convinced the kidnapper because Gene added, "I thought so. I'll be waiting to transfer the money as soon as I receive the photo."

He paced several more times, each time coming a little bit closer to Mae's hiding place, but then he halted with his back to her. "She'll be sorry she treated me like an imbecile. I'm not as stupid as she and Ryan think I am."

A charley horse squeezed Mae's right calf, and she bit down hard on her bottom lip to keep from crying out. She eased out of her high heel shoe and flattened her foot to ease the discomfort from the leg cramp. As the pain receded, Mae peeked around one of the boxes to see what was taking him so long to leave the storage room. If she stayed in this position much longer, more of her muscles would seize up.

Gene rubbed his hands together like an overdramatic movie villain. Really, the man had all the panache of a clown. No wonder Ryan and Yasmine treated him like the unwanted stepchild of the family. But that might make Gene the one to keep a closer eye on because even a well-behaved dog would turn on its master if provoked enough. Mae suspected Gene had been slapped down too many times by his siblings to not lash out when they least expected it.

"Yes, they will regret their actions, of that I will promise." With that strange pronouncement, Gene finally strode out, closing the door behind him with a welcomed click. Mae breathed in and out to lower her accelerated pulse, then stood and carefully stretched her muscles. She'd heard of Tibbit's Cemetery recently and racked her brain to recall the info as she paced over the same ground as Gene to work out the charley horse. On her third trip, she recalled the news story about a trio of data centers being built surrounding the defunct cemetery. No one would think to look for Emily there.

She picked up the binder clips and restacked the boxes, moving the stool to its proper place by the door. As she left the room, the idea to leave an anonymous tip about Emily's whereabouts formed. Yes, she could use the burner phone to ensure no one knew her identity, but she wouldn't call the police. She would phone that reporter who had an interview scheduled with Ryan on Friday. That would be safer for her, and it might drive another wedge between the siblings. She also suspected Yasmine or Gene was her mysterious contact. The more info she had about their actions, the more leverage she'd have with that person. Perhaps she would come out of this smelling like roses after all.

EMILY BLINKED BACK TEARS OF PAIN AND FRUSTRATION. THE THIN MATTRESS did little to protect her from the cold concrete floor, and the blanket her captor had tossed in smelled like it had been in a damp place for years. She shivered without any covering since she'd rather freeze than sneeze all night from the musty fibers.

The urge to pray once more filled her soul. She used to have a close relationship with God, but that had slipped to the wayside with the unfounded accusations against Jay, then his untimely death at his arrest. Jay had been a good man, a godly man who had served others his entire life. His faith in God's sovereignty and kindness toward those He had called to himself had never wavered. Even when the officers had come to arrest him, he had been shocked, yes, but gentle with them. Not fighting it but firm in his belief that he would be exonerated.

Fifteen years later, his name still bore the stain of an unresolved embezzlement charge, one that had tainted their entire family with the ugliness of an untreated tumor. While in rehab, Emily confronted her own cowardice in not pursuing the matter in the days after her husband's death. She admitted her own fear back then was she would find out Jay wasn't innocent. But she didn't want to leave this earth without trying to clear his name. Then when Jetta had brought the envelope to her, Emily had taken that as a sign she had been moving in the right direction. Having Jetta and Seth assisting her meant she was no longer digging on her own.

If she'd known her feeble efforts would lead to these attacks on her daughter and herself, she never would have begun the journey. The price had become too high to pay. She'd already sacrificed her husband to the embezzler. She would not do the same with her youngest.

Jetta had been through so much, with breaking up with her abusive boyfriend and then his assault on her. Her pregnancy as a result of rape broke Emily's heart, especially because Jetta had concealed it from her until she'd arrived in Virginia. Jetta still hadn't told her siblings about the baby, and Emily hadn't spilled Jetta's secret either. That was Jetta's decision, and Emily suspected her daughter wouldn't say a word until she'd decided whether to keep the baby or give it up for adoption. Emily wasn't sure which one would be best for Jetta and her mental wellbeing. That Jetta loved her baby was evident, but would the reminder of how it had been conceived be too much for her to bear as the baby grew? Would she grow to resent the child? Would another man ever want to raise the child of a rapist?

Seth's strong, handsome face popped into her mind. Emily had been grateful for the young man's assistance since he'd moved next door more than two years ago. He'd quickly become the go-to guy for moving furniture or carrying heavy objects. While he had a friendly outward demeanor, Emily had long suspected it hid a broken heart.

His inner strength reminded her of Jay, and she suspected Seth shared her late husband's faith. A faith she had begun to notice more and more in Jetta too. A faith she should return to herself.

The door opened and two figures entered. The light from the hallway backlit them enough that she could tell both wore black clothing with black gloves and ski masks, leaving only their eyes visible. Emily shrank back on the mattress as they approached without a word.

"No!" Her scream ripped from her throat as one of them grabbed her arm and yanked her to a sitting position.

"Another sound, and we duck-tape your mouth," the man growled in her ear.

She nodded her understanding and bit back another cry as the second man moved to her other side.

The two men hauled her upright and dragged her to the door. Emily fought to get her good foot underneath her to help ease the weight on her shoulders to no avail—they were moving too fast for her to assist. At what appeared to be the outer door, the men paused. One yanked a black hood from his back pocket.

Emily opened her mouth to protest but one look at his hard eyes had her snapping it closed. The man put the hood over her head but thankfully, didn't tighten the drawstring Emily had spotted. Then a cool breeze swirled around her. Within seconds, she was bundled into the back of a vehicle—an SUV she thought—as the floor was higher than a sedan trunk. The hatch slammed shut and the vehicle roared off.

Emily lost track of the many twists and turns or how long they'd traveled before the vehicle slowed. The sounds of other vehicles faded as the road became more bumpy and less smooth, leading her to think it was unpaved. No gravel crunched underneath the wheels and no outside sounds gave her any clues as to their location. All she knew for certain was it must be away from people. Her heart pounded so hard, she was certain it would be heard by her captors.

She didn't think either of the two men had been the one who interrogated her, but they might have been the ones who had grabbed her from the rehab center. Then the car halted, and the engine died.

The hatch opened and they hauled her out, leaving the black hood on her head. They again used her arms to move her away from the vehicle. Emily was in too much pain from her injured leg bumping along the ground to protest. If this was the end, she didn't want to spend it begging for more breaths from ones who obviously didn't care.

Then she was abruptly thrown onto the ground. Her head connected with something hard. Pain, this time in her head, overwhelmed her, and she welcomed the darkness that heaved her into oblivion.

TWENTY-THREE

Seth flipped onto his back, trying to get comfortable but his bed had morphed into a hard plank. Jetta's harsh words, coupled with her revelations about her ex, had him tossing and turning. Hearing how her ex had treated her had ignited a flame of anger he thought long doused. In the quiet of his bedroom, images of his mother whimpering as yet another man thought he had the right to use his fists on her face because of some perceived slight invaded his mind. Seth had learned it didn't matter the reason—the men wanted to prove their power over his mom, and, by extension, him.

The timing of Jetta's breakup suggested someone else might be the father of her child, but something about her haunted eyes made him question whether Kyle had left her alone. Jetta's fragility made him want to slay whatever dragons she battled, much as his younger self had attempted with his mother. Which brought him to the real reason he couldn't fall asleep.

Did he care for Jetta only because he sensed she needed protecting? Could he be mistaking love for his own need to keep a woman he cared for safe? Those questions tumbled around his brain like clothes in a dryer.

To distract himself, he picked up his phone and began scrolling through social media. Then he migrated over to his email to find Leslie Updike, his FinCEN contact, had sent him a message at 11:13, two hours ago.

Seth,

I checked with the guy who originally looked into the embezzlement allegations before Ainsley's death, and he said he'd recommended not arresting Ainsley because the evidence was circumstantial at best and "rather flimsy." He said the only thing tying Ainsley directly to the missing funds was a bank account in Ainsley's name in the Cayman Islands, which had been opened a few months before the investigation commenced. So not long enough for Ainsley to have siphoned off the millions of dollars Topher Robotics claimed he had taken.

Also, his notes indicated the agent had called the bank and asked to see the documents Ainsley supposedly sent to open the account, but the bank had no records of which documents had been used, which is against standard procedure at that branch. I verified this with the bank directly as well. Since you'd sent me Dolores Green's name, I asked about her account too. Same thing—no notation of which documents had been submitted to verify her identity.

Seth paused in reading to draw his own conclusion from what Leslie found out—that anyone could have opened the two accounts and made those electronic deposits. Then he continued reading her email.

The other interesting thing is that Topher Robotics laid claim on the funds in those two accounts and the bank wired the money back to Topher after the company presented documents showing Ainsley and Green had illegally taken the money. I asked to see the documents in question, only to be told the paper copies had been shredded and the online notes only said "documents."

This whole thing smells of yesterday's catch. And before you ask, I think bribes were paid to the Cayman Islands bank to obscure the accounts and their activity, but after all these years, there's too little of a paper trail to prove it.

You owe me more than a coffee for this!

Leslie

Seth sent a quick thank you to her, then forwarded the email to Jetta with a short message:

Not great news but I don't think we should be too discouraged. Talk soon. Seth

His phone buzzed in his hands. Brogan's name flashed on the screen.

"Hey, Brogan." Seth glanced at his watch to note the time. One-fifteen. Late for even his colleague to call unless there was breaking news that needed a photographer. "Another fire?"

"No. Do you know where Jetta is?"

Seth frowned. "At her house asleep, I hope. Why?"

"I just got an anonymous call on my office line from a burner phone."

Fallon had insisted his reporters forward their office landlines to ring to their personal phones after hours in order to not miss any scoops.

"The caller, who took care to disguise their voice so I haven't a clue about gender, said Emily Ainsley could be found at Tibbit's Hill Cemetery." Brogan coughed, then continued. "It's in Sterling, out Route 28 past Dulles Airport."

Seth couldn't believe it. It sounded too fantastical to be true. "Did the caller say how they knew this info?"

"No, they simply repeated Tibbit's Hill Cemetery and hung up. I tried calling back, but it rolled to an automated message saying the caller hadn't set up the mailbox, so I couldn't leave a message." Brogan paused, saying something under his breath about late-night drivers. "I'm nearly to your house."

Seth was already slipping into jeans. "I'll meet you at the end of the driveway."

Brogan disconnected without bothering to reply.

As he shoved his bare feet into a pair of sneakers, Seth contemplated texting Jetta with the news. But if it did prove to be a wild good chase, it would be best not to worry her. Too much anxiety couldn't be good for the baby, and Jetta was already carrying around more than enough.

Soon Seth slid into the passenger seat of Brogan's SUV and clicked his seatbelt into place. "Have you called the police?"

"I thought you might have the contact number to make things easier. I'd really rather not have to get a dispatcher to understand the urgency without knowing the background."

"Good idea." Seth checked the notes app on his phone for the contact info of Detective Oldfield, then punched in the number.

The detective answered after five rings, his voice sleepy. Seth hated waking the man up, but he was certain the detective wouldn't mind once he heard what Seth had to share.

"My name is Seth Whitman. We met yesterday morning at the shooting in south Arlington. You might have heard Jetta's mother, Emily Ainsley, had been kidnapped from her rehab facility around the same time as the shooting."

"A colleague mentioned that since the two women are related."

The man's voice sounded marginally more awake now. Seth cleared his throat, trying to find the words to succinctly related the circumstances. "My colleague at *The Northern Virginia Herald*, Brogan Gilmore, received an anonymous call a few minutes ago saying Emily Ainsley could be found at Tibbet's Hill Cemetery in Sterling."

"What?" Detective Oldfield's voice sharpened. "Tell me again."

Seth repeated the information. "We're headed to the cemetery now. We're coming from Falls Church and about to hop on the Dulles Toll Road. Should be there in about twenty minutes."

"I'll alert Fairfax County PD to send any patrol officers in the area to that location and meet you there."

"Okay." Seth remembered to add, "I haven't called Ms. Ainsley yet—didn't want to get her hopes up if this turns out to be a hoax."

"I see." Detective Oldfield didn't comment on whether he'd call Jetta.

Seth let out a breath as Brogan accelerated on the highway. The GPS on the vehicle's dash screen showed their ETA at seven minutes. "Thank you."

"Wait for backup," the detective said. "This could be a trap."

Seth said they would be careful and disconnected. He relayed the conversation to Brogan. "I didn't think about this being a way to lure Jetta to a lonely spot." He most certainly did not like to think about what might have happened had she been the one to receive the tip and not Brogan.

"Which is why we'll go in as slow and quiet as possible. Here's the turn." Brogan eased off the highway and onto a road lined on both sides with rectangle buildings about three stories tall. "Kind of ugly, aren't they?"

Seth peered in the darkness to see a sign illuminated by two small spotlights: Visions Data Center. "Yeah, but since they are not near any residential or retail businesses, they didn't have to make them pretty. I took some shots of a new center on the outskirts of Centreville that had been designed by a leading architect—very eye catching. These are functional but not attractive."

"Keep your eyes peeled for the left turn coming up, as I don't want to flip on my high beams unless I absolutely have to."

Seth peered into the darkness for the road, then pointed to a narrow slit between two buildings. "There, it's sandwiched between those two structures."

"Got it." Brogan eased the SUV into the tight, single lane gravel road with buildings on either side. They bumped along for a few hundred yards before the buildings ended. Ahead, the headlights picked up a wide expanse of open space. Soon, they could see a low, wrought iron fence with a stone monument marking the cemetery's entrance.

Seth waited until Brogan had neatly turned the car around until it faced the alleyway, then both men exited and conferred near the monument, which appeared to have a brief history of the cemetery on a plaque attached to the stone. "Should we split up or stick together?"

"Together," Brogan said. "It will be less confusing when the police arrive, I think."

Using their phones' flashlight app, the two entered the small cemetery and headed to the left. The light played over the simple graves with some names visible and others lost to age and weather. The scent of recently mowed grass tickled Seth's nose. Mature trees ringed the cemetery on three sides, providing a buffer between the data centers and the loved ones buried here.

They reached the back of the cemetery without spotting Emily. Seth had been so sure the caller was telling the truth. "Let's check the right side," Brogan said.

Seth moved in that direction, using his light to illuminate the way. Even with the flashlight, he tripped over something but managed to stay on his feet. He swept his light back over the area and spotted a broken piece of concrete. Still nothing. He raised the phone toward the copse of trees. The light caught something shiny, and he quickened his pace until he spotted the glow of a cast. "Brogan! She's over here."

Seth dropped to his knees beside the woman lying on her side, her lounge pants torn and dirty. She had a black hood over her head, and he carefully removed it. Her hair, usually so smooth and in place, lay in tangled knots around her shoulders. "Mrs. Ainsley? Emily?" He touched her cheek. Warm. Thank God, she was alive.

Behind him, Brogan requested an ambulance while Seth examined Emily as much as he could without moving her. He had no idea the extent of her injuries.

She stirred, then opened her eyes. "Seth?"

"I'm here. Help is on the way."

"Oh, Seth." Tears spilled down her cheeks. "Help me sit up."

"I don't want to hurt you more." He tried to dissuade her but the determined set of her jaw, so like Jetta's, told him to save his breath and help her. As gently as he could, he raised her to a seated position, her back against a tree.

Scratches marred her cheeks, and the palm of her hands had lacerations, as did her left knee. She began to shiver. Shock.

"Do you have a blanket in your SUV?" Seth directed his question to Brogan, who took off at a jog while still on the phone. He returned his attention to Emily. "It will be all right. You're safe now."

"Jetta?"

"She's safe too." He wouldn't be the one to tell Emily about the shooting. All that could wait. "I didn't call her yet. Wanted to make sure you were here and okay."

"Good." Emily's eyes slid closed as Brogan returned with a blanket.

"It's one Melender and I use for picnics." He handed it to Seth, who tucked it around Emily.

"I'll call Jetta. She'll be mad she's not here but glad her mom's been found." Seth pulled up Jetta's contact info as flashing lights and a siren heralded the arrival of the emergency personnel. He prayed for the right words to say to calm her as quickly as possible. When she picked up, he tried to inject confidence into his tone. "Jetta, it's Seth."

"What's wrong? Is it Mom?" Tension filled Jetta's voice.

"Your mom's fine, Jetta." Seth looked at Emily, who had opened her eyes at the sound of her daughter's name. "We found her, and she's going to be okay."

He held the phone to Emily's ear and mouth. "Seth is telling the truth. I'm a little more banged up, but I'm alive and free." She listened for a moment longer, then repeated assurances she was okay before nodding to Seth to remove the phone.

"She really will be okay." As he spoke to Jetta, a police cruiser, an SUV, and an ambulance crowded the small cemetery parking lot. "The cavalry has arrived. As soon as I know what hospital they're taking your mom to, I will text you. Promise."

"Thank you, Seth. I don't know how you found her, but thank

you." She alternated between crying and hiccuping. "I'm so happy, I'm crying. Again."

"I will let you know as soon as I know more, but I need to go now." Seth wanted to stay on the phone with Jetta, but he had questions to answer and Mom to assist. His heart warmed at her thanks, and he prayed perhaps God would use this to strengthen Jetta's faith and heal her heart.

TWENTY MINUTES LATER, JETTA SLID BEHIND THE WHEEL, PRAYING THE SAME prayer over and over again. *Lord, please keep me safe. Let Mom be okay. Thank you for her return to us.*

On the way to Stone Springs Hospital, where Seth had texted the ambulance was taking Mom, the repetition calmed her. But she couldn't help glancing in her rearview and side mirrors because the sense of someone following her wouldn't leave. In the darkness, no one pair of headlights stood out in the light traffic, so she put her paranoia down to a residual response to her mother's kidnapping.

The Emergency Department parking lot had plenty of spaces, so she picked one closest to the entrance and hopped out. The front of her stomach tightened, then relaxed. Panic flared for an instant before she remembered having a few contractions before and asking her OB-GYN about it. Braxton Hicks contractions or false labor. Nothing to worry about. The lights inside the ER had been muted for the overnight hours, and a quick sweep of the waiting area didn't show Seth in any of the chairs or couches.

The check-in desk had two empty seats. Jetta turned around to scan the area again, which held a pair of elderly women huddled together and a younger man with a beard holding a stuffed bear. No Seth or employees.

The automatic doors leading back to what Jetta assumed would be the patient cubicles swished open, and a man in maroon scrubs came out and headed to the desk. "So sorry you had to wait." He slid into one of the empty chairs. "How can I help you?"

"I'm Emily Ainsley's daughter, Jetta. I was told my mom was being brought here by ambulance."

He asked her to spell the last name as he entered it into the computer. "Ah, yes. She requested Seth Whitman to accompany her, but left word to bring you back as soon as you arrived. I'll need to see your ID, then we can go back."

She fished out her wallet and showed her driver's license.

The employee eyed the license. "Thank you, Ms. Ainsley. If you'll follow me?"

She did so, having to trot to keep up with his longer legs. Once through the automatic doors, she blinked under the brighter lights. Medical personnel bustled about, whisking open curtains to cubicles on either side of the rectangle-sized area. The desk clerk stopped midway down the right side. "Knock, knock."

Without waiting for a reply, he peeled back the curtain. "I have your daughter, Mrs. Ainsley."

Jetta stepped forward, her gaze fastened on the bed where her mother lay. "Mom!"

Emily held out her arms, and Jetta needed no further invitation. She enfolded her mother in a loose hug, not wanting to hurt her by squeezing too tight. "I'm so glad you're okay."

Jetta stepped back and glanced across where Seth stood on the other side of the bed. "Thank you."

He rubbed the back of his neck as it turned pink. "Thank the anonymous caller who tipped Brogan off about where Emily could be found."

Seth hadn't told her the details when he'd called, but she could get them later. Right now, she only wanted to hold her mother's hand and be reassured she was truly okay.

"Here, you sit down." Seth brought the chair around to the right side of the bed so Jetta could sit.

She touched his arm, unable to get out the words of gratitude filling her heart because of the lump in her throat. He nodded, then smiled at her mother. "I'll be in the waiting room if you need anything."

After he left, Jetta stroked her mother's hand. "I was so worried when you were gone. I couldn't help thinking this was all my fault. If we hadn't started poking around after getting that envelope, none of this would have happened."

"No, my sweet girl." Emily squeezed her hand. "If anyone is at fault, it's me. I decided to pursue the truth and opened this particular can of worms."

Jetta sighed. "We're nowhere near finding out the truth about Dad or who the embezzler is." Frustration threatened to release more tears, but she'd had enough with the waterworks. She wouldn't cry any more, or at least not today.

"We can pray."

The assurance behind those simple words coupled with the sweet peace in Mom's eyes made Jetta smile. "We can certainly do that. I've missed praying with you."

"I have too. I might have wandered a bit away from God after your father's death, but He's brought me back. I'm only sorry it took such terrible circumstances to remind me of who I had been ignoring."

"Shall I start?"

Emily nodded, and Jetta closed her eyes. "Dear Jesus, thank you for restoring Mom both to your fold and to us. Help her recover from her ordeal, and please, if it is your will, let us find out who was behind the embezzlement. You know how much Dad loved you and served you. We would so much like to restore his good name."

"And keep my darling daughter safe from harm," Emily added her prayer. "Give her wisdom as she contemplates her future and protect the baby she's carrying. Help her to see your hand in her life despite the difficult circumstances and not be afraid of embracing a future full of hope and love. Amen."

Jetta echoed her mother's amen, deciding not to comment on the last line of the prayer. She suspected Emily had been matchmaking with Seth, and while she wasn't as opposed to that idea as she'd initially been, she still couldn't see a future that included a man.

"I see your daughter has arrived." A woman wearing Scooby Doo scrubs and a stethoscope around her neck stood by the partially open curtain. "I'm Patricia, one of the ER nurses. The EMTs did a cursory examination of your mother, but we need to do a more thorough one, plus x-ray her leg to ensure nothing shifted in all her travels. The doctor will be by in a few minutes."

Her mom released Jetta's hand as the nurse left. "Why don't you wait with Seth while they take care of all this."

"You sure? I can stay." Jetta wanted to stay by her mother's side, but Mom had that determined look in her eyes that told her arguing would be futile.

"Yes, I'm sure." Mom pointed a finger at Jetta. "You need to tell that young man your feelings."

"What?" Jetta's cheeks heated at her mother's words. "He's just a friend."

"Jetta Lynn Ainsley."

At her mother's use of her full name, Jetta froze.

"I didn't raise you to be so foolish as to throw away a chance at love because you're scared."

"I—"

"I'm not finished." Mom shifted on the bed as the same nurse returned with an older man wearing dark blue scrubs with bright orange dancing crabs.

They certainly made interesting scrubs these days. Jetta recognized her lame attempt to distract herself from her mother's words.

"But I see I'll have to finish this conversation later."

Relief poured over Jetta like warm caramel sauce over ice cream. She leaned down and kissed her mother's cheek, then told the nurse she'd be in the waiting room. As she left, Jetta couldn't ignore her mother's assertion she had feelings for Seth. She wasn't ready to take a closer look at her heart, but she did acknowledge her mother had hit the bullseye on one thing. She was terrified of falling in love with the wrong guy and repeating the same mistakes she made with Kyle. Her confidence in herself to make a good decision when it came to love hovered around zero. With a baby on the way, her heart wouldn't be the only thing on the line.

CHAPTER

TWENTY-FOUR

Seth stepped outside the emergency department, the cool night air not enough of a deterrent to stay inside. He wished he could go for a run or hit the gym for some reps on the weight machines to burn off his nervous energy. Adrenaline still coursed through his body, buoyed by finding Emily's mother alive and mostly unharmed. The shine in Jetta's blue eyes had his heart racing for an entirely different reason. He told himself not to hope this meant she would be more open to pursuing a relationship with him, but his foolish heart leaped to that conclusion on its own.

He turned the corner, following the sidewalk around to the left. His phone buzzed, and after checking caller ID, he answered it. "Hey, Brogan."

"How is Mrs. Ainsley?"

Background noise indicated Brogan was likely still at the cemetery with law enforcement. "Not sure, as a doctor hadn't seen her when Jetta arrived. She's with Emily now, and I'm outside walking. Any updates?"

"Not much, but I did hear that one of the data centers recently installed security cameras, and it might have captured the vehicle used to transport Mrs. Ainsley to the cemetery."

"Maybe there will be something useful on the footage that will lead to whoever kidnapped Emily." Seth cut through one of the hospital parking decks. "Anything else recovered from the scene that might help ID the culprit?"

"Not that the cops are sharing, but the forensics team canvassed the area. I'm leaving in a few as things are winding down, and I need to get some shuteye before our ten o'clock interview this morning."

"Okay, thanks for the update." Seth exited the garage and turned right to take the path back to the ER. He'd nearly forgotten they had an interview—he checked the time on his phone—in less than six hours. Maybe he could grab a nap while waiting to hear how Emily was doing.

When he entered the waiting room, he spotted Jetta coming through the automatic doors. "Jetta? Everyone okay with your mom?"

Her hand braced the small of her back and her shoulders slumped. "Yes. The doctor came to examine her. Since the cubicle is so small, Mom sent me out and told me to put my feet up while they did. They'll also x-ray her leg afterwards, so it will be a while before I can rejoin her."

"Can I get you something to drink or eat?" Seth bit back more questions as she eased into a chair.

"I didn't think I could sleep before but now I can hardly keep my eyes open." She stifled a yawn behind her hand.

"Be right back." Seth went to the front desk to talk to the employee, whose name tag he now noticed read "Farhan." "Excuse me."

Farhan looked up from his computer screen. "How can I help you?"

"My friend's exhausted. Her mom's back with the doctor, and it will be a while before she's finished. Is there anywhere she can rest while she waits?"

"That's the kidnapping victim's daughter, right?"

Seth affirmed it was, figuring someone couldn't keep that juicy bit of news to themselves when Emily was brought in.

"She must be so relieved her mom was found and will be okay." Farhan clicked some keys. "Since we're not too busy, I can put her in one of the overflow triage areas. It won't be secluded, but there's a bed in there she can use."

"Thank you. I'll go get her." Seth hustled back to find Jetta had moved to one of the couches and had fallen asleep on her side. He decided not to wake her and returned to the desk. "She's asleep on one of the couches. Could I have a blanket instead of making her move?"

"Sure, that's an easy one. Be right back." Farhan scooted his chair back and left while Seth returned to keep an eye on Jetta. He wasn't able to completely shake the sense she was still in danger despite her mother's safe return. They weren't even close to identifying who had been stealing money from Topher Robotics unless the answer was right in front of them and they couldn't see it.

Farhan returned holding a white cotton blanket. "Here you go."

Seth thanked him, then draped it over Jetta, who barely stirred. He sat in the chair next to the couch and contemplated all they knew. He opened the notes app on his phone and began jotting down his thoughts and questions.

Jay Ainsley had been troubled by something at work in the months leading up to his death. Would Emily have his work calendar?

Someone at Topher Robotics made sure a paper trail for a fraction of the stolen money pointed to Jay, leading to his arrest, which apparently led to his heart attack. Was there any question it was caused by something other than the enormous stress he'd been under? Why did

Topher Robotics not sue Emily to recover the rest of the money they said Jay stole? Or launch an investigation into where the other money was?

As far as Seth knew, the Ainsleys didn't live an extravagant lifestyle. The Cayman Islands bank account yielded only a few million dollars, well below the number reportedly taken over many years. He composed an email to Mr. Warner to ask if he could find out when the embezzlement started and how long it continued.

Someone with insider knowledge sent Jay an envelope to help exonerate him but it wasn't delivered until fifteen years later. Who sent the envelope?

The papers hadn't been very useful because the financial institutions hadn't been named, only bank account numbers. But they did show dates and amounts, so perhaps with other info, a forensic accountant could piece together exactly what happened. Seth sent his FinCEN contact an email asking for recommendations for a freelance forensic accountant.

Dolores Green had been accused of altering invoices from SafeSense to Topher Robotics, but she denied any culpability. Then Fiona Everly left SafeSense to work for Topher. Coincidence?

Someone followed us to Dolores's house, then took potshots at us. Jetta received an anonymous phone call warning her to stop or the next time wouldn't be only fired shots.

Seth rubbed the back of his neck as the list grew longer. Nothing seemed to make any sense, especially the kidnapping of Emily. It was as if there were more than one entity behind everything, and only by separating the incidents and information would they be able to get a clearer picture. He tapped his fingers on the arm of the chair.

Was it that simple? Were they trying to put together a puzzle with too many pieces and so could never see the forest for the trees, as one of his foster dads used to say?

Possibly, but how to split up the list would need to wait. He yawned as the long day tackled him like two sumo wrestlers. He checked on Jetta, who slept on, then tried to find a comfortable position in the chair. As sleep beckoned him, he prayed once more for Jetta and Emily, and for wisdom in figuring this out before someone made good on their threat to seriously harm Jetta.

Ryan pounded the weight bag with his right hook, then a left jab. He swung his leg up in a round kick to connect with the hanging punching bag. The bag swayed from his attack as he danced the boxer's moves around it, delivering blow after blow with his gloved hands interspersed with kicks from his bare feet. The five a.m. workout invigorated him, firing his brain cells into overdrive.

He slammed the bag with his left foot, visualizing the board chair's smug face. An uppercut with his right sent the bag swinging as he smashed his father's interfering mouth. Ryan continued well beyond his usual workout time until his muscles quivered and sweat drenched his body. He ripped off his gloves and grabbed his water bottle, downing the contents in a few long swallows.

The door to his downstairs gym opened, and his wife stepped inside wearing a silk bathrobe over her matching pajamas. Pink polish glistened on her toes, a girlish touch that amused him in his sixty-two-year-old wife.

"Come to watch me attack this bag?" He blotted his face with a towel, then he clocked her serious expression—and his cell in her hand. "What is it?"

She blinked back tears, and his heart clogged his throat. "It's your father."

"What happened?"

"He's alive. Your mother called. The housekeeper found him in his office slumped over the desk when she brought him his morning coffee. He was unresponsive, and he's been taken to the hospital. They're running tests to see if it was a heart attack or stroke."

Ryan nodded as Sage related more information while keeping a serious expression on his face. While he wouldn't have wished his father harm, he couldn't help but see how the timing of his father's illness would play into his hands to keep the board on his side—and ready to quash any other hostile takeover bids.

"Ryan?"

He swiveled to see Sage staring at him, concern in her eyes. He offered a tight smile. "I'm okay—shocked, of course."

His phone buzzed in Sage's hand. She glanced at it. "Gene's calling."

Ryan did not want to talk to his brother, not yet. "Tell him I'm in the shower but to come to the office as soon as he can. And call Yasmine to tell her the same." He didn't wait for Sage to agree to his commands but left knowing she would. She was a most excellent wife, never complaining of his long hours at the office. Maybe soon, he would be able to enjoy the fruits of all his labors with her. The idea of a months-long tour in an RV of the Southwest US buoyed him through his shower and dressing.

Forty-five minutes after learning of his father's health crisis, Ryan convened a closed-door meeting with his siblings.

"What happened to Dad?" Gene asked as he sipped coffee he'd brought with him.

"I spoke with Mom, and she said the initial tests indicated he had a heart attack." Ryan leaned against his desk, opting to stand while his brother and sister sat in the pair of visitor club chairs.

"Just like Jay Ainsley." Yasmine sounded shaken.

"Who?" Gene frowned.

"The head of accounting Dad accused of embezzling millions of dollars," his sister snapped back. "Surely you remember? The media hounded us for months."

Ryan bit back a groan as her words reminded him he had an interview with Brogan Gilmore at ten this morning. He would have to cancel, of course, in light of his father's hospitalization. "Let's not jump to conclusions."

"I'm not jumping to conclusions," Yasmine huffed. "I'm pointing out it's weird when Dad had a checkup last month and was pronounced in excellent physical health that he would suddenly have a heart attack."

"He's eight-seven, for goodness sake," Gene responded. "Didn't that Ainsley guy have some sort of hidden heart condition?"

Ryan didn't want to listen to their squabbles about inconsequential things. "That's enough. Our father is fighting for his life, and we have to decide what that means for the future of the company."

Yasmine narrowed her eyes. "It doesn't mean anything, dear brother. We continue on as before."

"That's not exactly true." Ryan waited until both his siblings looked him straight in the eyes. "I have Dad's power of attorney, so that means I control his shares of the company until he's back on his feet."

"What?" Gene shot to his feet. "That would give you..."

"Fifty-two percent of the shares and thus control of the company." Ryan crossed his arms and tried not to smile too broadly as Gene gaped at him. He'd suspected Yasmine and Gene of plotting with shareholders to sell the company to Maxwell Technology, but his father's heart attack had spiked their plans.

"Are you sure about that?" Yasmine stayed seated, her expression calm.

"I can show you the document if you'd like."

"I'd check what your power of attorney covers." Yasmine reached into her briefcase beside her chair. She brought out a folder, which she handed to Ryan. "Dad also gave me power of attorney—specifically to control his shares of the company."

Ryan wouldn't respond until he'd seen the document. If that were true, that meant his sister would block his attempt to salvage the company. One glance at the page confirmed his sister's words. He closed his eyes, seeing all his hard work to save the company draining away like an old battery.

"Yes!" Gene pumped his fist into the air. "Why didn't I hear about this?"

"It appears no one did apart from Yasmine." Ryan didn't have time for his brother's joy or his sister's smugness. "You do realize if Maxwell Technology succeeds, they will break Topher Robotics into pieces. People will lose their jobs."

"But we'll be rich." Gene rubbed his hands together. "This is the best news I've had all day."

"You're rejoicing? If Dad survives, he'll have another heart attack over what the two of you have done to the company he founded." Ryan couldn't believe his siblings would be so unfeeling.

"You thought you were the favored child, but I guess you found out the hard way Dad didn't trust your business judgment." Yasmine got to her feet. "The only thing Dad loved was this company. Not me and certainly not either of you. If I happen to destroy his life's work, so be it. At least I'll have enough money to leave this area and never look back."

"Get out, both of you. You make me sick." Ryan turned away, unable to look at his brother and sister. His heart ached for his father, who had made his life as CEO miserable, but Yasmine had been right—Peter Topher cared more for his namesake company than for his three children. Maybe he shouldn't want to preserve his father's legacy, but Ryan had invested too much of his own life in

Topher Robotics to back down now. If a fight was what they wanted, he would be more than happy to oblige. In fact, he wouldn't cancel the interview with the journalist but use it to start his own campaign to win the shareholders to his vision for Topher Robotics.

TWENTY-FIVE

"Jetta?"

She opened her eyes a crack, her body not ready to leave the warm embrace of sleep. "What?"

"A Fairfax County detective is here to talk with you." Seth held a cup of something hot and steaming under her nose. She sniffed in the welcome aroma of hot chocolate. If she couldn't have caffeine from coffee, at least she could drink hot chocolate.

She pushed to a seated position and brushed her hair off her cheek. "Give me a minute," she said to the man wearing rumpled khakis and a wrinkled button-down shirt.

"Take your time." He flipped pages in a small notebook while she tried to blink the last vestiges of sleep from her brain.

It wasn't going well, but the hot chocolate would help. She reached for the cup, and Seth handed it over. The first sip was heavenly. "Hmm. Where did you find this?"

"A Cuppa Joe via DoorDash." He held up his own insulated paper cup. "I knew they opened at four for the shift change crowd, so I put in the order."

She'd slept for nearly three hours, but her body craved even more. "Any news on my mom?"

"She was taken for the X-ray about half an hour ago, so we should hear how she's doing soon." Seth resettled in his chair, his five o'clock shadow now more like a scruffy beard.

The desire to run her fingers over his jawline had her raising her hand, but she covered the gesture by shoving it through her own tangled locks. She must look a mess, but she couldn't care less. More sips of the deliciously creamy cocoa gave her brain enough of a kick she thought she could carry on a reasonable conversation. "I'm ready."

"I'm Detective Mason Harwell, assisting with the investigation into your mother's kidnapping." The older man tapped his pen against the notebook. "There's not much to report about your mom's abduction. We did request the security camera footage from the data center, but that will take some time. Forensics is sifting through all the trash we collected, but most of it appears to have been there for weeks, if not months."

"Maybe Mom will remember something useful." Jetta drank more hot chocolate.

A nurse came over to them. "Ms. Ainsley? Your mother's back from X-ray."

"Okay." Jetta rocked in her seat, careful not to spill her drink, to build a little momentum to stand. Who knew being pregnant would make simple things like rising from a seated position difficult?

"Is Mrs. Ainsley able to answer some questions?" Detective Harwell stood as well.

"I think so," the nurse said. "Follow me."

Seth hung back. "I'll check in with Brogan while you two talk to Emily."

Disappointment he wouldn't be by her side made Jetta almost ask him to come with her, but she held her tongue. His presence beside her would only fuel her mother's determination to play matchmaker between them. Better to not encourage Mom to see a future where Jetta most certainly did not, despite her growing affection for Seth.

"After you." The detective gestured for Jetta to go first, then fell into step behind her. Soon, they arrived at her mother's cubicle. Mom had her eyes closed when they entered but opened them when Jetta touched her arm.

"Hey, sweetheart." Her mother's voice was stronger than before, and Jetta hoped that meant she'd gotten a little sleep too.

"Hi, Mom." She introduced the detective. "He has a few questions for you, if you feel up to it."

Mom nodded.

"Walk me through what happened yesterday." Detective Harwell settled into one of the plastic chairs with his notebook open.

"I'd gone to the bathroom in my room. When I came out, two men dressed in scrubs with facemasks and gloves grabbed me. One of them said if I squealed, they would hurt Jetta."

Jetta covered her mouth with her hand to hold back a cry as her mother detailed the men bundling her out of a back door of the building, across the grass, and through the hedge to a waiting van.

"We found your slipper by the hedge," Jetta interjected when her mother paused to sip some water. "That's how we knew someone must have taken you, as you couldn't have walked that far on your own."

"They kind of half carried me, and I remember deliberately kicking it off to leave behind a clue." Mom gazed at Jetta. "I knew you'd find it and realize something had happened to me."

The detective cleared his throat. "What happened next?"

Her mother continued her tale, and Jetta shuddered as she listened to what her mother had gone through—being stuffed into the van and driven for hours before she was deposited into a room with only a mattress on the floor.

"Any idea as to why they kidnapped you? There was never any hint of ransom," Detective Harwell said.

"I don't think it was about money, or at least, it wasn't about getting money specifically for my return." Emily's brow wrinkled as if she was trying to puzzle something out. "Jetta, did you tell him about your father and the embezzlement?"

"No, but I did mention it to the officers I spoke with at the rehab center." Jetta sketched the basic outline of the original case and what they had done so far to try to uncover the truth after her mother had received the envelope. "We have a lot of pieces but haven't been able to put together a full picture."

Detective Harwell jotted down notes, then refocused on the recent kidnapping. "Why do you think the accusations against your husband and your kidnapping are connected?"

"Because someone came in—disguised with a ski mask and wearing gloves too—to ask me about Topher Robotics and some secret project called Vie." Mom shivered. "The person wasn't happy when I said I had no idea what they were talking about. But the person knew all about my trying to clear Jay's name of the embezzlement charge."

Jetta crossed her arms, resting them on top of her rounded belly. "Why would they think you knew about the project?"

"I haven't the faintest idea." Her mother sighed. "Then the two men who'd taken me returned last night, grabbed me, and left me in the cemetery. I never saw the other person again."

Detective Harwell asked more questions, but her mother didn't have more to add to her original recollection. He stood. "Thank you for your time, and I hope you'll recover from your ordeal." He handed Jetta his business card, then addressed Mom. "Please call me if you recall anything else."

Her mother thanked the detective. As he left, the doctor returned. "Mrs. Ainsley, good news. Your recent excursion didn't damage your leg. The bones are still healing nicely."

"I sense a *but* coming," her mother said.

The doctor laughed. "But since we also had your chest x-rayed, we found a small white spot on your lungs, which indicates you have an infection, probably pneumonia. So we'd like to keep you for a day to get some antibiotics going through an IV."

She coughed. "Now that you mention it, I have felt more congested and some pain when breathing, but not all the time."

"We caught it early, so with the antibiotics, you'll be feeling better soon." He touched her mother's hand. "A nurse will be by to let you know when we have a room ready for you upstairs."

After he left, Jetta scooted her chair closer and took her mother's hand between both of hers. "I'm sorry, Mom. I know you want to go home, and not be in a hospital again."

"But I won't be going home, will I?" Mom sighed. "I don't mean to sound ungrateful, but change is hard."

"Saying goodbye to the house you lived in for so long must be difficult too." Jetta drew in a breath. "May I pray for you?"

"That would be wonderful." Emily closed her eyes, and Jetta did the same. Then she lifted up her mother before the Lord, praising God for her safe return and asking for her healing. She closed with a petition that they would clear Jay's name as well.

"Amen," Mom echoed when Jetta finished. "Thank you, my dear."

Jetta smiled. "Of course. It's nice to share faith with you."

"I shouldn't have strayed after your father died, but God has brought me back into his fold." Mom coughed, reminding Jetta of her mother's fragile health.

The nurse whisked back the curtain. "Mrs. Ainsley, they're ready to move you to your room."

Jetta rose to move out of the way as the nurse began unhooking the medical equipment. An orderly came in and raised the siderails on the bed.

The nurse turned to Jetta. "You can check in at the front desk in about half an hour to get the room number."

Dismissed, Jetta returned to the waiting room. Seth sat, elbows on knees, his attention fixed on his smartphone. She paused to study him, admiring the way his long-sleeved t-shirt conformed to his impressive arm muscles. Long legs encased in faded blue jeans put him over six feet tall, a nice contrast to her own five feet, six inches. His rumpled brown hair and growing beard added to his overall physical appeal. Then there was their kiss. The kiss had rocked her to her toes. Even the baby had seemed to leap for joy at the contact.

But while she admitted to being attracted to the outward package, it was the inner man who tugged at her own heart. She'd seen his gentle nature, his kindness, his compassion, his willingness to help. All of those attributes made him irresistible, but resist him she must, although not for her own sake but for his. He might say now he wouldn't mind raising another man's child, but when he heard the rest of the story, he might change his mind. She thought too highly of him to ever tie him to her and the baby, no matter what her heart had begun to tell her.

Seth shut his vehicle door and shouldered his camera bag before walking toward Topher Robotics. He hoped the early morning run with Bingley, plus the gallons of coffee he had consumed, would keep him alert during their interview with Ryan Topher.

As he held the door for a pair of women exiting the building, he prayed once more for Jetta, who he'd left resting with Bingley. She'd been cool toward him, expressing thanks for taking Bingley out but not trying to engage in conversation beyond the essentials. Maybe it was because they both were exhausted after being in the hospital with Emily, but somehow, he thought it was due to her having second thoughts about a relationship with him that went beyond friendship.

With an effort, he shook off his thoughts of Jetta to focus on the upcoming interview. He entered the building and spotted Brogan chatting on his cell by a group of club chairs to the right of the reception area. He dumped his camera bag onto the low table and removed the digital camera, looping the strap over his head. While he waited for Brogan to finish his call, he snapped a few pics of the lobby.

"Ready?" Brogan pocketed his phone. "We're right on time."

"Let's do this." Seth slung the bag on his shoulder, then followed Brogan to greet the receptionist, who verified their appointment, gave them visitor badges, then called Ryan Topher's assistant.

"Ms. Stanhope will be down in a few minutes." The receptionist smiled, then answered the ringing phone.

Brogan and Seth stepped to the left of the desk to wait closer to the bank of elevators. "Any updates on Mrs. Ainsley or the kidnappers?"

"Not since I texted you what Jetta said her mother relayed." Seth raised his camera to capture a wall of water glowing from the sunlight pouring in through the floor to ceiling windows. He probably wouldn't use it for the story, but it would make a nice addition to his personal portfolio.

"Hmm, yes. I did some digging this morning to see what I could find on Vie, and the rumor mill has been rampant with whether Topher actually has such a wearable device or if he's fanning the flames to stave off Maxwell Technology's bid."

The elevator doors swished open, and a middle-aged woman wearing low heels and a no-nonsense expression headed their way. "Mr. Gilmore, Mr. Whitmore, I'm Mae Stanhope, Mr. Topher's executive assistant. If you'll come this way, Mr. Topher is expecting you."

Inside the car, Ms. Stanhope pressed the top floor, number fourteen.

"Have you worked for Mr. Topher long?" Brogan smiled at the woman.

"I've been his secretary since he became CEO."

"How long have you been with the company?"

"Twenty-six years." Ms. Stanhope shifted from one foot to another, then back again.

A potentially nervous response to Brogan's innocuous query. Interesting. Seth studied her from his position in the corner of the elevator while Brogan asked a few general questions about the company. The woman wore her graying brown hair in a low bun at the nape of her neck. Silver hoop earrings adorned her ears, and she wore a plain gold band on her left ring finger. The collar of her suit jacket showed some wear around the edges, and the plum color of the outfit appeared a little faded as if from frequent washes. Not a woman with expensive tastes, at least in clothes and jewelry.

The soft ding of the elevator indicated their arrival on the fourteenth floor. Ms. Stanhope stepped out and turned to the right, hurrying a little bit as if she couldn't wait to get away from them. Even more interesting. She stopped in front of a door at the far end and pushed it open without knocking. Inside, a small anteroom held a desk with a name plate reading "Mae Stanhope," plus a bank of filing cabinets against one wall.

Ms. Stanhope rapped on the closed door at a right angle to her desk, then entered. "Mr. Topher? Mr. Gilmore and Mr. Whitman are here."

She turned to Seth and Brogan. "Mr. Topher will see you." She stepped back to allow them to enter the room.

Brogan went first and Seth followed him inside the spacious corner room with floor-to-ceiling windows. Thick drapes in muted shades of burgundy stood open on the west-facing wall of the office but closed on the east-facing wall, likely to block out the morning sun. As Seth had expected, the room had the decor of a successful businessman, with expensive furniture and objects d'art.

Ryan Topher rose from behind a massive antique partners desk, his hand outstretched to greet Brogan, then Seth. "Do you want any coffee or water before we get started?"

Neither one did, so the CEO gestured toward a leather loveseat and two matching club chairs grouped in one corner. Seth figured the man was trying for a more informal approach to what he thought would be a puff piece.

"Mr. Topher, thank you for agreeing to meet with us today." Brogan pulled out his notebook and pen.

"Please, call me Ryan." The man smiled, but Seth detected concern behind the expression in the way his mouth tightened at the corners.

"Will your siblings be joining us?"

At Brogan's question, Ryan frowned. "I thought this was a profile of me."

"It is," Seth interjected, holding up his camera, "but we wanted some pictures of the three of you for the story."

His explanation relaxed the frown lines on Ryan's face. "I'll ask Mae to have them come by toward the end of our time." He uncrossed his legs as if preparing to step out to chat with his assistant, but Seth stood.

"I'm happy to relay that to Ms. Stanhope while I ask her about potential places for the photographs." Seth glanced around the space. "Your office is too bright with the morning sun, even with the curtains drawn. I'll take a few photos here, but I think another location, maybe in one of your labs, might be more interesting."

Ryan considered his request, then nodded. "Mae's been with the company for years, so she'll know which spots might work."

"Thank you." Seth left Brogan to interview Ryan. Outside, Ms. Stanhope sat typing on her keyboard. "Ms. Stanhope?"

"Yes?" She removed her reading glasses.

"I'd like to photograph Mr. Topher with his siblings at the end of the interview. He said you could let them know?" He smiled and leaned closer. "I was also hoping you could show me some good spots around the building for taking pictures. You must know all the places with natural light and interesting backgrounds."

She seemed to thaw a little at his compliment. "I'll let Ms. Yasmine and Mr. Gene know about the photograph, then show you a couple of spots that might work."

He waited while she sent the emails, then followed her back to the elevator. She took him not to the ground floor, but the fifth. "Right this way." She moved to the left down a short hallway, then used a keycard to access a locked door.

Inside, Seth stepped into large open space. Skylights and large windows on three sides let in tons of natural light. The open floor plan held not cubicles but workstations where people wearing white lab coats worked on various mechanical objects. A low hum of activity filled the space. "The robotics department, I presume?"

"This is where the magic happens." Ms. Stanhope's words might have been flippant, but Seth interpreted them as sincere based on the woman's rapt expression.

"It's rather amazing." He lifted his camera and snapped some photos, capturing the sense of accomplishment in the room. "This does have great natural light but it's a bit too busy for a group shot of the siblings."

"I have a few other places in mind too." She motioned him to follow her. Back in the elevator, she punched the ground floor. "We have a garden between the buildings that might work for what you have in mind."

"Great." Seth let a few moments of silence build before adding, "I appreciate you taking me around to these spots."

"You're welcome." Some of the stiffness left her shoulders.

"Given how long you've been with the company, you must have known the founder, Peter Topher."

To his surprise, Ms. Stanhope sniffed as if fighting back tears. "I can't believe he's in the hospital."

"Hospital?"

"He had a heart attack last night, or at least that's what the doctors suspect. His wife found him slumped over his desk this morning."

"I hope he recovers." The timing of the elder Topher's health crisis seemed a little too good to be true, but perhaps the man had a tricky heart. "Had he experienced heart trouble before?"

"Oh, my goodness, no. The man's always been as healthy as a horse." The doors slid open, and she led the way to a side door around the corner from the elevators. "Everyone's shocked by the suddenness of this attack."

Once she unlocked the door with her key card, Seth held the door open for her. "I imagine so."

The sun shone on a well-tended garden, highlighting trees beginning to turn from green to gold, orange, and red. Fall mums added splashes of color to the flowerbeds while evergreen bushes, trimmed into submission, provided a backdrop. Wooden benches set back from the gravel pathways added to the charm of the space. "What a lovely oasis."

"This was the senior Mr. Topher's idea. He wanted to create beauty in the midst of all the brick and mortar of the buildings."

"I'd say he succeeded." Seth wandered around to scope out possible places for the photos. He found several areas he thought would work as backgrounds for the sibling photos. "I think this will work nicely for the pictures of the three Tophers."

"Very well." She checked her watch bracelet. "Mr. Topher can only spare an hour, so I'll have Ms. Yasmine and Mr. Gene come here at ten-forty-five. Will that give you enough time?"

Fifteen minutes would be tight, but he could make it work. "Sure. I'll go back and snap a few while Brogan wraps up his interview."

Seth and Ms. Stanhope returned to Ryan's office, where Seth rejoined Brogan in Ryan's office to take some photos while Brogan finished his interview. He concentrated on capturing Ryan, tuning out his answers to Brogan's questions as he worked. All too soon, Ms. Stanhope came back in to remind them of the time.

Brogan gathered his phone and notebook, Seth his camera and bag, then the four of them went back downstairs and out to the garden. Seth had Ryan sit on one of the benches for some solo pics while they waited for his siblings. Brogan asked a few additional questions to wrap up his interview.

Then an attractive woman, who Seth recognized as Yasmine Topher, appeared, wearing a dark-blue skirt suit and a white blouse. "Why on earth didn't you cancel this, Ryan?" Yasmine glared at Seth, then Brogan. "We have the emergency board meeting at eleven-thirty because of Dad being unresponsive in the hospital."

"Dad always put this company first, so I thought I would honor him by doing the same," Ryan retorted with an edge to his voice as if warning his sister to be careful with her words.

"Since when do you care about the company?" Gene Topher strolled up in his own dark suit.

"I care, which is why I'm fighting to keep it in the family," Ryan hissed between his teeth.

Seth stepped in before the siblings came to physical blows. "Gene, would you please join your brother on the bench? Yasmine, stand behind your brothers." Seth situated the two brothers so that Yasmine was framed in the middle.

As he snapped a series of photos, Brogan asked Gene and Yasmine a few questions about Ryan's leadership over the years. From their replies, Seth gathered the trio didn't see eye-to-eye on how Ryan was running the company.

"I thought this was a profile of Ryan." Yasmine followed Seth's instructions to lay a hand on each brother's shoulder.

"It was, but with the hostile takeover bid by Maxwell Industries, it has become a bigger story." Brogan shrugged as if he had no control over that.

Seth rearranged the siblings several times, snapping photos while Brogan continued with his questions. Finally, Ms. Stanhope cleared her throat. "Mr. Topher, it's eleven."

Ryan stood. "That's all the time we have for you today."

Seth stepped over to where he'd laid his camera bag as Brogan thanked Ryan for his time.

As Ryan, Yasmine, and Gene headed for the door together, Brogan tossed out, "Oh, one more question, if you don't mind."

The siblings turned in unison, Ryan raising an eyebrow.

"Why are Yasmine and Gene conspiring with Maxwell Technology on the hostile takeover of Topher Robotics?"

CHAPTER

TWENTY-SIX

"Mrs. Ainsley, your vitals are strong, so how about we spring you from the hospital today?" The attending physician winked at her as he scribbled notes on her chart.

"That sounds great." Emily couldn't wait to leave the hospital, although returning to the rehab center wasn't appealing. "When will that happen? I'll need to give my daughter a time to come get me."

He glanced at the wall clock. "How about noon? I'll get the discharge paperwork started now."

"Wonderful." She grabbed her phone the minute he left her room and texted Seth.

> Would you mind picking me up from the hospital?

His immediate reply brought a smile to her lips.

> Of course. What time?

> Noon. Thanks!

253

He sent a thumbs up emoji in reply. Emily tapped her phone against the bed, then dialed Jetta.

"Hey, Mom. How are you this morning?"

"I'm fine. They're discharging me. Would you come get me around noon? And bring a Jersey Mike's sub, the one with turkey and provolone. I'm tired of hospital food."

"You must be feeling better if you want a sub. What time should I come?"

"Noon would work. I'll be waiting in the lobby." Emily should have felt bad about omitting to tell Jetta she'd also asked Seth to come, but how could she not when Jetta was determined to push Seth away. Anyone could see how much the young man cared for her daughter—and how much Jetta cared for Seth. Her youngest daughter had it in her head that she needed to distance herself from Seth because of the baby, but Seth wouldn't care. Emily suspected he already loved the little one as much as he did Jetta. Emily viewed Jetta's reluctance to let her feelings for Seth grow as more fear-based than fact-based, and she aimed to do what she could to help bring them together.

She didn't have time to contemplate the wisdom of her decision, as medical personal came in and out of her room with various papers and instructions ahead of her discharge.

"Ready to be sprung from this joint?" Seth grinned as he entered her room.

"More than ready." Emily patted the folder beside her. "I have all my discharge papers, so I am just waiting for a wheelchair."

He eyed her leg, still in its cast. "Did they say how much longer you'd have to wear that cast?"

She grimaced. "Maybe another week. The kidnappers dragging me about put strain on the bones. But enough about me. Do you have any updates on the investigation?"

"Nothing concrete, but Brogan and I did interview Ryan Topher this morning and take some pictures of him and his two siblings."

Seth shook his head. "Those were the most awkward family photos I've ever taken. None of them wanted to be near the other."

"Jay always said the Tophers were a close-knit family."

"They certainly didn't seem all that close to me. The two younger ones appeared to resent Ryan's decisions." Seth paced to the window, then back. "Brogan asked mostly softball questions about Ryan and the company, then did the classic, 'one more question' as we were getting ready to leave."

"About the embezzlement?"

"No, about why Yasmine and Gene were conspiring with Maxwell Technology on the hostile takeover of Topher Robotics."

"Is that true?" Emily couldn't believe any of the siblings would try to damage their father's company in that way.

"All of them vehemently denied it, but while Ryan appeared shocked, the other two seemed more angry than surprised."

"What did they say?" Curiosity tugged at Emily. While Peter Topher had still been chairman of the board when Jay worked there, Ryan, Gene, and Yasmine had been more involved in the day-to-day running of the company.

Seth pulled out his phone. "I had put away my camera, but Brogan had asked me to record his asking the question for his story. All three had given permission for recording the conversations earlier, but Brogan wanted to focus on their facial expressions rather than making sure he was recording." He tapped the screen, then held out the phone toward Emily.

A male voice, presumably Brogan's, asked the question. A moment of silence, then two males and a female talked over one another in a jumble of denials. Then one of the brothers said, "How dare you accuse me of such an action!"

Emily shot out her hand. "Stop it."

Seth complied.

"Play that last bit again."

He brought the phone closer to Emily and played the recording again, this time a little louder. Her pulse accelerated, and a wave of dizziness swept over her as she listened to the voice of her questioner. She raised a trembling hand to her temple. "That's the voice of the man who asked me questions about Vie. He's the one who kidnapped me."

"You're sure?" Seth replayed the recording a third time.

Emily nodded. "He tried to disguise his voice, but that's the one. Which brother was it?"

"Gene."

"The neglected middle child." She gave a half smile, remembering hearing her own middle children complaining in mostly a teasing way about their lot in life to be overlooked and forgotten.

"I'll text the detective to let him know." Seth sent the message while Emily digested the fact that Gene Topher had kidnapped her.

The why eluded her, unless he thought she knew more about the new technology under development than he had access to, which made no sense, given he worked for Topher and she hadn't set foot on the company campus in years.

"Mrs. Ainsley?" A lanky Hispanic man pushed an empty wheelchair into the room. "I'm here to give you a ride in my chariot to the lobby."

"Wonderful." Emily allowed the hospital orderly to assist her into the chair while more questions pummeled her mind. Was Gene also the one who embezzled millions and blamed Jay? Possibly. Maybe the police would look into it more closely with this new evidence of his illicit activities.

Seth trailed behind them as the orderly took her to the lobby. Emily thanked the man once he parked her beside a couch.

"Will you be okay here while I get my car?"

Seth's concern showed Emily once again what a caring individual he was. If only Jetta would see that it was genuine and not some act designed to fool women. But his comment reminded her she needed to come clean about something else too. "Actually, my daughter is coming to give me a ride."

He raised his eyebrows. "Does she know you asked me to come as well?"

Emily shrugged. "I might have not said anything about inviting you."

"Mrs. Ainsley—"

"I've told you to call me Emily."

"Emily." Seth dragged her name out to more than three syllables. "Jetta has made it clear she's only interested in friendship with me."

"She's making a mistake." Emily leaned forward, trying to get Seth onboard.

"It's her decision—not yours—and I will respect her decision. This"—he gestured to himself and her—"isn't going to help things."

From behind Seth, Emily spotted her daughter entering the lobby.

"Mom?" Jetta looked from Emily to Seth and back again. "What's going on?"

Emily sighed. "Don't get mad at Seth. I asked him to give me a ride too."

Her daughter narrowed her eyes. "Why would you do that?"

Emily paused, then decided she might as well be honest. "Because I think you're making a big mistake throwing out a chance for a relationship with him because you're afraid."

Jetta's mouth dropped as she stared at her mother. Then she snapped it closed. "Well, we both can't give you a ride, so who's it going to be?"

Emily considered. "I'll go with you," she told her daughter. "But before you take me back to the rehab facility, we need to talk." She knew that mulish set of her daughter's mouth and jaw and hastened to reassure Jetta. "Not about Seth and you, but because I know who organized my kidnapping."

"You do?" Jetta swiveled to glance at Seth, then back to her mother. "Who?"

"Gene Topher."

~

Jetta jiggled her leg as they waited for Detective Harwell to join them in the windowless interview room. Her mother rested serenely beside her at the table, which was bolted to the floor. Two empty chairs sat across from them while Seth leaned against the wall to her left, his bulk filling the small space and sending her nerves into overdrive. Every time he shifted, she noticed. To be honest, every time he breathed, her heartbeat increased with anticipation he would speak to her.

She should feel safer with her decision to friend-zone him, but she didn't. She missed his light touch on the small of her back when he guided her through a restaurant or store. She enjoyed feeling like a princess every time he hurried to open her car door or pull out her chair. The baby somersaulted, reminding her of the joy on his face when he'd felt the baby move, his hand warm underneath hers on her stomach. Their one, amazing kiss...

"Ms. Ainsley?"

Jetta blinked at Detective Harwell's question. "Sorry, lost in thought." She avoided meeting her mother's eyes but caught the slight smirk on her face. Great, Mom probably guessed she'd been thinking of Seth and would use it in her campaign to get them together. Not going to work. She had her little one to think of and couldn't afford to take any chances by picking the wrong man. Again.

"Mr. Whitman, would you please play the recording?"

Seth leaned in between Jetta and her mother and set his phone on the table in front of the detective, then hit the play button. The conversation Jetta had already heard filled the room as she breathed in the subtle scent of citrus and soap. Her shoulders relaxed, and even the baby seemed to settle his—or her—antics at the smell of Seth. She seriously needed to get a grip and concentrate on the interview with her mother.

She tuned back into the conversation to hear the detective ask her mother if she was sure the person who interrogated her was Gene Topher.

"Yes, I'm sure." Emily shot Harwell a look Jetta long recalled from her own childhood. Mom was getting exasperated with the repeated questions.

"You said you were in pain. Could that have clouded your—"

"Hearing? No." Her mother hugged her body. "I'm not some elderly woman who can't remember her name. I have an excellent memory, and you can ask me six ways to Sunday if I'm sure the man who came into the room where I was being held captive was Gene Topher, and the answer will stay the same. Yes."

Behind her, Jetta could have sworn she heard a muffled snort from Seth, but she didn't turn around to confirm. Instead, she focused on the implications of what her mother said. She leaned toward the detective. "Have you had a chance to look into my father's case?"

"I reviewed the notes from the arresting officers as well as the internal investigation into his heart attack while in custody, although his death occurred in your home," Harwell said. "I also chatted with one of my colleagues in the white-collar crimes unit about the case. After Mr. Ainsley died, Topher Robotics declined to assist us with our investigation, and that essentially closed the case."

Jetta frowned. "They didn't want to find out where the other millions of dollars went? Because I thought they only found a couple of million in one offshore account in Dad's name."

"My colleague, who joined the department only a few years ago, said the case notes indicated hostility on the part of Topher Robotics when they requested access to the company's financial records to trace the missing money. Without an active suspect and Topher Robotics insisting we stop looking into it, there was nothing else we could do."

"But Gene didn't ask me about the missing money," her mother said. "He asked me what I knew about something called Vie."

"Suggesting what, exactly?" Jetta massaged her forehead to stave off the beginnings of a headache.

"There are rumors the company is developing new wearable AI technology." Seth moved to Jetta's left as if to join the interview. "It's supposed to be lightyears ahead of the competition."

"So worth millions." Emily summed up what had coalesced in Jetta's mind. "Which Topher needs because someone has continued to siphon off money for years."

"Mom, we don't know that for sure." Jetta had dismissed Mom's earlier assertion that the original embezzler hadn't stopped stealing money.

"They got away with it once and blamed my husband. Of course they would have stopped when things were hot, as they say, but when the police investigation fizzled, then of course, they would start up again. They feel entitled to that money, they feel they've earned that money, and they might be more clever about it, but mark my words. They are still taking what's not theirs."

TWENTY-SEVEN

Mae added a small pitcher of real cream to the coffee service on the large silver tray. At board meetings, Ryan always insisted she serve the coffee as if she were some maid in a British mansion. This one should be rather contentious, with the question that reporter had lobbed at the siblings earlier that day. A smirk threatened to break out across her face at the memory of the shock on Ryan's face and the flashes of guilt on Yasmine and Gene's. But she couldn't afford to be seen as anything but the loyal assistant, so she tamped down her inner joy at the turmoil. She checked that the tray had two steaming pots of coffee, sugar and other artificial sweeteners, and cream, then lifted it and marched to the large, opulent conference room.

But the door wasn't left ajar as it usually was for her to easily push it open and bring in the coffee. Mae glanced around, but no one lingered in the corridor. With no readily available surface on which to lay the tray so she could twist the door handle, she was stuck. Ryan hadn't told her not to bring the usual coffee, but the firmly shut door suggested otherwise.

With a huff, she set the tray on the carpet, opened the door a fraction, then hefted the tray. She wobbled a bit with the heavy lift but held the tray steady. Now she could push her way inside like usual.

She did so and discovered an empty room. A look at the large antique sundial remade into a clock on the wall indicated the meeting should have started fifteen minutes ago, and Ryan always wanted coffee served during the recap of old business so she could take notes during the new business portion.

She moved to the side table and set down the tray. The board members had arrived, and they had entered this room—their folders still rested on the table—but where had they gone? Mae checked her phone but no texts from Ryan indicating a change in plans.

Then it hit her. They had gone to see Vie in action, Ryan's attempt to stave off a hostile takeover. Of course, she wasn't supposed to know about that, so she'd wait here and hope she wouldn't have to reheat the coffee.

Twenty minutes later, voices drifted down the hall to the conference room. Mae stood to check the insulated pots by removing the lids. Wisps of steam rose from each pot, indicating the liquid was still hot enough. She pasted a welcoming smile on her face as the first board members came into the room.

"Good morning. Would you like coffee?" As they settled into their chairs, she greeted them and poured decaf and regular coffee using cups and saucers already on the credenza. Ryan, Yasmine, and Gene entered last, and all but Yasmine declined coffee. Her hostess duties done, Mae retrieved a steno pad and pencil from a stash in one of the credenza drawers and slipped into her usual corner chair.

Ryan opened the meeting with old business, which took only a few minutes to review, then launched into the new business. "As you know, Maxwell Technology is launching another bid for a hostile takeover of Topher Robotics."

"Will you show the shareholders the video of this morning's demonstration before the vote?" Chester Cane called out. "That would spike their move."

"Or it could make them even more determined to carve up this company," Brooke Williams replied.

"Would that be such a bad thing?" Phillip Lane interjected. "I, for one, am getting tired of promises of great things to come that never materialize. Your father was a visionary, but even he overpromised and under-delivered. I think it's time to let go."

Ryan slammed his fist down on the table. "I will not allow the company my father built from nothing be destroyed in this manner."

Mae's pencil made barely a sound as she recorded the discordant conversation.

"We're hemorrhaging money, and now I think we can see where it's all been going," Greyson Reed said. "The accounts are a mess. This never would have happened under Jay Ainsley."

"Need I remind you that Jay stole millions from us?" Ryan stood, his hands on his hips as he glared at each member.

His posture reminded Mae of a warrior trying to rally his troops, only Ryan lacked the gravitas to succeed.

"Did he?" Elwin Carl, one of two original board members, lobbed the question into the sudden quiet. "Seems to me that was never proven."

Gene jumped in for the first time. "We found an offshore account in his name with a couple million dollars in it. How is that not a smoking gun of his guilt?"

"But according to our internal audit conducted after his death, more than twenty-two million dollars had gone missing." Elwin let that sink in, then asked, "Where was the rest of it?"

"He must have hidden it somewhere—he was an accountant. Obviously he knew how to move and hide money," Ryan snapped.

Mae recorded the conversation as the debate continued for several minutes, then Yasmine set down her coffee cup with a loud clink.

"This is all very productive, but we need to vote on what the board will recommend to the shareholders during tonight's emergency meeting." She smiled her innocent, I'm-just-a-girl-so-what-do-I-know smile. "My father looked at the evidence and decided Jay was indeed guilty of taking the money, and rather than subject our employees to the fuss of an internal audit to discover the how and where of the deed, put it behind us so we could concentrate on doing what we do best—developing new ways robotics can assist in making people's lives better."

Not surprising to Mae, Yasmine's words derailed the embezzlement talk and refocused the group on the vote. Soon members were registering their *yays* and *nays* related to Maxwell Technology's proposed takeover bid.

"Mae, what's the official tally?" Ryan's request was a formality, as everyone had been keeping track.

She cleared her throat and stood, as she always had when delivering the results of a board vote. "Of the fourteen members present at this board meeting, eight voted against the bid and six voted in favor. Therefore the board will recommend shareholders not accept Maxwell Technology's offer."

Ryan allowed himself a small smile, but Mae wasn't sure he could claim victory yet, if the expression on Gene's face was any indication. The middle sibling pursed his lips as if sucking on a lemon, but the determined look in his eyes told of more trouble to come.

"This concludes our meeting for today. See everyone tonight." Ryan shook hands with several of the other members who voted against the takeover.

Chatter filled the room as Mae put down her steno pad and began gathering cups and saucers. Some members left immediately, as did Yasmine and Gene. Ten minutes later, she returned to her desk to catch up on emails. Her desk phone rang.

"Ryan Topher's office."

"May I speak with Mae Stanhope, please?"

The unfamiliar feminine voice had a pleasant, conversational undertone.

"Speaking?"

"Ms. Stanhope, my name is Agent Leslie Updike with FinCEN. Are you familiar with our agency?"

Mae gripped the receiver tighter as her palms began to sweat. She tried to think why someone from the financial crimes agency would be calling her but decided it was probably related to the takeover bid. "Yes, of course. How can I help you, Agent Updike?" Good, her voice sounded steady and friendly.

"Would you be able to come to our office in Vienna for a chat?"

"What's this about?" Mae wanted to come across as confused but her tone held a strident note.

"I'd rather not say on the phone. We'll expect you in an hour. Here's the address." The agent rattled off the address, which Mae dutifully wrote down, then repeated out loud at the agent's request.

"Oh, and Ms. Stanhope, please don't mention this meeting to anyone." The agent said goodbye before Mae could agree.

She replaced the receiver, then glanced at the computer clock. 12:40. Since Ryan took lunch at noon, she usually went at one, but today, he had been holed up in his office since returning from the board meeting. She composed an email saying she had an appointment, then left. Walking to her car, she tried in vain to stay calm, but the feeling of birds coming home to roost wouldn't leave her. Her day of reckoning had arrived but at least she had a rather large bargaining chip to trade.

SETH MUNCHED ON A CHICKEN SANDWICH, WISHING HE WERE EATING WITH Jetta and not alone in his car. After helping Emily into Jetta's vehicle, he'd said goodbye and watched them drive away. Each time he parted from Jetta was hard, as he couldn't help but think it might have been the last time he would be with her. He bowed his head, allowing a wordless prayer to flow from him to God, the only thing he could do in the circumstance. Respecting Jetta's boundaries meant not pushing for his own agenda, which translated in waiting. His phone buzzed, drawing his attention outward.

"Hello?"

"Seth?" The female voice sounded slightly familiar to him, but he couldn't immediately place it.

"Speaking." He rewrapped the remainder of his sandwich, his appetite waning as it did whenever he pictured a future without Jetta.

"It's Leslie Updike. I have an update on the case you asked about."

"You do?"

"Mr. Warner sent over documents that showed someone at Topher Robotics had been stealing money for years—and it wasn't Jay Ainsley."

"Wait, he had documents?" Seth thought Warner had been upfront when he and Jetta had visited about what papers he had in his possession, but the man hadn't mentioned additional documents beyond the invoices.

"Copies, not originals. But enough to show someone else was responsible for some of the embezzlement."

Although reeling from this knowledge, Seth latched onto the modifier Leslie had used. "Some, but not all?"

"That's correct. This person appears to have stolen roughly a quarter of a million dollars from the papers Mr. Warner sent."

"Is this person still an employee at Topher Robotics?"

"That's all I can give you at this time." She sighed. "To be frank, I almost pushed this to the back burner, but my boss reminded me that Topher Robotics is in a fight to fend off a takeover bid from Maxwell Technology, so this became top priority."

"Will you keep searching for what happened to the rest of the money? There's still millions of dollars unaccounted for if this person only took $250,000."

"This is the beginning of what will likely be a long process."

"I appreciate the heads up." He decided to share about the

invoices. "Leslie, Mr. Warner did pass along invoices he thought might be dodgy for Jetta and I to investigate. We did and found almost all of them were legit except for one from SafeSense. The person I talked to claimed Topher Robotics brought the faulty invoices to their attention and that they'd fired the person responsible, a long-time employee named Dolores Green."

"Mr. Warner's email said something about that, but since we had clear evidence in what he did pass along, we haven't investigated the invoices yet. Anything else you found out?"

"We went to see Ms. Green, and she vehemently denied altering any invoices, claimed her finances were an open book."

"Dolores Green," Leslie said. "I'll put her on my list of people to talk to."

Seth hesitated, his mind flashing back to the shots fired, his fear for Jetta and her unborn baby driving him to throw himself over her body as he brought them to the ground. He suppressed a shudder, then decided to tell Leslie. "We visited her, and someone took potshots at us as we left."

"What?"

Leslie's shock echoed in her voice as he sketched out the details, then found the detective's info to pass along to her.

"Thanks. I'll give him a call and see how this might be connected with the embezzlement case."

"You're officially reopening it?" He hoped so, for Jetta and Emily's sake. No one had been officially interested in the truth in a very long time.

"It's unofficially official. We're in the gathering data stage right now. Is there anything else I need to know?"

"This isn't for public knowledge, but Emily Ainsley was kidnapped." As Leslie gasped, he hastened to add, "She's okay, and I don't know where the investigation stands, but she did identify Gene Topher as the masked man who visited her where she was being held." He didn't share the topic of their conversation, since it wasn't something FinCEN would have jurisdiction over. However, he did feel Leslie needed to know one piece of pertinent info. "I can't comment on the gist of their conversation, but Emily was warned to back off the embezzlement investigation."

"I'm glad she's all right. This is getting weirder and weirder."

"I agree." He could hardly wrap his mind around the news someone other than Jetta's father had been involved the embezzlement, or at least part of the stolen money. Like Leslie said, this was only the tip of the iceberg. Who knew what FinCEN's investigation would uncover? "Will you let me know when it is official?"

"Sure. In the meantime, be careful. It sounds like someone isn't too happy with how you're stirring the pot."

He thanked her for the call and disconnected, tapping his fingers on the steering wheel. He would compose a text to Jetta recapping the conversation, then check in at work. With any luck, he would have a light afternoon and could squeeze in a visit to Mr. Warner, who had a lot of explaining to do.

CHAPTER

TWENTY-EIGHT

Jetta stepped back into her mother's room to say goodbye. She'd given her mother privacy to get checked over by the resident doctor after her brief hospital stay. The entire staff, from the front desk to the nursing staff to the cleaners to the security officers, had gone above and beyond to make Mom feel welcome. As they should, since Mom had been snatched right from under their noses.

She rubbed the small of her back as another spasm of Braxton Hicks contractions shuddered through her body. She needed to sit with her feet up, but that would have to wait until she'd walked Bingley and checked her email for a contract from Become Clutter Free, a company specializing in downsizing family homes, to help with Mom's house. At least that was one decision she could make without tying herself into knots.

"Jetta, you look about done in." Her mother smiled at the aide who'd helped her into bed. "I know I am."

Jetta sank into the chair as the aide left. "I'm always tired."

"I remember feeling that way too." Mom studied her, the compassion in her eyes soothing Jetta's fraying nerves. "I also recall how out of sorts I could be. Your poor father never knew what might set me off. Some days, he could do nothing right in my eyes."

"Hmm." No way was Jetta answering that. Her mother didn't need any more ammunition in her quest to bring her and Seth together.

"I forgot to ask Seth at the hospital, so maybe you know the answer."

Jetta braced for yet another well-meaning push toward matrimony from her mother.

"Are you going to the shareholders emergency meeting tonight?"

The question made no sense to Jetta. "Shareholders meeting?"

"At Topher Robotics. Seven p.m."

"Why would I attend that?" She didn't want to point out the obvious—that only shareholders could attend, of which she wasn't one.

"Because you're a shareholder." Mom's serene expression was in stark contrast to Jetta's open-mouthed reaction.

She snapped her jaw shut, and closed her eyes, counting to ten to avoid yelling as confusion muddied the waters of her brain. Maybe she was experiencing some alternative reality in which she owned stock in Topher Robotics, something her mother had never mentioned before. "What are you talking about?"

Her words came out snappier than she'd intended, but Jetta was too cross to care at the moment.

"I didn't realize this until recently myself, but your father owned shares of Topher Robotics as part of his compensation package. A few months before he died, he transferred ownership of those shares to you."

"I was ten years old. How is that even legal?"

"It is if you have a custodial account, which you did with me as the custodian until you turned eighteen." Her mother sighed. "I think Dad knew he was going to be accused of embezzlement, and he wanted to protect us if they came after him for repayment. Moving the stock out of his name to yours did that."

Jetta studied Mom. "Why didn't you say anything earlier? I've been over the age of eighteen for seven years now."

"I only found out when I was cleaning out some papers in the office before my accident. For too long, I couldn't bring myself to go through Dad's things. It took me years to give away his clothing."

That made sense. Her mother had been both sad and mad for so long after Dad died. Jetta hadn't understood the anger, but now that she knew the full picture, she did. "But surely you got notices about shareholder meetings, etc."

"I didn't because your father had opened a PO box and used that as the address for the notices. I found that too, but of course, since he'd only paid for a year, that had closed, and the notices were likely returned. He'd used his work address as the alternate one for the PO box, according to the paperwork I found."

Another question occurred to Jetta. "How do you know I still own the stock, since it's been so long and the notices were returned?"

"I called the shareholder number and confirmed it. I also updated the address, but it's still addressed to me because we both have to be present to remove me as the custodian on the account." Mom pushed herself up in the raised bed to a more seated position. "I think you should attend. Seth can't because he's not a shareholder, but I think he should drive you and wait outside in case you need assistance."

Jetta narrowed her eyes. "This isn't another of your ploys to throw us together romantically, is it?"

"No, dear. This is a suggestion to get insider information and perhaps more answers to what happened to your father." Her mother patted her hand as if placating a child.

She resisted the urge to squirm and ignored the voice whispering that her mother had guessed Jetta wasn't as opposed to that idea as she let on. She could not view Seth in that way because he was too honorable a man to be trapped with a woman with her baggage and a child not his own.

"Seth is a big, strong man capable of keeping you safe."

Her mother's words reminded Jetta how secure being in Seth's arms had made her feel, how she loved his protectiveness towards her and the baby. Besides, Jetta shouldn't beard the lion's den solo. Time to admit her mother had a point. "Okay, I'll text him."

"Good. After everything that's happened, I don't want to worry about you."

Her mother did have a few new worry lines around her mouth and forehead, so perhaps that wasn't far from the truth. Jetta sent a text to Seth outlining Mom's idea, then stood. "I need to rest if I'm to stay awake during the meeting."

"You'll update me as soon as you can?"

"Of course." She kissed Mom's cheek, then left. Her heart skipped a beat as she made plans via text to meet up with Seth ahead of the meeting. Even her baby appeared to somersault with glee at the thought of spending more time with their handsome neighbor. No matter how sternly Jetta talked to herself on the drive home, she couldn't shake the fissure of anticipation at seeing Seth again.

MAE STANHOPE ADJUSTED HER SKIRT AND CROSSED HER ANKLES AS SHE waited for Agent Leslie Updike to join her in the small room. The vase of fresh flowers, light blue walls, and comfortable chairs around a round table wasn't at all what she expected. No stark interrogation room with a bright light and bolted down furniture. She could have been in someone's study.

The door opened, and a woman wearing slacks, a button-down pale-blue shirt, and a jaunty silk scarf as a headband entered, carrying an armful of folders. "Sorry to keep you waiting. I'm Agent Leslie Updike with FinCEN."

Mae shook the woman's outstretched hand.

"May I get you anything? Water? Coffee?" The agent smiled as she set her folders down.

"No, thank you." Mae's nervousness returned with the agent's entrance. She told herself not to worry, there was nothing to find. She'd been so very careful, and when that nice man, Jay Ainsley, dropped dead of a heart attack, the case had died with him.

"If you change your mind, let me know." Agent Updike placed the top folder in front of her, then clasped her hands on top of it. "I appreciate your coming here late on a Friday afternoon to help with our inquiries."

That gave Mae the opening she'd been waiting for. "I have no idea exactly how I can help you and with what inquiries. You were very cryptic on the phone."

"I apologize for that. I'm sure you understand the nature of our investigations must be kept close to the vest, as they say." Agent Updike opened the folder. "But I'm sure you can clear up a few points."

Mae wrinkled her brow. "Do I need a lawyer?"

"That is your right, of course, but you're not under arrest nor have I read you your rights. Right now, it's just a chat. But a lawyer will give this entire thing more gravity than it deserves." She shrugged.

Mae bit her lip. The woman seemed friendly and open, but she hadn't gotten away with millions by being foolish. "Okay, I guess."

"Great. If at any time during our conversation you want an attorney, say the word."

Agent Updike confirmed with Mae her full name, address, date of birth, and years at Topher Robotics. "What position did you start at with the company?"

"As an admin for the accounting department." Mae answered more questions about her rise through the ranks to her current job as executive assistant to the president. The questions put her at ease.

"So it would be fair to say you have acquired an excellent understanding of the inner workings of Topher Robotics." The agent met Mae's gaze.

"I would say that's true." Mae straightened in her chair at the implied praise.

"You worked for Jay Ainsley."

"Not directly. I was one of three general admins in accounting."

"What did you think of him?"

Mae considered her answer before replying. She didn't like questions about Jay but couldn't object without the agent wondering why. "As I said, I didn't really know him."

"But surely you must have formed an opinion of the man. He was head of a department where you worked"—she consulted a piece of paper in the folder—"for seven years."

"He didn't interact much with administrative assistants."

Agent Updike raised an eyebrow. "No? By all accounts, including your fellow admin, Mr. Ainsley was very personable. One said, 'He always inquired about my family, even remembering the names of my two dogs.'"

Mae shifted in her seat. Jay had been all of those things and more, but she didn't want to talk about him. "Maybe we chatted a few times."

"Did you like him?"

"Of course." That was something Mae could answer truthfully.

"Then why did you blame him for your embezzlement?"

The question, even though Mae told herself to expect it, hit her between the eyes. Mae worked her mouth, but no sound came out. Heat poured through her body, flushing her cheeks.

"Here." Agent Updike placed a cold water bottle in Mae's hands.

Mae uncapped it and drank, grateful for the cool water. She could recover from this. "Sorry about that. Got a little flustered, as happens when you hit a certain age." She herself was well past menopause and the accompanying hot flashes, but the agent couldn't know that for sure.

"I can see why you would be, considering you redirected $250,000 of company funds for your own purposes." She selected a page from the folder. "Once we knew where to look, we found out how you used that money to pay for your father's nursing home care."

Mae firmed her lips, not saying anything as the agent removed sheet after sheet detailing exactly how Mae had accomplished the embezzlement. Even though she couldn't clearly see the documents, she recognized the logo she'd created for the fake invoices. No doubt they could prove what the agent said they could.

When Agent Updike stopped laying out the evidence, Mae drew in a deep breath to shore up her inner strength and prepared to lay the groundwork to using her bargaining chip. "You've done your homework."

"We have. Why did you blame Jay Ainsley for your crimes?"

"Because someone told me to." She thought she detected a slight widening of the agent's eyes at her statement, but she wasn't sure. Before she asked for a lawyer, she wanted to see how much they knew. "Someone found out what I was doing and demanded I take even more money from the company. At first, we didn't attempt to frame anyone, but about six months before Mr. Ainsley died, this person told me to lay a trail blaming him for the embezzlement. All of it, including what I'd taken." She paused. "I was paying it back, bit by bit. I planned on replacing all the money I'd taken."

"I see that you had begun doing that but then you stopped because this person told you to continue the embezzlement?"

"That's correct." Mae took another sip of water and waited for the question that would reduce her culpability.

"What's this person's name?"

"For that, I'll need a lawyer—and a deal." Mae smiled, expecting the agent to gather her papers and leave the room to consult with someone who could authorize such a deal.

But she didn't. Instead, Agent Updike clasped her hands together on top of the now-closed folder. "Before you do that, keep in mind that the charges against you will extend beyond embezzlement."

Her words sent a fissure of unease down Mae's spine. "But I only took money."

The agent's grim countenance alarmed her. "You might think your crime hurt no one outside of Topher Robotics, but someone has been targeting Jay Ainsley's widow and daughter, even kidnapping Mrs. Ainsley. You've admitted to stealing money for this person. Who's to say you didn't assist in other ways too?"

"I had nothing to do with anything like that." Mae couldn't believe they would try to pin any other crime on her. She didn't hurt anyone. She would never physically hurt anyone.

"That may be true, but until we know the name of the person you claim pushed you to steal millions, yours is the name we will pass along to the local authorities investigating those crimes." Now the agent rose and carried the folders to the door.

"Wait!" Mae could see no way out. Deal or no deal, she would speak now or be lost to her husband forever. He would forgive her for the money, but never for anything else. "I want a lawyer, then I'll tell you what I know."

TWENTY-NINE

Seth leaned against the wall across from the auditorium to watch the shareholders of Topher Robotics enter for the emergency meeting. He reminded himself for the umpteenth time to not make this more than it was—a request by Jetta's mom to keep an eye on her daughter. Jetta acquiesced because she didn't want to upset her mother. While Jetta hadn't told him that in so many words, he had read between the lines of her texts to decipher the real reason for her request.

Jetta had promised to keep him updated via text on the proceedings behind the soon-to-be closed doors. Meanwhile, he observed those entering and prayed for Jetta's safety and the resolution of the case. Even though what they didn't know seemed huge, other pieces had begun to fall into place. Emily's revelation that Gene was behind her abduction had raised even more questions, and Seth had done further digging into the middle Topher sibling's life.

From company photographs, he surmised Gene usually took a back seat to his more outgoing brother and sister because Gene was never in the action but always on the fringes of those photos. The police indicated they would be investigating Emily's assertion of

Gene's involvement in her kidnapping, but Seth itched to confront the man himself.

His phone buzzed.

> Still waiting on the Tophers. Mood is uneasy. Scuttlebutt is board decision wasn't unanimous.

> Thx. Stay safe.

A group of people approached, and Seth recognized the Topher siblings. He stepped behind a leafy tree in a huge pot to avoid being seen. He didn't want questions as to why he was lurking in the hallway outside a closed-door shareholders meeting.

> Tophers arriving now.

After the doors closed behind the Tophers and their entourage, Seth glanced around the now-empty corridor. Maybe he could slip inside the room without anyone noticing, as he didn't want to miss the action. But every door he tried was locked, even the side doors. So much for that bright idea.

He returned to his corner behind the large plant and sat cross-legged on the carpet, then maneuvered the pot a little to shield his hiding place. He didn't want anyone disturbing him or asking him to leave the hallway. His phone buzzed in silent mode.

> Meeting underway. Board voted against the merger.

> Any idea how close was the vote?

> Someone behind me said it was very close.

A divided board meant Ryan Topher didn't have as much control over the company as he projected during their morning interview and photo session. The trio of dots indicated Jetta was adding more.

> A shareholder stood to ask who controls Peter Topher's shares, since he's in the hospital. Apparently, Ryan doesn't.

Who does?

> Yasmine.

Seth sent a shocked face emoji at that response.

How did that go over?

> There's a lot of shouting. Wait, Ryan's managed to calm everyone down. They're calling for a vote.

Seth waited, but Jetta stayed silent for about fifteen minutes, presumably while they voted.

> We have a break while they tally the votes. I'm heading to the bathroom.

People exited, and he craned his neck to see Jetta, spotting her hustling to the restrooms to the left of where he sat, still hidden by the green plant. Other people milled about on their phones. Yasmine Topher strode out and headed toward him, pausing on the other side of the plant in the small alcove.

Another text buzzed in, this time from Leslie, his FinCEN contact.

> Just a heads-up we have confirmation about Gene's involvement in Emily Ainsley's kidnapping. We've passed that along to the local police.

> Good. Anything new about who was behind the embezzlement?

A little progress. Still sorting through everything.

> Appreciate you letting me know.

Leslie sent him a thumbs-up emoji. Seth quickly updated Jetta with Leslie's info. Then the hairs on the back of his neck prickled, but before he could look over his shoulder, something hard and round pressed in between his shoulder blades.

"Hand me your phone, and no funny business. This is a gun against your back." The conversational tone to the man's voice chilled Seth more than the weapon's proximity to his heart.

He held up his phone. A gloved hand took it.

"Here's what's going to happen. When everyone returns to the auditorium, you're going to slowly get to your feet. Then we'll take a walk together."

Seth noticed people streaming back through the double doors. The results must be in, much faster than he'd anticipated.

To his right, Yasmine stepped out of the alcove and paused, her head down over her phone but her back now to the auditorium. "I'll get the girl."

Then she left, leaving Seth stunned—and fearing for Jetta's life. *Dear God, please keep her safe!* The prayer looped over and over as people left the area to return to the meeting.

When the doors closed, the man prodded him with the gun. "Let's go. Nice and slow, big guy."

Seth rose to his feet, his mind racing with the revelation of Yasmine's involvement. Was she the secret embezzler? He had read something about embezzling being a pink crime, one mostly perpetrated by women, but nothing seemed to point to the youngest Topher's guilt, probably because she'd cleverly directed it to Jay Ainsley instead.

"Walk to the left toward the far exit." The man moved slightly behind him on his left, the gun now against his side.

Seth noted which door and moved through the now-empty corridor. He tried to remember from their brief tour if the company had security cameras, but even if they did, he doubted footage of his abduction would be made available to the authorities. They made it outside without seeing anyone, further lowering his chances of being found. A black SUV with tinted windows and Maryland plates pulled up to the curb.

"In the back."

Seth opened the door and slid inside. The man stood in the open doorway, his gun trained on Seth while the male driver twisted in his seat.

"Hold out your wrists."

Seth did as the driver instructed. He kept his face blank as the man zip-tied his wrists together. Tight. Once secured, the driver turned back to face the windshield. Seth didn't see the blow coming from the side in time to move. The crack of a gun butt against his temple sent him sideways and into darkness. His last conscious thought was another half-formed prayer for Jetta's safety.

THE ROOM BUZZED WITH ANTICIPATION AS THOSE WHO HAD LEFT DURING THE break returned to their seats. Jetta shifted in the padded theater-style chair, trying to get comfortable. The baby kicked his displeasure at her movement—or maybe he too was tired of all this sitting. She decided standing in the back would be preferable to feeling like a whale stuffed into a sardine can. She offered excuses as she made her way from the middle of the row to the aisle. Once against the back wall, she sent another text to Seth.

Vote results are in.

No response. She frowned but maybe he was on another call. Ryan stood at the podium and brought the meeting back to order. He called on one of the board members to read the results of the vote.

"The vote on whether to accept Maxwell Technology's takeover bid carries, with a margin of 432 to 412."

The room erupted in cheers and boos. Jetta texted Seth the results. Nothing from him. She slipped through one of the doors and into the corridor. Detective Harwell, along with several uniformed police officers, approached her.

"Ms. Ainsley, I didn't realize you would be here." Detective Harwell paused before her.

"I didn't either, but apparently my father passed along his shares of the company to me in the months before his death." She craned her neck around the man to see if Seth was in his spot by the potted tree. Then the significance of the police presence registered. "Are you here to arrest Gene Topher for kidnapping my mom?"

"We will be in touch once we have more information." The detective's noncommittal answer seemed to indicate she'd guessed right.

"Ms. Ainsley?"

As the police contingent headed into the auditorium, Jetta turned to see a young woman dressed in a business suit. "Yes?"

"Mr. Whitman asked me to give this to you." She handed Jetta a piece of paper, then walked away.

Jetta unfolded the paper.

Jetta,

I know who's behind the embezzlement. Meet me outside through the doors to your left.

Seth

She frowned. Why write her a note when he could text her? She sent him a series of question marks as a text, then waited but received no reply. She didn't like this, not at all. Every instinct screamed this was a setup. She hesitated, her desire to know the truth about the embezzlement warring with her caution. Spinning on her heel, she'd taken three steps toward the designated door when she halted. Everything she knew about Seth told her he wouldn't ignore her texts unless he was unable to answer. She tried calling his phone. It rang several times before rolling to voicemail. She disconnected without leaving a message.

Tapping her phone against her leg, she pivoted until she spotted the potted tree. She would check over there first, then decide whether to comply with the note's instruction. Once at the tree, she studied the carpet around it. Nothing. Using the wall for leverage, she crouched to peer into the pot. Dead leaves littered the soil. Someone really needed to take better care of the live plants.

Jetta plunged her hand into the leaves, feeling her way around the trunk. She brushed against a hard object with her fingers. After tugging it out, she stared at the phone covered in dirt. Sinking onto her knees, she blew the debris away and flipped the phone over to access the card holder. As she'd expected, the credit card she pulled out had the name Seth Whitman on the front.

Someone had taken Seth.

She struggled to her feet and stumbled against the wall.

"Are you okay?"

Jetta met the worried gaze of an older man, his graying hair and glasses giving him a fatherly appearance. "A little off balance, that's all." Then she added, "I need to find someone in the auditorium, but still feel a bit unsteady. Would you mind walking with me there?"

"Happy to help." He held out his elbow in a courtly gesture, and she gratefully took his arm. Together, they made their way back to the auditorium.

Once inside, she scanned the room and spotted the police near the front. "I need to speak with one of the officers."

The man nodded and walked her to the small cluster of uniformed officers standing a little behind the detective, who stood talking with the Topher siblings.

Jetta didn't bother trying to get Harwell's attention but instead thanked her escort before tapping the arm of the closest officer. "Hi. I'm Jetta Ainsley."

"Emily Ainsley's daughter, right?" The young Hispanic officer whose nameplate read P. Rodriguez shifted his focus to her. "How can I help you?"

"I think Seth Whitman's been kidnapped." Jetta explained about the note and finding Seth's phone in the potted tree. He listened intently.

"Give me a minute." Officer Rodriguez stepped over to the detective and whispered in his ear. Detective Harwell looked at Jetta, then at the three Topher siblings. He said something to the officer, who returned to Jetta.

"If you'll come with me, please?" The officer took her elbow in his hand.

Jetta walked with Officer Rodriguez out of the auditorium, but the cop didn't stop there. He continued to the outside door, his fingers biting into her arm.

"Hey, you're hurting me." She tugged, but he only gripped her tighter.

He shoved her through the door and into the darkness. Too late, Jetta realized this was the direction the note told her to go. At the curb, a black SUV idled.

She spun, her movement breaking Officer Rodriguez's hold, and dashed for the door, but the cop caught her in two strides. "Let's not do anything foolish, Ms. Ainsley." His punishing grip on her upper arm made her swallow a cry of pain as he forced her toward the waiting vehicle.

Jetta opened her mouth, intending to yell for help, but Rodriguez hissed in her ear, "If you scream, your boyfriend will die."

She shut her mouth as another cramp hit her midsection, making her stumble. Rodriguez heaved her upright, cursing as he bore more of her weight. She shot a prayer heavenward for her safety and for Seth's—and that whoever was behind this would be caught.

The cop yanked open the back door and manhandled her into the vehicle and onto someone lying across the seat. The door slammed shut and the car sped away before she could get her bearings, sending her sprawling across the other person.

She somehow managed to push to a seated position. The light from passing street lamps illuminated her backseat companion's still form. It was a man with muscular arms and torso. She touched the side of his head, and her fingers came away sticky. The man groaned, relief pouring over her Seth wasn't dead.

THIRTY

Ryan pinched the bridge of his nose in a vain attempt to ward off the ache building in his head. He couldn't believe he'd lost control of the company his father had built from scratch, especially with Vie mere months away from being operational. Even his telling the shareholders about the wearable AI device's release date hadn't swayed the more vocal ones adamant to get their big payout with Maxwell Technology's takeover.

"Mr. Topher?" A young woman, whose name he'd forgotten, stood in front of him. "Will you be needing anything else from me tonight?"

"No, you can type up your notes and email them to Mae and myself in the morning." No point in making the employee work longer than necessary. He would definitely not be putting in the overtime he had been. Mae's cryptic text apologizing for not making the meeting because of an emergency bothered him. She had been his executive assistant since he'd ascended to the presidency, and her absence at such a crucial meeting was out of character.

He moved from the wings, where he'd disappeared for a few private moments after the results had been certified, and down the stage steps. Then he clocked the uniform police officers close to his siblings. This didn't look good. He hustled over. "What's going on?"

Yasmine, her eyes bright with unshed tears, nodded to Gene. "They're saying he was behind the kidnapping of Emily Ainsley."

"That's absurd." He turned to his brother. "I'd heard she was making a fuss again about her husband's embezzlement, but to accuse you of kidnapping her is bizarre. Perhaps she's developed a mental disorder and is going to accuse me of something heinous next."

"As I was informing Mr. Topher, we have enough evidence to arrest him for the crime." A tall detective nodded to one of the uniformed officers, who stepped forward and took Gene's arm.

"I'm arresting you for the kidnapping of Emily Ainsley." He pulled out a set of handcuffs and snapped them around Gene's wrists.

As the officer recited the Miranda rights to Gene, Ryan said, "Don't say a word. I'm calling our lawyer. He'll meet you at the station."

Gene nodded, his gaze sliding away from Ryan's as the officer took his elbow in a loose grip.

After confirming which station Gene would be taken to, Ryan called the firm's attorney to arrange for representation. Something about Gene's expression troubled him. The detective followed the officers out of the room, leaving Ryan and Yasmine alone with a handful of other shareholders, who had been gawking at the scene.

Ryan touched his sister's shoulder. "Let's get out of here." She nodded, and they left, heading to Ryan's office for a private chat. "How could there be evidence of kidnapping?"

She sank onto the loveseat while he took one of the club chairs flanking the couch. "I have no idea."

He leaned back in the chair to regard his youngest sibling as the prickle of unease that had arrived when the reporter had asked Gene and Yasmine why they were conspiring with Maxwell Technology for the takeover grew into flock of geese. Her guileless gaze reminded him of how easily she'd manipulated their parents during their childhood. She never received the blame for any of her shenanigans and often managed to get him or Gene to take the fall. In a flash, he realized he'd been holding a viper close to his breast all these years, that his sister—who should have put the company first—had been out for herself.

"It was you." He whispered the words, then cleared his throat and spoke louder. "You're the one who embezzled the money, not Jay."

Yasmine laughed. "What are you talking about? Jay Ainsley was arrested for embezzling millions of dollars. You and Dad saw the evidence."

"But we only recovered a fraction of what went missing. Where's the other money?"

"He spent it." Yasmine relaxed against the loveseat. "You haven't seen me spend like a sailor, have you? You're tired. The vote went against you and now you're—"

Ryan tuned out her words, focusing on what he knew about his sister. Her love of pretty things. Her frequent trips to Europe in search of new art for her office and home. The pieces, always carefully within what her balance sheet could afford, displayed with such pride. Then the surety of why and how and what she'd spent the money on overwhelmed him. He sank his head into his hands.

"Ryan?"

The fake concern in his sister's voice angered him. She was the reason Maxwell Technology had been successful. She'd been bleeding the company for years. He had no doubt she didn't stop with Jay's death. "It was never enough for you, was it?"

She widened her eyes. "What are you talking about?"

"The job, the generous salary and benefits, access to the company jet and other perks. You wanted more." No, it was more than that. "You thought you deserved more."

Anger sparked in her eyes as she dropped her I'm-just-a-girl façade. "You bet I do. I should have been CEO, but no, dear old Dad couldn't get past the fact I was female, and didn't I know companies needed strong men to run them? I would have taken Topher Robotics farther than you ever could. Look at your legacy. You've lost the company Dad spent his lifetime building. Good thing he's already had an attack because this will break his heart."

She rose to her feet. "Bye, brother dear. I'm going home to celebrate my windfall with a glass of wine."

He let her leave without trying to stop her. For a long time, Ryan sat in the semi-darkness of his office, thinking about how to right the wrong perpetrated against an honest man and whether he had the guts to turn his own sister over to the authorities. All his life, he had tried to do what he thought would please his exacting father, who trumpeted family fidelity above all else. It was time for him to do what was right for him, not his father and not the company.

"Wake up, Seth."

The soft whisper of his name penetrated the darkness, bringing him back to the light. His head pounded worse than the one—and only—time he'd downed too many beers at a frat party in college. The vibration underneath clued him in that he was in a vehicle. Memories filtered into his brain. The man who'd pulled a gun on him and forced him outside and into an SUV. Stickiness on his cheek and the metallic scent of blood filled in more gaps. The man who'd abducted him must have hit him in the head to knock him out.

As the vehicle turned, his body rolled to the left. He reached out but found his wrists bound together. Someone caught his bicep and kept him from falling off the seat. He hadn't imagined her voice then. He'd been hoping he had dreamed Jetta calling his name, for that meant she was safe. He opened his eyes to darkness, the faint illumination of the vehicle's dashboard the only light. Seth used his shoulder and bound hands to push into an upright position. Nausea swept his body at the movement, and he slammed his eyelids closed again while taking shallow breaths to avoid losing the contents of his stomach. After a few minutes, he cautiously opened his eyes, grateful to find the world had stopped spinning.

"Seth?" Jetta spoke very quietly over the hum of the engine.

"Just a minute." He breathed the words as the SUV slammed to a stop, the driver cursing as a deer bounded across the road.

"No talking." The man in the passenger seat raised his gun as if to emphasize his command.

Fine by Seth. He wasn't sure he could get out any words without throwing up, so staying quiet would be best. The driver gunned the engine, throwing Seth backwards against the seat. He gritted his teeth as pain exploded in his head.

He would not pass out, not when Jetta needed him, but the vehicle's swaying movement made it impossible to keep his eyes open and not vomit. He closed his eyes, willed his stomach to settle down, and prayed. The nausea faded as he poured out his heart to his heavenly Father for their safety and rescue.

Seth wasn't sure how much time had passed when the SUV shuddered to a halt and the driver put it into park but didn't cut the engine. Seth opened his eyes and reached his bound hands toward Jetta, who clasped them in her own. "You okay?"

"I said no talking." The man shoved his gun in Seth's face. "Or do I need to clock you in that big head of yours again?"

Seth shook his head, fighting another wave of nausea. He gritted his teeth and sucked in air, willing his stomach to calm down.

"I didn't think so." The man snorted. "Not such a big guy now, are you?"

You wouldn't be either if someone had hit you on the head and bound your hands. Seth wisely kept that comment to himself. Both men waited without speaking or making a move to exit the vehicle. In the outside darkness, no lights provided any clue as to where they were. The SUV's headlights shone on a gravel road with trees on either side. Someplace rural, which could be in the middle of nowhere or down the street from civilization.

A phone buzzed, and the passenger answered. "Yeah, we're here with the two packages."

He listened, then dropped a string of curses. "You ordered us to grab these two and you're saying you've changed your mind? What are we supposed to do with them now?"

He yanked open the door and climbed out, shutting it with enough force to shake the entire vehicle. Seth leaned into Jetta's shoulder, trying to comfort her as best he could. This didn't sound good at all. More importantly, whoever had ordered them snatched was backpedaling, which meant they had suddenly become a liability instead of an asset.

The man returned to the vehicle, sliding into the seat without closing the door. "She will regret this."

"What's going on?" The driver turned to his companion. "Are we going to get paid?"

"Shut up and let me think!"

"No, you tell me what she said."

"Out of the car." The passenger exited the vehicle again and the driver did as well, leaving the car running and the doors closed. The two men met in front of the hood, their bodies silhouetted in the headlights.

Seth wasn't going to waste this chance to escape. "Can you reach the door lock button on the passenger side?"

Without waiting for Jetta to reply, he looped his hands over the headrest on the driver's side and launched himself onto the middle console. As his knees hit the hard surface, the door locks clicked with a satisfying *snick*.

"Hey!" One of the men had spotted his movement and rounded the hood, but Seth had his legs over the console. The other man headed toward the passenger side of the vehicle. Seth would not let them get their grubby hands on Jetta again.

He didn't pause but maneuvered his body into the driver's seat. Once there, he used his bound hands to put the car into drive. Pressing down on the accelerator, he gripped the steering wheel at the bottom with both hands as the SUV lurched forward.

One of the men banged on a back window. Jetta screamed. Seth gave the vehicle more gas, and it leapt forward.

In the rearview mirror, he spied the passenger raising his weapon, the red of the taillights giving the scene an otherworldly appearance. "Get down!"

The gunshot shattered the hatch window right before the gravel road turned. He nearly lost control of the vehicle as he navigated the tight left, his fingers tingling and his wrists burning. But he managed to keep all four wheels on the gravel.

"Jetta, you all right?"

"Yes."

His heart zinged with relief at her voice and confirmation she was okay. Now to figure out where they were.

"The driver took his phone, but the navigation system is displaying the map with our location."

Excellent. With his limited ability to steer, he couldn't take his eyes off the winding road. "Can you read the map and tell me where we're headed?"

She leaned forward between the front seats. "Not quite sure, as it appears we're on some unnamed road. But it looks like we'll connect with Dry Mill Road soon."

"Okay." His hands ached from the zip ties and strain of managing the wheel. He thought about stopping and having Jetta drive, but fear their kidnappers had called in reinforcements kept him in the driver's seat. "Do you see anything you can use to cut these zip ties?"

"Nothing back here, but I'll check the console." She opened the compartment. "Nothing. Maybe there's something in the glove compartment. Could you stop for a minute so I can switch to the front passenger seat?"

"Let's get to the main road first. I don't want to stop until we're farther away from those guys." He wrestled with the wheel as the SUV hit a pothole.

"Okay." She sat back, and he missed her closeness.

Which was ridiculous. They'd shared one kiss, and while he longed to repeat it, she had pulled even further away of late. That hadn't stopped him from developing a burning need to not only protect her but to cherish her all the days of her life. He glanced at the map, which showed their blue dot only a few feet from the road. Sure enough, as they rounded a slight curve, the headlights showed a paved road up ahead.

He halted the SUV a few feet from the verge. "I think it's safe if you want to get in the front seat."

"Can you unlock the doors?"

He did so and she climbed out. Was she moving slower than usual? He couldn't be sure, but something seemed off. Once she was settled in the passenger seat and he'd relocked the doors, she immediately rummaged in the glove compartment. "I don't think there's anything sharp enough. Wait, here's something." She held up a pair of nail clippers. "This will work. Give me your hands."

He held them out. Before starting, she clicked on the interior light. As she worked on cutting the thick plastic, he studied her. Beads of sweat dotted her flushed face. A slight grimace twisted her lips. He recognized the signs of suppressed pain, having seen his mother ignore her own aches for so many years as a child.

The tight bands encircling his wrists broke with a snap, releasing him and flooding his hands with a tingling sensation as unrestricted blood flowed to his fingers. "Thanks."

She replaced the clippers in the glove compartment, snapping it closed with a gasp.

"You're not okay." He twisted in his seat and reached for her, but she shrank back against the passenger door.

"I'm fine. Please, let's go."

He glimpsed tears shimmering in her eyes before she snapped off the light.

"If you turn right, we'll be heading back toward commerce."

Seth bit his lower lip to keep from pressing her to tell him what was wrong and checked for traffic. His wrists ached and his fingers tingled as he pulled onto the pavement, but it was his heart that hurt the most.

No matter how many times he glanced in her direction as he drove through the darkness, Jetta never turned her head from gazing out the passenger side window. Her arms cradled her belly, her shoulders drooped with fatigue. She shivered from the cold air blowing into the SUV from the broken rear window. He had no jacket to give her to warm her up, and he couldn't stop until they were in a safe place.

Since he couldn't make her accept his help, he did the only thing he could think of—prayed for her and the baby's safety, as well as giving thanks for delivering them from their captors. As they continued toward civilization and safety, underneath his prayer hummed his sadness at her rejection of his assistance. He fought back tears at his inability to reach the woman he loved, but as his mother had taught him years ago with her continual bad choices when it came to men, you could love a woman with your whole heart, but you couldn't save her unless she let you.

CHAPTER

THIRTY-ONE

Emily put down her phone after another fruitless attempt to get in touch with her daughter. Jetta had promised to call as soon as the shareholder meeting broke up, but other than a text saying the votes had gone in favor of Maxwell Technology's takeover bid, she'd heard nothing for more than an hour.

A knock at the door had her turning with a smile, sure it was Jetta, but an aide poked her head inside. "Visitor for you, Ms. Ainsley." The aide ushered in a woman about Emily's age.

Emily frowned at the unfamiliar face. "Do I know you?"

The woman shook her head. "I'm Dolores Green. May I sit down?"

"Okay." Emily's curiosity heightened as the woman pulled the chair closer to her bed.

"I'm sure you're wondering why I'm here." Dolores ploughed ahead without waiting for a response. "Your daughter and a friend, Seth something, visited me earlier this week."

Now Emily placed the woman's name. "You altered invoices from SafeSense to Topher Robotics."

"That's what the paper trail indicated." Tears filled the other woman's eyes. "But I didn't. I had no idea about the bank account in the Cayman Islands in my name with thousands of dollars. I never opened the account. Yes, I worked in accounting but as an administrative assistant. I was never a CPA. I wouldn't know the first thing about altering invoices and embezzling money."

Dolores's grief appeared genuine. As tears spilled down her cheeks, Emily handed Dolores a box of tissues. She suspected there was more for the other woman to share, so she waited quietly while Dolores regained control.

"Sorry about that." Dolores blew her nose, then wadded up the tissues. "I've racked my brain trying to figure out who could have set me up. I'm a simple woman. I live alone with my dogs. I can't imagine who I could have harmed so much they'd do such a thing. I lost my job and can never work in finance again. It's been very difficult to find a job."

When Dolores didn't immediately continue, Emily said, "It might not have been personal."

That brought a fresh round of tears. "That makes it even more terrible, doesn't it? That someone picked my name out of a hat and said, 'I think I'll destroy this woman's life for the fun of it!'"

While Dolores sobbed, Emily patted her shoulder as she thought about everything the woman had said. Once she'd quieted, Emily put her theory into words. "I think someone was in a very desperate situation. They needed to shift the blame from themselves to someone else, but who? They picked my husband because he was the only person outside the Topher family who held a C-suite position at the company. They picked you because you're unassuming and unappreciated or overlooked at work."

"Yes, that's true. My contributions were always ignored or downplayed. I was a nobody. One of my dogs, a darling little shiatzu named Holly, was sick, and I was trying to raise money for her treatment through a local animal rescue organization. She'd been a rescue dog. Someone anonymously donated a large sum of money that paid for her care." Dolores blew her nose. "Of course, that was right before

I was accused, and my SafeSense bosses assumed I had been the anonymous donor, using the money I had taken."

Emily listened as Dolores recounted more details. With each word, she believed someone had scapegoated Dolores much as they had done her husband. Another innocent victim because of someone's greed. "Someone stole millions from Topher Robotics, millions that have never been recovered. If Jay had lived, I think the case against him would have fallen apart. But he didn't, so they swept it under the rug after a cursory internal investigation that snagged you in its net." The more she talked, the more the scenario made sense to Emily. "I doubt the person responsible for all of this has stopped. They would have felt emboldened to continue embezzling money, especially after getting away with it."

"That might be true, but how can we prove it after all these years?" The hope in Dolores's eyes tugged at Emily's heart. "I tried to contact Seth and Jetta to see if they've learned anything but received no reply. Then I remembered Jetta mentioning your accident and that you were in a rehab facility in Reston. I thought I'd come see you in person to make sure you understand I didn't have anything to do with what happened to your husband."

"I believe you. I know my daughter and Seth are trying their best to find out."

Dolores blotted her cheeks with a fresh tissue. "You still don't know the identity of the person who stole all that money?"

"Not yet." Emily's cell rang, and she picked it up, hoping it was Jetta. But an unfamiliar number flashed on the screen, sending her pulse skyrocketing. "I'm sorry, I need to get this."

"I'll leave. Thank you for seeing me. If you find out anything, please let me know."

"Will do." Emily waved goodbye as she swiped to answer. "Hello?"

"Ms. Ainsley, this is Officer Brody. Is your daughter with you?"

"Jetta? No, she's not, and I've been trying to reach her for more than an hour." Emily gripped the phone tighter.

"We found your daughter's phone on the sidewalk outside of Topher Robotics but no sign of her."

Emily pushed herself to an upright position in the bed. "Is Seth Whitman around?"

"Was he on the Topher campus too?"

"He was. He went with Jetta to the shareholders meeting, although he couldn't attend since he doesn't own shares. Please, you must find my daughter. She's close to nine months pregnant and under a lot of stress."

"We will do everything we can to find her, ma'am. We'll be in touch as soon as we know something. If you hear from her, please call this number."

Emily thanked the officer and disconnected. Hugging the phone to her chest, she prayed for Jetta's safety, for her unborn baby, and for Seth. That young man would do everything in his power to keep her daughter safe. She prayed her daughter would give her fear about making a mistake with Seth over to God and see what a fine man Seth was, one who Emily believed was very suited to be Jetta's helpmate. Seth would love Jetta's baby as his own and never hold its conception against the child or her daughter. *Please God, help Jetta to see Seth for the man he is, and keep them both safe.*

After praying, she reviewed her conversation with Dolores. Something had jogged a memory of Jay muttering to himself a few weeks before he died. What was it? Then it came to her in the proverbial flash of remembrance. *They've been discounting her for years. She's flown right under their radar.*

And with that memory, Emily knew who had taken the money. She had no proof, but FinCEN had the authority to dig deep into the person's finances. She found the FinCEN contact and dialed, praying her hunch would pay off and this nightmare would soon be over.

Jetta shifted in her seat as the pain built in her belly. She huffed out small breaths, willing the fake contractions to go away. Her doctor had said stress could bring them on, and she'd certainly had a stressful day. But the contractions lasted longer than they had previously and seemed at regular intervals.

Wetness dampened her jeans. She peed her pants? Then realization struck. It wasn't urine but amniotic fluid. Her water had broken.

She was in labor.

In a car in the middle of nowhere.

Alone.

"Jetta?"

Not totally alone.

Seth touched her arm. She sucked in a breath as another contraction hit her, this one stronger and longer. How many minutes had passed since the last one? She struggled to remember but couldn't seem to catch hold of a thought as the pain ripped through her body.

"You're in labor. I'm pulling over."

She wanted to argue, but the tightening of her stomach yanked her attention back to the baby, who apparently was ready to come several weeks early. She most certainly wasn't ready, not when she hadn't decided what to do once baby arrived.

Then managing the indescribable pain of the contraction took all of her concentration. She bit back screams while scrambling to remember what the nurse had said during the online birth classes she'd taken. Short breaths? No breaths? How could she breathe anyway?

When her muscles relaxed, she noticed Seth had stopped. Panic clawed at her throat. She couldn't give birth in some stranger's SUV in the middle of nothing. "Where are we?" An inane question, given she really didn't care, but she needed to talk about anything other than what was happening inside her body.

"The Loudoun County Fairgrounds."

This being late September and evening, no one would be around.

It was just her and this baby she wasn't sure she wanted, and Seth, the man she did want but kept pushing away for his own good.

Jetta yelped as a contraction shuddered through her body, doubling her over. She clutched her stomach, the pain all she could think about, all she could experience. As the contraction lessened its hold on her, Seth's voice registered.

"Breathe with me." He met her gaze, his steady and calm. He held out his hand, and she slipped hers inside. Her own breathing slowed in time with his. In, out. In, out.

Then the pain began to build again. She squeezed his hand as hard as she could and threw her head back against the seat. Her feet plowed into the floorboards, lifting her bottom off the seat. A guttural cry escaped her lips. She could not do this. She did not want to do this.

"Breathe, sweetheart, breathe. Short, panting breaths when the contraction hits."

Seth walked her through the breaths until the contraction eased. "I don't think the baby is going to wait until we can flag down help."

"No...way...to...call?" *Please, let him find a way to get help.* She would not do this in a car, she would not do this from afar. Good grief, she must be addled if she was making nonsensical Dr. Seuss rhymes.

"We're on our own unless someone sees our hazards and stops."

His voice held no hope of that happening, as much as she prayed for it. Tears spilled over and down her cheeks as fear and panic jostled for dominance inside her. "I don't want to do this." Her body refused to listen as it built momentum designed to expel the baby she had been harboring for so many months.

"I know." He laid his hand alongside her cheek for a split second, the warmth of his touch easing her panic a fraction. Then Seth opened his door as a sharper, stronger contraction nearly overwhelmed her, wrenching a scream from her that echoed in the enclosed space. He was leaving her to do this alone?

Through the haze of pain, she made out his figure as he jogged around the hood to her side. She barely kept up with his movements as he opened the passenger back door, then hers. "We need to get you into the back seat."

"No." She shook her head, sending strands of hair whipping back and forth. "I can't." The need to push saturated every nerve, but she clamped her legs together, not willing to give in, not here, not now.

"Yes, you can. We can do it together. We have to." He leaned his forehead against hers, the compassion and love in his eyes stealing the final shred of her resolve.

"Okay."

At her agreement, he eased her legs out of the car, then supported her body as she tumbled out of the vehicle and into him. He absorbed her weight with ease. She screamed as a contraction drove her to her knees. Only Seth's strong arms kept her upright. He lifted her up onto the back seat, swinging her legs around so her back was to the passenger side door.

"Don't move. I'll be right there."

A brief pressure on the top of her head, then he closed the door. As she struggled to manage another contraction, she focused on that moment. On the expression in his eyes. On what she'd learned over these months of being around Seth. He was an honorable man. He wasn't at all like her ex. He would never knowingly hurt her.

God had brought him into her life, allowing her to see what true servanthood looked like on this fallen planet. If Seth had lived while Jesus walked the earth, he would have been first in line to wash someone else's feet. He would have served the lepers, given hope to the hopeless. His love of Christ shone through all his actions, especially in his gentle treatment of her. Her mother had been right.

She could trust him with her life.

She could trust him with her baby's life.

A peace stole over her, washing into the nooks and crannies of her mind, overflowing the pain and fear of this baby's conception. A blast of cool air from the shattered hatch window hit her at the same time as another contraction. Seth climbed into the back seat, crowding her space as he closed the door. He rubbed his hands together, the smell of something sharp and citrusy filling the space. "I found some hand sanitizer in the console."

She bit back another yell as the pain built and built and built, but she couldn't take her eyes off the man opposite her. "Seth."

She must have whispered the name because he didn't pause in leaning over the backseat and rummaging in the hatch area. He plopped back on the seat, something in his hands. "I found a couple of sweatshirts. I think they're clean."

"Seth."

He shifted closer, his hand capturing hers. "Yes?"

"Help me." She whimpered through the contraction as the urge to push increased. "I...trust...you."

"Thank you." Seth squeezed her hand, as a tear rolled down his cheek. He was crying. Not because he was sad, but because her words had made him so happy. Of that, she was sure. With a groan, she surrendered to the birthing process, thanking God for bringing this man into her life for such a time as this.

THIRTY-TWO

Seth trembled as he held the sweet baby girl, so tiny in his hands. Once he'd helped Jetta remove her jeans and underwear, the birth had progressed like lightning. "She's perfect. All fingers and toes accounted for."

He wrapped the infant in one of the sweatshirts and laid the bundle in Jetta's arms, umbilical cord still attached. A knock at the window startled him. He glanced up to see flashing blue lights and the figure of someone standing by the back door.

"I think it's a police officer." He used the second sweatshirt to wipe his hands before opening the door and stepping out into the cool night, closing the door quickly behind him.

"License and registration, please." The officer shone his flashlight over Seth, illuminating the blood and fluids covering his clothing.

"This is not my car." His body shook as the adrenaline began to drain. "But that's not important. We need an ambulance."

"Are you hurt?" The suspicion in the other man's voice doused Seth with the equivalent of cold water.

"No, but the woman in the backseat just gave birth to a girl." The miracle of that awed Seth, but he focused on getting the officer to believe he was telling the truth. Later, he could bask in the joy of what the arrival of Jetta's baby meant for him. It was enough she'd trusted him to deliver the infant. "She needs medical attention."

To his credit, the officer didn't argue. "Sir, please move to the hood of the car and place your hands on the vehicle."

Seth did as the officer said, waiting while the man shone his flashlight through the driver's side window and into the backseat. He opened the back door and spoke to Jetta, their conversation too low for Seth to hear. The officer must have called for an ambulance because a wailing siren soon became discernable. Seth sagged against the SUV, his legs turning to spaghetti, grateful more help was on the way.

The officer backed out of the vehicle and closed the door. "There's a hospital five minutes down the road, so the EMTs will be here soon. She and the baby appear to be doing well."

Seth nodded and slipped into the driver's seat of the SUV. "Ambulance should be here soon. You okay?"

"Yeah, thanks to you." She offered him a sleepy smile, one more beautiful than any he'd ever seen.

Flashing lights and loud sirens heralded the arrival of the EMTs. "Things will likely get a little crazy, so I'll say this now, while it's only the three of us. Thank you for trusting me to help bring your daughter into the world. It's the most precious gift anyone's ever given me."

"Oh, Seth. I—"

The opening of the back driver's side door made him miss whatever Jetta had been about to say. He slid out of the vehicle to give her privacy as the EMT did her job. While Jetta and her baby were cared for by the paramedics, Seth filled in the officer about the evening's events, including the fact that two kidnappers might still be wandering around the woods several miles from the fairgrounds. When they loaded Jetta and her infant into the back of the ambulance, Seth promised to call her mother as soon as he could. As the ambulance drove away, Seth once more said a silent prayer of thanksgiving for bringing the littlest Ainsley into the world safe and sound. He couldn't wait to plan a future with what he already considered his girls.

SETH ADJUSTED HIS GRIP ON THE VASE OF PINK ROSES, THEN LOWERED THE three pink balloons to exit the elevator on the maternity floor. Nerves zinged through his body, nearly overpowering him, but he soldiered on, telling himself to stop second-guessing his decision to come despite Jetta's ignoring his texts. A restless night's sleep hadn't helped his mood, and waiting for visiting hours had further tied his insides in knots. But the Scripture about all things being possible with God looped in his mind, giving him the courage to face Jetta and see if the amazing woman of last night who delivered a baby—a baby!—in the backseat of their kidnapper's SUV still wanted him in her life. While her words about trusting him had sounded sincere, he well knew how the cold light of day could wash away good intentions. Hadn't his own mother proven that time and again?

But Jetta wasn't his mother, nor did he wish her to be. She was a woman who had been deeply hurt by another man, a blow he prayed she would be able to work through one day and accept Seth into her and her darling girl's life. He had never wanted anything more than he wanted to be Jetta's husband and her baby's father. He didn't care about the circumstances of the infant's conception or that he wasn't the biological father. He had fallen in love with the baby as he'd fallen in love with her mother. The two were a package deal, one that he had no intention of separating. If growing up in foster care had taught him one thing, it was that families could be created as well as made, that the important thing wasn't genes but love and respect for one another. He prayed once again that Jetta would give him a chance to show her and her daughter how much he cared for them both.

The door to Room 2345 stood ajar, and he knocked gently on the frame. "Come in," sang out Emily. Good, maybe her mother would help ease any awkwardness between them.

He entered to find Emily sitting in the bedside chair holding the baby. Something looked different about his neighbor, then he smiled. "Your leg cast is off."

Emily's grin stretched wide. "I bullied the doctor into getting it off sooner since I had to see my latest granddaughter in person. He's a grandfather himself, so he understood, but I have to wear this leg brace and use a walker for a few weeks."

Seth turned to the bed where Jetta's attention appeared to be directed toward her mother and the baby. He approached with his offerings of flowers and balloons. "Hey, how are you?"

"Tired." She met his gaze briefly before ducking her head.

At her short response, he faltered. Maybe he shouldn't have come after all. His hope things would be different after the drama of last night's birth shattered, but he wouldn't give up so easily. However, his nervousness made his palms slick with sweat, and he feared he would drop the vase if he didn't set it down soon. "I thought pink was an appropriate color, given the baby's gender."

Jetta made no response, nor did she tell her where to put the vase. This wasn't a good sign at all, but maybe fatigue and the shock of the birth were responsible for her less-than-hospitable welcome.

Emily glanced toward the bed, but when her daughter didn't make a suggestion, she sighed. "I think there's space by the window."

Seth stepped around the bed and carefully set the vase on the wide sill. The balloons, attached to the vase, danced as they floated toward the ceiling, stopping when the ribbons became taut. He returned to the foot of the bed. "The baby is all right? And you? I stopped by but wasn't able to see you because visiting hours were over and I'm not..." He couldn't finish the rest of the sentence—that he wasn't granted access to Jetta and her baby because he wasn't family. "But I came as soon as I could this morning."

"Thank you for the flowers and balloons." Her words had a perfunctory tone, which hurt worse than dropping a dumbbell on his foot.

"You're welcome." He shoved his hands into his pockets and wondered how long he should stay, given the cool reception.

"Seth, please give me a hand."

He welcomed Emily's directive and stepped closer to where she sat.

"Take the baby so I can get out of this chair."

"I probably shouldn't…" But Emily thrust the infant into his arms before he could finish his thought. He gathered the precious bundle, wrapped in a white blanket with blue and pink stripes at the top. A little pink cap covered her head. Her rosebud mouth puckered as she slept.

She was the most beautiful thing he'd ever seen.

"Hey, little lady." He shifted the baby in his arms, tucking her in close to his chest. "You gave us a scare last night. Guess you wanted to be on the outside to see what all the fussing was about."

Emily stood and pulled a walker forward. "I'm going to get a cup of coffee. You two need to sort out whatever"—she waved a hand in a circle—"this is, or I'm bringing back a knife to cut the tension."

Seth cuddled the baby as Emily left the room. So it wasn't him imagining things. Even Jetta's mom could feel the tension between them. The silence built between them like a brick mason adding to a wall. He rocked the sleeping infant back and forth, wishing he knew the right words to say. The wall clock ticked off two minutes before he couldn't stand it any longer and decided a softball question might loosen things between them. "Do you have a name picked out for her?"

"No."

He snuck a glance at the bed, but Jetta had turned her head toward the window, away from him and her baby. Her stiff posture and crossed arms gave him scant hope things would thaw between them. Maybe talking about what he'd learned about the case might help. "I spoke with a detective after the ambulance left last night and gave them a description of the two men who grabbed us. They had the vehicle, which had been stolen. No surprise there."

No reaction from Jetta.

He directed his words and attention to the baby cuddled in his arms. "The police called me while I was driving to the hospital to say they'd picked up the two men who'd taken us, along with the cop you said had put you in the vehicle."

"Someone from the Loudoun County Police Department came by for my statement this morning."

She'd spoken an entire sentence—that was encouraging. He had so much to tell her, but her withdrawn demeanor locked the words inside him.

A nurse came into the room, glanced his way, then headed over to Jetta. "What do you need, Ms. Ainsley?"

Seth's heart sank at the implication Jetta had pushed the call button rather than ask him for assistance.

"I'm very tired. Can my baby go back to the nursery for a while?"

The nurse nodded toward Seth, a smile tipping up the edges of her mouth. "Your husband seems to be handling baby just fine."

The misunderstanding brought heat to his cheeks, and he dipped his head toward the infant, sensing now was not the time to let Jetta see how pleased he was to be mistaken for her spouse. Maybe one day...

"He's not my husband."

The harsh words doused his happy haze with the finesse of a bucket of ice water. He whipped his head up, but Jetta spoke to the blanket on her bed. *Please, look at me.* If she would only meet his gaze, he was sure they could figure this out, whatever this was, together.

"In fact, I don't want him in my room or around my baby."

Seth froze, shock at her blatant rejection turning him into a statute. He opened his mouth but couldn't push any words past the lump blocking his throat. He wasn't sure what he could say to that statement anyway.

The nurse frowned, her head swinging from Seth to Jetta. "Has he done something wrong?"

"No, I just don't want him around." Jetta hunched down in the bed, turning on her side away from Seth.

"Okay." The nurse approached Seth, holding out her arms for the baby.

Seth didn't try to fight it. Jetta had determined to shut him out, and he wouldn't argue, not here in front of the nurse. Maybe later, when Jetta had regained her composure or had more time to think, she would realize her mistake and they could work through things.

For now, he dropped a kiss on the baby's head much like he'd done with her mother last night. Then he carefully transferred the precious bundle to the nurse and hustled out of the room, tears dampening his cheeks before he'd taken more than two steps. At the elevator bank, he swiped at the moisture on his face before punching the down button with more force than necessary.

"Leaving so soon?"

The teasing note in Emily's voice sliced into him, making the wound her daughter had inflicted bleed even more fiercely. Hurt once again clogged his throat, but this time, he got the words out. "Jetta told me she didn't want me around, that I had to leave."

"Oh, Seth. I'd so hoped..."

"Me too." He couldn't hear what Emily had hoped for him and Jetta, not when his heart resembled raw hamburger. The hurt mixed with anger, filling him with the driving need to pummel something until he could make sense of Jetta's actions. Maybe someone would be up for sparring at the gym. The elevator dinged and the doors opened. "I've got to go."

Without waiting for an answer, he slipped into the waiting car. Forty-five minutes later, he strapped on boxing gloves and stepped into the ring to meet his opponent, a muscular man nicknamed The Beast. He bumped gloves with The Beast, then took the first swing, connecting solidly with the man's jaw.

As they traded punches with Clancy refereeing, Seth tried to give his anger and frustration over Jetta's decision to excise him from her life to God. But the thought that wouldn't leave him alone was an old friend, one who reminded him of the many times the women in his life had deserted him. First his grandmother kicked him and his mother out of her house, which exacerbated his mom's downward spiral. Then his mom refused to work her plan to get him back. Now Jetta shut him out of her and her daughter's life.

The Beast landed a vicious uppercut, sending Seth against the ropes with a split lip. He spat out the blood, then nodded to Clancy he would be returning to the fight. The older man shook his head as he allowed them to continue.

Enough with these useless thoughts. Seth would pummel this guy until he rammed those thoughts away, physical pain his only companion. Maybe then his heart wouldn't ache so much.

CHAPTER

THIRTY-THREE

"Why did you push him away?"

Mom's strident question pulled Jetta from the brink of sleep. She pried open her eyes, as lethargy tugged at her body. "Mom, I'm tired." So exhausted from the harrowing kidnapping and backseat delivery. Seth's kind eyes and calm demeanor as he talked her through the birth flashed across her mind, but she shoved that picture away as firmly as she had sent him packing. "Can't we talk about this later?"

Her mother peered down at her, opened her mouth, then snapped it closed. "I'll be back in two hours."

Jetta had already let her eyelids drift closed as she sensed her mother's departure. Sleep once more claimed her, but her dreams brought Seth back into her life in a jumble of scenes. Seth laughing as she tossed a ball to Bingley. Seth lifting anything remotely heavy without complaint. Seth protecting her from the kidnappers. Seth holding her while she cried after her mother's kidnapping. Seth leaning closer, his lips capturing hers in a kiss so gentle, so sweet, she hadn't wanted it to end. Then a crying baby entered her dreams.

Seth held the squalling infant, one big hand cupped around the little one's head, an expression of love so intense, it took her breath away.

"Ms. Ainsley, your daughter's hungry."

She struggled back to full alertness as the baby's cries increased. She was alone in the room with the nurse and the crying newborn in the portable crib. Disappointment Seth wasn't there filled her, but of course he'd left. She'd said she didn't want him around, and he would never presume to stay if she said go. She pushed to a seated position, rubbing her eyes like a toddler to erase the lingering effects of the nap. "How long was I asleep?"

The nurse checked the clock. "It's been about two hours." She refilled Jetta's plastic mug with water, snapping the straw lid down before handing it to Jetta. "Drink some water, then we'll get baby latched on."

Jetta complied and soon held her daughter as they both learned this nursing thing. The nurse left, and Jetta enjoyed the quiet sounds of a feeding infant. She marveled at the baby's soft blonde fuzz. Love for the infant pulsated throughout her body, a love she hadn't been sure she would feel given the circumstances of the baby's conception. But she did love this little one, fiercely and completely.

"Am I interrupting?" Mom pushed her walker into the room.

"Come on in, Mom." Jetta stared down at her baby, not wanting to read the scold she was sure would be in her mother's eyes. She knew Mom only wanted what was best for her and now her granddaughter, but Jetta didn't want to hear how badly she'd behaved with Seth. As she dozed off and on throughout the night, she hadn't been able to recapture the peace she'd experienced in the backseat. Instead, her feelings were too raw and fresh, which she attributed to the dopamine and oxytocin released at the birth. She still couldn't wrap her mind around the fact she was a mother of a daughter, and that meant she had a momentous decision to make about the baby's future. Then she'd had a panic attack upon arriving at the hospital related to memories of the rape. It had taken her a long time to calm down.

Plus there was Seth's role in delivering the baby. He'd seen things, done things, to help bring the baby into the world. How could he ever view her romantically after the messiness of the birth?

So she'd panicked when he arrived, the hope shining on his face. Hope she wasn't sure she could reciprocate. Telling him to leave was the only way she could think of to give her the space she needed to figure out her and her daughter's future.

"How's my darling granddaughter doing?" Mom made a little cooing noise as she leaned over the bed to gaze at the baby still latched to Jetta's breast.

"She's okay. I think we're getting the hang of nursing." Jetta detached the baby and put her on her shoulder to burp.

"Oh, honey. You're going to need to put a little more gusto into those pats or the baby will never release a burp." Mom sank into the chair. "Babies aren't that fragile, you know."

"I know." Jetta didn't, but she did trust her mother. She increased the pressure, and the baby let out a decent burp.

"You see?"

"I see you're going to be a bossy grandma."

Mom laughed as Jetta positioned the baby on the other side.

"I'm also going to tell you you're making a big mistake, shutting out that young man of yours."

"Mom, I do not want to discuss Seth." Jetta glared but Mom wasn't fazed.

"I don't want to have a discussion." Mom skewered Jetta with The Look, the one that said *you're gonna listen to what I have to say.*

Jetta sighed. "Have your say then."

Mom nodded once. "Thank you. I only have one question for you."

"Which is?"

"Have you prayed about this?"

The question wasn't the one Jetta had expected. "Of course, I've prayed." She had prayed that God would keep Seth safe from danger, that she would be able to give him up, and that he would one day find a woman worthy of his love. It couldn't be her. She was too broken, too hurt to ever be ready for loving a man like Seth.

"I meant have you prayed about the rape?"

Her mother's words stopped her cold, anger boiling over in a nanosecond. "How dare you ask me that!" Her heart beat faster. "I've prayed God would bring justice, that he would heal me body and soul, that he would give me love for this baby. Of course I've prayed about it."

Her mother's steady gaze bore into her as the baby squirmed in Jetta's arms. "But have you prayed for God's help in forgiving your ex?"

"He doesn't deserve my forgiveness!" The words tore out of her, shattering the fragile peace the birth of her baby had granted her. "He stole my virginity, my dignity. He took what wasn't his to take and ruined my chances to find a good man."

"A good man like Seth?"

"Yes, like Seth." Sobs shook Jetta's frame so hard that the baby whimpered. She didn't object when her mother rose and took the baby from her arms. "But I'm too broken for anyone to want."

"Oh, Jetta. You're not broken. God doesn't look on you and see someone who's broken beyond repair. God looks on you and sees a sinner washed in the blood of Christ, his precious son. In Jesus, you're whole and clean." Mom rocked the baby. "He even brought you a man who understands what you've been through and has the patience and love to come alongside you as you work through things."

She shook her head. "No, you don't understand. Seth deserves someone who doesn't need fixing."

Mom kissed the baby's head. "You're wrong, but you'll need to figure that out for yourself."

Jetta ignored the tears slipping down her cheeks—and her mother's words. She was trying to do the right thing, the honorable thing, and save Seth from sacrificing his happiness on someone as messed up as she was. Sure, he would probably say he could love her and another man's baby, but over time, his love would fade into resentment at having been stuck with claiming a child not of his own flesh. If she believed otherwise, she would cave and ruin his life. That wasn't something she wanted to risk.

Seth slowed his speed to a light jog after completing six miles, a little longer than his usual runs, but he needed to expend the extra energy on physical exertion, or he'd end up back in the ring for round two with The Beast. His ribs, knuckles, and jaw still ached from the previous encounter four days ago, the bathroom mirror telling him every morning and evening as he brushed his teeth what a fool he'd been to fight the other man. At least Brogan and Fallon hadn't said much about his battered appearance when he'd shown up for work the following day.

The story Brogan had written about Maxwell Technology yanking its takeover offer after the arrest of the middle Topher sibling for Emily's kidnapping had been picked up by the national papers, including one of Seth's photographs from their interview. While the two men responsible for kidnapping him and Jetta had been caught, they had lawyered up and weren't talking. Seth had mentioned Yasmine's proximity to the kidnapper who had pulled a gun on him and that he'd thought she'd said something about getting the girl—meaning Jetta—but the detective said no evidence linked the youngest Topher with their kidnapping. Maybe he'd misunderstood.

In fact, the police were treating both abductions as being perpetrated by the same individual—Gene Topher, who had kept his mouth shut so far, according to Brogan's sources. Seth's texts to Leslie to inquire about FinCEN's investigation had been unanswered beyond a cryptic "stay tuned" sent three days ago. Which meant he had no new information and no one to hash things out with, given Jetta's unresponsiveness to his calls, messages, or texts. Emily had called asking if he would take Bingley for runs and walks, raising his hopes that Jetta would interact with him when he picked up and returned the dog. Those hopes fizzled when Emily texted the leash would be looped over the side gate handle and Bingley would be in the backyard for him to grab without bothering Jetta or the baby.

So he put a lot of mileage on his running shoes, pouring out his heart to God as he pounded out the miles with Bingley at his side. As if sensing Seth was thinking of him, the dog gave a soft woof as he spotted a squirrel racing up a tree near the sidewalk. He tightened his grip on the leash. "Don't get any bright ideas about chasing after that squirrel."

Bingley panted but didn't reply. Seth dropped to a walk, bringing the dog to heel as they rounded the corner on their street. In front of Jetta's house stood an unfamiliar vehicle, a white Lexus SUV, parked at the curb, no driver inside. Pain blossomed in his chest as he surmised the owner was visiting Jetta, who apparently allowed others into her life but not him. But he reminded himself sternly he had no right to her heart, no matter the kiss or words she shared during the stress of giving birth in the backseat of a car. He could not —he would not—hold her to promises made under those circumstances. Instead, he would honor her wishes for him to be on the periphery of her life and show his love for her by caring for her dog while she adjusted to motherhood.

Whether or not she noticed his contribution.

He slipped Bingley into her backyard, draping the leash over the outside handle of the gate, then headed to his house for a shower. Forty-five minutes later, he slathered butter on a baked potato to accompany the steak he'd broiled in the oven. He resisted the urge to check to see if the white SUV still sat in front of Jetta's house. No good would come of spying on his pretty neighbor, even if he loved her. He ate in silence, both of his roommates out for the evening.

After cleaning up the dishes, he retreated to the dining room, where he'd set up an old door across two sawhorses. A black cloth covered the door, allowing him to arrange his photographs on its stark background. Might as well figure out which pictures to submit to an Arlington gallery for a potential spot in an upcoming show on local photographers. For the next couple of hours, he sorted through his collection, culling out the ones he thought might fit the show's theme of "The Unexpected Shot." He needed a dozen photos, although if chosen, only half of those would be on display—and for sale.

His phone buzzed with an incoming call as he selected his top twenty choices, and he answered without checking caller ID. "Hello?"

"Seth, it's Leslie Updike."

He straightened, his brain switching from photographs to fraud. "Tell me you have news."

She laughed. "I have news. We got a lead on the identity of the person behind the embezzlement."

"Who?"

"I can't say yet, but we've managed to pinpoint some accounting crumbs that point directly to this person."

"Does that mean this is an official investigation?"

"This is an official investigation. We have several forensic accountants working on unraveling the trail and delving into the finances of the suspected embezzler."

"Thanks for the update." He wasn't sure it was much of an update, but at least it gave him an excuse to text Jetta. After saying goodbye to Leslie, he composed a quick text to Jetta with the update and hit send.

His phone buzzed, signaling an incoming text. He snatched it up only to bite back disappointment that Emily's name flashed on the screen along with a message.

> Have you heard any updates from your
> FinCEN contact?

Seth recounted what Leslie had told him, adding he'd texted the info to Jetta.

Emily's reply floored him.

> Good. I told them to check out Yasmine Topher. I think she's the one behind the embezzlement.

> Why?

> Because she's been overlooked by her father and her brothers. She's smarter than all of them, but Peter is too old-fashioned to allow a woman to helm his company. I think that made her mad enough she got even by taking the money. Jay never liked her, called her "all sweetness and light until you crossed her."

> Interesting. From what Leslie said, they are gathering information and should have enough to arrest someone soon.

Emily responded with a thumbs up emoji.

> Praying for you.

He hearted her response, then returned to narrowing down his photographs, his mind split between concentrating on the task at hand and seeing how nicely Yasmine Topher fit the profile of an embezzler. As he worked, he couldn't help noticing how silent his phone stayed. No vibrations indicating an incoming text. Seth swallowed his disappointment for hoping Jetta would respond to something related to the embezzlement, even if she ignored his own entreaties.

He'd had a lifetime of experience that should have doused the hope in his heart that this time, the outcome would be different. But his foolish heart wouldn't listen to his brain, and he clung to the memories of their sweet kiss and her trust in him during the birth of her daughter.

THIRTY-FOUR

Jetta paced back and forth, jostling the fussy baby up and down with every step. Her daughter, whom she hadn't named yet, refused to settle down. Eight-thirty p.m. The baby had nursed well and burped, her diaper was fresh, so Jetta wasn't sure what the problem was. Her mother had offered to cut short her rehab stay and move back in to help, but Jetta deflected the offer. Mom meant well, but Jetta needed to see if she could handle motherhood on her own or not. Being a single mother was a huge responsibility. Thus far, she felt like an utter failure.

Seth's text about the FinCEN investigation should have cheered her that answers to who was behind framing her father and stealing the money would be forthcoming eventually, but she'd had to resist the urge to throw her phone against the wall. Her OB-GYN had said her emotions might be raw and see-sawing for a few weeks after the birth, but Jetta hadn't realized how far her moods would swing.

The visit earlier that day with a representative of a Christian adoption agency hadn't gone well either. The woman had been nice and presented her options with how an adoption might work— open, closed, somewhere in between. Jetta had no idea she had to think about whether she wanted to be part of the baby's life or not. The decision whether to give her baby up to another set of parents seemed momentous enough without having to figure out how involved she would want to be with the adoptive family.

The niggling idea she didn't have to decide wouldn't leave her, that she could simply agree to let Seth be part of her and her baby's life, and all would be rainbows and unicorns. Okay, maybe that was putting too much of a happy spin on things, and Seth didn't deserve her sarcasm. She shifted the baby to her other shoulder, then resumed pacing and patting. The baby let out a loud belch.

"Better?" Jetta rocked back and forth as the infant's cries softened to a whimper. Another burp escaped, and her daughter snuggled down on her shoulder. She eased into the glider chair Mom had surprised her with when she came home from the hospital. She suspected Mom had corralled Seth into putting the chair together, since she spotted the box next to his recycling bin, but she was grateful to have the chair.

With a push, she set it in motion, and the baby soon drifted off to sleep. Jetta's body relaxed as quiet descended on the house. She'd close her eyes for a few minutes, then put the baby in the bassinet and get something to eat, as she'd only nibbled a few bites of her scrambled eggs and toast.

Seth leaned over her, his warm chocolate eyes shining with a love so intense, so pure, it stole her breath. She reached up, allowing her fingers to brush the shadow along his jawline, marveling at the contrast of the rough texture with her smoother skin. He brushed a strand of hair from her face, his gaze fashioned on hers. "Do you see me, sweetheart?"

She dropped her hand, confusion clouding the moment. "I see you."

"I'm real. I'm here. I'm waiting for you to see me."

"I do." She struggled to her feet, the baby suddenly in his arms, not hers. The sight of his big, strong biceps flexing to cradle her infant daughter brought tears to her eyes. The baby didn't stir with the transfer, simply slept on as peaceful as a lamb.

Bingley's wet nose on her bare foot jolted her out of the dream and back to reality. It took a few minutes for the vestiges of the vivid dream to receded and for Jetta to recover her bearings. Seth wasn't there. She was in the baby's room. Her daughter stirred but didn't awaken as the dog nudged Jetta again, this time with a soft whine. Shadows had deepened while she had slept with only the nightlight on in the baby's room. She checked the time on her phone. Nine-thirteen. She'd been asleep for only about twenty minutes or so.

Jetta pushed Bingley out of the way so she could lay the baby in the bassinet, covering the infant with a blanket. Time for some decaf tea and to finish her omelet if Bingley hadn't gobbled it up, since she'd left it on the kitchen counter. But when she moved toward the door, the dog blocked her way.

"Out of the way," she whispered.

Bingley responded with a low growl, something he had never done before. She placed her hand on his collar intent on moving him aside when she heard something. She dropped to her knees beside the dog and listened. Yes, someone was moving around downstairs.

Her fingers slipped as she grabbed her phone. If she called 911, she would have to speak, something she didn't want to do unless absolutely necessary. She didn't want to draw the intruder's attention to herself and her baby. She'd text Seth and ask him to call 911. Without giving herself a chance to reconsider, she sent the text, adding she was turning off her phone to avoid detection. She didn't want any buzzing or beeping to alert whoever had broken into her house. She would stay with Bingley in the baby's room and wait for help to arrive.

Then she heard footsteps coming up the stairs.

Seth lifted the thirty-pound weight in a bicep curl with his left hand, completing twenty reps before switching to his right. He continued alternating every twenty reps until he'd worked each arm with a hundred repetitions. After replacing the weights, he debated whether he should add sit ups to his regime or call it a night. His phone buzzed, distracting him from his late-night workout.

Jetta's name flashed on the screen, lifting his heart until he read her brief message.

> Intruder downstairs. Baby's sleeping. I'm
> there with Bingley. Call 911 for me. Will wait
> in baby's room until help arrives. Turning off
> phone to avoid detection by intruder.

His heart rate skyrocketed at the news. This wasn't how he wanted to hear from Jetta. With Gene Topher's arrest and FinCEN investigating Yasmine, he thought the danger to Jetta was over, but apparently not. He prayed for her and the baby while dialing 911. After relaying what little info he had to the dispatcher, he ignored her admonition to stay put until first responders arrived and dashed out the back door.

He slipped through the side entrance to Jetta's backyard, then eased up onto the patio. He paused outside the sliding glass doors leading to the dining room, listening for any noise that would indicate where the intruder was. Hearing nothing, he jiggled the handle to slip the lock. He'd noticed it was loose last year and had pointed it out to Emily, who hadn't seemed overly concerned. Now he was glad she hadn't fixed it. The door lock disengaged, and he slid it silently back on its runners. Once inside the house, he gently closed the door to prevent any intruders from escaping easily and crept toward the front of the house.

Nothing stirred. The study door stood open, and he glanced inside as he passed. Someone had turned on the desk lamp, and he glimpsed papers strewn across the desk and spilling out of an open filing cabinet drawer. Someone had been searching, but for what?

Emily had said she'd gone through Jay's papers searching for clues as to who the embezzler might be but found nothing.

A noise from upstairs made him hurry. Hugging the wall, he climbed the stairs. At the top, he paused to listen again. Bingley growled, and a woman's voice commanded Jetta to quiet him.

Seth eased toward the baby's room, the door partially open. He flattened himself against the wall and concentrated on slowing his breathing to keep as still as possible—and to hear what was happening inside the room.

"You will tell me what your father has on the embezzlement." A familiar female voice demanded.

"I don't know what you're talking about. My father was the one accused of stealing that money." Jetta's voice sounded strained, as if she were hanging onto to her composure by a thread.

You can do it. Hang on a little longer, my darling. His silent encouragement turned into a prayer God would help her until he could figure out how to rescue her. While every fiber of his being wanted to burst into the room, he couldn't risk it with the baby and Jetta inside. The other female may have a weapon, so he needed to get the lay of the land before he did anything.

"Your mother told Gene he was collecting information about the embezzler."

The mention of Gene clued Seth in that Yasmine Topher was in the room with Jetta, but why would she risk confronting Jetta? She'd gotten away with embezzlement for years without anyone being the wiser.

"She never said anything to me, and she's been through all his papers," Jetta said. "Please, I don't know anything."

Yasmine mimicked her last words, the sarcasm coming through loud and clear. "You are pathetic. You and your mother thought you could figure out what my own brother had no idea was going on right under his nose. He underestimated me, and so did you."

The baby whimpered, and Jetta must have made a move to the crib because Yasmine snapped, "Stay where you are."

"She needs to be fed. She'll start crying harder soon."

"Then you'd better tell me what I need to know."

"There's nothing to tell! If my father had evidence, we don't know where it is." Jetta appeared even more distraught as the infant's wails increased in volume.

"Your precious baby's getting worked up. You'd better stop messing around and tell me the truth. Where's the evidence your father hid?"

Seth sensed time was running out. He needed to act fast, or Jetta and her baby might not survive. He shot a prayer heavenward and concentrated on Yasmine's voice as she harangued Jetta over the baby's screams. Once he had been very good at figuring out where people were by listening to their voices. His life had depended on being able to slip by open doors without notice. Yasmine's tone changed slightly, telling Seth her back was to the door. Time to make his move.

THIRTY-FIVE

Jetta struggled to keep Bingley quiet and her own emotions in check as the baby wailed her displeasure and Yasmine cursed Jetta's obstinance in not revealing where Dad had hidden his evidence about the embezzlement. Jetta had no idea what the woman was talking about, but the youngest Topher sibling's presence in her house had revealed the answer to the *who* in the original embezzlement case. Yasmine had taken all that money and blamed Dad for it. Jetta would bet Yasmine was still redirecting company funds into her own account. Why didn't concern her—that could be sorted out later. If she did have a later. The compact pistol in the other woman's hand gave Jetta grave doubts she would live to see another day. Yasmine hadn't gotten away with embezzlement for more than fifteen years without having an exit plan.

Had Seth seen her text? She wouldn't blame him if he decided to ignore her or had blocked her number. *Please, God. Let Seth have seen my text and called for help. Please keep my baby safe.* She couldn't ask for safety for herself, not when she'd made such a mess of things after the baby's birth.

Yasmine turned her back to the door, directing her tirade at Jetta, who cowered on the floor with Bingley across the room from the baby's bassinet. Something moved in the doorway behind Yasmine, then Seth sprang at Yasmine, pinning her arms to her sides from behind in a bear hug. Bingley broke Jetta's hold on his collar and lunged for the woman, biting the hand that held the gun.

Yasmine screamed and dropped the weapon. Seth kept her arms immobile as she thrashed about while Jetta scrambled on all fours for the gun. She kicked it under the dresser, then dashed for the crib and her sobbing baby. Picking the infant up, she held her daughter close to her chest as sirens split the air. Her daughter's cries simmered to a whimper as Jetta rocked her in her arms.

Yasmine continued to struggle and curse, but Seth didn't loosen his hold. His gaze sought Jetta's, concern and some deeper emotion flaring in their brown depths. "You okay?"

Jetta nodded, her legs shaky, but she didn't want to sit down until Yasmine had been secured by the police. "You came."

"Of course I did." His quiet words soothed her jagged nerves, as if his coming was never in doubt.

Yasmine wailed louder, her words jumbling together into incoherence. Jetta's head ached from the constant noise, first from her baby, now Yasmine.

Seth shook Yasmine with enough force to snap the woman's head back and forth once. "Shut up. You've caused enough trouble."

Bingley gave one sharp bark as if to echo Seth's admonition, and the combination must have made an impression on Yasmine because she firmed her lips and didn't utter another sound.

In the silence, a pounding on the front door alerted them to the arrival of police. Jetta hurried down the stairs with her baby and let them in, explaining Seth was holding the intruder upstairs. The next hours were a blur of feeding the baby, giving her statement to a detective, and trying to stay out of the way as crime scene techs gathered evidence of Yasmine's break in. The woman herself had been led away in handcuffs after an EMT had treated the minor injury Bingley had inflicted on her hand.

"How did she get in?" Jetta asked the detective when he stopped by to check on her as she waited on the living room couch for the all-clear so she could return the sleeping baby to her bassinet.

"We found a pair of picks on Ms. Topher's person, and the front door exhibited scratches around the lock, so she must have picked it to gain entry," Detective Morell said. "It shouldn't be much longer, as the crime scene techs are nearly finished in the baby's room."

Through the living room archway, Jetta caught a glimpse of Seth as he stood in the foyer talking to another officer, Bingley leaning against his leg. Seth absently rubbed the dog's head as he spoke. Her hero, the man who had come without question despite her awful treatment of him. The detective rose. "Let me check with the techs, and I think we can get out of your hair for tonight, or what's left of the night."

"Thank you." Jetta returned her gaze to Seth, who glanced her way. He spoke to the officer, then headed into the living room.

"Hey." He stopped a few feet from the couch, Bingley sitting beside him. "How are you holding up?"

"I'm tired but glad it's over." A yawn split her face as she shifted the sleeping baby to her other arm.

"Want me to hold her for a while?"

"No." She caught the flash of hurt in his expressive eyes before a blank expression returned. "I'd like you to sit beside us for a while."

For a moment, she thought he might turn down her olive branch and leave, but then he moved to the couch, settling to her right, his thigh brushing against hers. Bingley resettled on the floor at their feet, his head on his paws. She drew in a breath, wanting to thank him but unable to find the words with her brain so exhausted.

Instead of speaking, she sighed and nudged his left arm with her elbow until he lifted it along the back of the couch. Then she slid into him, snuggling her head on his chest. He hesitated for an instant before placing his arm around her shoulders and tucking her closer against him.

With another sigh of contentment, she closed her eyes, her body relaxing fully for the first time in hours. Days, really. Her mind stopped racing, her breath evened out, and she slept, implicitly trusting this man would keep her and her little one safe.

SETH TOSSED THE BALL TO BINGLEY, WHO RACED AFTER IT WITH A HAPPY bark. He repeated the exercise several more times before placing the ball in the basket inside the back door. Five days had passed since Yasmine's arrest, and while Jetta wasn't shutting him out any longer, she wasn't exactly inviting him into her life with open arms. Instead, he existed in a kind of limbo where she welcomed his help with Bingley but didn't initiate anything more intimate than exchanging updates on the case.

He refilled Bingley's water dish in the kitchen, then turned to leave.

"Seth?" Jetta stepped into view, her hair damp and her feet bare. "You got a minute?"

"Sure." He dropped onto one of the bar stools to avoid dragging her into his arms and kissing her senseless. Despite the hot-cold treatment, he couldn't take his eyes off of her whenever she was in the same room as him. Motherhood agreed with her, giving her a glow that enhanced her natural beauty. He hoped she'd decided to keep the baby and longed to hold the as-yet unnamed infant.

"It's been a crazy few days, hasn't it?"

"Yep." He and Brogan had co-written a series of articles detailing Gene and Yasmine's behind-the-scenes machinations to sell Topher Robotics to Maxwell Technology, as well as Yasmine's embezzlement of millions of dollars. Turned out she had a secret room in her house even her husband hadn't known about filled with black market antiques, including a missing painting by Vincent van Gogh. Once in custody, she had kept quiet until a search of her home revealed the hidden room and its stash of priceless art. Then she'd bragged about how she'd stolen the money from right under the noses of her "idiot brothers."

In return for testifying against his sister in the corporate espionage charges, Gene confessed to his role in kidnapping Emily Ainsley. Gene also pointed the finger at his sister for the snatching of Jetta and Seth, a charge she tried to deny until the bank records of a secret account showed money paid to the two men arrested for their role in taking Jetta and Seth. According to Brogan, Yasmine couldn't spill facts quick enough, showing off how smart she was and how stupid everyone else was. Providing additional information about Yasmine's guilt was Ryan's executive assistant, Mae Stanhope. Mae had revealed she had inadvertently given Yasmine the idea to embezzle funds, since Mae had done so to pay for her father's hospice care.

What became crystal clear was Jay Ainsley had had nothing to do with the embezzlement. The charges against him had finally been dropped, his good name restored. The police could find no evidence Jay's heart attack had been caused by anything other than abnormal stress from worrying about the company's finances. Peter Topher was recovering from his heart attack, which doctors attributed to his skipping his high blood pressure medicine a couple of times because he'd forgotten to refill the medication. Dolores Green also had her happy ending, with Mae confessing she had simply picked Dolores out of the SafeSense company directory as the patsy for the altered invoices.

Leslie's update two days ago had floored him with FinCEN's findings that Maxwell Technologies had engaged in corporate espionage related to its takeover bid. Apparently, the fake FBI agent had been part of their attempt to find out how close they had come to uncovering the embezzler at Topher Robotics.

"What's next?" Jetta leaned against the counter, her gaze fastened on his face.

"You tell me." He longed to move around the counter and take her in his arms, but he needed her to make the first move.

"We could…" She swallowed, then tried again. "We could date."

Date. Not exactly what he was looking for, but he'd take it if she truly meant it. But she needed to know he wasn't interested in merely dating her. He wanted to court her, old-fashioned as that might be. "I'm not interested in dating you, Jetta."

Her eyes widened. "You're not? But I thought…"

"I want more." He let his words hang in the air between them, willing her to accept his offer. He would give her the space she needed to fully heal from what he suspected had been rape by her ex. Seth didn't need to know the details, just that she trusted him to put her and her baby first.

"I don't know if I can give you more." The pleading expression on her face nearly made him give in and accept her lukewarm terms in order to spend more time with her.

But he wasn't going to settle for less. That much he had learned about himself over the past week. "That's okay."

Her shoulders sagged. "Great."

"No, you misunderstood me. It's okay that you can't give me more, but I can't date you without wanting more."

"You'll leave me?" Her voice broke, tears leaking out of her eyes.

"I'll be right next door, but I can't see you. Not as more than a friend." He spoke very gently as if trying to calm an injured animal.

"But I want to see you."

How to make her understand this was breaking his heart? He loved her too much to not pursue a relationship with his whole being. He decided to go all in, lay it all out on the table.

"No, what you want is someone to go out with on a Friday or Saturday night in a casual relationship. You think I'm not strong enough to know what you need or my own mind. You think I don't *see* you, but I do. I see you—all of you—the good, the bad, the broken, the whole. I love every bit, but you're too scared to let me."

Tears streamed down her cheeks. "I don't want to ruin your life as mine has been ruined."

He forced himself to stay still, praying she would have the

courage to tell him her deepest, darkest secret, to bring it into the bright light so it would lose some of its terrible power over her.

She shuddered, then whispered, "One night, a few weeks into the new year, I awoke to see Kyle in my bedroom. It had been more than two months since I'd broken up with him, but there he was. He told me I owed him for all the dinners and theater tickets and sporting events he'd taken me to, that he was there to collect. I screamed, but he slapped me. I tried to fight him, but he was too strong. When he finished, he told me no one would believe he forced me since he had a key to my apartment. He also reminded me he knew people in high places." She cleared her throat. "I decided I would take my chances and went to the hospital for a rape kit, then I spoke with a police officer, who offered to call a locksmith to change the locks on my apartment that very night. He was right about his connections. He managed to cut a deal and got community service. But I got the judge to give me a restraining order with the threat of the plea bargain being revoked if he trespassed it."

She met his gaze. "So you see, I'm damaged goods because of him."

"Oh, Jetta. Your life isn't ruined because of one man's terrible actions." He gave in to temptation and moved to stand in front of the weeping woman. He cupped her face in his hands, using his thumbs to wipe away her tears. "If that's true, then my life is in pieces too because of one mistake I made when I was a kid. I won't rush you. I know you need time to heal, to find your way forward. But, my darling, I want to be there beside you, holding your hand, cheering you on."

Her eyes sought his, the hope flickering in their depths spurring him to continue. "I want to help you raise this little girl, to be there for you both through life's ups and downs. I want to study God's Word with you and help teach your daughter about God's love."

"You do?" The wonder infusing her voice fanned the hope in his heart.

He kissed her forehead. "I do, with my whole heart. That's why I can't date you. I want to court you and your baby. I'll go to counseling with you, whatever you need. I'm here for the long haul. I'm not going anywhere."

"Oh, Seth." Her smile took his breath away. "Will you stop talking long enough to kiss me?"

He brought his lips closer to hers, hovering above them. "Jetta Ainsley, may I court you and your beautiful daughter?"

"Yes, please." She pressed her mouth to his in a kiss that sealed the promise of a future between them.

All too soon, Jetta pulled back, placing her fingers across his mouth when he would have covered her lips again. "Wait, I wanted to tell you I've decided on a name for the baby."

"You have?" The soft expression on her face made his knees weak. "What is it?"

"Sadie."

The name took a moment to register, and even then he wasn't sure he'd heard her correctly. "Sadie? As in..."

"Your little sister's name."

A warmth rushed over him at this woman's thoughtfulness in giving him a sense of closure from his childhood. "You're sure?"

"I'm sure. Sadie suits her. Sadie Emma Ainsley."

"That has a lovely ring to it." He captured her lips with his for another toe-tingling kiss.

When he broke the kiss, both of them breathless, Jetta added, "So does Sadie Emma Ainsley Whitman."

THE END

Acknowledgments

For some reason, writing *Justice Denied* didn't progress as smoothly as the story for book one (*Justice Delayed*) did. While I had a firm idea about the plot and the characters, my writing time on the book resembled the Swiss cheese approach—lots of holes between time at my keyboard. That resulted in the book being rather a hot mess that I had to wade through and untangle.

But thank goodness I had some help along the way. On the financial crimes front, I read the excellent *Embezzlement: How to Detect, Prevent and Investigate Pink-Collar Crime* by Kelly Paxton, CFE, PI. When I contacted Kelly through her website, she called me back almost immediately and answered my questions about how to make the embezzlement part of the plot believable. Any mistakes I've made are entirely mine.

When I finally had the book in shape, I needed beta readers, and several readers stepped up to the challenge: Lisa Stillman, Laura Bowman, Connie Hill, Gail Oines, and Cindy Ervin Huff. Thank you so much for reading through the manuscript and offering your thoughts on the story and characters. I couldn't have arrived at this moment without you!

I'm always grateful for the support of my family, especially my husband and Mom (aren't mothers the best cheerleaders?). God has indeed blessed me with the ability to write, the support to do it, and the readers to read my work.

Sarah

About the Author

Sarah Hamaker loves writing books "where the hero and heroine fall in love while running for their lives." She's written romantic suspense novels and nonfiction books, as well as stories in *Chicken Soup for the Soul* volumes. As a AWSA certified writer coach, her heart is encouraging writers. She's a member of ACFW; ACFW Virginia Chapter; and Faith, Hope and Love. Her podcast, "The Romantic Side of Suspense," can be found wherever you listen to podcasts. Sarah lives in Virginia with her husband, four children, and three cats.

Connect with Sarah!

Website: sarahhamakerfiction.com

Newsletter: https://sarahhamakerfiction.ck.page

BookBub: https://www.bookbub.com/profile/sarah-hamaker

Goodreads: https://www.goodreads.com/author/show/1804799.Sarah_Hamaker

YouTube: https://www.youtube.com/channel/UCzI8JVSzbms6MoQbFc6SiLQ

LinkedIn: https://www.linkedin.com/in/sarah-hamaker-7295a01/

Other Books by Sarah Hamaker

The Seeking Justice Series

Journalist Brogan Gilmore had been a rising star when an unethical shortcut on a story leads to his fall from grace. A chance encounter with convicted murderer Melender Harman a few months after her release from prison provides Brogan with a chance for career redemption—if he can land an interview with her.

After serving her 17-year sentence, Melender has one objective: To uncover the truth about what happened to her cousin the night the toddler disappeared. When Brogan pursues her for an exclusive story, she reluctantly agrees if he'll help her reexamine the original investigation into Jesse's presumed kidnapping and murder.

While re-investigating the case, Brogan struggles to keep his objectivity as he begins to believe Melender's innocent of the crime—and starts to envision a possible future together. Then a shocking discovery throws their relationship—and investigation—into turmoil.

As Brogan and Melender come closer to solving what happened to Jesse, will their budding relationship survive the truth?

The Cold War Legacy Trilogy

Compelling stories about ordinary women uncovering extraordinary secrets of the past that could cost them everything.

The Cold War Legacy Book One: The Dark Guest

The Cold War is over, but The Wolf is still at the door.

"Once I started reading *The Dark Guest*, I could not put it down. The story captures the reader in the first chapter and doesn't let go until the last. Sarah Hamaker has created wonderful characters to root for as she takes them on a dangerous, twisty journey to the truth."

—Patricia Bradley

Author of The Natchez Trace Park Rangers Series

When Violet Lundy isn't cleaning rooms at Happy Hills Assisted Living Facility, she loves spending her free time with resident Rainer Kopecek. Hearing his stories of the dangerous life he led behind the Iron Curtain in East Berlin makes her own life seem more tolerable. But when Rainer is found dead and his room in disarray, Violet suspects foul play.

Dr. Henry Silverton lives among his books, teaching and writing about the Cold War. A letter about an East German traitor known only as "The Wolf" propels Henry out of academia and into Violet's life. Together, they embark on a perilous quest to uncover the truth about Rainer's death and the traitor's identity.

Can Violet and Henry uncover the secrets of the past before one of them ends up as The Wolf's next victim?

The Cold War Legacy Book Two: The Dark Atonement

A translator and a medical researcher team up to find a long-lost scientist with an innovative cancer treatment.

German translator Lena Hoffman thought her grandfather died years ago. But the unexpected arrival of a cryptic postcard seems to indicate otherwise. As Lena delves into her grandfather's past and uncovers information about him and his cancer research work in East Germany four decades ago, she unwittingly puts her own life in danger.

Dr. Devlin Mills works as a cancer researcher at the National Institutes of Health and lives across the hall from Lena, although they've never formally met. But when Lena is nearly run down by a vehicle, Devlin finds himself thrust into the role of protector. As their lives intersect, the pair find themselves in a race to discover the whereabouts of her grandfather—and whoever wants to silence him—before the past catches up with the present.

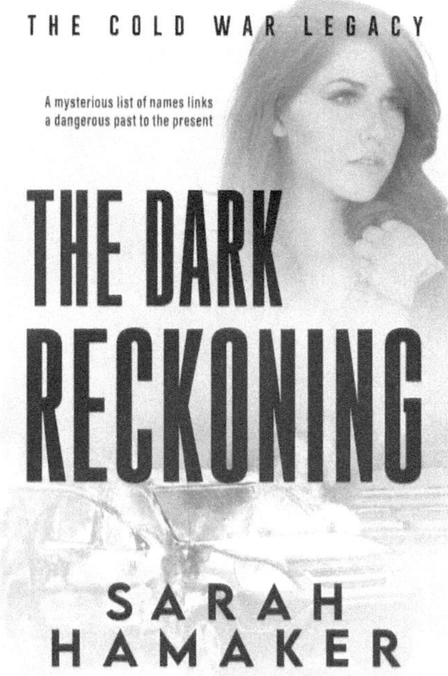

The Cold War Legacy Book Three: The Dark Reckoning

A mysterious list of names links a dangerous past to the present.

When Isana Thomas finds a smartphone among the cherry trees, her life is put in jeopardy. Isana discovers the phone belongs to Lillian Hillam, whose son, Cyrus "Cy" Hillam, works at The Heritage Museum with Isana. But Lillian is missing, and someone doesn't want the pair to find her.

Cy can't believe his mother would disappear without telling him, not after his father's suicide when he was a child. Then kidnappers claiming to have Lillian contact him, asking to exchange her life for a list of names. Cy and Isana must delve deep into his parents' past to find the list and save his mother's life.

But someone doesn't want them to succeed and will do anything to stop their search. Will Cy and Isana uncover the truth about the list before their lives are snuffed out?

Love Inspired Suspense

Dangerous Christmas Memories

A witness in jeopardy…and a killer on the loose.

Hiding in witness protection is the only option for Priscilla Anderson after witnessing a murder. Then Lucas Langsdale shows up claiming to be her husband right when a hit man finds her. With partial amnesia, she has no memory of her marriage or the killer's identity. Yet she will have to put her faith in Luc if they both want to live to see another day.

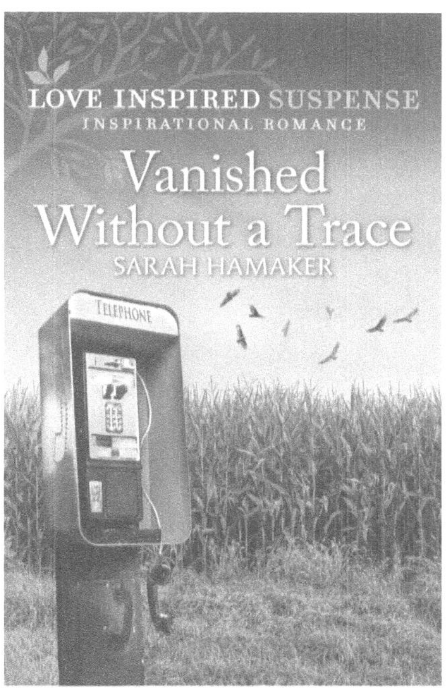

Vanished Without a Trace

A missing person case. A new clue. And a fight for survival.

After nine years searching for his missing sister, attorney Henderson Parker uncovers a clue that leads him to Twin Oaks, Virginia—and podcaster Elle Updike investigating the case. Partnering with the journalist is the last thing Henderson wants, until mysterious thugs make multiple attacks on both their lives. Now they'll have to trust each other...before the suspected kidnappers make them disappear for good.

Standalone Romantic Suspense

Illusion of Love (Seshva Press)

A suspicious online romance reconnects an agoraphobe and an old friend.

Psychiatrist Jared Quinby's investigation for the FBI leads him to his childhood friend, Mary Divers. Agoraphobic Mary has found love with online beau David. When David reveals his intention of becoming a missionary, Mary takes a leap of faith and accepts David's marriage proposal.

When Jared's case intersects with Mary's online relationship, she refuses to believe anything's amiss with David. When tragedy strikes, Mary pushes Jared away.

Will Jared convince Mary of the truth—and of his love for her—before it's too late?

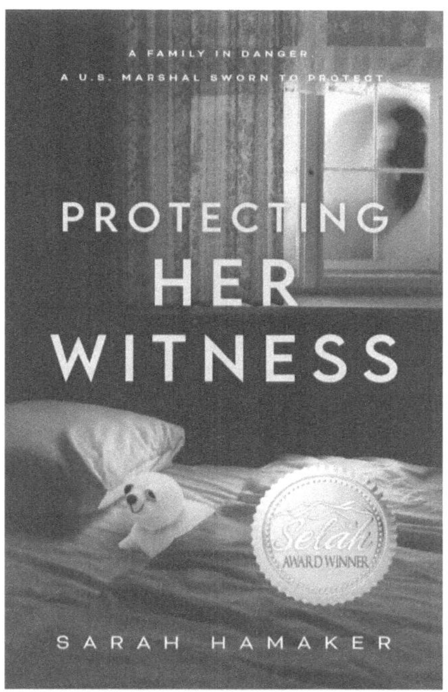

Protecting Her Witness (Seshva Press)

A family in danger...a U.S. Marshal sworn to protect.

U.S. Marshal Chalissa Manning has been running from her past and God for most of her life. When she meets widower Titus Davis and his son, Sam, her well-built defenses begin to crumble. But someone is targeting Titus and Sam, and it's up to Chalissa to both protect them and to find out who is behind the attacks.

As the threats pile up, will Chalissa be able to keep the family she's grown to love safe?

Novellas

Christmas Cold Case (Seshva Press)

All she wants for Christmas is to solve her parents' murders—and stay alive.

Noelle Chastain has returned to Twin Oaks to discover who killed her parents thirty years ago. When the Shenandoah County Sheriff's Office declines to reopen the cold case, citing lack of new evidence, attorney David Keener steps in to help her search—and keep her safe from someone who doesn't want her digging up the past.

Will they find out who's behind the increasingly personal attacks on Noelle before she suffers the same fate as her parents?

Deadly Diamonds (Seshva Press)

The race to find missing diamonds puts a widow in danger.

Three years ago, Dulce Honeycutt's life imploded when her husband died after a robbing a jewelry store and her 18-year-old son, Kieran, landed in prison as an accessory. The uncut diamonds were never recovered, and when rumors fly that she and Kieran know where the gems are hidden, their lives are in danger.

Veteran insurance investigator Miles Sharp believes Dulce knows more about the diamonds than she's revealing. But as the attacks on the beautiful widow's life multiply, he struggles to maintain his professional objectivity. Is Dulce a victim or is her story a sweet web of lies?

Mistletoe & Murder (Seshva Press)

Alec Stratman comes home to Twin Oaks, Virginia, after his Army retirement to contemplate his reentry into civilian life. Instead he's greeted with the murder of his beloved Great-Aunt Heloise.

For Isabella Montoya, the loss of Heloise Stratman Thatcher goes beyond the end of a job. Heloise had encouraged Isabella to follow her dreams and helped fund her studies. Now, accused of her mentor's murder, Isabella is scrambling to prove her innocence.

Since his great-aunt had written glowing letters about Isabella, Alec is unwilling to believe the police's suspicion of the former housekeeper. Instead, he works to help clear her name.

Will Isabella and Alec be able to navigate the secrets that threaten to derail their budding romance and uncover the truth about Heloise's death before the killer strikes again?